SURRENDERED DREAMS

Surrendered Dreams

MICHAEL P. O'KANE

ISBN: 978-1-7395705-2-1

This is a work of fiction. Names, characters, places and incidents either are products of the author's imagination or are used fictitiously. Any resemblance to actual events or locales or persons, living or dead, is entirely coincidental.

MENMA BOOKS

www.menmabooks.eu

Ballyhillow, Leap, Skibbereen, County Cork, P81 RK51, Ireland

PREFACE

In my old alma mater, St Columb's College in Derry, we had a famous Latin teacher who drummed into his pupils term after term, year after year, two tenets he firmly believed in. The first was that "violence begot violence" and the second was that "abuse of power in politics and religion" was the root of all evil.

To reinforce his theorems, he pointed to the two World Wars that cost tens of millions of lives and, instead of bringing peace, spawned another potentially more devastating Cold War, and to warring religions throughout the ages.

To prove his strongly held views, he lined up the entire class of thirty of us, took out his trusty leather strap and gave the first boy six of the best, three on each hand, then handed the weapon to the boy he had just punished, who in turn had to repeat the punishment to the next in line and so on until the end of the line was reached.

It was a lesson well learned, as far as I was concerned. I assiduously avoided violence and politics thereafter by immersing myself in a journalistic career. Not all my fellow pupils in that class fared so well. Young men from County Derry and Tyrone joined the IRA campaign of violence in the late Sixties. Some died, and others ended up in prison. In that class was John Hume, then a quiet, thoughtful student. He had his mind set on the priesthood but, after university, became heavily involved in the Civil Rights Movement to win back the rights denied to the Nationalist minority since the establishment of the Six Counties. He learned the lesson well; he was totally against violence and ultimately won peace for the North of Ireland.

Maybe because of that Latin teacher, *Surrendered Dreams* developed into an anti-war/anti-violence novel, illustrating how the shock waves from armed conflict afflict the lives of ordinary people. Belligerents on all sides justify their actions in the name of freedom, justice, and self-defence or to settle old scores; innocent victims are simply written off as "casualties of war".

In the late Sixties, I was assigned by *The Irish Press* to the reporting staff of the Dáil and Seanad, and it was there that I first took an interest in politics. I really could not avoid it, for in the newsroom of *The Irish Press* I was surrounded by men and women who had fought in 1916 and in the Civil War that followed—among them men like Paddy Cregan, reputed to have cycled from Limerick to Dublin to join the rebels; Máire Comerford, who was in the thick of the fighting until the surrender; and the imposing Maurice Liston, who steadfastly refused to discuss the events of that memorable Easter Week in which he played a major part.

Like all unresolved conflicts, 1916 came back to haunt us in the late Sixties, and working in the Northern Office for the *Press* we could see the signs of another conflict being sown. What we did not foresee, however, was how the bombings and killings would become part of everyday life. In the three decades between 1970 and 1990, thousands of people lost their lives.

It was during that period that I was told about a foreign woman in a nursing home in County Tyrone recovering from a stroke; she had lost her husband and only son, both of them members of the Provisional IRA. When I met her, she told me the story of how her family came to Ireland and the hardships they had endured both in their Bavarian homeland and in Ireland. It was then I had the idea that someday it might provide material for a novel.

Although *Surrendered Dreams* is largely a work of fiction, I have tried to accurately recount events pertaining to the story that took place in Europe, America, England, and Ireland in the late 19th and 20th centuries. For this, I must express my gratitude to the staff of the National Library, who were so helpful during the weeks of research.

I must also acknowledge the help of my journalist colleague Helen Quinn, who burned the midnight oil pouring over early transcripts to iron out inconsistencies and make the story readable.

And thanks also to a family friend, Blanaid Dwyer, who gave me the benefit of her great knowledge of the German language when I needed it to authenticate the story.

I am indebted to another journalist colleague, Maurice Sweeney of Menma Books, for his patience and understanding during the long process of putting the novel together.

And last but least I have to acknowledge the encouragement and understanding of my wife Elizabeth and my children while I was writing, and rewriting, and endlessly rewriting............for years!

Michael P. O'Kane, 2024

CONTENTS

BOOK I

CHAPTER ONE

MASSACRE IN A BAVARIAN VALLEY

Helmut Wagontraper pulled the door behind him on the log cabin, bumping it with his shoulder to make sure it was shut tight before slipping the stout metal bolt into position. He took a couple of steps backward and let his eyes run the length of the building to see if any of the windows had been left open. When he was happy that everything was secure, he took a lock from his pocket, slipped it through the hole in the bolt and snapped it shut.

His wife Rosa watched in silence from the front gate as he made the final checks. He was such a careful man, leaving nothing to chance. Even though the cabin was situated high on the mountainside and unlikely to attract unwanted visitors, he left nothing to chance. There were lots of hillwalkers in the summer, and a deserted house was a handy place to shelter from sudden rainstorms. Securing doors and windows did not completely guarantee to keep the cabin secure but it helped. In any case, he was well aware that people would force doors or windows if they needed a place to bed down for the night; in winter, wild animals seeking refuge from the snow and frost would burrow under walls and force their way through the floor timbers.

He saw her looking at him; she was anxious to be on her way.

"We won't be coming back here," she said impatiently.

"Whether we come back or not, I don't like the idea of strangers in my home," he called to her.

He stood a while longer looking at the house, his eyes misty. The only sign of life left was a thin wisp of smoke spiralling lazily upward into the chill morning air; embers in the open fireplace still had not breathed their last.

The stout chimney breast was the most outstanding feature of the cabin, built to funnel smoke from the open fire. It acted as a bulwark against bitterly cold winds that swept the mountainside; inside, stones absorbed heat from the fire and kept the house warm on cold nights long after the last of the firewood had been reduced to ash.

His brothers helped him cut stone for the breast from a rock exposed by floodwaters on a bend of the river in the valley below. They hauled it block by block up the mountainside on horse drawn litters. He was very proud of that chimney; he had designed and built it himself.

Apart from the gable wall the remainder of the cabin was constructed with pine logs. Doors and windows he fashioned with tools loaned by his father; walls built plank on plank, joints lagged with black sheep's wool and bound with sticky blue clay to keep out draughts in winter and insects on hot summer nights. There was no shortage of building materials; the farm was surrounded on three sides by endless tracts of forest. He could still remember the overpowering smell of sap oozing from the bark as he felled the trees.

Helmut had built a house to stand the test of time, a home for Rosa and himself for the rest of their lives, where his children and his children's children would grow up. Alas, that was not to be; he was leaving, and in his heart, he knew that the likelihood of ever seeing their home again was remote.

He wrenched the wooden handle of the door one last time to make sure it held fast and put the key in the pocket. As he walked to the gate, he fastened the coat buttons one by one until he reached the fence where his wife and son were waiting for him, holding the reins of the horses that would take them on the first stage of a journey to a new life. Cattle grazed on the upland meadow, blissfully unaware of the sad parting of a family to whom the mountain farm had been home.

"I never thought I would see this day," Helmut said to Rosa, drying the tears from his cheeks with the sleeve of his coat.

"We are alive—that's the most important thing," said Rosa. "We survived the Anarchists, and we must thank God for that. And please God, we will be happy in the new life that lies ahead of us."

When Helmut had settled his wife on the mare, he lifted his son Johann up behind her and slapped the animal on the rump to get it moving. He took the reins of the packhorse that carried what few worldly belongings they could manage, mounted his own animal and set off down the mountainside after them.

"Schau nicht zuruck," he called out to them. *"Wir mussen unser Pech hinter unslassen."*

And they went their way, wet eyes staring straight ahead down the steep track to the valley, terrified to take one backward glance in case it would bring them more bad luck.

When the cabin was out of sight, they paused to have a final look around the mountainside. Helmut lifted his head and filled his lungs with the smell of heavily scented air. This is how he wanted to remember their mountain home, bathed in sunshine and reeking of sweet-smelling clover.

The first flowers of spring had already pushed their heads through the cold earth along the edge of the forest. He had cleared hundreds of trees to make grazing land for the animals, but here and there, stumps that had defied his best effort to dislodge them still scarred the landscape. Primroses used the ugly roots for cover against frosty nights to give themselves a head start during the first days of spring.

"Wherever we go in the world," said Rosa sadly, "we will never find another place as beautiful as this."

It was the first day of May in the year of Our Lord, eighteen hundred and seventy-seven, and the family was leaving the lovely valley of Hoffenfeld for a new life in a faraway country called America.

Helmut and Rosa Wagontraper grew up together in that Bavarian valley, their Alpine homes separated by a stream that came down the hillside from snow-clad peaks above. The noisy water marked the boundary between their farms; it was also a source of cold clear liquid to drink and wash in, and for watering farm animals. At the end of its course, it ran under a small bridge before tumbling into the main river that snaked along the valley floor.

Life in Hoffenfeld revolved around the river. In spring, there was good fishing; on hot summer evenings, it was a place to cool off when the day's work in the fields was done; on warm days when school was over, boys and girls gathered around deep pools to swim and play games. There on its grassy banks, youngsters experienced close physical contact with one another that roused their first feelings of sexuality. Love came early to young people in the valley. While still in their puberty years, it was the custom to pair off and barring death or some other major upset, they would remain together and marry before they came of age. Helmut was seventeen and Rosa two years younger when the match was made, and two years later, they were married.

Life was good for the young couple and even though the Wagontraper farm already supported his mother and father, and older brother Kurt and his wife Lilly and their infant son and Helmut's younger brother Pieter. The young couple was given a small cabin near the main house. Rosa's dowry of four cattle joined the Wagontraper stock, and both she and her husband worked and saved for the day when they could afford a farm of their own.

Those first years of married life were filled with love and tenderness and making plans for the future. In that fertile valley, people lived well. Christenings, weddings, church holy days, even funerals, were all excuses to meet and celebrate. A year after they wed, Rosa produced a son for her husband. They called the boy Johann, and he was the focus of their world as he cooed and gurgled his way through babyhood to take his first faltering steps on the cabin floor. No sooner was the boy weaned than Rosa fell pregnant again, and Helmut had to extend the small cabin to accommodate his expanding family.

He had an extra bedroom ready for the arrival of their second son Noel in the summer of 1872. Rosa was disappointed it was another boy for she wanted a sister for Johann. Valley custom dictated that she could have one more try for a girl, but either way, that would be the end of her family. Valley folk were discouraged from having large families because everybody was acutely aware that there was a limit to how many people the land could sustain; thus, couples were discouraged from having more than two children. This was the valley people's way of ensuring an adequate supply of boys and girls for the future without overpopulating the land. Records were kept in the Catholic church, and on the feast of the Annunciation each year, the priest gave an account of births, marriages and deaths for the preceding year and how the population had changed; in this way, everybody knew exactly where they stood.

Since the home farm was already supporting so many people and, as was the custom, it would pass to his older brother after his parents died or retired, Helmut knew he would have to get a place of his own. Neither he nor his parents had money to buy another farm in the valley, so he decided to create a new holding on the mountainside. It was bitterly cold there in winter and difficult to maintain stock indoors for months on end, but people in neighbouring valleys had carved out decent farms for themselves, and he felt there was no reason why he could not do the same. There was plenty of unclaimed land up there, and though the soil could not be tilled because of the danger of erosion and landslides, upland meadows provided an abundance of grass for six months of the year, and he would have to depend on good crops of hay to see his animals through the winter.

He made several trips to the mountain and eventually decided on a sloping expanse of high meadow facing south over the valley, sheltered from the worst of the cold winds by high trees.

Helmut's parents were not enthusiastic about their son's plan to live on the mountainside where snow clung to the slopes long after it had disappeared from the valley; but he was determined, and they could not deter him. There was a strict rule in the valley that only necessary servile works would be carried out on Sundays, but Helmut was so anxious to get his house built that, against his parents' wishes, he and his brothers went up the mountain on Friday evenings and worked non-stop until it was time to descend again on Sunday evening to get ready for their normal week's work on the home farm.

They started building when the good weather came in early summer, and by September, when the days began to get short, they had a cabin secure enough to live in. Kurt and his brothers slept there at weekends, but Rosa had to remain at the farm because she was still nursing her baby. She used her spare time to make heavy curtains for the windows and thick straw mats for the stone floor. Horse-hair mattresses were brought from Innsbruck; an airing rack was borrowed from her mother-in-law to dry the children's clothing; mirrors and pictures and other items given as wedding presents helped take the bare look off the dark cabin walls.

The couple decided—against the advice of parents on both sides—to bring their belongings up the mountain so that they could move in before winter. When everything was ready, they rounded up their stock on the last day of September and drove them up the steep mountainside.

Kurt's parents were worried that baby Noel would not survive sub-zero temperatures and insisted they leave the baby behind; Rosa's sister-in-law, Lilly, had weaned her own baby, and it was arranged that she would nurse Noel until the couple returned for him in the spring.

The Wagontrapers, together with Rosa's family and neighbours, came to see them off, and there were hugs and handshakes all around and tributes to Helmut and Rosa for their initiative and hard work in creating their own homestead. After several glasses of mulled wine and a lot of tears the families bade the young couple farewell.

Although taught from childhood that it was bad luck to look back when setting out on a journey, the three could not resist waving and calling out to their families until they reached the lower edge of the forest and disappeared from view.

Rosa had a lot of misgivings about leaving Noel.

"It's going to be a long, lonely winter without him," she told her husband as they laboured up the steep mountain track. "I wish you had taken your father's advice and stayed in the valley until spring. We won't get any work done on the farm in any case when the snow comes."

"The sooner we get settled in the better," he insisted "Looking after the animals will keep us busy, and by spring we will be ready to start a full season of farm work. The time will pass quickly Rosa. You'll see."

She knew there was no point in arguing further with him, but she could not get rid of the feeling that it was not right to leave her baby behind. She should have insisted that Noel come with them.

The horses snorted and stumbled as they climbed uphill, and by the time they reached the cabin, the breath from the exhausted animals hung like frozen spray in the chill air. It was not yet winter, but in the shade of the trees, the temperature was almost at freezing point.

The couple managed well during those first few weeks. It was cold, but there was a lot of sunshine, too, and they had time to make the cabin comfortable before the first heavy snowfall came at the end of October. There was a break in the snow for another two weeks, which gave Helmut a chance to complete a lean-to behind the cabin to provide shelter for the animals. Naked to the waist, he worked from dawn to dusk cutting saplings for the walls of the cowshed and splitting logs for a stout roof to take the heavy snow that he knew would come early in November.

As she went about her chores, Rosa watched him through the open window. How lucky she was to have such a husband, strong in mind and body, devoted to her and the children. He was just like his father—independent and proud; he would put up with any hardship so long as it was for the good of his family. She should have felt happy, but she missed her youngest son terribly and suffered a lot of discomfort from her breasts, for she was having trouble stemming her milk. As she and Helmut snuggled against one another to keep warm in bed at night, she also worried about becoming pregnant again. Helmut worked so hard that he had little energy for anything else, but sometimes, in bed, a fire began to burn in Rosa's thighs, and when he responded to her need for him, she drew every ounce of passion from his tired body. Afterwards, when he lay exhausted beside her, she prayed to the Virgin Mary not to punish her craving by making her pregnant.

In the days before Christmas, the weather was still fine, and they expected visitors from the valley, but nobody came. Snowdrifts normally made access to the mountain impossible, but that year, the falls were remarkably light, and there had been no strong winds to cause drifting. They found it hard to believe that the family would let Christmas pass without coming to exchange greetings and swap presents.

Rosa suggested that if nobody arrived by the end of the festive season, they should take Johann and set off down the mountain to be with the Wagontrapers for New Year's Day. Helmut was worried about leaving the farm in case a sudden fall of snow prevented them from returning, but Rosa persuaded him to go because she was pining to see her baby son.

On Christmas Eve, they prepared the festive dinner, thinking somebody would surely arrive the next day. When they did not, Rosa sensed something was wrong.

"If anything out of the ordinary happened," he reassured her, "somebody would have made the journey up the mountain to tell us."

So they waited, still convinced that Christmas would not pass without visitors.

In the idyllic Hoffenfeld Valley, people lived, for the most part, in splendid isolation. Once or twice a year farmers travelled to Innsbruck or Munich to sell their produce. They brought back clothes and shoes for the women; jars of sweets and toys for the children; tobacco twist by the yard; barrels of German beer and bottles of wine and schnapps.

Long journeys through the mountains in Bavaria carried the risk of attack by robbers, so the farmers travelled in groups, armed and ready to come to each other's aid if set upon. The valley farmers were a tough lot, well able to defend themselves.

These trips to the market were also important because it was one of the ways they kept contact with the world outside their valley. The only other source of news was the priest who came from Innsbruck once a month to say Mass. He heard Confession and gave Communion and, instead of a sermon, kept them up to date on what was happening in the country at large under King Frederick William IV, an unhappy monarch who ruled an increasingly unsettled Germany from his palace in Berlin.

"You are doing well compared to the rest of the country," the priest told them, "and you should be thankful to God. In the southern states, life is very hard, especially in winter. Food is scarce and there are frequent riots led by political and anarchist groups who are exploiting the fears of rural communities and fuelling unrealistic expectations among impoverished industrial workers.

"Cities and towns are crowded with people who have been displaced by the war between France and Austria, among them thousands of farmers like you, hard-working people who have lost land, homes and possessions. There is plenty of work for them in Germany, but the pay is poor and food prices high, and families have to work from dawn to dusk just to get enough money for food and clothing.

"Violence orchestrated by radicals seeking to overthrow the established order is a daily occurrence. One group led by a mad Russian, Mikhail Bakunin, and calling itself the Anarchist Movement, wants workers to seize factories and run them for their own benefit."

The priest said Bakunin had been forced to flee Russia years before to avoid arrest and moved south to Europe, where he set up secret societies and preached revolution. Bloody bands of terrorists spawned by these movements terrorised the countryside; they kept on the move to avoid clashing with the national army.

Problems in the world outside Bavaria had begun to impinge on the traditional way of life in the quiet alpine valleys. After the defeat of Austria by Prussia in 1866 Chancellor Otto Von Bismarck formed the North German Confederation of States. Southern states including Bavaria valued their independence too much to join until Bismarck dragged them into the Franco-Prussia War in 1871 and eventually they were annexed to the German Reich.

Bismarck got involved in conflict with the Roman Church which led to a state of affairs known as the *Kulturkampf*—the struggle of civilizations. Laws passed by the Protestant-dominated Northern majority allowed him to take control of education and the appointment and dismissal of clergy.

Religious orders were dissolved, and many Catholic priests and bishops were dismissed, imprisoned or deported.

The Jesuit priest from Innsbruck kept the staunchly Catholic population of the Bavarian valleys informed of what was going on during this troubled period, explaining the political power struggle in the world around them. He was particularly worried about another Anarchist movement led by a Frenchman, Proudhon, a disciple of Bakunin. Its aim was to destroy the concept of private property and establish an order in which everything belonged to the working classes. Proudhon did not have a lot of success in Europe as a whole, so he concentrated his efforts in Germany, where the political situation was volatile.

"Already," the priest warned, "marauding bands of workers are roaming the countryside, looting villages and farms, stealing crops and livestock and murdering people.

"Some of these attacks have taken place not too far from München," he warned. "You must be on your guard against them. My advice is to set up a watch system in the valley and make plans to defend yourselves just in case."

Word passed among the Hoffenfeld farms about the threat of intruders, and all able-bodied men were told to assemble with weapons at the Wagontraper farm on Christmas Day. The plan was to use the traditional Christmas get-together to organise sentries for the New Year, people who would keep watch day and night and alert the valley farmers to any approach of strangers. The priest was due back in the valley to celebrate Mass on Christmas Day, and he would be in a position to give the gathering the latest news about the movements of the Anarchists.

The Wagontrapers decided that if the threat of attack became imminent, the women and children in their own household should be moved up the mountain to stay with Helmut and Rosa until the danger passed. Helmut's father Pieter and his sons would stay behind to defend their home.

In Innsbruck, a young Jesuit priest, Fr. Sebastian, and four altar boys were rehearsing ceremonies for the Vigil Mass on Christmas Eve when the main door of the church burst open and mounted horsemen appeared in the centre aisle. Terrified worshippers who had been listening to the choir practising Christmas carols cowered between pews when the mounted intruders discharged their rifles in the air, bringing shattered glass and strips of lead from huge stained-glass windows high above crashing to the floor. Chunks of plaster moulded and painted by craftsmen a hundred years before fell from the ceiling, showering the pews below and sending up clouds of dust as it disintegrated.

Two horsemen trotted up the centre aisle and forced the terrified animals to jump the white marble altar rail. They grabbed the priest's arms and hoisted him up between them; they threatened to pull him apart if he did not tell them where chalices and crosses, and other valuables were hidden. Terrified altar boys collected gold and silver patens and chalices, wrapped them in the altar cloth and handed them over. They pleaded with the horsemen to set the tortured priest free.

The robbers jumped the horses over the altar rails again, dragging the half-conscious priest with them, his feet frantically kicking the air like a puppet on strings. They took him out of the church onto the street, tied him by one hand to the branch of a tree and began to question him. They wanted to know about the valley people—"rich farmers whose bellies were full while the rest of the country starved." They knew priests visited the valleys regularly and had information about where the best pickings were. Fr. Sebastian, eyes bulging with pain from a dislocated shoulder, could have told them the truth—that he never visited the valley people and knew nothing about them, for valley parishes were Fr. Damien's domain. But he knew they would not believe him and would surely kill him. So he told them what they wanted to hear. Hoffenfeld was a valley of full and plenty, and it was not far away. The harvest had been good, and the barns were well stocked for winter.

After threatening to return and burn the church if they found he had told them lies, they rode off to rejoin the main body of horsemen at the edge of town, leaving the young priest still swinging from the tree by one mangled hand.

Fr. Sebastian was in pain but felt no guilt for telling the bandits what they wanted to hear. Fr. Damien had told him only a couple of days before how the tough Hoffenfeld farmers were organised to beat off any attack from Anarchists. In his anger he had sent them into a trap from which, God forgive, none of them would emerge alive.

"They are Satan's disciples, and if they are to be dispatched to Hell's fire where they belong the valley farmers are the ones to do it," he told the terrified altar boys as they cut him free. Despite his aching limbs and the deep anger inside him, he felt good about what he had done.

The priest was carried to the convent beside the church, where the nuns put his dislocated shoulder back into place and cleaned the wounds on his hands caused by the rope. Though in great pain, he told them that if he fell asleep, he would be awakened the moment Fr. Damien returned from an outlying parish where he had been hearing Confessions. He couldn't wait to tell his superior how he had sent the Anarchists into the trap set by the Hoffenfeld farmers.

When Fr. Damien returned late that night to Innsbruck and heard what happened, the blood drained from his tired face, and he became physically ill.

"The farmers are not properly organised yet," he shouted in anguish at Fr. Sebastian. "They did not expect an attack before Christmas, you fool. They will be caught completely off guard!"

His first thoughts were to get back on his horse and ride through the night to warn them, but he knew it was too late. The gang had too much of a start on him and, more than likely, were already in the valley plundering and killing. In the depths of depression, he went into the freezing church and knelt in the darkness to pray, oblivious to the flurries of snow drifting through the shattered windows high above him.

"Blessed Mother of God," he pleaded, "be with your people this night, for they are sorely in need of somebody to help them." He knew in his heart that unless God gave them a miracle, they were beyond help, for the Anarchists were ruthless, and they had the element of surprise on their side. The valley people had relied on him to give them advance warning;

instead, his young curate had delivered them into the hands of a band of murdering thieves.

❁

Outside Innsbruck, the main body of Anarchists—nearly fifty mounted men in all—set off for Hoffenfeld. They stopped at an inn on the way long enough to consume whatever food and drink was available, and when the innkeeper and his wife demanded payment, the unfortunate couples were locked inside the building and the place set on fire. Ignoring the pathetic screams for help from the owners and guests trapped in the blazing building, they rode off, swilling the remains of the beer they had commandeered in the name of the Anarchist revolution.

There was a difference of opinion as to when they should attack. Some flavoured finding a place to shelter for the night and move in at first light; in winter, farmers did not get up early because there was no outside work to be done, and they would still have the element of surprise. Others thought it better to press on into the valley under cover of darkness and the falling snow; the wind would muffle the sounds of their arrival. After much discussion, it was decided that they should go ahead with the night attack; the raid would be over before dawn, and that would give them the morning to organise transport for the fruits of their night's endeavour. They could be out of the valley and on their way to Munich before noon, well clear of Innsbruck in case the national army was alerted.

Some of the leaders thought it was a mistake not to have killed the priest because there was a possibility he might send a rider to Hoffenfeld to warn the farmers. Orders were given that anybody seen on horseback on the road was to be shot just to be on the safe side.

When they reached the foot of the valley, the gang dismounted and gathered around to get their final orders. Ten captains were selected, each assigned four men; each group would be responsible for securing three homesteads. The plan was that small parties of men would be dropped off as they progressed up the valley and only when the last group was in position would the coordinated attack begin. The signal to move against the farmers was three shots in quick succession. When the situation was under control, they should check out what supplies were available and have all produce loaded and ready to move by dawn.

Lights showed in the windows of a farmhouse when the first group dropped off; the remainder of the column moved up the valley and disappeared into the darkness. The waiting men, huddled knee-deep in the snow, knew it was going to be a long night for it would be hours before the last group got into position three or four miles up the valley and the signal given. It grew colder and the biting wind was blowing into their faces. They paced up and down to try and keep warm, but as the hours passed, the cold became more intense. They leaned against their horses to try and get some heat from the animals' bodies.

It got so cold that when the lights went out in the farmhouse the men decided to move in and get it over with so that they could enjoy the heat inside.

"No matter what happens," the leader warned, "It has to be done without a shot being fired or we are in trouble with the others. Any gunfire will alert the farmers before everybody is in position."

The freezing men were confident they could overpower the household without gunfire. They had knives and they would slit a few throats if need be, and it would be all over in a couple of minutes.

They tied their horses to a fence downwind and went on foot through the soft snow to the house. The front door was shut but not locked. The pair let themselves into a large room where a fire was burning. In the flickering light of the embers they could see there was nobody there.

Three doors opened off the room, two to one side and one on the other. The single door turned out to be the scullery. The two on the other side led to bedrooms. Both appeared empty until one of the men noticed movement in a bed in the corner. He lit a lamp, and sure enough, he could make out the bent form of an old woman fast asleep. She was the only occupant of the house, the lone sentinel whom they had earlier seen snuff out the lamp in the parlour before retiring for the night.

The woman's eyes flickered and she recoiled in fear when she awoke to see the faces of strangers bending over her. One of them hit her with the butt of his rifle and broke her neck before she had time to utter a word.

When they were sure there was nobody else at home, they searched for anything of value. They found neither money nor valuables but were happy to settle down to enjoy food and drink and the warmth of the fire until the signal came from the top of the valley. It would be time enough then to see what was in the barns and what kind of transport was available to move it.

Near midnight three shots shattered the Christmas Eve peace. The raiding parties moved swiftly; locked doors were forced off hinges and the sleeping occupants of farmhouses were shot as they tried to get out of bed. Those still awake were overpowered and killed before they realised what was happening. The gang shot anything that moved—man, woman or child, even dogs and cats. Caught completely by surprise, the families had no chance to defend themselves.

Intermittent shooting continued before a deathly silence descended on the valley. The attack was so well co-ordinated that most of the families were killed within minutes of the start of the raid. Some farmers who managed to get to their guns exchanged shots with the raiders but were soon overpowered. Within half an hour the Anarchists had all the homesteads in the valley securely under control.

The first group of raiders had the easiest task. The old lady had left the front door of the farmhouse on the latch so that her son Johann Muller and his wife and their two daughters who were visiting a neighbour's farm would not disturb her on their return. Muller's elder daughter Maria and Holstein's son Pieter wanted to marry, and the match was to be sealed that night. The families sat around the fire in the Holstein kitchen and toasted the future of the youngsters. The women made plans for a spring wedding and embarrassed Maria and Pieter with speculation that they might be grandparents by the time another Christmas came around.

Three shots rang out in the darkness, echoing through the valley. The men by the fireside looked up, sensing danger, and got to their feet.

"I'll get the guns just in case," said Pieter Holstein, making for the bedroom where they were racked neatly on a wall. There was a crash as the front door flew open, and he turned around to see men wearing long black coats and carrying rifles burst through and start shooting. In the first hail of gunfire, the two wives slumped backwards on their seats, eyes bulging, hands desperately clawing at their stomachs where blood pumped through holes made by the bullets that had ripped into their tight bodices. A second volley hit Muller and Holstein and Pieter simultaneously as they stared in disbelief at the red holes drilled in the bodies of the women. The men moaned as the bullets struck, bowling them backwards over the furniture. The fire began to spit and spark wildly as flying blood spattered the glowing logs.

The girls screamed, except for Maria Muller, who knelt on the floor and pressed her hand to Pieter's head to try and stop the spurting blood. As the sticky redness flowed through her fingers and onto her lap, she pushed him away in horror, dug her nails into her skull through a mop of thick black hair and screamed. Maria and her younger sister Marita and the Holstein's daughter Rita were roughly herded to one corner of the room.

When the raiders were satisfied there was nobody else in the house, they dragged the bloody bodies of the dead men and women through the front door one by one and dumped them like slaughtered animals in the snow outside.

Cowering in the corner of the room, the stunned girls fell silent as the bodies were dragged through the front door, leaving a trail of blood across the floor. The raiders picked up bottles of schnapps the farmers had been drinking and drained them to get some heat back into their freezing bodies. They warmed their hands and backsides at the fire while they kept an eye on the girls.

"No point in killing them yet," said one of them. "They're not bad looking for farm girls. We'll have fun with them tonight and decide what to do with them in the morning."

The killers searched the house for money. They upended beds and mattresses, pulled out drawers, smashed delph and pottery, and prodded chairs and cushions, hoping to find something of value. One went to the barn to check what was there, but the place was in darkness, and he returned to the house and told the others it was a waste of time—it would be easier to check when daylight came. He had a rope which he cut into short lengths and roughly bound the girls' hand and foot. The younger of the two men dragged them one by one to a bedroom and dumped them on the floor.

They found more schnapps and beer and bottles of wine and drank their fill until a warm glow enveloped their tired bodies. The older man went to check on the girls from time to time to make sure they were still securely tied. He rolled Maria over on her back, put his hand inside her blouse and squeezed her breast until she cried out in pain. He opened the blouse fully to expose both breasts to the lamplight. The sight of the half-naked woman and the drink made him randy, and he felt like having her. He put his face down to kiss her, but she turned away, shaking. Annoyed, he pulled roughly at her breasts, squeezing and twisting the soft flesh until she screamed in agony. The second man appeared in the doorway; seeing the half-naked girl gave him the urge to find a woman for himself.

The older man cut the thong around Maria's feet and walked and dragged her half-naked to the front of the fire. There were blood marks on her chest where his ragged nails had dug into the white flesh. He tried to kiss her a second time; she turned her head away again. He hit her hard with his fist, but the girl was in such deep shock from the brutal killings she was hardly conscious of the blow. In his fury he pulled at her leather skirt until it came apart and ripped off her undergarments until he exposed her thighs. He prised her legs apart with his boot, lay down on top of her and forced himself into her until she screamed in agony. The harder he pushed, the louder she screamed until something tore inside her belly, and she slipped into unconsciousness. He raped the limp young body.

The second raider carried the smaller Muller girl, Marita, into another bedroom, untied her feet and began to strip her. She made no effort to resist, for she had heard the screams from Maria when the raider beat her.

He opened her blouse but found there was nothing there, no breasts, no nipple; it was hard to know whether she was a girl at all. Disgusted, he left her and went back into the bedroom for Rita Holstein.

She was better—a plump, rosy farm girl. He took his time, caressing and kissing her until he was ready for her. Her body recoiled when he forced his way inside; then she relaxed her muscles to try and ease the pain, gasping for air as he violated her. She shut her eyes tightly and held her breath to blot out some of the pain, but she could not rid her mind of the sight of bullets ripping through the body of her mother or the screams of Maria.

When the raiders had satisfied their lust, they celebrated with more schnapps and beer and boasted to one another about the way they had ridden the women.

The younger Muller girl, traumatised after the killings in the Holstein parlour and terrified by the screams of her sister and Rita Holstein as they were stripped and raped by the men, believed it was only a matter of time before they came for her again. Her hands were still tied, but the man who came into the room had cut the rope on her ankles to get between her thighs before he discovered she was not what he wanted and left her. When she heard one of the girls being dragged into the parlour, she struggled to her feet and walked to the bedroom window. She lifted the latch with her mouth and slowly forced the wooden frame open with her head. She jumped as high as she could until her stomach was over the window ledge, balanced her body and then tumbled headlong into snow piled against the outside of the house. She scrambled to her knees, pushed herself upright against the wall and stumbled knee-deep through the snow, avoiding the bloody bodies of her family dumped outside.

It was freezing cold, and she realised she would die unless she could get something to cover herself, but first, she had to get rid of the binding on her wrists. She made for the barn; there would be tools there, something to cut the rope with. And there would be hay there too in which she could keep warm. She pushed the metal bolt back with her elbow until the door swung open.

She couldn't see in the dark but felt around until her face touched the cold steel of a scythe hanging on the wall. She forced the rope binding her wrists against the razor-sharp blade until it came apart and she was free. She rubbed her hands together to get the blood circulating in her cold fingers. She knew she had to move quickly, for once they discovered she was missing, they would come after her; it would be easy to follow her footprints in the snow.

Marita realised she had to get away from the Holstein house quickly and seek help for her sister and Rita, but she also knew that she could not survive outside without warm clothing. In the blackness she felt around with stiff fingers until she found a horse blanket; there was nothing else; she wrapped it tightly around her and walked off into the night.

As she made her way along the frozen river, she heard horsemen shouting and cursing near the homesteads of neighbours. The voices of the raiders and the screams of their victims carried a long way in the still night air. It was then she realised there was nobody to turn to for help. Her neighbours in the valley were all under attack.

She hid for a while in some bushes, pulling the blanket tightly around her, but there was snow in her shoes and her bare legs were frozen as she plodded through deep drifts; her fingers were numb from holding the heavy horse blanket around her shoulders. Marita felt she would die from the cold if she did not find shelter soon.

Her instinct for survival was strong. She would never make it out of the valley to Innsbruck unless she could find a horse, but she was too scared to approach any of the farmhouses or barns where they were stabled. Then she remembered that Helmut and Rosa Wagontraper had a new farm on the mountainside and were spending their first winter there. Had they come home for Christmas, she wondered? Or might they still be up there? If they had come down to the valley, they were probably dead too, but even so, the cabin was still there, and she could find warmth and shelter if she could reach it. She got to her feet again and trudged slowly onward, lifting her bare legs high with each step to avoid stumbling in the deep snow. She had to find the mountain cabin; there was nowhere else to go.

When the others returned at dawn to check the haul from the farm, they found the two men asleep in a drunken stupor in front of the dying fire in the Holstein House. A girl lay dead on the kitchen floor, her naked buttocks in a pool of her own blood. Another lay naked in one of the bedrooms, hands still tied behind her back, shivering on the cold stone floor. It appeared somebody had escaped through the window of the bedroom. Snow during the night had almost completely covered the tracks, so they looked no further.

The anarchists did not even bother to wake their drunken fellow travellers. The captain shot both of them dead where they lay snoring on the floor. He then shot the shivering naked girl with no more concern than he would have for putting an injured animal out of its misery.

They harnessed four horses to a large cart, loaded all they could from the Holstein barns and joined a long column of men, animals and vehicles making their way out of the valley. The last group had orders to torch every house and building as they retreated and to shoot any animals left behind.

The Wagontraper family fared no better than the Holsteins. Helmut's older brother, Kurt, was sitting in the barn with a bottle of schnapps, keeping watch for a fox that had been killing chickens, when he heard horses approaching. He opened the door and saw strange figures walking towards him. He took the safety catch off his shotgun and discharged a warning before making for the house. The intruders returned fire with rifles, and he was hit twice before he got halfway across the farmyard. Kurt moaned and fell forward in the snow.

"That's the end of our fox," said his father inside the house when he heard the shots.

Suddenly the front door crashed onto the floor and in came men wielding rifles. Helmut's father and mother, Kurt's wife and child and Helmut's baby son Noel and the youngest brother were all around the fireside. For a moment they stared in amazement at the intruders; Kurt's father was first to realize what was happening and lounged towards the wall where two shotguns were hanging.

The gunmen opened fire as soon as he moved, and he and his wife and two sons went down in a hail of bullets. Only the terrified Lilly was left standing, screaming in the middle of the room. One of them held her at gunpoint while the others went through the other rooms to make sure there was nobody else there. They dragged the bleeding bodies outside and dumped them in the snow.

The leader of the group beat Lilly to make her tell where the family kept money and valuables, but the girl was so terrified that she could not give them a coherent answer. They ransacked the house and took everything of value, then helped themselves to as much food and drink as they could. One by one, they raped the terrified young woman, leaving her bruised, bleeding body on the floor like somebody who had been savaged by wild animals. She was so numb with shock that she felt nothing when one of them stood over her and put a bullet through her heart.

The Anarchists shot and killed and raped at will that night in Hoffenfeld. In the morning, a convoy of riders and wagons assembled along the frozen river until the order was given to move out. They left behind a smoke-filled valley that once was home to thirty hard-working farm families, none of whom had been spared.

The leader of the Anarchists was happy with the proceeds of the raid.

"It only proves", he announced proudly to his men as they set off, "that God helps those who help themselves". The whole operation had been carried out with military precision and with only three casualties among the fifty people involved in the raid—the two men shot dead as they lay asleep drunk, and one killed when a shot was fired from a barn as the raiders approached. It was one of the largest hauls they had ever taken, and it would fetch a lot of money from merchants in Munich. The stupid priest in Innsbruck knew what he was talking about—the Hoffenfeld had been a prize indeed.

On Christmas morning, Helmut Wagontraper struggled through the snow on his mountain farm with a bale of hay on his shoulder toward the lean-to shed where the animals were housed. Though his body was bent over under the bulky load, out of the corner of his eye he noticed movement at the edge of the forest. At first he thought it was deer gnawing the bark of a tree, but as he focused his eyes in the grey dawn, he realised it was human. The form moved from one tree to the next as if spying on the cabin. He dropped the hay, went to the shed for his gun and made his way around the trees until he had the stranger between him and the cabin. Helmut fired a warning shot, and the blanket-clad intruder fell forward in the snow.

He slowly approached the crumpled form, moved the blanket away with the point of his gun and turned the body over on its side with his foot. He found himself looking at the face of a girl; terrified eyes stared back at him from a pale, round face. He put down the gun and tried to help her to her feet, but she was too weak to stand up.

"In God's name, what are you doing here?" he shouted. "How did you get here? I might have shot you!"

She stared back at him and tried to move her lips, but no sound came.

He carried her cold body to the cabin, shouting to his wife to get out of bed and help him.

Rosa was already awake, wondering what the shooting was about at that time of the morning. When she saw the lifeless girl, she thought Helmut had shot her.

"I only fired a warning shot," he told his terrified wife. "The girl is almost dead from the cold. He lit the fire and boiled a pot of water while his wife massaged the girl's arms and legs to get the blood circulating again in her frozen limbs.

When the water was warm enough, they gently eased her naked body into a bath, lowering her slowly until her whole body was immersed. Rosa noticed black marks on her wrists and ankles—obviously the girl had been bound hand and foot. It took a long time before the young body came back to life and colour back to her skin. They dried her and tucked her into bed and stayed with her until she fell asleep.

At midday, Rosa heard the girl sobbing. She was sitting upright on the bed with a blanket around her, head bowed, her young body convulsing. She mumbled about her mother and father and the Holsteins, about shooting and pools of blood on the floor.

"I'll never see my mother or father again, never, never, never…" she cried, staring at the floor. "They're dead, all dead…"

The couple thought the girl was raving when she told them what had happened at the Holsteins; how strange men with guns had attacked the farm during the night and killed everybody in the house. She had managed to escape through a window and heard shooting and screaming from other farms as she struggled up the valley to find the path to their cabin. The more the girl talked, the more Helmut realised that something awful had happened.

"Please go and help my sister and Rita," she pleaded. "If you don't, the men will kill them too."

Helmut, dressed in heavy clothes, recovered his gun from the woods and filled his pockets with ammunition.

"Don't go alone," Rosa begged him. "Get help from some of the other farms or from Innsbruck. If what the girl says is true, they will kill you too."

"If the girl is telling the truth," he replied, "there is no time to get help. I must get home and make sure my parents and brothers and my son are okay. They will come with me to help the Holsteins."

He had a terrible fear of what lay in front of him as he trudged through the snow, for he was sure that despite her state, the girl was telling the truth; he was expecting the worst. As he made his way downwards, he came across tracks in the snow where she had climbed the steep path to the cabin; it was a miracle the girl had survived the freezing temperatures of the night.

No story, no matter how horrible, could have prepared Helmut Wagontraper for what he found that Christmas morning. From the moment he crossed the frozen river at the foot of the mountain, there was a smell of death in the air. Smoke from the smouldering remains of farmhouses and outhouses covered the valley floor like a blanket, and when he got the first whiff of it, he recognised the smell of burning flesh. Each farm he passed had the same awful stench; homes and outbuildings had been gutted; all that remained were blackened stone chimneys, standing like headstones in a graveyard for giants. When his parents' home came into view, the remains of the house and outbuildings were still emitting clouds of black smoke. The cabin adjoining the house where he and Rosa had started out on their married life was a pile of smouldering ash; the gable wall was a black hulk of stone; smoke from the ruins still rose through the chimney.

Where the barn once stood, he stumbled across the body of his brother Kurt, lying on his back. One side of his chest was torn where he had been struck by a shotgun blast; his life's blood had already drained away, mixing with the snow to form a sheet of red ice under him.

In what had been the parlour of their home, he found the charred remains of a man and woman whom he knew instinctively were his mother and father. In a bedroom lay the body of his sister-in-law, the lovely Lilly, naked from the waist down, her chest a mass of bloody flesh where she had been shot at close range. In a corner, he found small bundles of charred flesh—the remains of the infants. One of them was his baby Noel but it was impossible to know which one.

He knelt down in the middle of the remains of his home and buried his face in his hands, intending to say a prayer but was so numbed by the carnage around him that not even the words of the Lord's Prayer would come to him; his mind was blank. He rocked to and fro on his knees, trying to come to terms with what had happened. The charred and mangled bodies around him were all that remained of his parents, his brothers, his infant son. This was not a bad dream; it was just like the terrified girl had described it—a nightmare. He wanted to cry, but the tears would not come.

His shoulders drooped under the weight of grief and guilt: grief for the irreplaceable loss he had suffered, guilt about not being at home when his family needed him most, that he did not come down the mountain before

Christmas to see them, that he had forced Rosa to live on the mountain with him and leave her baby behind to die.

He knelt there until his body stiffened from the cold. It was too late to do anything to help them in this life, so he poked around the remains of the barn building until he found a shovel; all he could do was give them a decent burial. One by one, he carried the mangled and charred remains to the banks of the frozen river and dug holes in the snow and gently laid them to rest beside one another: his mother and father, brother and wife, younger brother, and finally the dead infants. He piled snow high on top of them and put stones to mark the spot. When spring came, he would put them in a proper grave in the valley cemetery so that they could rest in peace. He stood over the makeshift graves, staring at the whiteness. For the first time, he began to cry. The tears helped drain some of the grief out of him, and when the sobbing stopped, he dried his face and turned away.

He could not bring himself to pray; his thoughts were now focused in another direction as anger built up inside him. He wanted revenge. Helmut wandered down the valley, checking for some sign of life, but he found none, not even a live animal. In the Holsteins, from which the Muller girl had fled, the bodies of her parents and the Holsteins lay in the garden, beside them the blasted body of the Holstein boy. He found the remains of a girl still smouldering in what had been one of the bedrooms and a second girl and two men in what had been the parlour. He knew who the girls were, but the men were strangers. The bodies were so badly burned they were barely recognisable. The two strangers had been shot at close range, their faces torn away by the gun blasts.

Helmut cocked his rifle when he spotted a lone horseman trotting through the snow towards him, but it turned out to be Fr. Damien, the priest from Innsbruck. When the two men met, they clasped one another and cried on each other's shoulders, bodies convulsing with grief.

"There's no point in going any further," said the old priest. "They killed everybody in the valley. There's not a living soul left."

Through the tears and sobbing, Helmut told the priest about the Muller girl. "Somehow she managed to escape from the Holstein's house and made her way through the snow up the mountain to my cabin," he said. "Whatever she saw and heard has left her deranged; Rosa is doing her best to help her." Helmut told the priest how he had found her in the snow. It was a miracle she had reached the mountain cabin in the freezing night-time temperature.

"We need to get some help and go after them," said Helmut. "I know revenge is a sin, Father, but they cannot be allowed to get away with this. They have to be made to pay for what they have done."

"I know how you feel," said the priest sadly, "but it's a waste of time. This band of murderers is so well equipped with arms, horses and supplies that even the national army is reluctant to confront them."

Helmut was confused, so Fr. Damien persuaded him to accompany him back to Innsbruck so they could send messengers to neighbouring valleys to warn the farmers. Fr. Damien was convinced the murdering band would strike again, probably after Christmas when the money from the sale of their booty from Hoffenfeld had been spent.

Apart from Helmut, Rosa, Johann and Marita, there were nine other survivors of the valley community. Two boys had been in hospital in Munched, and two families were with relatives in Innsbruck for Christmas.

Fr. Damien recruited workmen from Innsbruck to recover and identify the bodies of the dead and put them in makeshift snow graves until they could give them a proper burial in spring. Fifty-two bodies were identified as valley folk, and three were strangers.

Rosa was frantic by the time her husband arrived back on the mountain two days after he had left. She had spent most of the time he was away on her knees, praying to the Virgin to keep him safe and bring back her baby Noel to her. When he did not return by nightfall of the first day, she was sure he too had been caught by the raiders and killed. She comforted Maria and Johann and kept herself occupied until he finally arrived home.

After what the girl had related to them as she recovered from her ordeal, Rosa was apprehensive, but she knew the Wagontrapers were a strong family and was confident that Helmut would find baby Noel and bring him back to her.

Her joy at seeing her husband again was short-lived. He came alone, white-faced and dishevelled. He told her baby Noel was dead together with all the members of his family; so too were her own father and mother and two brothers. She stood in the middle of the cabin as if in a trance, staring in disbelief as he recounted the full horror of what happened not only to their families but to everybody else who had been in the valley on Christmas Eve. There was no easy way to tell her; she had to know the truth.

Rosa walked out into the freezing cold and Helmut watched as she trudged around the cabin until her feet had worn a deep path in the snow. He and Marita and the boy sat inside in silence. She returned as suddenly as she had left and began to prepare the evening meal as if nothing had happened.

When they had eaten, she went to her bed, and there she remained for two days, oblivious to the world around her. Even in her shocked state, Rosa could not erase from her mind the scenes of horror described by Marita, and she prayed that her own family and Helmut's had not been tortured before they died. Now that all hope of seeing any of them alive again had gone, she tormented herself over the death of her infant son. Had he been killed as he slept, or was he burned to death in the fire? Did he have the comfort of somebody's arms around him when it happened?

She could not get out of her mind the sense of foreboding she had in September when she left the boy behind with Lilly. She wanted to bring him to the mountain, but the Wagontrapers would not let her. It was their fault her baby was dead; she should not have listened to them. If she were a proper mother, she would have insisted on bringing him and he would still be alive.

Helmut spared her the circumstances in which he found the bodies, especially those of the younger women who had been stripped and raped before being killed. Nor did he tell her that he could not distinguish the body of his own son from his brother's child, so badly charred were the remains. In the morning, he found her kneeling in a corner of the room, sobbing quietly. Alternatively, she prayed to God and his Holy Mother to look after her baby son in heaven, then suddenly broke into a fit of cursing, blaming God and his Mother and the Wagontrapers and Helmut for the death of her beautiful son. When her mood changed, she was on her knees again, thanking the Virgin Mary for bringing her husband home safely and for sparing the life of Marita Muller.

"We have Johann, we have Marita, and we have each other," Helmut tried to console his wife. "We must be thankful for that. Remember whole families have been wiped out, gone forever."

Marita Muller did not expect good news about her sister or Rita Holstein. The men who had attacked them had behaved like animals from the moment they burst through the door. They had tortured and raped her sister and Rita and tried to do the same to her, even when she was plodding through the snow after she escaped. She had hoped that they might still be alive, that they would kidnap the girls so that they could continue to use and abuse them. She was not surprised when Helmut told her they were dead. She lay awake all night trying to make sense of what happened. When she could not, she took over the household chores from Rosa, who wandered around aimlessly, demented at the loss of her baby son.

The family did not venture down to the valley again that winter, not even to attend a Special Mass for the victims of the massacre. When the snow began to melt in spring, Helmut took a pick and shovel, and Rosa and Marita Muller and Johann and himself went down to the river to bury their dead.

He dug two graves—one for his mother and father and the two boys, the other for his brother and his wife. He placed one infant on top of Kurt, the other with Lilly. He made a stout wooden cross, etched the names with a red-hot poker and carved *Emordet von den Tuefels Jungern*—murdered by the Devil's Disciples.

He recovered the bodies of Marita's parents and sister on the Holstein farm, and together, they made the sad journey down the valley to bury them with the remains of her grandmother. Marita asked Helmut to take Pieter Holstein's body as well so that he could be buried with Maria, to whom he was to be married. The charred, frozen remains were all laid to rest in the same grave. On a wooden cross, Helmut etched: *Vereinigt fur Immer*—United Forever.

The last thing he did before returning to his mountain home was to put *For Sale* notices on both farm holdings. He had made up his mind that whatever the future held, neither Marita nor the remnants of the Wagontraper family would ever till that blood-stained land again.

Anarchist bands remained active throughout Bavaria for another year. Even where farmers had time to organise, they were no match for horsemen trained and led by former army officers. The more the farmers resisted, the more casualties they suffered; in the end, many decided to save their lives by fleeing the valleys altogether, abandoning homes and crops to the rampaging gangs.

Many never returned, settling instead in adjoining countries or moving eastwards to start a new life in industrial cities and towns. A few emigrated to German colonies in Africa and further afield and others packed their belongings and set off for America—a new land of opportunity everybody was talking about.

The Jesuits in Innsbruck had a lot of information about this great country across the ocean where there was so much land that it was being given away free to encourage people to come and live there. It was three thousand miles from one coast of America to the other, and in between, there were millions of acres of rich farmland drenched in sunshine, land where crops grew all year round. You could get a thousand acres from the government; all you had to do was fence it off. Other emigrants had made fortunes digging gold from rocks and rivers in a place called California. It sounded too good to be true, but Fr. Damien insisted that while the stories might be exaggerated, it appeared America truly was a land of opportunity.

Helmut expressed an interest in going there and the priest made a special visit to the mountain farm to discuss it with him. Fellow priests of his order had been to America and found it a wondrous place, he told his friend.

"The country is so vast it stretches almost from the North Pole to the Equator and from the Atlantic Ocean on one side to the Pacific on the other. In some parts it's like Bavaria with cold winters and hot summers, but in the south they never have a fall of snow. The winters there are hotter than our summers!"

To anybody thinking about emigrating, he advised certain practical steps: "Once you leave for the New World, it's unlikely you will ever have the opportunity to return to Bavaria. My advice is to save all the money you can for the next few years.

"Rosa and little Johann and Marita Muller and yourself must learn English," he told Helmut. "That is the language of the new country. A good knowledge of English and a bit of education combined with your farming skills and money from the sale of your farms will ensure a sound future for you and your family."

Helmut and Rosa talked at length about what the priest had told them and, by the end of the summer of 1873, had made up their minds that America was where the future lay.

When they told Marita about their decision, she surprised them: "I made up my mind a long time ago to leave Hoffenfeld," she said. "I will sell the farm, and it will be enough to get me to America and make a new start."

In August when the harvest was over, the family loaded surplus potatoes, butter and cheese onto carts and sold them in the market at Innsbruck. They gave the money together with the proceeds of the sale of the farms to Fr. Damien for safekeeping. They planned to work the mountain holding for two more years, by which time they would have enough to pay for the voyage, money to buy stock and tools for a farm in America and hopefully have enough left to buy or build a small home.

It was decided that Marita and Johann would board with the nuns at the convent in Innsbruck to get an education and learn English. Fr.

Damien also arranged for one of the sisters to attend the valley church once a month to teach English to the Wagontrapers and anybody else who was interested in going to America. Through wind and snow and rain, Helmut and Rosa made the difficult journey down the mountain and sat in the front pew for Mass so that they could be near the teacher for the English lesson that followed. Neither of them could write the complicated language, so they had to rely on sounds made by the teacher.

My name is Helmut.

I am a farmer.

I live in Bavaria.

I have a wife. Her name is Rosa.

I have a son. His name is Johann.

The simple phrases were difficult at first, but Helmut and Rosa repeated them over and over until they became familiar with them.

At Christmas Helmut went on horseback to Innsbruck and took Marita and Johann home for the holidays. As they sat around the glowing fire in the festive evenings, they played word games with the children to improve their English. Helmut and Rosa had a far better vocabulary because while they were learning to speak words and phrases, the youngsters were being forced to learn the grammar first. Sometimes the older pair put words in the wrong order and laughed at their awkwardness. But all were so enthusiastic that no matter how many mistakes were made, it did not discourage them.

At Easter Fr. Damien brought Marita and Johann home from school when he rode up the valley for the Stations of the Cross on Good Friday. Some of the farms had been sold, but many were still derelict; there were plenty of people looking for land, but the Bavarians were a superstitious people and, after the massacre, referred to Hoffenfeld as "the dark valley." Prospective buyers were also put off by fear that the Anarchists, who were still active in Germany, might strike a second time. Some farms lay idle to see if the youngsters who survived the massacre or relatives of the murdered families would take them over.

There was a fine new house where the Wagontrapers home had stood, and the owners assured Helmut that if he went to America, they would tend the graves as if they were family.

In the two years since that awful night in the valley, Marita developed into a pleasant mature girl. The nightmares became less frequent with time, and she began to behave like a normal girl again. Around the farm she and Johann were inseparable. Watching them running through the upland summer meadows on carpets of purple and white clover and alpine blooms, Helmut was reminded of his own happy childhood, of summer days lolling on the banks of the gentle river.

Marita was no longer the flat-chested girl that had been roughly cast aside by the intruder on the night of the massacre. She had blossomed into a pretty sixteen-year-old, her body curved and lithe, clothes stretched tight over hips and buttocks. She had long dark hair which she plaited, revealing a perfectly formed neck and head. She knew from the blood coming from her thighs every month that she was now a woman but also had odd sensations inside her at times, a hunger that food or drink would not satisfy. She wanted to ask Rosa about it but could not pluck up the courage.

Sometimes she awoke during the night to the sound of Rosa and Helmut making love on the other side of the curtain in the small cabin; she knew exactly what was going on for the nuns had explained to her what happened between a man and a woman and how life began in the womb. Some of the girls at school knew a lot more than she did and showed her how to arouse her body by stroking the inside of her thighs. She wondered what it would be like to be with a man, somebody who clasped you so tight that your body and his became one.

When she heard the moans of their lovemaking, she pictured them in her mind, rocking together on the bed, until her own heart beat faster and she felt the flush of blood through her veins. Then images from the past intruded and she found herself back in the Holsteins and the blood spurting from the bodies of her mother and Mrs. Holstein and she could hear the screams of her sister and Rita as the men raped them. Several times she woke to find Helmut and Rosa standing over her bed, shaking her to end the nightmare. They knew it would be a long time before the terror of that night was erased completely from the girl's mind.

She was lovely to look at and most of the time happy and bubbling with excitement, especially when she talked about the life that lay before them in a new country. The convent had made her competent and confident and the nuns taught her poise and etiquette and how to take care of her body and how to show it off to the best advantage when the time came to look for a husband. She had dark eyes, pale cheeks, and when she let her black hair hang loose around her shoulders, looked more Latin than German. She stood out in the company of others her age for they were mostly buxom farm girls whose main concern was to show prospective husbands that they would make strong farmhands and produce healthy, robust babies.

In normal times, Marita would have already been spoken for by one of the boys in the valley. But almost all of those she knew when growing up had been murdered and new families had younger children. In any case Marita had lost interest in boys, in finding a man to marry. When she dreamed of love now it was always with older men and she had this curious vision over and over again that after she went to bed with a man he left, and she never saw him again. It did not worry her for she had set her mind firmly on leaving Bavaria and no man and no love affair would deflect her from her plan. She had money, she had some education and by the time she was ready to go she would have enough English to make her own way in America. Even if Helmut and Rosa changed their minds, she was determined to go alone.

As the time to leave Bavaria approached, Marita thought a lot about what she was leaving behind—her dead sister, her parents, and especially her grandmother, to whom she had been more attached than anybody else and from whom she had learned so much as a child.

The old woman had been brought to Hoffenfeld as a bride when she was only eighteen years old. She had been born and grew up on another farm near the City of Hanover in one of the northern states, where her family were market gardeners. While visiting relatives in Munich she met and married her Bavarian farmer husband, which was how she came to live in the valley. Her grandmother described in detail the wonderful things she had seen in her lifetime in the great world outside Bavaria. She had visited Holland and Belgium when she was a girl and boasted that she had "dipped her toes in the cold North Sea."

The old woman told her grand-daughter some of the secrets she had learned when she was growing up. Lots of young men—and a few older ones too—had approached her parents after she left school to know if they might court her.

"My mother made it clear she would not entertain any approaches until after my nineteenth birthday," she said, "no matter what they had to offer. This suited me because I wanted a few years to enjoy myself before burdening myself with a husband and children.

"So I had lots of boyfriends and I coaxed them into buying me bangles and necklaces and even clothes and shoes. I became very clever at using my feminine charms to get what I wanted!

"The trick is to promise a lot, take what they've got, give as little as possible and then dump them before things get too serious," she laughed.

"What most men really want is to make love to you and while you never say yes, you never say no either. You have to keep them on a string, like a puppet. When you are older you will understand this.

"Remember, once a man makes love to you, it changes your life forever. He thinks you belong to him and will brag about his conquest to his friends. But remember, when one man has his way with you, others regard you as soiled goods."

Like her grandmother, Marita Muller was a great talker, especially on summer evenings when they sat outside in the shade of the cabin and Helmut and the boy were still attending to chores about the farm. The girl seemed to know a lot more about life than Rosa. Rosa realised that despite her youth, her companion was very wise in the ways of the world.

Marita confided that in Innsbruck the nuns let her out sometimes to carry messages to nursing sisters in the hospital and it was fascinating to see how busy the city was. In the streets she saw magnificent, gilded coaches and horses with polished harness and shining brass buckles, and men with tall hats and long tails; there were uniformed soldiers marching up and down with rifles over their shoulders, guarding the Mayor's house. There were shops selling ladies' clothes and food and buttons and books, almost anything you wanted—there seemed to be a shop for everything.

"There are fabulous buildings called hotels where people stay when they come to visit the city on business or on holiday," she said. "All day long, carriages stop outside to drop people on the steps of these huge establishments, and porters remove luggage and follow the guests inside.

"I tried to get inside once to see what it was like, but the uniformed doormen would not let me pass," she said.

"One big shop had a great sign saying it arranged passage to America and I asked for information, but the staff would not talk to me without my parents," she added.

She was warned by the nuns to stick to the main thoroughfare when she ran errands because there were urchins about and danger of being set upon in narrow side streets.

Marita had no intention of straying for it was the fashionable main streets that fascinated her. Women in splendid dresses and magnificent coats strolled arm-in-arm with their gentlemen in the evenings or stood on the pavement chatting with friends.

"On a fine Sunday hundreds of couples parade arm in arm about the city," she told the starry-eyed Rosa. "They walk up and down the same streets for hours meeting friends and admiring each other's clothes. When the weather is wet or cold, they congregate in cafes and bars to drink coffee and beer. In winter they crowd onto open-air ice-rinks, holding hands as they skate in circles; some are so skilled that they would make you dizzy just looking at them."

Rosa listened to the girl's stories and marvelled how someone so young could know so much and describe everything so vividly.

When she had the older woman's full attention, Marita lowered her voice so that Helmut would not hear and told her about women in Innsbruck called prostitutes. They never married but allowed all sorts of men to make love to them, and she had been told they were paid lots of money. The women earned their living this way, and the more beautiful the girl, the more money she could get from a man who wanted to share her bed for a night.

"Some of them earn so much that they can afford to live in fine houses," she whispered. "Men take them on holiday to famous resorts in Italy and France and buy them expensive clothing and jewellery. Some even have their own coaches and livery and servants to cook for them and to look after their houses.

"I once asked the nuns about them," she laughed. "They were horrified and warned me not to mention such people, for they were *Brides of Satan*."

But Sister Xavier took her aside and confided in her. "Not all those women are evil," she said. "It's the only life many of them have ever known for, and they often start when they are only twelve or thirteen years old. You have to have pity on them. While young and beautiful they are showered with money and the good things of life, but when they get older and their beauty disappears and men no longer desire them, most end their days in institutions or die in agony from horrible diseases."

Rosa couldn't believe what she was hearing from the sixteen-year-old. She found it hard to imagine that such women existed and was dubious about what the girl was telling her. How could women go to bed with different men all the time and not have a house full of babies?

Marita explained that these women had ways of ensuring that even though they went to bed with a different man every night and maybe even two on the same night, they would not have any babies. Her grandmother had told her all about this. Any woman could stop herself from having babies if she didn't want them or if she already had too many.

"The trick is to exhaust your husband with lovemaking for a couple of weeks and make sure he stays away from you for the next two weeks."

Rosa was sceptical. From experience she knew it was not as simple as that.

"Anyway, if you do get pregnant and don't want a baby," Marita explained matter-of-factly, "there are herbs which you use to make a brew and after drinking it for a couple of days the bleeding will start again and the baby is gone. My grandmother told me all about that."

Rosa had never heard such wild stories in her life. All her mother told her before she got married was that her man would put a seed inside her that would grow and grow until it became a baby big enough to be born. She did not know until her wedding night how her husband got the seed inside her, and she was terrified when Helmut hurt her so much. She had no idea either how she would know when a baby started or how long it would grow inside her, nor about the fear and pain she suffered when the time came for Johann to be born. As for the other matters, she was disgusted that Marita had even mentioned such terrible things. She could not imagine refusing to make love with Helmut whenever he wanted her and was horrified at the thought of any woman refusing to bring her husband's child into the world once it had started in her womb. She warned Marita not to speak of such things again for if Helmut found out he would be very angry.

But Marita insisted she had seen her grandmother pick the herbs along the riverbank and make the brew for her own mother and that's why she never had another baby.

On the second anniversary of the massacre, a special Mass was arranged, celebrated by Fr. Damien. Afterwards, the new valley folk got together for a Christmas drink that went on late into the evening. While they were having supper a man arrived on horseback from Innsbruck to tell Fr. Damien that Fr. Sebastian was dead. His frozen body had been found hanging from a tree in the grounds of the church that morning, and it appeared he had been there all night.

Fr. Damien was shocked by the news but not surprised. Since the massacre, the young priest had been unable to rid himself of the feelings of guilt for the deaths of the valley people. The older man watched him deteriorate mentally and physically as the months passed until, eventually, he became so deranged that he could not even say Mass. He spent his last days pacing to and fro in front of the church, reading aloud from the New Testament. In his Missal he left a note for Fr. Damien saying how sorry he was and asking the forgiveness of God and the people of Hoffenfeld.

Fr. Damien took a personal interest in the dark-haired Muller girl while she was at school in Innsbruck. The nuns regarded her as a good scholar, quick to learn and hard-working, especially in English, in which she was far in advance of other pupils. She was so keen that the sisters allowed her to read prayers in English during their meals, a chore normally reserved for novices.

For Marita it was a chance to read and speak the language she was so keen to master, to hear herself say the words out loud and have the nuns correct her when she got the pronunciation wrong. They encouraged her to think about becoming a nun or perhaps a teacher. But Marita made it clear she didn't wish to be a nun, or a teacher, or a missionary, nor even a wife. She was going to America, and nothing would deflect her from that course.

She already had visions of the life she would lead there, and the kindly Sisters would have been shocked if they could have read her mind. For Marita had concluded that she could get much more out of life as a *Bride of Satan* than a *Bride of Christ.*

She and the Wagontrappers had already made their plans. When the time came, they would gather their belongings, say goodbye to the valley, and set off on a five hundred-mile journey to Genoa in Italy to begin their great sea journey to the new world.

CHAPTER TWO

JOURNEY TO A FAR AND DISTANT LAND

On that Spring morning as the family left the hill farm, Rosa and Johann took Helmut's advice and resisted the temptation to have one last look back at their cabin home. They rode with heads bowed as the horses carefully picked their way down the steep incline. Heavy dew hung over the fields and the tall grass was disturbed only by the occasional wave of cold air rolling down the hillside from the snow-capped Alps. The pungent odour of pine needles mingling with the scent of sweet-smelling clover and the first flush of fresh grass was everywhere; it filled their lungs, intoxicating them, stealing their breath away.

Ahead the wide expanse of valley floor spread out before them; far below, the river snaked along between emerald-green meadow grass and newly ploughed fields. At this time of year acres of alpine flowers lay like a carpet on the ground sloping down to the river, bathing the valley in a blue haze of morning light. The scent of blossoms was everywhere, and for the first time Helmut felt weakness in his resolve to leave. He might never see anything like it again except perhaps in dreams, but he knew that wherever he went, this overpowering smell of clover and flowers and sweet grass would linger in his senses for the rest of his life.

When they reached the river, other smells invaded his subconsciousness: memories of the acrid stench of burning flesh and smoke from gutted homes and charred remains that filled the air the morning after the massacre. It was from this smell of death that he and Rosa and the boy and Marita were fleeing.

The new people in the valley were strangers so there was nobody to say goodbye to. They crossed the river to pray at the family grave before taking the road to Innsbruck for the last time. When they reached the town, they went first to the church to thank Fr. Damien for all he had done for them since the loss of their families and the help he gave them to prepare them for what lay ahead.

When they were parting, Helmut took the key to his cabin from the pocket of his greatcoat and gave it to the priest.

"It's yours now, Father, to do with it as you will," he said sadly. "Give it to some young couple who need a place of their own. If not, maybe the nuns could use it in summer to get away from the heat in Innsbruck."

He handed over a note in Marita's neat handwriting, passing ownership of the hillside farm to the priest.

As a final act, they knelt before their friend, who placed his hands on each of their heads and prayed silently. When he had blessed them, they lifted their bowed heads to see tears in his eyes.

"May God travel with you to the new world," he said, "and may it bring you good fortune and a happy future. God knows you have already had more than your share of trouble and misfortune in this life. Place your trust in Him and always remember your loved ones in your prayers".

"I hope this is not the end of our friendship," said Helmut sadly. "Please God we will meet again someday."

"It's unlikely," said Fr. Damien, "unless the Bishop decides to get rid of me to the mission fields in America, but I am getting a bit old for that now."

They spent their last night in Bavaria at the convent in Innsbruck, where Marita went to school, and set off after dawn the next day with three horses and a packhorse. The nuns were sad at parting with Marita, but as soon as they were out of sight, the girl dried her tears, tossed her long, shiny hair over her shoulders and lifted her face to the sun. This was the day she had been looking forward to for so long and she had no regrets at leaving her childhood home or the convent where the nuns had educated her in the ways of the world. They were on their way to America to a new life and she had set her sights firmly on the future.

Fr. Damien gave them a map on which he had marked in blue the route they should take and put an X on places in the mountains where the remnants of the Anarchists still operated and warned them to be extra vigilant. The marauders were no longer the force they had been; their numbers had been drastically reduced in skirmishes with the National Army during the previous two years. They were now forced to concentrate on softer targets, preying on stragglers on the mountain passes. The priest advised them to stay on the main routes, make sure they travelled in company and always find shelter before dark.

He warned Helmut to take it easy, or the horses would never make it through the Alps. At the end of each day, the animals should be well looked after, and they themselves must have plenty to eat and drink—it was their best safeguard against falling ill. The long journey on horseback would tax their stamina to the limit, especially Rosa and the children.

The priest had changed their money into gulden and also managed to buy some English gold sovereigns for them.

"Gold coins of any description are in demand in most countries of Europe, and when you get to America, you can exchange them for dollars, which is the local currency."

The nuns, worried about the family carrying so much money and the risk of being robbed on the long journey, made three soft leather body belts into which they sewed the coins. The belts were worn by Helmut, Rosa, and Marita and pulled tight around the waist to make them less noticeable. The women's belts had the side next to their skin covered in silk so that the leather did not cut into the tender midriff while they were on horseback.

The nuns laughed as they fitted the money belts. Marita had no problem, for when they tightened the belt, she looked slimmer and more attractive than ever in her clothes. Rosa was plumper, and it was impossible to fit the belt, so it would not show through her dress. The sisters tightened it until she had difficulty breathing and quickly loosened it again when she became faint. They advised her to wear a loose-fitting coat but warned that once they moved down out of the mountains into Italy, it would get very hot and humid, and she would have to discard heavy clothing. They advised it might be better at that stage to put the belt on the boy until they were aboard the ship.

If Marita had not been present when the nuns were pulling and hauling at her, Rosa would have told the good sisters what the real problem was. The thing that she did not want to happen had happened and at the worst possible time. She was pregnant and she had agonised for a whole month before they left over whether to tell Helmut. He had to know sooner or later, but she was afraid if she told him before they set out on their journey, it would put all their plans in jeopardy. Almost certainly, he would have insisted they stay on the mountain for at least another year, maybe even two or three, until her baby was strong enough to travel. That would have been a big disappointment to everybody, and she felt certain that Marita would have gone to America without them; the last thing she wanted was to split the family.

When she first discovered she was pregnant, Rosa thought about telling Marita, remembering that she claimed she had a remedy to stop the pregnancy. But she was scared to try anything like that—it would be flying in the face of God to even think about getting rid of her baby once she had conceived it. So she decided to tell nobody until they were well on their way to America and it was too late to turn back.

They were making the journey at the best time of the year, Fr. Damien assured them, when the notorious Atlantic storms were most benign. But it could get monotonous at sea, and they should bring plenty of fresh fruit aboard ship for he had heard nothing but bad stories about the food handed out by the sailors. In any case he estimated that if everything went well and there was no major hold-up, the family should reach America by mid or late June.

Rosa thought about what Fr. Damien had told them. If he was right and the journey took less than two months, she would have four months to settle down in the new country before the baby was born. Already she was feeling some sickness, but it would pass, hopefully before they had to board the big ship for the final leg of their journey across the ocean that separated Europe from America. One thing did worry her; the priest had warned about another hazard of the sea, an illness called seasickness that gave a lot of discomfort to a lot of people. Food brought the sickness on, but not to eat at all was just as bad. The only advice he could offer was to get as low as possible into the bowels of the ship where the rolling that caused the illness was less noticeable.

The money belt was very uncomfortable, but she solved the problem by taking it from around her waist and wearing it like a bandolier under her dress; lying between her breasts, it was hardly noticeable.

Helmut's plan was to travel on horseback over the lowest pass through the Alps—the Brenner—to the town of Merano, then west along the Venosta Valley towards the Swiss border and south to Bormio and Tirano in Italy. The nuns gave them a letter to deliver to the convent in Bormio, where arrangements had been made for them to rest for a couple of days before beginning the long haul west to the Swiss border and Lake Como. They could break their journey again for a couple of days at a convent in Lecco if they felt they needed to. Then they would be out of the mountains and on to more level terrain and the weather should be much better for the last part of their journey to Milan.

They planned to sell the horses in the north Italian industrial city and make the final leg of their overland journey to the port of Genoa by railway, which Fr. Damien said would be the most exciting part of their trip. Helmut reckoned that the money from the sale of the horses and saddles would be enough to pay for the rail journey and their passage as far as Gibraltar. After that they would have to open one of the money belts to buy tickets to England and again for the long sea passage across the Atlantic.

It was the first time that any of them had ever made a long journey on horseback, the first time any of them had been beyond Innsbruck. As they climbed towards the Brenner Pass, staying in the saddle became difficult. The remains of winter snow formed banks on either side of the road; in several places, they came across great boulders dislodged from the mountain by winter storms and sent crashing down into the Pass.

The travellers were hemmed in along the narrow roadway by massive outcrops of barren rock thrusting needle-sharp tips up into the clear blue sky. As they ascended, they came across more piles of rubble where parts of the mountainside had collapsed under the weight of snow, causing rockslides that partly blocked the roadway.

This was the main commerce route from Austria and Bavaria southwards into Italy. There was a lot of movement through the Pass, mainly people on horseback but also wagons laden with wooden crates and barrels of beer and coal for the factories in Innsbruck and sacks of grain for the flour mills. Many of the carts were covered with canvas to protect cargo against the unpredictable weather in the mountains. The carthorses—big, heavy animals the likes of which he had not seen in the valley—fascinated Helmut. As many as six were used to pull one wagon, and he marvelled at the way they moved as a team, sharing the burden. They were hitched together by chains and heavy black harnesses, polished brass rings and buckles glinting in the sunlight. But it was the sheer power of the teams of horses that amazed him as they dragged their cargoes up steep inclines, their breath sending clouds of steam into the cold mountain air. The wagons did not have shafts, but between each pair of horses was a wooden trace, the ends of which were connected by chains; the horses took the strain of the trace, and drag lines hauled the heavy load behind.

Movement around them diverted their attention from the arduous journey, and time passed quickly until the sun was overhead and they had reached the most difficult stage of the Pass, nearly twenty miles on their way.

They stopped to eat chunks of fresh bread and homemade cheese washed down with fresh milk from the convent. They had salami with tomatoes and salt.

When they resumed the climb in the afternoon, it turned cold and began to rain. Wind drove the icy drops so hard into their faces that they could hardly see where they were going; the horses began to stumble as they missed their footing. Helmut decided that it was too dangerous to continue. They dismounted and walked the animals until they reached an inn where they could sit out the storm. Everybody had the same idea and the place was crowded, but the innkeeper took pity on Johann, who was shivering from the wet and cold and found one room for the four of them. Inside was warm and comfortable, and they had a hot meal in the evening. After the others had gone to bed, Helmut went downstairs and drank beer with the men and swapped stories about life in Bavaria and Italy. Few had heard about the place called America where they were going and listened with interest as he related what Fr. Damien had told him. His audience couldn't believe that such a paradise existed and especially that you could get as much land as you could work for free. Helmut insisted that what he told them was true, for it had come from the mouths of missionary priests who had been there.

The others were fast asleep when he let himself into the room in the early hours of the morning but too much beer made him snore loudly waking Rosa and Marita and they had to cover their heads to get back to sleep.

In the morning the rain had stopped and the sun was shining. They were advised by the innkeeper to stay where they were for another day because there had been rockslides in the Pass and after the storm torrents of water were cascading down the mountain road. He warned that heavy rainfall and melting snow killed people in the Pass every year.

Helmut cursed the delay so soon after leaving Innsbruck and they sat around the inn all day getting the latest reports from occasional travellers who had braved the conditions. All advised him not to move until the weather improved; it was too dangerous, especially with the boy and women. The storm had caused a landslide at one point, and getting around the blockage was perilous.

They ate well and that night Helmut drank lots more beer and nodded off beside the fire downstairs and had to be awakened from a deep sleep by Rosa who came looking for him in the early hours of the morning. He instinctively felt for his money belt. They had been warned by Fr. Damien that there were lots of people just waiting for a chance to get their hands on easy money. The belt was still around his waist, intact.

"You will have to be careful in future not to drink too much," Rosa chided him, "for the loss of our money would be disastrous."

By the time they were ready to resume their journey next morning, traffic had built up on the steep incline leading up the northern side of the pass. As was the custom among those who regularly used the route after a rockslide, they travelled in convoy.

When they reached the scene of the landslide, it was an incredible sight. It seemed as if half a mountain had collapsed. The sheer weight of the boulders had pushed one section of the roadway ten feet to one side, and part of it was hanging over a flooded stream. Horse-drawn carts and wagons had to turn back, for there was no prospect of the road being cleared for several days. It was still possible for people to make their way around the blockage by dismounting and walking the animals along the edge of a fast-flowing stream.

Helmut was determined there would be no more delay, so he tied the horses together and led them in single file around the danger. Then, he went back and walked the boy and the women along the rugged path to safety.

He was glad when the Pass was behind, and they were moving downhill. Gradually, snow disappeared from the roadside, and in the evening, they reached the town of Vipiteno in Italy and turned westwards for St. Leonard and Merano. It was getting late, and they found an inn for the night. They were tired after trekking all day, and the most difficult part of the journey had yet to come.

While undressing for bed that night, Helmut noticed that Rosa was not wearing the money belt around her waist.

"It was cutting into my hips with the rocking of the horse," she lied, "so I took it off and put it over my shoulder instead. It's much more comfortable this way. I'll change it back to my waist when the journey on horseback is over."

When the others were asleep in the room the couple made love and afterwards slept soundly in each other's arms. If he had noticed her expanding waist or swollen breasts, Rosa would have told him about the baby, but he was so anxious to have her that he did not suspect anything unusual. She knew she would have to tell him soon, as she could not hide the bump much longer; if she could keep it a secret until they reached Milan, at least there would be no turning back at that stage.

After their lovemaking, Helmut made sure she put the money belt around her waist before he doused the lamp, but as soon as he began to snore, she took it off again, wrapped it around her hand and hid it under the pillow. In the morning, she was up and about before he was awake. When they went downstairs for breakfast, she lied that she had already eaten from the saddlebag, and she drank black coffee while the others had a tasty meal of salted herring and smoked bacon.

Rosa felt ill and needed to get out in the fresh air to avoid being sick. She knew from experience that this was only the beginning; it would get a lot worse before she got better, but she had to put up with it. Her greatest worry was the seasickness Fr. Damien had warned them about when they went aboard the ship. She might be able to cope with it, but would it harm the baby?

They set off along the mountain road with the morning sun on their backs. It got warmer as the track turned and twisted between high mountains on either side. They began to climb again, and the horses laboured up steep, stony roads that led to the highest point in the second obstacle they had to negotiate, the Jaufenpass. Helmut urged them to keep going while they had good weather; he was anxious to get over the Pass and down the other side that day.

After forty tortuous miles, which brought them clear of the Jaufenpass, they stopped to rest in St. Leonard, a sleepy town that still seemed to be in a state of hibernation. Although tired and aching from the long trek through the mountains, they got back on the horses as soon as the meal was over and covered another twenty miles through the Passiria Valley to reach the town of Merano, where they stayed the night.

Next day they moved off along the Venosta Valley where the road ran close to a picturesque alpine river, the Adige. The route meandered to and fro to avoid having to criss-cross the river which was in flood from melting snow. The fast-flowing water left deep scars on the valley floor where meadows showed signs of being ravaged by years of floodwater.

Now and again, invisible clouds of cold air descended from the mountains, and the chill made it difficult to breathe. But it revived Rosa and helped ease the discomfort she was feeling from her heavy clothing and the warm sunshine. Every five miles they dismounted and rested the horses, freeing them to graze on the sweet grass along the river. It was a peaceful valley, not unlike Hoffenfeld, but a lot warmer at that time of year. When they stopped to water the horses, Johann discovered a pool in the river, and he and Marita splashed around. They searched for minnow and hurled flat stones across the glassy surface, counting the skips before the momentum died, and they sank to the bottom in a flurry of ascending bubbles. Marita taught the boy how to time the bubbles so that he could tell the depth of the water.

Gradually, the scenery changed, and instead of fields of meadow grass, the land was used to grow grapes and soft fruit. Helmut marvelled at the neat terraces of vines following the contours of the hillside and stepped one above the other in perfect symmetry, facing south to catch the full force of the sun. When the vineyards reached all the way down to the roadway, they stopped to examine the bushes that would eventually bear heavy bunches of fruit. Each plant had four or five embryo clusters of flowers hanging from long branches trained to grow laterally along wire supports.

Helmut told them how his father had once bought barrels of black grapes in Innsbruck to try and make wine and there was great excitement at home crushing the fruit to extract the juice before it was stored in big jars in the barn to let it ferment.

"But he got something wrong, and the wine tasted like vinegar, and the mushy mess had to be dumped in the river," said Helmut. "After that any grapes he brought home were purely to eat fresh. I still remember the sweet taste when we squashed the berries between our teeth and played games spitting the pips to try to hit each other."

They travelled forty-eight miles that day—the full length of the valley. In the evening the vineyards gave way to fields of corn with green stalks that would eventually produce husks of yellow grain. Helmut knew about this corn, but they had never been able to grow it in Hoffenfeld as the season was too short.

They stopped to eat from the saddlebags and set the horses free to graze by the roadside. Marita approached a farmhouse and asked for wine to have with the remains of their cheese and dry bread. The farmer's wife did not understand a word of German, but when the girl pointed to a wine bottle and glasses on the table, she brought a pitcher of red wine. She also gave her a present of six hard-boiled eggs, which they shelled and ate with the bread and cheese.

They left the valley behind and turned south on the road to Bormio, skirting the border with Switzerland. They still had another tortuous climb ahead of them through the high snow-covered Stelvio Pass. They stopped at the first inn they came to and had a meal and a good night's sleep.

Fr. Damien had warned that the Stelvio was an even more difficult climb than the Brenner and to make sure the horses were well fed and watered before they attempted it. The pass was more than nine thousand feet, the highest pass in Europe accessible to vehicular traffic. The weather was good, and the road had been completely cleared of winter rock falls. The only hazard was from speeding coaches anxious to pass slower carts and wagons. The heavy traffic made the climb more difficult, and several times, they had to lead the horses off the road and wait until it eased. The unwritten rule was that ascending carts and coaches had right of way; if heavy vehicles stalled, there was a risk of rolling backwards on the steep mountain road and smashing into others directly behind.

Helmut found the pass far more picturesque than the Brenner, and when they reached the top, he let them dismount and rest for a while to admire the view and watch the antics of coaches and carts jockeying for position on the narrow roadway. Once they got over the Pass the terrain became easier, and despite a lot of stops they reached the town of Bormio late in the evening, arriving tired, sore, and hungry at the door of the convent where they hoped to spend the night.

The nuns were surprised to see them travelling such a dangerous road at such a late hour but made them welcome. They already had word from the convent in Innsbruck to expect the Wagontrapers. The sisters filled tubs with hot water for the weary travellers and gave them oil to rub into tired limbs to ease aches and pains. Some of the nuns were Bavarian and delighted to have somebody from the home country to talk to.

They had been told in advance that the families were survivors of the infamous Hoffenfeld Christmas Eve Massacre. The nuns wanted to get from them a first-hand account of what had happened on that awful night. Helmut told them how Marita had escaped, sparing none of the details. The nuns had heard about the Anarchists, but Helmut's story brought home to them the full horror of what happened. When they asked the girl about it, she shook her head.

"I don't want to talk about it," she said sadly. "I want to try and forget what happened."

The sisters also wanted to find out about America. Mother Superior was coming to visit in August, and they had been told that she might want some of the community to go to Rome to learn English before being sent to a hospital in a place called Chicago, one of the biggest towns in the New World. They listened wide-eyed as Helmut passed on information given to him by the priest. Helmut and Rosa suggested they should all meet sometime in America, for if Chicago was one of the main towns, it should be easy to find the convent there.

The nuns were in awe when they heard how much English the Wagontrapers had learned and insisted that the family teach them a few words and phrases. In the morning, the guests had to give another English lesson at breakfast.

"Gut morning, Miss Muller," the sisters chimed. "We take coffee now."

The nuns fussed over them and, at the same time, learned as many English words as they could. Marita told them it would make a good impression if they all greeted the Mother Superior on her arrival by saying: "Good day, Mother Superior. You are welcome", but the heavy German accents made it sound quite different. Nevertheless, the girl wrote it down, and Johann parroted it a hundred times, and in the end, the sisters were quite happy that they nearly had it right. The nuns were sorry to see them leave. The family had brought a bit of excitement into the dull routine of life in their convent isolated in the mountains. The sisters promised to remember them in their prayers until they were safely ashore in their new country.

They set out from Bormio well refreshed, and Helmut was determined to move faster that day and make it as far as Tirano, close to the Swiss border, where they would stay the night. The journey took them along a pleasant mountain valley, the Llina, through which flowed the Adda River. No sooner had they resumed their travels, however, than they had to stop again because Rosa was ill, and when Marita took Johann to a stream to play in the cool water the young mother-to-be was in so much distress that she blurted out to her husband about the baby.

He stared at her in disbelief and railed at her for keeping it a secret. He couldn't understand why she did not tell him before leaving the farm, why she let him take her on such an arduous journey and put herself and the baby in danger.

"Unklug, unklug, Frau!" he scowled at his wife, but he knew there was no turning back at that stage. However, the news meant they would have to travel more slowly and take more rest.

"We will have to take things easier," he told the sobbing Rosa. "Riding on a horse is not good for you or the baby. We will not start out any day until your sickness has passed and you are well enough to travel. There will be no more long days on the road. Once we get to Milan, you will have time to recover. After that we are finished with the horses—the rest of the journey will be by train and ship."

His anger cooled, and he comforted his wife until the others returned, but he would not let her straddle the horse again in case it caused her to lose her baby. He showed her how to ride side-saddle but she found it difficult to stay in that position for any length of time. After three hours on the road, Rosa became ill again, and they had to stop. There was no inn, but he found rooms in a farmhouse where they had a meal, and the two women and the boy went to bed early. Helmut stayed up late drinking with the surly farm owner with whom he had great difficulty communicating. The only thing they worked out between them was how much he was to pay for meals and beds for the night. Helmut said that money was not a problem and he saw the first flicker of real interest on the face of his crafty host.

Helmut didn't trust him and, to make sure he didn't try anything during the night, took his pillow and blanket from the bed and slept against the door so that it could not be opened without disturbing him. There were no strange goings on during the night, but in the morning, when he went to saddle the horses, it was clear that the saddlebags in the barn had been searched. Everything was disturbed, but nothing was taken; whoever rifled them was looking for one thing only—money.

Rosa was ill, but Helmut was anxious to get away from the farmhouse, so he told her to mount up, and they would stop and rest by the roadside until she was well enough to go on. They were hardly out of sight of the farmhouse when she became ill again. When they dismounted and she and Marita were alone the girl asked her what was wrong. Rosa told her about the baby. The girl was taken aback by the news but hid her shock and lied that it was great news and how pleased Helmut must be, and Johann too, when he found out he was going to have a new brother or sister. Rosa confided that Helmut was not too happy with her for keeping it a secret, and she was worried that it would add greatly to her discomfort during the long sea journey to America.

They travelled another fifteen miles that day before seeking a place for the night. All they could find was a disused barn, as the region was very poor. The farmhouses were not very substantial, and Helmut wondered how people survived the winters there. They ate what food they had in the saddlebags and drank water from the river and settled down to sleep on dry hay.

The still night air was warm, and Marita lay awake for hours listening to insects flitting around the barn, occasionally colliding with the door and window. The four of them cuddled up alongside each other in the hay and had a good night's sleep.

While Rosa was getting over her sickness in the morning, Helmut lifted the boy up behind him on his horse and set off in search of a farmhouse where they might buy some food and fresh milk.

Marita offered to ride ahead to see if she could find a place to eat but he would not permit it. A girl riding alone in strange countryside could be in danger. She had become quite an accomplished horse-woman since she had come to their mountain farm, and when he emerged from the barn in the morning, she had already saddled the horses and was taking them to the river to water them.

When Helmut and the boy had gone, Marita sat down to talk to Rosa about her sickness. If it became too much for her, too difficult to bear, the older woman complained, what would she do?

"If only your grandmother was here, she'd know what to do," sighed Rosa.

Marita smiled but said nothing. Her grandmother was not there but *she* was there, and *she* knew what to do. And what's more, when she took the horses to the river earlier, she had seen the dark hairy leaves of the herb her grandmother had told her about. She picked some and put them in her saddlebag, just in case.

"What would you say if I told you I had some of grandmother's remedy in my saddlebag?" she said nervously.

Rosa knew from the girl's face that she was not speaking in jest, but much as she would have liked to, she was too terrified even to think about trying that remedy.

As the hours passed, she felt worse. The sickness sapped her energy; she could not eat or drink without retching; she was holding everybody up, and soon she and her baby were going to become a burden to them all. She recalled the anger in Helmut's voice when she told him she was pregnant. How different it was from the times she was pregnant with Johann and Noel.

"I have some of the herbs to make the brew," said Marita. "If you are so ill, you should think about drinking some of it. You have to make up your own mind, but under no circumstances are you to mention it to Helmut."

They travelled all afternoon and since there was still no place to lodge, Helmut sought a room in a farmhouse again. There was only a widow and two children in the house and the young woman was glad of the money they gave her in advance for she appeared to have little or nothing to live on. There wasn't much food, but they had bread and cheese and some dried fish, and she gave them milk that she kept cool in a can in the stream.

While Helmut, Rosa and Johann sat outside in the summer night air, Marita borrowed a tin can from one of the farm children and boiled leaves in water until they produced a pint of black fluid. As soon as it cooled, she poured the dark brew into an empty wine bottle and corked it with a piece of raw potato. The widow eyed her suspiciously, wondering what she was up to. Before she went to bed, the girl packed the bottle upright inside her saddlebag to make sure it would not spill.

In the morning, it rained heavily, and they were forced to remain indoors. Rosa spent hours trying to vomit on an empty stomach, and Marita did her best to comfort her with sips of water, but it was of little use. Her body heaved and heaved until her muscles ached with the retching. Between bouts of vomiting and crying, she pleaded with Marita to do something to help her. The girl nodded and went to fetch the bottle.

When Rosa took the first sip, it tasted so foul that she could not swallow and spat it out, but Marita gave her more and held her nose until she swallowed it. Rosa thought she was going to die. It burned her throat. She cried out as it slid down into her aching, empty stomach, but the girl held her tightly and forced more into her mouth and pinched her nose again until she swallowed. Tears were running down Rosa's cheeks, but Marita did not stop until the last of the brew was gone from the cup. Helmut heard his wife sobbing, but he knew from experience that he could do nothing to help her once the sickness came. It would pass in another week or two and she would be fine again.

Marita whispered to her that she would have to drink the same amount the next morning and the remainder in the evening, and hopefully, it would put an end to her suffering. Although weak from the effects of sickness and the brew and frightened about what she was trying to do, she did not complain. They travelled a further fifteen miles that day after the rain cleared and arrived at the pleasant town of Sondrio. They stayed the night in a small hotel where the manager was so concerned about Rosa's condition that he advised Helmut to bring her to the local doctor. But Marita warned Rosa not to go, as the doctor might discover she was trying to get rid of the baby.

In the morning, Marita forced her to drink another full cup of the brew before they set out for the town of Colico on the shores of Lake Como, which they reached in the evening. They stopped for a while to admire the wide expanse of water and the rugged beauty of the mountains surrounding it. Marita recalled how Fr. Damien, in his efforts to explain how big America really was, told them if Lake Como was dropped in the middle of America, you would have trouble ever finding it again. They tasted the water, expecting it to be salty, but it was fresh, though a bit brackish. They found an inn near the shore and rooms for the night and had a meal and slept well.

Rosa called Marita in the morning to tell her she was feeling a bit better. She had no morning sickness, and for the first time, the smell of food from the kitchen did not make her ill. She felt like something to eat.

"First," the girl told her, "you have to drink more brew. Then if you still feel like it you can have some food."

This time Rosa sipped the foul-tasting fluid herself little by little until the cup was empty. It still tasted like poison, but at least she did not have the awful sickness with it. She no longer felt like eating and instead decided to go back to bed for a couple of hours.

When they eventually set out that day Marita told her to straddle the horse; she was really determined to use every method she knew to help Rosa get rid of the baby and riding astride the horse might finally dislodge it. When Helmut pointed out she must ride side-saddle Rosa said it was much more comfortable.

They had been on the road for less than an hour when Rosa slumped over the horse's neck, writhing in agony, and had it not been for the boy riding alongside, she would have tumbled to the ground. Helmut eased her down from the saddle. Her body jerked a couple of times, and she went limp in his arms. He carried her down to the lake, and Marita poured cold water on Rosa's ashen face until she opened her eyes and began to moan. Helmut went back to the road to see to the frightened boy and the horses.

Rosa knew something had happened inside her. The pain and the sickness were gone, but her hips and thighs were numb. Marita smelled the sickening odour of blood, and when she put her hand under Rosa's dress, her fingers touched the hot, sticky liquid oozing from her thighs. She knew then that Granny Muller's remedy had worked just as she told Rosa it would. The bitter black brew had got rid of the baby.

When Helmut returned, Rosa told him she had a problem and he should take the boy away for a while and Marita would see to her needs. He was reluctant to go, but she became angry, and he left.

Marita was excited and scared by the enormity of what she had done. She stripped Rosa to the waist, sat her down in the cold lake water and began to wash the red stains. Her swollen stomach convulsed a couple of times, and blood stained the water around her. Finally, a little sack appeared. Rosa turned her face away, and when the sack emerged from her thighs, Marita pushed it with her hand out into the water. Rosa cried when she saw the tiny form of her baby float away. The girl comforted her until the sobbing eased, then helped her back to the tall lakeside grass, where she dried her and dressed her. Marita told her to lie down and rest for a while before she called her husband and son to tell them that she had lost her baby.

A distraught Rosa eventually told her shocked husband how sorry she was but promised she would start another baby as soon as they got to America.

"It's not your fault. That long journey on horseback was just too much for a woman in your condition," he said. Little did he know that it was Marita who had brought about the miscarriage using a bitter brew handed down through generations of her grandmother's family.

They rested that afternoon, and while Helmut comforted his wife, Marita took the boy and went in search of transport to bring Rosa to the convent in Lecco. A farmer showed no interest until she produced a shiny gold piece. Half an hour later, he appeared with a horse and cart with hay in the back for Rosa to lie on; minutes later, they were on their way.

They climbed from the lakeshore, and it soon became clear why the farmer had to be coaxed by gold to make such a journey. The roadway was carved out of sheer rock towering over the lake—a succession of winding, zigzag terraces scaling one of the highest ridges in the Alps. Where mountain torrents cut across the tortuous roadway, wooden bridges had been built, and Helmut wondered how such a feat of engineering was even possible at that height. The farmer explained that the road was called the "Galleria" and was closed most of the winter when avalanches caused landslides and smashed bridges. It was so dangerous that nobody used it after dark at any time of the year. The views were awesome but spectacular. When the road reached its highest point on the cliff face, they could see Switzerland, and Johann watched ferries steaming up and down the lake between Como and Colico.

"They look like ants crawling on the water," he said to his father.

Rosa grew stronger as the day went on, and when they arrived at Lecco, she was able to walk from the cart to the convent door. Marita paid the driver, and he left to try to get home before dark. They rang a bell several times before a hatch in the convent gate opened and a face peered out, and Helmut explained why they were there. He handed over the letter given to him by the nuns in Innsbruck and the face disappeared for two or three minutes. Then the gate swung open without warning, and they were ushered into a deserted courtyard. Without a word, the nun led them to some bedrooms, unlocked the doors and disappeared.

They stayed there for two nights, and though they were well fed and had comfortable rooms, not a single word passed between them and their hosts for this was a contemplative community, all the members of which had taken a vow of silence. They were given a room each with one candle placed beside a barred window illuminating stone floors and walls.

Well rested, they set off on the third day for Milan. Rosa was still weak and shaken after losing the baby, and Helmut made inquiries before they left if there was a coach service available. There was not, but he was advised that when they reached Bergamo, about thirty miles away, they could sell the horses and saddles and there was a daily coach service to Milan.

They rode for a couple of hours, rested a while, rode for another couple of hours, rested again, and though progress was slow, Bergamo finally came into sight in the afternoon. This lifted their spirits. They found a place to stay that night, and while Rosa slept, Helmut and Marita took the horses and saddles to a blacksmith and asked if he could find them a cash buyer who would give them a reasonable price for them. The smith recognised a bargain when he saw one and purchased the lot himself, knowing he could sell them at a good profit. He counted out the lira under the girl's watchful eyes, and they shook hands on the deal and parted. On the way back to the inn, Marita bought two stout wooden chests complete with locks and keys, and they carried them up the narrow hotel stairs and packed all their belongings into them, ready for the morning coach to Milan.

Although they paid four full fares and extra for the trunks, the coach was so crowded that Johann had to sit on his father's knee for the entire journey, and Marita was annoyed when the man beside her nodded off several times and let his head fall on her shoulder. She complained to the driver about overcrowding, and eventually, he allowed her to sit with the luggage at the back but warned that if she fell off, it was her own doing, and he would not be responsible. Apart from short stops to change horses, the driver kept his team at a steady canter, and they arrived in Milan and drove into the City Square just as the bells were ringing the midday Angelus.

The shaken passengers alighted, their luggage was unloaded and stacked on the street, and the coach was gone as fast as it had come, leaving them standing bewildered in the hot noonday sun. They sat on the trunks for a while and watched pigeons swirling around, hoping for some scraps of food from the new arrivals. Apart from the group deposited so unceremoniously from the coach, there was not another soul in sight in the square.

Nothing went exactly to plan, Helmut thought, but despite everything that had happened, at least they were in Milan and not too far behind time; if they were lucky enough to get a train that day, they could be in Genoa by nightfall.

The hot sun burned their skin as the temperature in the square moved upward to its daily high and they were forced to seek refuge in the shade of the porch of the Cathedral nearby. One of the passengers was English, and Marita overheard him say there would be a long wait for transport because the city came to a complete standstill at that time of the day. They moved their belongings inside the Cathedral, where it was cooler, and passed the time looking at the stained-glass windows through which bright sunshine splashed light and colour on dark walls and pillars. Magnificent paintings and frescos adorned the ceilings. Helmut and Rosa spent a while in prayer before the dazzling white altar, but Marita wandered around trying to work out the meaning of Latin inscriptions. Since the massacre, she had not prayed, and even in the surroundings of the magnificent church, she was not moved to say a prayer for her dead family. The nuns were devout and kindly women who dedicated their lives through God to helping other people, but Marita had long since made up her mind that there was no God and if there was, he was not her God. Whatever beliefs she had as a child, she deliberately pushed to the back of her mind since that awful night. If there was a God, he existed only for those who helped themselves and for the rest of her life that was exactly what she intended to do—think only of herself.

Helmut went outside a couple of times to check if any transport was moving, but there was still nobody about, and the heat was unbearable; it was two hours before there was any movement. At first, it was just a few tourists on their way to visit the cathedral, followed by some cyclists crossing the square from one side to the other; then a few horse-drawn carts came into view and eventually some horse cabs and a few coaches. Within half an hour, the square in front of the cathedral was a hive of activity; there was so much noise that Helmut had to shout at Rosa to make himself heard above the grating of iron-shod wheels on stone paving. Coaches and carriages sped in all directions as if fleeing the Black

Death; everybody seemed to be in such a mad rush. The din jolted the exhausted travellers back to life. Helmut hailed a cab from the Cathedral steps and asked to be taken to a hotel near the station so that they could make their departure the next day more convenient. Luckily, it was only a short journey as the cabby drove like the Devil, and the women were terrified as the carriage lounged from side to side and slewed around street corners, steel-rimmed wheels sliding sideways on the cobblestones. He cursed everybody else on the road, shouting at them to get out of his way. The shaken passengers were glad when the swaying coach finally bounced to a halt.

The family rested in comfort that night with good food and wine and lots of coffee in the Hotel Cavour on the Place Cavour overlooking the public gardens. After dinner Helmut was offered cigars by the waiter and, unsure what to do, took two. But as soon as he lit one, he began to choke when the acrid smoke entered his lungs. The others laughed as he struggled to get his breath back.

The hotel was six storeys high, and they were on the fifth floor, a long way up the stairs, but the view over the park from the bedroom was magnificent. They were awake early the next morning, and even at that time, thousands of people were making their way along the streets to offices and factories. According to the hotel manager, Milan made everything from a needle to an anchor, but it was best known for its leather goods, particularly shoes. Johann asked what an anchor was, and the manager laughed and told him that before he got to America, he would know all about anchors, for they acted like brakes in the sea when ships wanted to stop.

Helmut went to the station to purchase train tickets to Genoa and enquired about the departure of ships for England. The ticket officer spoke German and was delighted to give his visitor a full report on what was available in his best German accent.

"Some cargo ships sail direct to the port of London," he said, "but the passenger service west from Genoa only goes as far as Gibraltar. After that, you have to take another vessel along the Atlantic coast of Spain and France to the English port of Liverpool. From there you can get direct passage to New York."

The enthusiastic railwayman proudly pointed to a huge map of Europe on the wall of his office with shipping routes east and west from Genoa clearly marked. The clerk said Helmut could have saved himself the long sea journey if instead he had travelled north to Munich. From there he could have gone all the way to the North Sea by railway and get a ship to America from Amsterdam or Bremen. He did not know that the last thing the family wanted to do was travel through Germany and face the risk of getting caught up with the Anarchists again.

The clerk gave him a train timetable and a list of sailings from Genoa for the following four days. Helmut was grateful for the help, but the clerk said it was nothing; he was delighted to get a chance to practice his German. Nevertheless, Helmut took a cigar out of his pocket and handed it over the counter. The two men shook hands, and he left.

They had the whole day in Milan and went out to have a stroll around the city. The hotel manager recommended they visit several historic buildings, but the women were terrified of getting into another cab, so they set off on foot. In the fashionable shops they tried on shoes and hats and dresses in the latest design and colours. Helmut bought boots for himself and an almost identical pair to fit the boy.

They went into a cafe and had bowls of soup and pasta and strong coffee and walked through streets lined with shops that sold goods of every description. They bought a brown paper bag full of hard-boiled sweets and sucked them until Johann got blisters on his tongue.

It was not until shops began to put up shutters that it occurred to Helmut that they had made the same blunder as the day before. Everything closed down at midday and everybody disappeared from the streets, and by the time the noon Angelus bells stopped ringing, the only signs of life were pigeons perched in the shaded eaves of high buildings and their own tired selves on the hot pavement below.

They found a cool spot in the shade and sat down to make a closer inspection of their purchases, but heat reflected from white walls and windows on the other side of the street became unbearable. Helmut knocked at shop doors and windows to try and attract the attention of somebody inside, but they were as deserted as the streets, and he got no response. What would he do if Rosa passed out on the street? What would anybody do in an emergency in this place? There was nobody to help.

They were forced to sit on the steps of a bank until siesta time ended and life returned to the city. They hailed the first cab that came along, and the women piled in with their shopping bags. Nobody cared when the driver flayed the buttocks of his unfortunate horses to make them go faster. They reached the hotel exhausted and shaken and vowed not to venture out again.

That night Marita suggested they should use the big bath beside their bedroom. They filled the white tub with warm water from a shiny gold tap, and she and Rosa got in at the same time. They washed each other and splashed about for more than an hour until the water began to cool. Johann pleaded that it was the turn of his father and himself. The women came out of the bathroom naked, laughing about their antics in the soapy water. Helmut blushed at the sight of them; he had not seen Rosa naked since they bathed in the river together as children. Marita saw his embarrassment and went into more fits of laughter.

Father and son used the same water as the two women and enjoyed the novelty of the big tub with its gold taps that spewed out hot and cold water on demand. While splashing about, Johann accidentally pulled the chain holding the plug and before they realised what had happened, the water disappeared. The pair dried themselves and dressed, and when the two women heard about the disappearing bathwater, they rolled around the bed laughing. Helmut had not seen Rosa so happy for a long time.

Next morning, they learned how to flush the toilet bowl and there were more howls of laughter when water gushed from the cistern to fill the bowl and just when it threatened to overflow it magically disappeared through the floor. Marita was the only one brave enough to use it at first and showed the others how to manage. Helmut wondered if they had baths and toilets and all that water to waste in America.

After breakfast the next morning, he paid the hotel bill with lira from the sale of the horses.

When they arrived at the station the platform was crowded. Helmut purchased three full and one-half tickets from Milan to Genoa. They had to push their way along the platform until they reached the long line of shining red and green coaches that made up the train. The windows of the carriages were so clean you could see inside: seating upholstered in black and green and red leather, curved cream ceilings with lights hanging from them, and panels between each compartment adorned with street scenes.

People peered through the glass to get a better look; others milled around impatiently waiting for the doors to open, eager to get aboard.

At the far end of the platform, there was a deafening hiss and great clouds of steam billowed from under the engine and streamed upwards until it got trapped under the glass roof of the station, where it mingled with thick black smoke belching out of a tall green smokestack. Johann's eyes danced with excitement at the hustle and bustle around them. He pleaded with his father to take him to the front of the train to see the great engine. Helmut was wary about leaving the luggage because there might be thieves about, so he asked the women to go with the boy.

The noise of escaping steam was deafening when they got close to the engine. The women were scared that it might explode but the boy tugged their clothes and urged them forward until they were alongside the iron monster.

Despite the deafening noise from escaping steam, Johann thought it the most beautiful thing he had ever seen. He was mesmerised by the magnificent green and red engine trimmed with yellow lines and bedecked with flags criss-crossed at the front. On the side of the steam tank was emblazoned the name—*Garibaldi*. Johann saw two men inside feverishly shovelling coal into an open fire, their faces black and sweaty from dust and heat. Eventually, they closed the door of the iron firebox and wiped their hands and faces with dirty rags. They shouted at passengers to stand back in case they were caught in a burst of steam; when some people did not move, the monster let out a long, shrill whistle that sent them scurrying, covering their ears with their hands to shut out the piercing noise.

Rosa lifted the boy and ran as fast as she could until they were well clear. Helmut smiled as the three of them came running along the platform and collapsed with fright on top of the luggage.

"What a monster," Johann shouted at his father. "It has only one lung and it's spitting steam and fire. We had to run for our lives!"

Eventually, the Guard arrived and opened the carriage doors one by one, starting with First Class compartments and working his way through Second and Third. The family had First Class tickets, and porters fussed over them and their luggage until they were aboard and comfortably settled in a compartment of their own. The coach was just like a hotel room with cushioned seats, framed pictures on the walls and carpet on the floor; they had a key to lock the door so as not to be disturbed during the journey.

The Guard, green flag in hand, walked the full length of the platform calling out a warning to passengers about urchins who specialised in snatching valuables from unwary passengers as the train was leaving the station. Sure enough, as the train chuffed and puffed its way along the platform, he heard a commotion, and when he looked out of the window saw three small boys hanging onto the outside of the carriages, one of them laughing and swinging a handbag he had wrestled from some unsuspecting passenger. They hung on with one hand until the train cleared the station, calmly hopped off, and disappeared into bushes growing alongside the railway track.

"Imagine risking your life for the contents of a handbag," said Helmut.

It took a long time to get clear of the city of Milan and it was only then that they realised just how big a place it was. Once away from the station, they passed dozens of factories and rows and rows of houses, terraced like the vines they had seen in the alpine valleys. Helmut wondered how so many people could survive in a place like that without land of their own or trees or a river or even a stream.

Once they left Milan behind, however, everything changed. The countryside was largely cultivated; fields were well tended with cattle and horses grazing on lush pastures and huge tracts of green grain waving in the breeze created by the train as it rolled across the landscape. The rails on which the engine dragged the heavy coaches travelled in long, straight lines, curving gently now and then to skirt a hill or avoid a river.

They crossed the lovely Plain of Lombardy. Looking backwards, they could still see the outline of the Alps, and ahead, the pointed peaks of the Apennine Mountains loomed in the brilliant morning sunshine. The flat countryside was a sea of green. They made several stops at small towns. Men in smart uniforms worked feverishly to get people off the train and get new passengers aboard so that the *Garabaldi* could be on its way again as quickly as possible.

Away from towns, activity in the countryside was not as hectic. All the planting had been done in spring and crops were now in their peak growing season. Vivid colours and the sweet country smells coming through the open carriage windows made it familiar territory to the Bavarian family. Early hay crops lay drying in the sun, ready for collection to be stacked for winter fodder. Women gathering the hay paused to wave to passengers; frightened animals grazing near the railway scurried away to escape the rumbling metal giant that had invaded their quiet pasture.

The train moved at such speed that Kurt and his family hardly had time to take it all in, but as they approached a high bridge over the River Po, the *Garibaldi* slowed to a walking pace, and they had a good look at the splendid feat of engineering. The river was in full spate because of the volume of water coming from the snow still melting in the mountains. Johann and Marita leaned out of the carriage window to get a better view of the swirling mass of dark brown water below. Helmut was glad when they reached the other side, and they left the angry foaming river behind, for the bridge appeared to be a frail structure with its feet in the river in danger of being washed away by the surging mass.

Marita spotted Mount Ebro in the distance, its peak rising so high into the heavens that it disappeared into the clouds. They left the plain and began to climb again. Travelling through the mountains, Helmut thought about the hard days they had to endure making their way over alpine passes on horseback. He hoped there would be lots of railways in America, for this was a most comfortable way to travel.

Almost three hours after leaving Milan, the *Garabaldi*, still belching black smoke and white steam, began its descent to the port of Genoa and the family had their first view of the Mediterranean Sea. It was just as Fr. Damien had described it—a patchwork of alternating shades of green and blue water stretching all the way to the horizon. Ships in the harbour appeared as toys on this great water, and Helmut wondered what chance one of those little ships would have in a storm on that vast ocean that stretched until it met the sky.

The family stayed at the Hotel des Quatres Nations chosen at the railway station when Marita saw a billboard advertising the fact that the manager spoke English. It was a pleasant enough place but not nearly as fine a hotel as the one in Milan and she was disappointed because they never met the manager all the time they were there.

There was a sailing to Gibraltar the following day, but Helmut was advised it was unlikely they would get aboard for it was a very busy sea route and sometimes people had to wait a week to travel. As it turned out, the normal service was completely booked out, as was another sailing four days later. He was disappointed by the delay and decided to make enquiries about getting passage among other vessels berthed along the quays. Eventually, he found one prepared to take him, but it was not due to sail for two days.

For the first time they had to dip into their gold coins to pay the passage. Rather than take all the money from one belt, Helmut thought they should open all three pouches, take a few coins from each and secure them again. That way, he argued, if one pouch was lost or stolen during the sea trip, their overall loss would not be so great, whereas if they used everything from one belt and lost or had one of the remaining two stolen, it would make things very difficult for them later. They were depending on the gold to get them started in their new life.

Rosa thought this was a good idea, but Marita was not so enthusiastic.

She did not want to part with more than her own fare, and when Helmut chided her about it she told him she was hanging onto her money for a business she planned to open in America. She told Rosa and Helmut that she was not interested in farm life and intended to settle down in a big town or city, and she would need all the money she had to get started.

The couple was taken aback by Marita's attitude, for they had assumed all along that she was part of the family and would settle down with them once they had found a farm in America.

"What would a young girl like you be doing all alone in a strange country?" a perplexed Helmut asked her.

Marita refused to discuss the matter further with them and did not part with any of her money. She paid her own fare.

Marita asserted her independence to show them that she was capable of making a life of her own. There was another reason. After the massacre she had put all her faith in Helmut and Rosa. He seemed so strong and capable, especially when it came to making plans for the future and arranging for them to emigrate. She looked up to him then as if he was her father. But from the day they left Innsbruck, a lot of things seemed to go wrong, and she began to doubt him, feeling that he might not be strong enough to survive in a new country. He had no idea how to deal with the situation when his wife told him she was pregnant. If it had not been for her and the secrets she learned from her grandmother, poor Rosa might have died before they ever got to Milan.

At least were now aware that she intended to strike out on her own when they got to America, and she was glad she had told them for she did not want to be burdened with the troubles of a family not her own.

Marita had done a lot of thinking since she first decided to go to America, and of one thing she was sure—she had no intention of ending up as some farmer's wife, producing a brood of children to be used as cheap labour on the family farm. If that was what she wanted, she could have stayed behind in Bavaria. The main reason she was going to the other side of the world was because she wanted something different from life.

The prostitutes in Innsbruck intrigued her. These *Brides of Satan*, as the nuns called them, seemed to live a grand life. She liked the way they dressed, the fine houses they lived in and the elegant gentlemen who escorted them. The women looked happy and carefree as they strolled around the streets hand in hand with their men; they seemed to want for nothing. She knew they had to sell their bodies to maintain a life of opulence, but that was all part of the game. Everybody had to make sacrifices if they wanted to get on in life. Look at the sacrifices a farmer's wife had to make, producing children and looking after them while burdened with the job of working alongside her husband on the farm. And all you had to look forward to in later years was the hope that your children would take care of you in your old age.

Fr. Damien had told Helmut that there was a grave shortage of women in America, so much so that the Government offered free passage from Europe for any girl who wanted to come to settle down there.

"If girls are that scarce," figured Marita, "then America is surely the place to be."

She had money—enough to buy a house. She would find other girls to work with her, and if what she saw in Innsbruck was anything to go by, she could make a lot of money by providing women for lonely men. She was obsessed with the notion that money was the key to happiness, the means to control her destiny. Never again did she want to be as vulnerable and defenceless as she was that night in Hoffenfeld, cringing in fear as men abused and tortured and murdered her family.

She was determined that any man who wanted to violate her would pay dearly for the privilege. And if and when a time came when she wanted to marry, she would make the choice and make the decisions about the kind of life she wanted to live.

The knowledge imparted by her grandmother about babies and how to prevent them and, even more importantly, how to get rid of them could be invaluable to her in such a business. The bitter brew worked for her grandmother and for her own mother, and she had made it work for Rosa, so there was no reason to believe it would not work for any woman as long as she had the dark green leaves to produce the potion. She kept some herb roots wrapped in a damp cloth in her trunk, and if she could get them to grow in America, they would provide a constant supply of brew when she needed it.

When Marita refused to share the total cost of the fares from Genoa, Rosa was annoyed by the girl's lack of trust but said nothing. She knew that this young girl was a lot more mature than she pretended to be and certainly a lot more world-wise than Helmut could ever imagine.

Considering all she had been through, Helmut thought Marita a pleasant and agreeable girl with a solid head on her shoulders. He had no idea how wise she was, but sometimes when she talked about life and what might lie ahead, he sensed a steely coldness in her, as if she still had a score to settle with the world over what happened to her family.

On May 20 they sailed out of Genoa on the barque *Spezia* bound for Gibraltar, a vessel laden with wines and shoes and clothing and sixteen passengers for whom there was very poor accommodation. The Wagontrapers shared one cabin and took turns sleeping in two single bunks.

After the initial interest in watching the crew make the vessel ready for sea, they spent a lot of time in the cabin. Once the land disappeared from view, there was nothing but flat water as far as the eye could see in any direction; luckily the weather was fine and there was no sign of the dreaded seasickness.

Passengers were told that the vessel had cargo for Marseilles and Barcelona, but the stops would be brief. In the French port, cargo was unloaded but the crew had to wait for more to arrive on the docks, and the family was allowed ashore for a couple of hours. In a market they bought freshly baked bread and cheese and fruit to help vary the diet of salted fish and pork provided by the crew.

Marseilles was a busy port; as far as the eye could see along the docks, ships were loading and unloading. Dockers argued and hurled insults at one another when something went wrong; everybody seemed to be under stress, over-excited.

The ship left port while they slept that night, and two days later they put into the Spanish port of Barcelona where they were allowed ashore for most of the day while cargo was discharged and more goods loaded. It was unbearably hot. The smell of food cooking in eating houses near the port and the rancid odour of decaying fish was nauseating in the stifling heat, so the family bought bread and tomatoes and cheese and found a shaded spot behind a grain store and sat down to eat. Bottles of wine were cheap and tasted good. They ate peaches and small, sweet oranges and apricots and black grapes. They purchased firm unripened fruit to bring back to the ship, for they had been told they would not reach Gibraltar for another four days.

At sunset the huge canvas sails were hoisted once again and the barque headed out to sea for the final leg of its journey. They sailed in ideal weather and a steady breeze for two days; then on the morning of the third day the *Spezia* ran into a storm.

It started when the blue sky clouded over, bringing with it a strong breeze that drove the vessel so hard that the crew had to take down some of the sails to slow it down. As skies darkened and the wind blew harder, white capped waves appeared; the vessel pitched up and down and lurched from side to side fighting the wind, battered on all sides by the heaving water. Every time the bow dipped into the waves white water swept the deck from bow to stern.

Helmut could not stand the buffeting inside the cabin, so he went topside to see what was going on. The sea all around them was in turmoil; foaming waves crashed headlong into the ship and the air was filled with spray. The vessel tossed around like a like a helpless toy as it battled to keep its bow into the waves. Crew staggered about the heaving deck stoically performing their tasks, bracing themselves against ropes and rails to avoid being washed overboard.

Helmut was shocked by the ferocity of the storm. The ship seemed to be in danger of being swamped. There was water everywhere, and the drenched deckhands battled the elements to secure crates and barrels that had broken loose from where they had been stored on deck. Part of the gunwale amidships had a gaping hole where a heavy crate had splintered the woodwork as it was swept overboard; water poured through every time the vessel pitched to port.

The ship itself turned and twisted, tottering momentarily on the crest of each wave before plunging down into the following trough. Sometimes the bow was still on its way downward when the next wave struck; Helmut was terrified that they would go under. But somehow, no matter how deep the trough between the waves, the prow always bounced upward again out of the water to meet the next wave.

When he got in the way of the crew, he was ordered below. He was glad the women had not been on deck to see the fury of the storm around them. They were thrown about a bit in the cabin as the vessel lurched from side to side, but none of them were hurt. Rosa suggested they should say a prayer that the storm would abate soon. She wanted to keep them occupied so that they would not fall victim to the dreadful seasickness. She prayed aloud, thanking the Blessed Mother for keeping them safe, and begged Jesus to bring their ship through the storm and protect them from illness.

Marita sat with bowed head as if she was praying, but her mind was on other things. She saw when Helmut returned that he was pale with fright, and she was worried that everything was not as it should be. It scared her, but uneasy as she felt, she could not bring herself even to say Amen to Rosa's prayers. God was not in Hoffenfeld when they needed him, and there was no reason to believe he was anywhere near them in the middle of this storm. Nothing would convince her that God existed; he was just a religious icon held up as an example of tolerance to encourage people to be good and accept any suffering that came their way. And even if she was wrong and there was a God and some kind of an afterlife, she would cross that bridge when she came to it. But for now, she intended to remain as long as she could on this earth and live every day as if it was her last.

Death no longer held any terror for her. She had faced it before and escaped when her family was murdered. Since then, she felt that once your time came to die, when there was nothing between you and the end, there was no point in fighting it. Everybody died sooner or later, and if the boat went down and she drowned, how much more acceptable that was compared to the violent end suffered by her parents and sister? Her grandmother had said that "death followed life just as night followed day", but "it was nicer to leave this world lying in a comfortable bed surrounded by your family than to die from hunger on the roadside or be trampled to death by a horse."

For the family huddled together in the cramped cabin it seemed like the end was not far away, especially during the night when sea water flowed under the door and Rosa screamed that the boat was sinking. They sat on the bunks to keep their feet dry.

At dawn, the bouncing of the ship eased, and the water slowly disappeared from their cabin floor. Helmut ventured onto deck and found the situation had changed for the better. The crew had secured the cargo that had broken loose in the storm and the ship's carpenter was patching up the damaged gunwale. The seas were not running as high, and the sun could be glimpsed from time to time through holes in the angry clouds.

As midday approached, the wind eased further, the waves got smaller, and the sun came out. Helmut brought the family on deck and joined other passengers to get some fresh air after being cooped up in the cabin all night. The crew gave them mugs of red wine and the captain apologised for the buffeting they had taken from the storm.

"Usually you get some warning," he said, "but this time it descended on us like a wolf on the fold and we did not have time to run for shelter.

"To make matters worse," he explained, "we have been blown so far off course that we have to make for Algiers in North Africa. We didn't intend to stop there, but it's the nearest port, and we need to make urgent repairs."

Some of the cargo was so damaged that it had to be dumped at sea. Bales of expensive cloth from factories in Milan bound for high-class tailors in England and France ended up tossing in the waves off the coast of North Africa. The passengers were bruised and sore from being thrown around, and although the Wagontrapers had escaped seasickness they were weak from lack of food, for they had eaten nothing for the duration of the storm.

In Algiers they purchased bread, cheese, dried fish, milk, and lots of fresh fruit but did not delay ashore; the women were scared of the dark, shifty-eyed beggars on the streets who openly carried knives and looked like they would cut your throat for a loaf of bread. They brought the food back to the ship and ate it on deck.

While the crew pumped water from the bowels of the *Spezia*, shipwrights came on board and fixed the rudder; others repaired sheets and sails damaged by the gale force winds.

Just before dark there was a flurry of activity; the repair men packed up their tools and went ashore, the sails were run up and the ship slid gently out of harbour on a light breeze and turned westwards into a blood red sunset.

Gibraltar came into sight on the morning of the seventh day after they left Genoa. The storm and the unscheduled stop at Algiers lengthened the journey by three days. The harbour was crammed with ships needing repairs after the storm. The *Spezia* had to anchor one whole day and night outside until a berth became vacant and they could get ashore.

Helmut found an inn with rooms not too far from the port area, and they rested there for three days before attempting the long sea journey to England. They had travelled nearly a thousand miles from Genoa; the sea trip to Liverpool was another 1,600 miles.

Marita opened her body-belt and gave Helmut money for her fare. The vessel on which they were booked was a paddle steamer, the *Princess Victoria*. It was the supply ship for Gibraltar and a lifeline with England for troops manning the garrison there; the Spanish authorities were hostile to the presence of an English outpost controlling access to the Mediterranean Sea and did not permit access overland through Spanish territory. The *Princess Victoria* ferried arms and food and troops and everything else the rock fortress needed to sustain life on this lonely outpost of the Empire.

The *Victoria* was a far different vessel to the *Spezia*. It had long, smooth sides of iron, great sheets of dark grey metal held together with thousands of steel bolts sweeping forward to a bow that looked sharp enough to slice through anything that crossed its path. It had no masts or sails, but in the middle, a curious sloping chimney belching black smoke just like the *Garibaldi*. On either side, paddle wheels churned the water into foam as the ship drove relentlessly forward through adverse tides and wind and white-topped waves.

Helmut counted more than a hundred passengers, most of them soldiers' wives and children on their way to England for the summer holidays. Marita and the boy listened eagerly to the English voices for words and phrases they could recognise. They were sorely disappointed at how little they understood of what was said. They did not realise that different accents were the cause of the confusion.

Johann stood at the stern and watched the great iron wheels on either side of the ship propel them through the water, leaving two white trails in its wake. Changes in weather seemed to hardly affect its progress except when the wind blew stronger and the high bow dipped low in the water so that spray from waves washed over it. Passengers moved around during the day, strolling about the deck chatting or playing games to while away the time. In bed at night, Helmut listened to the steady clump-clump-clump of engines far below in the bowels of the ship, turning the giant wheels.

"What kind of machines are they," he wondered, "that never miss a beat and never need to take a rest?"

The vessel made one stop at Vigo in Portugal to take on coal. Crossing the Bay of Biscay during the night they ran into a storm and for the first time the wheels slowed down and the ship began to roll from side to side as Atlantic waves crashed into her broadside. In their cabin Marita and Rosa felt ill and Helmut brought them on deck to get some fresh air.

It was two o'clock in the morning, and it seemed everybody had abandoned their cabins to seek respite in the open air. They held onto rails and ropes and stairways to avoid being thrown about as the ship wallowed in the Atlantic swell. Most passengers were physically ill, retching until it seemed they were going to heave up their insides. Children particularly were in great distress and mothers were so ill themselves they could do little to help them.

This was the dreaded seasickness they had been warned about; it continued throughout their last night at sea until the *Princess Victoria* left the coast of Brittany behind into the calmer waters of the English Channel and sailed into Plymouth Harbour. It was their final port of call before Liverpool.

The weather cleared and their stop was short, and they steamed out of Plymouth at noon in bright sunshine. Travelling North up the Irish Sea, the coast of England was visible all the way. That evening they watched the sun setting like a great ball of fire over Ireland.

Helmut raised his arm and pointed to it: *"Die sonne geht in Amerika unter"* he told them.

Though it was dark when they sailed up the Mersey River, Liverpool port was a hive of activity, men loading and unloading ships under lanterns swinging from long poles that bathed the quays in yellow light. When the *Princess Victoria* tied up, there were queues of horse-drawn cabs and carts waiting to ferry passengers and baggage to hotels and guesthouses. Rosa, Marita and Johann guarded their belongings on the cobbled quay while Helmut searched for a cab. He was gone a long time, but they didn't mind because they were glad of the opportunity to find their feet on dry land again after their experience in the Bay of Biscay. Helmut came back with an open cart; it was all he could find, for the cabs had already been taken by soldiers' families. After a bumpy journey to the hotel, they went to bed for their first proper night's sleep since they had left Genoa.

Helmut woke next morning to the sound of heavy cartwheels grating on cobblestones. Although it was after eight o'clock it was dark outside, for the city was shrouded in thick dark fog. One solitary gaslight was in view outside the hotel window, but the fog closed in around it, strangling the warm light before it had a chance to spread its incandescence.

They had never seen anything like this thick dark mist that reduced visibility to a couple of feet and blotted out God's daylight. When Helmut ventured through the front door of the hotel, he felt the cold dampness; tiny particles of black grime clung to his hands and face. He heard traffic on the street, but all he could see were dark figures moving about like ghosts in the shadows. The cold dust-laden air in his lungs took away his breath and started a fit of coughing that did not stop until he was back in the warmth of the hotel. The porter explained that fog was a regular occurrence in the city due to factory chimneys that pumped tons of smoke particles into the air. When there was no wind to blow them away, they hung at rooftop level, forming dark clouds that shut out the light. It would not clear until a good wind came.

He warned Helmut to keep his family in the hotel until the fog lifted for apart from being unhealthy it was dangerous when you did not know your way about. Helmut could not understand how carts and coaches and cabs used the dark streets in the thick fog without causing major accidents.

He was annoyed at being confined to the hotel, as he was anxious to get to the shipping office and find out about vessels going to America. The women were delighted with the comfort of their rooms; the seasickness had taken its toll, and they were tired and lacked the appetite to eat a decent meal. Rosa, in particular, was unwell. The miscarriage had drained her physically and emotionally, and before she had a chance to recover, the seasickness had sapped whatever strength she had left.

Rosa's poor health also caused her bouts of depression and several times she confided in Marita that she had a premonition she would not live long enough to see America.

The girl dismissed her fears as a lot of nonsense.

"We are about to set out on the last leg of our journey, and nothing is going to stop us," she said firmly. "The fog will clear, and Helmut will find a ship and we will put up with whatever discomfort comes our way knowing that within ten days of leaving Liverpool we will be in America.

"You and Helmut will get the farm you have been dreaming about, and you will build a new home, and you will have a whole new life in front of you. That's the way we planned it, and that's the way it is going to be, and you should forget the past and think instead of a bright new future ahead of you".

"No more doubts or superstitions, Rosa," she chided. "Put the old life behind you and only think of the future. From now we have to think about the new life that begins the moment we set foot in America."

But no matter how convincing Marita tried to sound, she could not get through to the older woman.

Marita sometimes had dark thoughts of her own, but she kept them to herself. They were more real when she was alone and her mind drifted back to the night of the massacre in the Holsteins' house. She could not get rid of the picture of her mother and Mrs. Holstein lying back on the couch with blood spurting through bullet holes in their dresses. Sometimes she woke in the darkness sweating, hearing again the pitiful screams for help from Maria as the brute raped and savaged her. It was all so senseless—they could have taken what they wanted; they did not have to brutalise or kill anybody. They could have raped them and satisfied their lust and taken all they could carry and go their way without resorting to torture and murder.

Rosa prayed a lot, fingering her Rosary beads, repeating incantations over and over without thinking what she was saying. The events of the past five years had taken a far heavier toll on her than on her husband or Marita. The loss of her family and infant son in the massacre and the miscarriage she had on the journey left her with intense feelings of guilt. She tried to make up for it by spending every spare moment on her knees, pleading with God and his Blessed Mother for forgiveness and protection.

Helmut was so preoccupied with arrangements for their travel that he hardly noticed his wife's deteriorating mental condition. Sometimes, when she cried at night, he scolded her, telling her to pull herself together or they would never get to America. Although he desperately needed to make love to her, she kept him at bay. He put this down to her fear of becoming pregnant.

Marita conversed a lot with the older woman, trying to cheer her up, but Rosa's continuous chanting of prayers and fingering of her Rosary beads irritated her, and the longer it continued, the more annoyed she became.

Marita sometimes felt guilty about not being able to pray herself, particularly for her parents and sister and her grandmother, who all believed fervently in the power of prayer when they were alive. But she could not do it. All the families in Hoffenfeld were good Catholics, good Christians who regularly attended Mass and did all the right things like helping one another and making sure babies were christened, and they gave generously to the Church after a good harvest. When large areas of Germany turned away from Catholicism, Bavaria remained loyal to the Church of Rome. The valley families were so strong in their faith that they had to be dissuaded by the priests in Innsbruck from taking up arms against the Bismarck Government in defence of Faith and Fatherland. What good did it do them? Where was their God that night when they needed him most?

At school they were taught not to seek revenge but to turn the other cheek when somebody hurt you. But being good and turning the other cheek when somebody punched you or kicked you or tortured and murdered only spurred evil-doers to even greater evil. They took advantage of weakness. In the valley, God gave the Anarchists a free hand to steal and rape and kill good people and get away with it. She decided that the only way to protect yourself was to fight evil with more evil and make sure you were still standing while those around you were on the ground. Heaven and Hell were invented to frighten people into being good.

Of one thing she was sure—if Fate ordained that she would die young like her sister, she would not go like a lamb to the slaughter; there would be no turning the other cheek to her attacker. If there was danger, she would strike first and kill if she had to, to survive.

Even when the girl was with the nuns in Innsbruck, Fr. Damien sensed that she had lost much of her faith; she blamed God for allowing her family to be murdered so ruthlessly. He took her aside a couple of times and tried to reassure her that bad things happened not because God authorised them or even tolerated them but because evil men were disposed to do evil things, and nothing could stop them.

"God could have made the world perfect", he reasoned with her. "He could have arranged things so that everybody only had good thoughts in their minds, did only good things and evil would not exist.

"But that would have reduced the human being to a puppet existence, his every thought and action dictated by God. So God gave us free will with the ability to do good and avoid evil. If some men found it easier to use the gift of free will to prey on their fellow man, God has no control over that.

"It is the price humanity has to pay for freedom of action", he tried to convince her.

The priest's theology was too deep for the girl's understanding, and even when she did, she could not accept his argument. Her ordeal at the hands of the marauders had robbed her of her family and what was left of her childhood.

Curiously one of the things that stuck in her memory was the fact that the groping rapist had rejected her because he found her immature and unattractive. Sometimes, as if to try and reassure herself, she stripped naked when she was alone and looked at herself in the mirror, at her breasts with their dark purple nipples, her flat stomach and the neat little dimple that formed her belly button. Her thighs were round and white except for the dark tuft of hair between them. A graceful neck and shoulders curved neatly around her chest to a narrow waist, broad hips, and rounded buttocks. From the rear, her buttocks were on the heavy side, but each cheek moved up and down independently as she moved—the way the nuns in Innsbruck had taught her to walk.

"Hold your head and shoulders steady," said Sister Attracta, "and let your hips sway naturally from side to side." She put a leather-bound copy of the Bible on the girl's head and made her walk up and down until she got it right. "If you are not going to be a nun, then you have to learn to walk, speak and behave like a lady."

She might have looked a bit scrawny when she was growing up, but Marita knew she now had the body of a real woman; the more she looked at herself, the more she was convinced that she could interest men on the lookout for a pretty woman. But any man who wanted the pleasure of holding those buttocks in his hands would have to pay dearly for the privilege. She had made up her mind firmly about that.

The only features that she did not like were her face and hair. She could not get it out of her head that her cheeks marked her out as a peasant girl. Her hair was straight and though shiny and healthy looking, added nothing to her appearance. Her grandmother told her she had beautiful hair and she should groom it every day to keep its lustre, but somehow it was too dark for her face. She had to do something about that and about her blotchy skin.

When she talked to Sr. Attracta about it the nun told her not to worry. Skin colour changed, and climate and food had a lot to do with it.

"When you get to America, the weather and the food will be very different from in Bavaria," she said. "The redness will disappear, and your skin will tan from the sun, and the colour of your hair will lighten. You have a good face and a healthy body, and that's the most important thing."

Her body was changing, and she was changing, and she began to feel that she now acted and thought more like a woman. Bavaria and her girlhood would soon be just a distant memory.

It seemed odd how her life changed so quickly. Could it be that fate had made it happen—had ordained the massacre—just to change one life, hers? That's the way it sometimes seemed to her—God or the Devil or Fate or some unseen hand had planned and executed the brutal murder of all those innocent people in that quiet valley so that Marita Muller would be thrown out into the world to live a completely different style of life. If the Anarchists had not come that night, she would probably be getting ready to marry one of the boys she had been teasing by the pool. She would sleep in his arms at night, content knowing she had a husband to love and babies to carry on his name. Before the killings, Marita had her heart set on a particular boy about the same age as herself, the younger of two sons. They had kissed and hugged and, at thirteen years of age, pledged their love for one another and were only biding their time until they were old enough to marry. Curiously, now she could hardly remember him; he was dead like the others, and his face was a blur when she tried to picture what he looked like.

She wondered whether, if there had been no massacre, she would have been content to spend the rest of her life as a farmer's wife? After all the things her grandmother had told her and taught her about the wonderful world beyond her Alpine valley would she have been content to live in Hoffenfeld? The wise old woman had aroused her curiosity and given her an appetite for a different life.

Since the murder of her family, she had two years to think about her future and how she would manage on her own.

She felt strong, particularly when she thought about her escape from the house that night to get away from the killers of her family, about the way she took control in an emergency and got rid of Rosa's baby when it threatened to delay their departure for America. She had no qualms about forcing Rosa to drink the bitter brew to abort her baby, nor did she feel any remorse when she pushed the poisoned foetus out into the lake waters with her bloody hands. It had to be done, and she did it.

Meals in the hotel in Liverpool were far different from what they were used to. The food was wholesome, but the family could not cope with the strong black tea or mugs of cold buttermilk offered as an alternative. They were served cheeses and sliced meats, and each day, they had hot meals of stew, steak, kidney pudding, roast beef, and lots of fresh vegetables that they found tasty and nourishing. Soft, creamy butter was spread thickly on freshly baked bread. The jams were delicious—sweet and sticky like honey but full of fruit that tasted as if it had just been picked.

The boy was amazed by the amount of traffic on the streets and spent his time outside the hotel listening to the curses of drivers as they whipped the sweating animals to make them move faster. He cringed as they squealed in pain from the beating. Gangs of children dodged in and out through the traffic picking up lumps of coal that had fallen from carts.

Hotel guests were warned not to go abroad at night for fear of being accosted on the streets, so Marita spent her days moving about the shops on the main streets, admiring window displays of clothing and furniture and jewellery. In a shop that sold underwear for ladies she bought several scanty items, wrapped them carefully in a parcel and concealed them in the bottom of her trunk. She felt these might come in handy in America.

Liverpool was not like Innsbruck or Milan. Many of the buildings were fine stone edifices but badly discoloured by the grime that clung to them. Even high church spires were black all the way to the top. An establishment offering wigs for women intrigued her. She tried on some of the hairpieces and particularly liked one with a shock of long blonde hair. It looked good on her, but when she heard that she would have to have most of her own hair shorn to get it to fit properly she lost interest.

More interesting were the side streets with dingy little shops selling second-hand furniture and old books and pictures, coins, guns and swords and army uniforms, even military decorations. These places were far busier than the main shopping streets and seemed to be frequented by the working class of the city.

She found the people friendly, often calling out a greeting to her as they passed and some of the boys whistled after her and tried to engage her in conversation when she laughed at their antics.

"Hi, love, fancy a walk along the Mersey?" and "What's a nice girrel like you dowin in a gaff like this?" The bolder ones wanted to know if she fancied a "bit of the other." Her problem was that she didn't understand a single word they said. It did not sound a bit like the language she had been taught by the nuns in Innsbruck. This worried her because the others depended on her to a large extent to make sense of this English-speaking world. She hoped the Americans spoke better English than these people.

She was puzzled by posters on billboards and lamp posts and disused doorways urging people to join the Salvation Army, which looked a bit odd because most of the members in Army uniform were women. She had never heard of women in an army nor was there any sign of rifles or other weapons with which to fight.

While browsing in the narrow streets she noticed women standing at corners offering themselves to men passing by. The women approached men walking alone and engaged them in conversation. Occasionally one stepped out in front of a man, opened her blouse and exposed her bare breasts. Most men had a look, stepped sideways, and continued on their way. But now and again, one would linger, exchange brief words, and the woman then walk away, followed at a discreet distance by her new acquaintance.

The girl knew instinctively that what she was witnessing was the same business carried on by the fancy women in the elegant houses in Innsbruck. The women were prostitutes and made up for their poor dress by showing their clients plenty of bare flesh to attract business; sometimes, they even encouraged a client by allowing him to touch her breast with his hand. There was no elegance or style about these women—nothing like the ladies in Innsbruck.

Marita followed one pair into a back street to see what happened. The woman opened the door of a small two-storey house and went inside, leaving it ajar for the man to follow. After he entered, two little girls emerged, and the door closed behind them. They played hopscotch on the street. Marita walked up and down, watching the door and the children playing outside. Several times, men approached, asking if she was offering "a good time", but when she shook her head forcefully to show she was not interested, they moved on. Even at that time of the day, lots of women were picking up men casually on the street and taking them to their houses or to hotels.

The door opened and the man stepped out, the woman behind him in a red nightgown. She handed him his hat and cane, kissed him on the cheek and smiled as he turned to walk back down the street. He had been with the woman for less than an hour and looked happy and well-satisfied with his encounter. The children continued the game for a few minutes until the woman, dressed for the street again, came to the front door and called them inside. She locked the door with a key and went back to her spot on the corner and began to approach more men.

Marita couldn't believe it! The woman was wearing a wedding ring, and she had two children. She was using her own home as a brothel. Where was the husband? Did he know what was going on? The small, terraced house in a Liverpool back street did not have the glamour of Innsbruck but the set-up was much more practical. What a good idea for getting started in America, she thought. This was much more discreet than a big house where men could be seen coming and going, and everybody knew what business was being transacted.

She saw white women approach black men, which seemed odd to her, and there were black women who had no inhibitions about approaching white men and going off into the back streets with them. What would happen if they became pregnant? How did they avoid it with so many men coming and going every day? Having a baby would wreck their business, and getting pregnant by a black man and having a coloured baby must be disastrous, especially for a white woman. How did they avoid pregnancy? Did they know about the dark, bitter leaves that her grandmother had shown her, or was there some other way of stopping babies? If they didn't know about the herbs in England, she could make a fortune.

Women dressed in the same uniforms she had seen on the billboards—the Salvation Army—sometimes approached the prostitutes and talked to them. She also saw other women in uniforms at street corners accompanied by a small band of musicians preaching and singing. The prostitutes ignored them and went on about their business. Passers-by abused the preachers, cursing them and telling them to go back to London as they were not wanted in Liverpool. It was then Marita realised the women were not in an army at all but were some kind of religious group.

After wasting two days trying to book passage to America, Helmut realised he had made a mistake in coming to Liverpool. They should have left the *Princess Victoria* at Portsmouth because it now appeared that the most frequent passenger service across the Atlantic went from the south coast of England. Liverpool was a huge port, but its trade was cargo business, with ships sailing to and fro around the globe. For some years, it also had a regular weekly steamship service to New York and Boston, but spiralling costs had forced the two competing shipping companies—the Inman Line and the White Star Line—to curtail the number of sailings. They cut their losses by pooling resources to run a couple of services each month. There were only two vessels booking passengers from Liverpool to New York during the following five weeks, but all the berths were already taken, and the first available accommodation was at the end of August.

Some cargo vessels also took passengers, but they were slow and uncomfortable, and everybody he talked to advised him against such a voyage. Many of the captains smuggled paying passengers aboard against the express orders of the ship's owners and thought nothing of putting them ashore at the first port of call if the owners found out.

"Seven weeks is far too long to wait," Helmut told the women. "We may have to travel back to the South Coast to get an earlier sailing."

He was faced with the choice of awaiting the return of the *Princess Victoria* from Gibraltar to return them to Portsmouth or take a coal boat to Queenstown on the south coast of Ireland to catch the transatlantic steamship service there. This latter course had the advantage of being the shortest route across the Atlantic. However, the trip across the Irish Sea to the southernmost tip of Ireland was slow, and the service to America was expensive. He was reluctant to spend more than he had to out of his cache of gold coins.

There was a service from Glasgow to America, but it involved a long overland trip by rail to Scotland. The hotel manager suggested instead that they take the Irish mail boat to Derry, on the North coast of Ireland and board the Scottish vessel, the *Clyde Clipper*, when it stopped in Lough Foyle to pick up mail on the outward journey to New York. The service was new, and since they were still trying to build up trade on the route, it was cheap; there would be no trouble getting passage, and they would be in America in about ten days. The next sailing was due to stop in Derry in four days, so they had plenty of time to get there. A mail boat sailed to Derry every day from the nearby port of Heysham. Helmut was delighted at the prospect of getting to America within two weeks and thanked the manager profusely for his advice.

CHAPTER THREE

BLOOD ON THE COBBLESTONES

Four days after arriving in Liverpool the Wagontraper family were on the move again—to Ireland. They dragged the wooden chests of belongings aboard the Heysham ferry and were still searching for seats in the crowded deck when the vessel glided away from its dock on the Mersey River and sailed out into a choppy Irish Sea; the English coast quickly receded into the morning mist.

It was so crowded they never found seats and were forced to squat on the deck near the stern. It was cold at first but as they left the land behind the vessel emerged from the mist into bright sunshine that soon warmed them. Passengers who had been indoors came on deck to enjoy the fine weather.

The family listened to talk going on around them but had a hard time trying to figure out what they were saying, and Helmut wondered about the English they had learned in the valley. Would they ever meet people who spoke the same language as the nuns taught them?

Passengers huddled in groups on deck and kept to themselves; they were quiet-spoken and not very friendly. For the most part they were poor-looking people, gaunt in appearance, badly dressed, and the children looked undernourished. The men were rough, weather-beaten; the faces of the women were hardly visible at all for they wore shawls over their head and shoulders; children, some of them barefoot, sat close to their mothers.

The women and children stayed apart from the men. They were all dressed very much the same—black or dark grey dresses down to their ankles with heavy shawls tied loosely around the waist. They reminded Marita of the dark-skinned women they had seen in North Africa when they sheltered after the storm; when the shawls slipped from their heads in the breeze, they revealed coarse long hair and pudgy red cheeks. She noticed that many of them also had red hair.

The men wore peaked cloth caps and jackets, reaching almost to their knees with stout steel-tipped boots that seemed several sizes too big. They drank dark brown liquid from crockery bottles, and the more they drank, the louder their banter; some sang songs and were applauded and cheered by their companions. They seemed to have an endless supply of bottles with them, and the songs continued one after the other for the journey. The children played games with empty bottles, tossing them over the side of the ship and watching to see how long they could stay afloat before being swallowed by the foaming wake.

The women conversed among themselves, but it was impossible to hear anything because they spoke in such low tones. They took no part in the drinking. They made sure the children did not stray too far and kept themselves busy attending to babies hidden under the shawls. And all the time they babbled away in a strange lilting tongue. They reminded Rosa of hens on the farm keeping an anxious watch on their clutch of chickens.

On the upper decks, passengers were better dressed. Stewards in neat blue uniforms served food and drinks throughout the voyage. The men had long curled moustaches and carried canes and paced up and down the deck like soldiers as if their constant activity would bring them more quickly to their destination. The Wagontrapers were not close enough to hear what was being said because of the noise of the ship's engines. When the ferry sailed up Lough Foyle and docked in the heart of the city, passengers from the upper decks disembarked first; only when the last of them had departed were Helmut and his family and a throng of second-class passengers allowed to push their way down a narrow gangplank to the quayside.

By the time they got ashore, finding transport was difficult because the first-class passengers had taken most of what was available. Many made their way on foot along the quays, carrying their belongings on their shoulders. One of the crewmen told Helmut that the shortage of cabs was due to trouble in the city earlier in the day, which kept a lot of the normal cabbies off the road. Armed men had attacked policemen, and a big search was going on in the city for the group responsible.

There was a hotel within easy walking distance, but the trunks were too heavy to carry, and they were forced to wait on the quay for almost an hour for a sidecar.

After the excitement of Liverpool, Derry was a sleepy, easy-going place. There were fewer people on the streets during the day, especially in the shops, and there was none of the traffic hustle and bustle they had seen in Liverpool or Milan. The pace of life was much more leisurely; people strolled around in the warm sunshine or stood in groups at street corners smoking and talking.

Marita and the boy went for a walk in the evening sunshine through the streets near the hotel. Many buildings were ramshackle and neglected, a drab place compared to Innsbruck. Even the sandstone facades of the more substantial establishments had great patches of green moss and wildflowers and weeds growing on ledges; many looked as if they were about to collapse, with gable walls propped up by stout wooden beams. There were plenty of shops, but they were small and poorly stocked, and there never seemed to be more than a handful of customers inside.

Although vehicle traffic was sparse, the girl had never seen so many people on bicycles; it seemed to be the favourite form of transport, especially among younger people. From her hotel window on the morning after they arrived, she saw hundreds of girls cycling to work, shouting to one another and laughing as they passed through the square.

Marita marvelled at the way they manoeuvred the cycles to make sure they avoided one another, long cotton dresses tucked neatly under their bums on the saddle to prevent the material from catching in the spokes of the wheels. Sometimes there were two girls on one bike, the second sitting on a carrier behind the other. There were squeals of laughter when the wheels went into ruts on the cobbled streets, causing the metal carrier to pinch their buttocks through light cotton skirts. She had never seen so many people on cycles.

But the thing that struck her most about the city was the number of people begging on the streets while she was out walking. Five or six children at a time pushed forward with outstretched hands in the hope of getting a coin, and no matter how little she gave, they thanked her profusely in their strange tongue. Begging women always seemed to have a baby tucked inside their shawl, and children hanging onto their long skirts had barely enough clothing to cover their young bodies; none wore shoes.

The beggars all had the same bewildered look about them. She could see it in the eyes of the women especially, a mixture of despair and pain. In Algiers, the women had only slits in their head covering where eyes should have been, and the men had a shiftiness that instantly put you on guard. These people were different, especially the women. They were poor, they were pleading, but you had the uncomfortable feeling there was a lot more to them. When they begged, their voices had no emotion, just a monologue of words that sounded like a litany of prayers, words that had lost their meaning. The most striking thing about them was the look of hunger on their faces.

She felt uncomfortable when she was near them. It was as if they were waiting and watching, biding their time for something to happen to change their lives and end their poverty. And she felt threatened when they crowded around her on the footpath, thrusting outstretched hands at her, pleading for help. She pulled her coat tightly around her and quickly retreated to the safety of the hotel, vowing not to venture onto the streets again. She urged Helmut to make sure to get tickets for the next sailing to America. The *Clyde Clipper* was due in two days' time, and she wanted to get away from the unhappy city as soon as possible.

Alone with Rosa that night, she confided that there was a smell of death about the place, and she could not rid herself of the eerie feeling she got every time she was confronted by the outstretched begging hands and pleading eyes. She had been told that poverty was a legacy of a great famine that had struck Ireland more than thirty years before, but Marita felt there was more to it than that. There were a lot of soldiers about, and where you had armed soldiers, trouble was not too far away.

Sometimes when she met mounted patrols on the street the riders whistled and howled and made rude gestures at her. They thought it was all good fun. The soldiers looked neat in their red and blue uniforms with white belts and fancy hats and polished rifles; but she was terrified of their attentions.

Helmut completed arrangements to sail on the *Clyde Clipper* the following Sunday, which meant they would be on their way in a couple of days. The arrangement was that they would board a launch on the river not far from the hotel, which would take them to where their ship was anchored in Lough Foyle, its last port of call before it sailed for America.

The family did not like the impoverished Irish city to which circumstances had forced them to visit on their journey to America, so they spent most of their time indoors, out of reach of the beggars and the soldiers who seemed to be around every street corner. Those last few days hanging about the hotel seemed endless, but they awoke early on Sunday full of excitement; this was the day they would set sail on the last leg of their journey to the New World and a new life.

Their final day in Derry coincided with the Feast of Corpus Christi, a major religious festival in a city that was predominantly Catholic. Helmut thought it would be a good idea to go to church to pray for a safe journey to America. They had not managed to attend Mass since they left Bavaria. Marita had no interest in going to Mass, but she agreed because she did not want to be left on her own in the hotel.

They were given directions to the Cathedral, and as they got closer, the streets became crowded with people making their way towards the great stone edifice on the hillside overlooking the city. Outside the church, hundreds of people stood around talking and smoking. When Helmut and his family went inside, it was only half full, but when a bell rang from the tower, the huge church filled in a couple of minutes.

Before Mass began, Helmut and Rosa and the boy knelt in prayer. Marita sat in the pew and looked around her. She was fascinated by the magnificent interior. There were not as many frescoes or stained-glass windows as in the churches in Innsbruck and Milan, but still, it was very beautiful. Light coming through tall leaded windows splashed around the marble altars and walls and glinted on mosaics of Joseph and Mary and the baby Jesus and the figures of Saints. Tall Roman columns of sandstone supported the arched roof; stalagmites of white marble soared upwards from its three altars.

She turned her attention to the priest when he climbed into the pulpit to give the sermon. The congregation fell silent, and Helmut and the others listened attentively, hoping that they could recognise enough words to follow what he was saying. But even though his voice was loud and clear, the priest was still difficult to understand.

He announced first that the total debt on the new Cathedral had been completely cleared, thanks to the generosity of the congregation and very generous contributions from businesspeople in the city.

He changed the subject to talk about the Corpus Christi procession to be held in the city that afternoon. To Marita, who understood some of the sermon, it was all very confusing. On one hand, he said it was the duty of every Catholic to attend the procession, to give public testament to the glory of Christ who had shed his blood for them; on the other, he was warning people to stay away,

"You all know who I am talking about," he continued, raising his voice and using an upright arm to reinforce his words. "This procession is purely and solely a religious occasion, and if the Fenians try to disrupt it and turn it into a political meeting, they do so at their peril and under threat of excommunication from the Church." He spat the words out one by one, slowly, deliberately, so that nobody could be in any doubt.

"There has been enough bloodshed and strife in this city in recent days and the Fenians are the cause of it. Today, we celebrate the feast of the Body of Christ, that body that shed blood so that we might be saved. There is to be no other bloodshed—that is Christ's will, and it is our will."

Rosa looked at Marita and shook her head. The few words they recognised made little sense, but Helmut guessed he was talking about the shootings in the city the day they arrived from Liverpool, the trouble that kept most of the cabs off the streets when the boat arrived.

When the priest turned to leave the pulpit, a section of the congregation began to cough and shuffle their feet; the young priest stopped immediately and turned to face the congregation again, his face red with anger.

"I'm warning you Fenians," he raised his voice and shook his fist to make sure he got his point across, "if you cause trouble, you will face excommunication and the wrath of God! I will not have you involve innocent people in your bloody work!"

A group of men near the back of the church stood up, started to sing and marched out in single file, leaving the incensed priest flailing his arms and shouting after them, repeating his warning that they were doing the work of the Devil.

It took a while for the congregation to settle down after the disruption, and when the time came to take Communion, people queued in the aisles and waited their turn to kneel at the altar rails and receive the host. It reminded Marita of the Bible miracle of the loaves and fishes in the desert. It took so long to place the bread tablets on the outstretched tongues of the throng that the Wagontrapers did not arrive back in the hotel until nearly two hours after they left. The visit to the church had been a tiring and confusing experience, except for Johann, who nodded off during the sermon and had to be carried all the way home on his father's shoulder.

The priest and his sermon were the chief topics of conversation as they ate breakfast in the hotel. The manager told them not to venture out during the parade in case there was trouble. Anyhow, he told them they could see everything from the balcony of the hotel, which overlooked the square where the Corpus Christi ceremonies were due to take place.

Helmut asked the manager about the group the priest had shouted at—the Fenians. Who were they, and why would they turn a religious procession into a political meeting? Rather than explain what it was all about, especially with his guest's poor English the manager replied simply that the Fenians were a rebel organisation who wanted the English to leave Ireland and let the Irish run their own country. He turned and walked away, leaving Helmut as confused as ever.

Long before the procession from the Cathedral began, the square began to fill with people anxious to find a space close to the platform where the ceremonies would take place. It was a warm day, and everybody was dressed in light summer clothes, adding to the festive atmosphere of the occasion. The women still had their heads covered, the older ones with hats and the younger ones with scarves. Marita was intrigued by the way young girls used the scarves to bind their long hair on top of the head. The begging women were there too, their heavy black shawls over their heads and shoulders and wrapped around their bodies. Some men wore soft hats and a few had bowlers, but the vast majority had flat tweed caps with peaks—the same ones they had seen on the boat from Liverpool. Small girls wore long white dresses and veils.

The barefoot children were there too, some begging, others dodging in and out of the crowd playing hide and seek, much to the annoyance of the adults.

Hotels, teahouses, shops, and public drinking houses did great business. Men and women stood around in groups outside the pubs drinking from the same crockery bottles Marita had seen on the mail boat. Hawkers were selling fruit and children queued with their pennies to get a sticky toffee apple or a poke of hard-boiled sweets. Marita realised it was the first time since they arrived in Ireland that she had seen people smiling and happy.

As the time for the procession neared it got hotter there was cursing and swearing and occasional scuffling as tempers frayed among men drinking the black beer.

At noon, a statue of the Virgin Mary was carried into the square. The crowd stopped drinking and fell silent. Behind the statue came the bishop and priests dressed in long white robes, followed by religious brothers and a large contingent of nuns with starched white headdresses and long black robes. Altar boys carried metal crosses, young arms struggling to hold them upright in the sweltering heat.

When the last of the boys had taken up position, the bishop, holding a tall shepherd's crook in one hand, led the throng in the Rosary, a litany of prayers heard only as a great mumble. As soon as prayers started, women made sure their heads were covered and the men removed their cloth caps, soft hats and bowlers. Prayers were followed by hymns, prayers, and more hymns. Everybody participated loudly in the prayers, but when it was time to sing, the men fell silent, leaving it to the women to carry it through.

The ceremony lasted for nearly an hour, and Helmut and Rosa and some other guests knelt down on the balcony when the bishop gave the final blessing. The procession reformed and slowly began to make its way out of the square.

Then a strange thing happened. A group of men near the stage where the bishop had been standing mounted the platform and faced the crowd. They pulled green sashes over their heads, wearing them like bandoliers, put on their peak caps and began to sing. It was difficult to hear at first, for the men were so few and the crowd so large, but gradually, as people near the stage joined in, the noise spread outwards like ripples from a pebble in a pond until it seemed everybody in the square was singing.

When it came to the chorus the voices got louder and the men on the platform punched the air with raised fists to give more emphasis to the words. The singing meant nothing to Helmut, but he sensed that the mood of the religious ceremony had changed.

By the time he heard the chorus for the third time, he was able to put some of the words together:

We will be true to Thee till death,

We will be true to Thee till death.

A lone priest mounted the platform, waving his arms and shouting at the men to stop, but they carried on as if he did not exist. People sang their hearts out and neither heard nor cared what the frantic cleric was saying. Sensing that the Fenians had taken control, the clergy abandoned any attempt to reform the possession, and the infuriated bishop and his retinue retreated quickly into a side street while nuns herded white-veiled girls and altar boys back to the Cathedral, leaving behind them a square filled with thousands of defiant voices singing.

Faith of our fathers living still,

In spite of dungeon fire and sword.

Helmut felt Johann tugging at his elbow, and when he turned to ask what the matter was, the boy pointed to a street beside the hotel. Soldiers were marching towards the square, four deep, rifles on their shoulders. While Helmut watched, an officer shouted orders, and the marching men stopped, formed two lines across the street junction and fixed bayonets to the muzzles of their guns.

The first line of men went down on one knee and pointed their rifles at the people in the square. When an officer gave the command, there was a loud crackle as the kneeling men fired a volley, and a cloud of acrid smoke hung briefly in the still air in front of them. Most of the people on the balcony scurried inside to safety, but Helmut froze in fear. He could not take his eyes off the scene. Before the first cloud of smoke from the rifles had time to disperse, the kneeling soldiers stood up and stepped backwards, and the men behind stepped forward and went down on one knee. Another command and loud crackling of gunfire again filled the air. This time Helmut and the women shifted their eyes to the crowd in the square. People nearest to the soldiers were on the ground; others staggered about, holding their hands over wounds where the bullets had struck. Some cried out for help; others stared at them in disbelief. The men on the platform were still singing as if nothing had happened.

The first volley had gone over the heads of the singing throng, but the second was fired into them, and a lot of people were struck down. The seconds ticked away, the singing faltered, then stopped altogether as the full impact of what had happened became clear. There followed an eerie silence broken only by the piercing screams for help from people writhing in agony on the ground.

Panic set in as word spread that the soldiers were shooting, and people started screaming. They pushed and shoved to get out of the line of fire, and in the confusion, old people and children were knocked to the ground and trampled underfoot. The wounded and injured were abandoned as the throng sought refuge in side streets.

After firing two volleys, the soldiers removed their bayonets, reformed into lines of four and calmly marched away as if nothing had happened.

They disappeared down the street beside the hotel from where Johann had first seen them coming. The few people who had remained on the hotel balcony were stunned by the events unfolding before their eyes. People who had fled indoors were praying or crying. The hotel manager ordered the doors to be locked and advised people to go to their rooms and stay there until the trouble was over.

Forty or fifty people injured in the shooting or trampled by the fleeing crowd still lay in the emptying square; some were deadly still, others moved in fits, bodies convulsing as the lifeblood drained out of them. A few who still had the strength to cry out waved their arms in desperation and pleaded for somebody to help them. The cries continued, but nobody went to their aid. Everybody was intent on getting away from the gunfire.

While the last of the stragglers were still leaving the square, Helmut heard the sound of approaching horses and wagons, metal wheels grating on the cobblestones. The noise got louder until a convoy of white vans appeared, and when they came to a halt, women in nurses' uniforms got out and hurried to tend the wounded. They worked feverishly among the stricken people. They put tourniquets on wounded limbs, swathed bloody heads in bandages and padded chest and back wounds with thick gauze pads to try and stem the flow of blood from the gaping bullet holes and keep them alive until they reached the hospital. The more seriously injured were put on stretchers and driven away in ambulances; the less serious were treated where they lay. Those beyond help were laid out alongside one another on the procession platform.

A couple of hours passed before the nurses, their immaculate white uniforms stained in blood, completed their work; when they left, gangs of men arrived with handcarts and brushes and shovels. They poured sawdust over the bloody areas on the square; they stood around smoking and talking in low voices to give the sawdust time to soak up the blood, then swept it into neat piles and loaded it back onto the carts.

While the workmen were cleaning up two black vans arrived, and Helmut counted as policemen collected thirteen bodies. After the vans left, the square was deserted, silent as a morgue.

Although what they had witnessed terrified them, Helmut and a few others from the hotel remained at their vantage point overlooking the square until the last bodies were removed. The whole bloody affair had taken nearly three hours from start to finish, but to the watchers from the hotel, it seemed like minutes.

Shaking with fear, Marita went to her room and locked the door. It was the second time in her young life that she had witnessed a massacre. The killings were no different from what she had seen in Hoffenfeld. Was there any place in the world where people could live their lives in peace? Was it possible the same sort of thing could happen in America?

She could not understand why no attempt was made to fight back. The men in the crowd numbered thousands, and the soldiers were fewer than fifty. What sort of cowards were these people who allowed their women and children to be slaughtered while they scurried off like rats without lifting a finger to help the injured or to strike back against the people who had done it? Why would soldiers kill people for singing at a church parade?

Helmut was shocked too and angry. This was what the young priest had been shouting about at Mass when he warned against turning the procession into an act of political defiance. The appearance of the green sashes had changed the nature of the gathering as the young priest predicted it would. Clearly, he knew more than he was willing to say in the church. He tried to warn them, but they would not listen.

"Why did the soldiers fire into the crowd when warning shots would have achieved the same result?" Helmut asked the terrified manager. "Why did they shoot people?"

"Clearly the attack was planned well in advance," answered the white-faced manager, "for not only were there soldiers hiding in the streets nearby before the Corpus Christi ceremonies began but the ambulances and nurses were there too and the cleaners with their handcarts and police vans to carry off the dead. This was a reprisal against the Fenians for a number of attacks on soldiers in recent weeks. Clearly a decision was taken by somebody in authority to punish the rebels and their supporters.

The problem now is that the Fenians will take revenge on the army and police, and God knows where it will all end."

Helmut was glad that they would be on the *Clyde Clipper* and far away from this dreadful place before the day was through.

The hotel gong summoned guests to afternoon tea, but few heeded the call. The family stayed in their room and packed the last of their belongings in preparation for departure. Each hour that passed seemed endless, and they became more and more anxious; they needed to get out of the hotel and away from this place as soon as they could.

Helmut and Marita counted what remained of the gold coins and extracted enough to pay the hotel bill and purchase passage for two adults and two children on the ship. They had to be more careful than ever with the money belts because he had been warned that crewmen knew that some emigrants had money with them, and poorly paid seamen would do anything to get their hands on it. Sooner than put any of the women at risk Helmut suggested that he should carry what remained of the gold as he felt he would be better able to defend himself if attacked.

Marita was not happy with the arrangement but, deciding that it was not the time to argue, handed over her money belt; the most important thing was to get away from this hellhole.

When the time finally came to leave, porters carried their bags and trunks downstairs to await the arrival of the carriage that was to take them to the ferry. As they waited in the foyer there was a commotion near the hotel, and they heard gunfire. One of the porters disappeared and returned a short time later to say that a group of men had ambushed soldiers and there were dead bodies in the street only a couple of hundred yards from the hotel.

Fifteen minutes later, they heard more shots. This time, they were told it was the soldiers firing at Fenians trying to escape through one of the city gates. There was panic among the guests, and the manager tried to relieve the hysteria by advising them to go back to their bedrooms, where they would be perfectly safe, until the situation calmed down.

Helmut and Rosa refused to go upstairs in case they missed their transport, but the manager told them it was a waste of time hanging around the foyer, as no cabby would venture onto the streets while the soldiers were on the rampage. The main hotel doors were closed, and the Wagontrapers reluctantly went back to their room, but not before Helmut threatened the manager that if they missed the clipper, it would mean another five-day stay in Derry, and he would hold the hotel responsible.

The women were terrified at the idea of having to go out into a city with so much trouble on the streets but were more scared at the prospect of being forced to stay in Derry for another week.

The situation became so tense that Rosa pleaded with her husband to find some way to get them to the ferry, for she did not want to spend another night in the place. And Marita made it clear that no matter what happened she was going to catch the ferry even if she had to walk to the river on her own.

Helmut knew that if they missed the *Clyde Clipper* their lives would be in danger. The tit-for-tat killings would go on and God knows where it would end. They were safe in the hotel for the moment, but if they had to wait around for the best part of another week for the next ship, he was afraid they would get caught up in some kind of a revolution and God knows what would happen to them.

They had left Hoffenfeld to get away from the nightmare of a massacre and now found themselves stranded in a strange city in a strange country thousands of miles away, in the middle of a civil war. He had to think of some way to get the family away from Derry. It was not a big city. The hotel was not far from the river, and he figured from what he knew that it might be possible to leave by the rear and walk through the narrow streets to the docks. If they could make it that far, he was sure they would have no trouble finding the ferry to take them to the *Clyde Clipper*.

He slipped out of the room and went downstairs to the porter and asked how far away the river was and how they might get there. Helmut gave the man a gold piece and, in return, got a rough hand-drawn map of the streets between the hotel and the docks with the shortest route marked out. The porter estimated the distance at about a quarter mile; even carrying their own baggage, they should be able to get there in twenty or thirty minutes at most. He warned Helmut that though there was no curfew in operation, the only people out and about were soldiers and police, and they were in such a rage over the shooting of their comrades that they would fire at anybody or anything that moved. It was a big risk bringing a family onto the streets in such a situation.

Helmut knew it was dangerous but had made up his mind. When he went upstairs to talk to the women, he told them the river was only twenty minutes away and they could walk there easily.

"I have a map to guide us," he said to reassure them. "Take only what is necessary and leave the rest behind, for we have to move quickly. One way or another, we will get out of this place today. Get ready as fast as you can."

Although fearful of what lay ahead the women extracted from the trunks their most important possessions, enough to fill one leather case each. Marita took only a few dresses she had bought in Milan and inside one of them hid the herb roots and the saucy underwear she had bought in Liverpool. The two women and the boy each carried one case and Helmut two, and they were well able to manage.

Helmut instructed the women and Johann what to do if they ran into any patrols; simply put down the bags and raise their arms in the air and he would do the talking. The soldiers would understand as soon as they began to speak that they were foreigners and had nothing to do with the killings in the city or with the Fenian rebels.

"But the one thing you must not do, no matter what happens, is run; this might give the soldiers an excuse to start shooting," he warned. "Most of the patrols seem to be outside the city walls where Fenians are hiding. We could be lucky and meet nobody on the way to the ferry."

They had to leave behind the large trunks bought in Italy that contained most of their clothing and a few mementos from their cabin home. Before they left, Marita tried to sell the trunks and contents to the hotel porter, but he said he was not interested. He knew they would have to leave the trunks behind in any event, and they would be his for nothing. Marita was annoyed by the crafty hotel employee and gave the manager instructions to store the trunks until she could have them picked up at a later date and shipped to America.

"That will take the smirk off his face," she said to Johann.

The family left early to make sure they got to the river before dusk. If they ran into a patrol, it would still be daylight, and the soldiers would see clearly that they were not a threat. The worst that could happen was an enforced return to the hotel.

The sun was low in the west as the porter unlocked the tradesmen's entrance at the rear, and they cautiously made their way through shaded streets that led to the river. The place appeared deserted, not even a dog to be seen. They walked between rows of small red brick homes which showed no sign of life except for tell-tale thin lines of smoke rising from chimneys and occasionally a slight movement of curtains in windows as they passed. It was so tense that they did not dare utter a word to one another. The only sound that broke the languid evening air was the noise of their footfalls on worn cobblestones. Now and again, they heard the crack of rifle shots that rang out over a city cowed and silent but the gunfire seemed a long way off. They heard the clatter of horses' hooves. This time, they sounded nearer, but the area they were in was a maze of narrow streets, and it was hard to know exactly where the horses were. In any case, it was unlikely that their paths would cross.

"Stay close together," whispered Helmut, "in case the soldiers appear."

He studied the rough map at each street corner and pointed the way forward, urging Rosa and Marita to keep moving. There was no more shooting, just the ring of metal horseshoes on cobblestones in a street somewhere nearby.

Johann touched his father's arm and whispered: "Poppa, there are horses coming!" Helmut looked up just in time to see a mounted troop wheel around the corner at the far end of the street, coming towards them at the trot. He dropped the luggage and raised his arms above his head.

"Schiebt nicht! Schiebt nicht! Wir sind eine deutsche Familie die nach

Amerika auswandert!" He shouted to make sure the soldiers could hear him above the clatter of the horses' hooves. But the troopers never faltered, and the horses broke into a gallop. They rode four abreast, rifles slung over their shoulders.

The two women went down on their knees, instinctively covering their heads with their arms. Helmut stayed on his feet, hands waving in the air, pleading with the horsemen not to shoot. But the words meant nothing to the soldiers, for in his panic, he did not realise he was calling to them in his native tongue.

Then all hell broke loose as rifles crackled in unison. Soldiers were shouting at one another, and their terrified horses reared up on their hind legs. Helmut turned his back on them and pulled Johann to the ground and lay on top to shield him from the hail of bullets. He could hear the clatter of the horses' hooves above the squealing of animals and the crackle of gunfire. He waited for the bullets to tear into his flesh.

The gunfire and shouting continued for a few minutes, then ceased as suddenly as it had begun. Helmut could not believe he had not been hit. He was alive, and the boy under him was alive, and he could see the two women lying to his right; they were terrified and crying but not in pain. The soldiers had only fired to frighten them, he thought. He quickly put his head down again when three more shots rang out.

He waited a while in the silence before he turned his head around to see what was happening, fearful in case any sudden movement might give the soldiers an excuse to start shooting again.

Fifty yards away, there were troopers lying on the ground, and beside them, riderless horses tossing their heads in the air, snorting. Two soldiers hung from their saddles, feet caught in stirrups, heads touching the ground. One of the horses was lying on its side, hind legs kicking pathetically in the air. There was no sign of life from any of the soldiers, no movement at all on the street except the tossing manes of frightened animals and the smell of fresh blood.

While he was still trying to figure out what had happened Helmut spotted a lone soldier beside his horse on the ground. He was trying desperately to extricate his foot from where it was trapped in the stirrup under the animal. He had a pistol in his hand, and there was blood on the side of his face.

The women lay completely still where they had fallen. Helmut could hear Marita sobbing, and he knew she was okay, but there was no sound from his wife, who was motionless. If she had been hit, he was sure she would have cried out unless a bullet had caught her on the head. Please God she was all right.

"Stay where you are and lie very still," he whispered. "Is anybody hurt?"

"Do something, Helmut. For God's sake, do something," Marita whispered. "Is Johann hurt?"

"The boy is not hurt," he said. "Now keep quiet and lie still."

Helmut had no way of knowing what had happened, and he was afraid even to lift his head to see what was going on in case the shooting started again.

They had walked into a street where rebels were lying in wait for the soldiers. When the mounted men entered from the other end, the troopers were momentarily distracted by the appearance of the family coming towards them with their arms in the air. They did not spot rifle muzzles protruding from windows and doorways until it was too late. They were caught in a volley of gunfire, ambushed. Fewer than twenty shots had been fired, and even though the soldiers had rifles and side arms, it was doubtful that they had managed to get off even a single round before they went down under a barrage of gunfire from the rebels.

After a few more minutes Helmut lifted his head to look up the street. As far as he could see, the soldiers were all motionless on the ground except for the lone trooper who had managed to free himself from his fallen mount; he was crawling towards them with a pistol in his hand.

He saw three or four people emerge from doorways. They moved among the bodies of the soldiers. They picked up pistols and rifles and stripped the men of their ammunition pouches. The wounded horse was still squealing, but it had lost so much blood that it no longer had the strength to kick its legs.

The crawling soldier had almost reached the spot where Helmut and Johann were lying when there was a shout from one of the men in the shadows. Realising he had been spotted, he crawled quickly over to the two women and put his pistol to Marita's head.

"On your feet, Fenian bitch!" he said, and when she got up, he stood behind her.

"Do what he says, Marita!" Helmut shouted.

The soldier fired a couple of shots at his pursuers, using Marita for cover. The men retreated into darkened doorways and shouted threats at him. Even though they had him outnumbered, they were afraid to come out into the open to attack him.

Helmut could not see the faces of the Fenians in the dark street, but he recognised the distinctive tweed caps with big peaks, the same ones worn by the men at the procession.

When the soldier got to his feet, he roughly pulled the sobbing girl close to him, keeping her between himself and the Fenians who flitted from doorway to doorway, stalking him like an animal but wary of the pistol he brandished in his right hand. His left arm encircled Marita's neck. Slowly, he backed away along the street, dragging his injured foot.

Helmut and Johann moved closer to Rosa who was breathing steadily but seemed to be in a faint. The boy shook his mother and begged her to wake up.

In the dusk, the gunmen followed the lone soldier until they passed the spot where Helmut and Rosa and Johann were lying. They did not even bother to glance in their direction.

He raised the limp body of his wife upright and managed to get his shoulder under her waist, and when he was sure she would not slip off, he struggled along the street towards the river with her, followed by the boy. He picked his way around the bodies of the dead soldiers and snorting horses and headed in the direction of the ferry.

The boatmen heard the shooting and were about to push off when they spotted the trio approaching the quayside. They helped get the woman and boy into the boat and quickly rowed out into the river. Helmut pleaded with them to stay a while, for there was a girl with them, and she had been taken hostage by one of the soldiers. They rowed around a couple of times, peering through the river mist for any sign of life on the dockside, and when they could wait no longer, set off into Lough Foyle. They splashed cold river water on Rosa's head and neck until she came out of her faint. When Helmut told her about Marita, she turned her face away and cried.

The terrified soldier used his hostage skilfully, dragging her backwards, arm firmly around her neck, pistol at the ready to shoot anybody who got too close. He fired a couple of shots when he saw them moving in the shadows, but as he retreated, they kept moving forward, biding their time. They were trying to get a clear shot at him, but he made sure the girl was always in the line of fire.

The more frightened the soldier became, the more he tightened his arm on her neck so that she had to struggle to breathe. He didn't care, as he firmly believed she had been planted on the street to distract their attention before the ambush, and he intended to shoot the bitch as soon as he was in the clear. When he had a chance to glance around, he could see the lighted windows of the hotel at the end of the street behind him and this spurred him on; once he got there, he would be safe.

In desperation, when she could not loosen his grip on her neck, the girl buried her right elbow into his ribs with all the strength left in her. He gasped as her sharp bone dug into his chest, winding him; the pistol fell from his hand. It clattered on the cobblestones, and when he stooped to try and recover it, she broke the grip of his arm and stumbled away, choking and coughing as she sucked air into her starved lungs.

The soldier, his hostage gone and the pistol on the ground, decided to make a run for the hotel. When he turned the last corner, he glanced back to see if they were still following him. An arm appeared out of a doorway beside him and drove a knife through his ribs into his chest. As he slid to his knees choking on the blood that filled his lungs, the blade was withdrawn, and one assailant held him by the hair of the head while another slit his throat. The soldier stared in disbelief, eyes bulging, feeling blood spurting out of his chest and mouth. He coughed a couple of times, then toppled forward on his face. His executioners slipped back into the darkness from which they had emerged.

Though they had no way of knowing what happened to Marita, Helmut and Rosa had no intention of going back to look for her. All they wanted was to get as far away from the soldiers and the killings as they could. But when they left the river behind and headed out into the safety of the Lough where the transatlantic ship lay at anchor, Helmut felt guilty about abandoning the girl, not knowing what was going to happen to her. He took ten pieces of gold and one ticket from his money belt and gave them to one of the boatmen with instructions to leave them at the hotel for Marita Muller. Once she was free and found them gone, he figured, the only thing she could do was go back to the hotel. She would get the gold and her ticket and follow them to America on the next sailing. The ferryman promised faithfully that he would get the money to the girl that night, and Helmut gave him two gold pieces to make sure he would honour his pledge.

No sooner were they rid of their passengers, however, than the rogues shared the gold between them. They could not believe their good luck that day. They even thought of going back to see if the belongings abandoned by the family were still in the street, for they could be worth a few pounds as well. But when they got ashore the place was crawling with police and soldiers and they decided to settle for what they had.

Marita stumbled back down the street the way she had come to try and find Helmut and Rosa, when suddenly another man with a rifle confronted her. He opened a door and told her to get inside. When she hesitated, he grabbed her by the hair and roughly pushed her into a dark hallway. She tried to cry out, but her lungs were so starved for air that no sound would come.

"If ye say wan word," said the man, "I'll slit yer throat."

When he closed the door, she fell down on her knees, still gasping for air. She didn't understand what he had said, but she was glad to be free of the soldier's death grip and the threat of being shot.

"Sit where ye are; be quiet as a mouse and ye'll be right as rain," said the man.

In the cold, dark place, she tried to figure out what had happened. She had seen the soldiers charging at them, heard the shots and thought they were all going to be killed. Even when the shooting stopped, she was afraid to move and lay on the cobblestones until she found herself being grabbed by the hair and hauled to her feet by the soldier. As he forced her backwards on the street, she saw Helmut and the boy kneeling beside Rosa on the ground. The soldier had his arm tightly around her neck and kept moving until she could no longer see in the dusk.

What happened to them? Had they been shot? She remembered Rosa lying motionless. She could be dead, but Helmut and the boy seemed to be okay. Where were they now, she wondered? Did they go back to the hotel, or were they hiding in some house near where the ambush happened? Maybe they were making their way to the river to look for the ferry. What if they were already on their way to the *Clyde Clipper?* Surely they wouldn't go and leave her stranded in this awful place!

Helmut had all her money. She had given it to him for safekeeping aboard the ship. Cold shivers ran down her spine at the thought that they might have gone and left her behind, penniless and without a friend to turn to for help.

Helmut handed over his tickets to the ship's bursar, and Rosa took the boy on deck and watched in the fading light until they could see the land no more. She felt sad about abandoning the girl after all they had been through, but she and Helmut had Johann to think about, and if they missed the ship, God knows what would have happened to them. Marita was resourceful, wise beyond her years and a survivor. She was convinced the girl would make it to America on her own once she got away from the wretched city.

But by the time the family knelt down in their cabin that night to thank God for sparing their lives, Rosa was filled with remorse for abandoning the girl. While her husband and the boy went through the ritual prayers, she could think of nothing but the lonely figure of Marita, maybe wounded and dying in the street when the soldier was finished with her. She cursed Derry, she cursed the people, she cursed the soldiers, but most of all she cursed the men with guns whose faces you never saw, men with cloth caps who sang hymns of praise to God one minute and killed soldiers the next.

Kneeling in the blackness behind the door, Marita had no conception of time. She could hear her own breathing and sometimes a rustle as the man moved about nearby. But she had no idea where he was exactly or if there was anybody in the house with him. Her knees were aching from the cold stone, and she shifted her position so that she could sit with her back to a wall. She heard him rattling with the rifle; he was still there.

"Ve come from Germany. Ve go to America. My family vaiting for me. The ship is vaiting for me. I have to go now." She spoke slowly so that he would understand and tried to get up.

"Quiet, woman," he said. "Ye're going nowheres. The others are well gone by now. Ye're on yer own."

She didn't understand.

"Please I must go to hotel," she insisted.

"Ye wouldn't have a prayer," he said firmly. "If the soldiers don't shoot ye the night they'll hang ye in the morning. Them English gentlemen are not fussy when it comes tae killing Irish."

She didn't understand a word he had said but persisted in telling him over and over again in broken English that she had to get back to her family to catch the boat to America that night. He paid no attention.

Much later he broke his silence. "Where did ye say yis was from?" he asked. "Are yis French or what?"

She understood. "Ve come from Bavaria, from Germany. Ve leave our farm to go to America to start new life."

"Heard of America, but nivver heard of that German place in me life. Anyways it's too far away to bother me head about," he laughed. "Git yer head down woman," he said. "We're stuck here fer the night."

After a while, she fell asleep with her face resting on her hands and awoke later with the sun in her eyes, rays filtering through a tiny fan window over the hall door. Her companion was gone. Her hands were dead from the weight of her head, but she managed to get to her feet and found the bolt on the door. Her fingers were numb, and she couldn't move it. She rubbed them together to get the blood back into them and tried the bolt again.

"Stay where ye're at, woman. Am tellin' ye—yer a goner if ye go out that door."

He was standing behind her with a knife in one hand and a lump of bread in the other.

"I have to get to hotel," she pleaded, her hand still on the bolt.

"Ye go nowheres wi'out me," he said firmly and motioned to her to get into the kitchen. On the table were two mugs of steaming hot tea and a plate with chunks of dark brown bread smeared with butter.

"Ate as much as ye can," he told her. "It might be the last bite ye'll see the day."

Hunger was the least of Marita's worries. She was still in shock after her ordeal and terrified of what was going to happen to her. She ate because he told her to, chewing the rough bread, but the tea tasted worse than the bitter leaves she had brewed for Rosa.

"What sort of a woman are ye that doesnay drink tae?" he asked. He took her mug, spooned sugar into it, then milk, and stirred it briskly. "Now drink it," he said. She took a few sips so as not to anger him and it tasted better than before. After that they ate and drank in silence. He lit a cigarette and began to blow smoke rings to amuse himself.

He was a thin man with mousy brown hair and pale skin stretched taut over pointed cheekbones. A long bony nose ran all the way down his face from sharp deep-set eyes to a pinched, narrow mouth. It was a comical looking face except for the narrow lips that gave him a mean appearance.

He had a revolver on the table in front of him and now and again removed the shiny bullets from the barrel, examined them as if to make sure they were okay. He then replaced them, spinning the chamber with his fingers. She knew he was one of the rebels, a Fenian, and he had helped kill the soldiers in the street the evening before.

Her kidneys were bursting and she needed to relieve herself urgently. There was a chamber pot under a sink in the corner. She picked it up and moved to the hallway, out of his view. But as she sat down, he came to watch. He stared until she finished, pulled up her knickers and fixed her skirt.

"Nice backside ye have there," he laughed. "Maybe I'll try it out for size later on." He smiled as he spoke, and though she didn't know exactly what he meant, she didn't like the way he was looking at her. He had the same leering look as the man who had stripped her that night in her bedroom when her sister was raped. She would have to be on her guard until she got away from him.

He seemed in no hurry to leave the house. There was a good supply of food and tea and milk, several tins of cigarettes and lamps and candles to light when it got dark. They were only a couple of streets away from where the soldiers had been ambushed, but he did not seem worried about it. During the night, he heard shooting in the area, but no soldiers appeared in his street. Now and again, he went on the alert when he heard horses nearby but relaxed as soon as they had gone. Several times he checked his rifle and pistol to make sure they were loaded.

He knew the army would cordon off the area when it got light so that they could recover the bodies of their dead comrades and conduct a house-by-house search of the street corner where the ambush took place. If they found evidence that any of the householders was involved in the killings, they would shoot the occupants and burn the place down. The Fenians had long gone; the only reason he was still here was the woman. He had been ordered to hold her until things calmed down and then take her to the mountains and get rid of her in case the soldiers got their hands on her.

He was sitting on the chair with his head back and his eyes closed. On the table in front of him were a tin mug and his revolver. A rifle stood against the wall in the corner, his cloth cap hanging from the barrel. For the first time she noticed his hands—long thin fingers, bony knuckles, sinews, and veins standing out like ridges in a field. At the slightest sound inside or outside the house, the eyelids flicked open. His senses were as sharp as those of an animal, that same animal instinct that allowed him to kill without thought for his victim.

BOOK II

CHAPTER ONE

A GOD-FORSAKEN PLACE

During the day, the sun's rays filtered through the kitchen window, illuminating cigarette smoke and dust particles turning and twisting in the warm air. Later, when it moved around, light reached the upturned face of the reclining figure on the chair and woke him. He rubbed his eyes, stretched his body against the wooden chair back and got up to make more tea. He lit a stove and, while the kettle boiled, toasted thick slices of bread until they were golden brown and smeared them with butter while they were still hot.

She was hungry and gorged herself on the tasty bread and melting butter. She put milk and sugar in the black tea, stirred it and took long gulps to wash down the toast.

He smiled as he watched her eat but she avoided looking directly into his eyes. When they finished, he grabbed her wrist and pulled her after him up narrow stairs. He pushed her ahead of him through a door into a bedroom and ordered her to get into bed and left. When he came back a few minutes later, she was still standing fully dressed inside the door, frightened and uncertain what to do.

"Please take me to the hotel to family," she pleaded, tears spilling down her cheeks. He took a pistol from behind his back and put it against her forehead.

"I won't tell ye again. Git yer clothes off. Everything!" he said coldly and pulled at her skirt to make sure she understood.

Marita shivered. When he took the gun away from her face, she unlaced her shoes and removed them, together with her stockings. He stood there in silence, leering while she took off each garment. He seemed amused when she folded her clothes and placed them neatly over the back of a chair. When she was naked except for her knickers, she covered her chest with folded arms and lay down on the bed, turning her naked breasts away from him.

He grabbed her roughly and forced her over onto her back. She could see the excitement in his face as he eyed her nakedness. He pulled at the knickers until he had them over her ankles.

"Ye're younger than ah thought and a good-looking bitch, too," he said, getting more excited at the sight of her bare thighs.

He ran the palms of his hands over the curves on her hips. She instinctively crossed her legs to protect herself. He put a hand over one breast and gently pressed.

Marita had been in the same situation before and knew the ordeal that faced her. There was no point in resisting. Better let it happen and get it over with. She didn't want to die in this awful place. She didn't want to lie in a cold grave like her sister and her mother and father. She was going to America. Let him do what he wanted and soon she would be free of him. If she could survive the horror of the murder of her family, she could blot this animal out of her mind too. She refused to look at him, staring instead at the ceiling and walls, anything to avoid his eyes. If he was going to rape her, she was not going to make it easy for him. She would not resist, but she wanted to make it clear that she did not want him.

He got off the bed and quickly took off his shoes, trousers and jacket but kept on his shirt and a frayed green woollen pullover. He looked stupid standing there with his buttocks and thighs naked, still wearing the pullover and stockings, and the thin, clownish poker face didn't help. He reminded her of a scarecrow.

He saw her staring scornfully at him and his face flushed with anger. He lashed out and struck her shoulder with his clenched fist.

"Bloody bitch! Who de ye think ye are?" he hissed. "I'll show ye who's the boss in this house!"

Shocked by the blow, she sat upright and tried to roll off the bed. He pushed her over on her back and climbed on top of her until he had her firmly between his knees. He lashed out again and hit her on the side of the face with the back of his hand; she felt blood in her mouth, running down her throat, choking her. She shivered as his cold buttocks came down on her warm stomach. While she coughed to try and clear the blood from her throat, he stroked her neck with his long, bony fingers.

His touch was gentle at first, but he got rougher as his passion flared. She kept her face turned away from him, feeling the blood and saliva dribbling from the side of her mouth. His breathing became more urgent, and his hands began to hurt her.

"Ye stupid bitch, ye stupid foreign bitch, "he snorted at her, "I'll show ye who's the boss!"

He squeezed her breasts and pulled at her dark nipples until she cried out in pain. He gave a nervous laugh as she writhed in agony beneath him.

"Now who's the boss, ye snobby foreign bitch?"

Terrified, she broke free of his grip, but he had her pinned down with his body, and all she could do was pound his chest with her fists to get him to stop. For a moment, he was winded by her assault, but he did not budge. The more pain he inflicted on her young body, the more excited he became. Slowly and deliberately, he brought the full weight of his body down on top of her. When he found the fold of soft flesh between her legs, he lurched at her, and she felt him force his way inside. His breath came in short, sharp bursts from his open mouth; his uneven, discoloured teeth resembled animal fangs.

Her body was numb with pain from the hurt to her thighs and the blows to her face. She closed her eyes and tried to blank out her mind to her suffering but instead found herself back in Hoffenfeld listening to the screams of her sister being raped. Now it was happening to her, and she could do nothing to stop it.

When he exhausted himself, his half-naked body collapsed on top of her, and she could feel the hot sweat and the pounding of his heart. He rolled over and lay beside her, caressing her with his hands and kissing the bruises on her breasts as if to soothe the pain he had inflicted on her. When he tried to kiss her on the mouth, she turned her face away and he struck her again. She didn't care; the animal had tortured and raped her, and all she felt for him was revulsion. If he had left his revolver within her reach, she would have happily put it to his head at that moment and pulled the trigger, whatever the consequences. He struck her once more with the back of his hand, cursed her, then stood up and put on his trousers.

After he had left the room, she lay on the bed and cried. The burning sensation inside and the ache in her back where he had doubled her over was so bad that she could not move her legs to sit up. The pain in her breasts and shoulders was unbearable. In her agony all she could think of was how she was going to get away from this animal, away from the house. If the family had gone without her, they were now on their way to America, but if they were still trying to find her, the people in the hotel would know where they were. She had to make her way back there or she was lost; she was convinced this madman would kill her when he was finished with her.

She got onto her knees and used the bedclothes to clean the blood and sweat from her body, but no matter how much she rubbed, she could not rid herself of the stench of him. The bruises were already swelling as if the skin was about to burst. She could feel blood and fluid oozing from her aching thighs.

Marita cowered in the room until the light began to fade, hoping against hope that he might be gone when she got downstairs. But he was still there sitting at the table, head back, eyes closed, gun, cigarettes and matches in front of him as if nothing had happened. She sat down opposite and stared at him. The bruises were still there, but the tears were gone; after Hoffenfeld, she had vowed she would never let a man hurt her. She was angry. She wanted to make him pay for what he had done to her. But the most important thing was to stay alive and wait for a chance to escape and find her way back to the hotel.

Even if Helmut and Rosa had panicked and gone without her, she was sure they would not leave her stranded. There would be a message at the hotel and maybe some money if only she could get there. The problem was the soldiers. What if they connected her with the ambush? They would show no mercy, and her English was so poor it would be impossible to convince them of her innocence. She wondered if the soldier who held her hostage had reached the safety of the hotel. She wanted to know but dared not ask the brute across the table from her.

That night he ordered her back to the bedroom and raped her again. She lay still throughout, thighs wide apart until he exhausted himself. She felt nothing but hatred for him. He was an animal, acted like an animal, and if there was a God in heaven, he would die like an animal. She lay still until she heard him snore, got out of bed to get dressed and went to sleep on the floor.

During the night the cold woke her. She heard voices in the kitchen, men talking. He was not in the bed. She crept to the closed door and listened. They were making plans to leave Derry the next morning. They talked about her, but she did not understand enough to know what was said.

Marita was convinced that he was going to kill her. She lay awake for the remainder of the night but fell asleep when daylight came. She awoke later to find him standing over her in the room, pistol in hand. He ordered her downstairs. He made tea and more toast with butter and cheese and told her to eat her fill, for they would get no more food that day.

The men who came in the night had taken the rifle with them, but he still had the pistol, which she saw him put inside the lining of his coat. He gave her a heavy black shawl to cover her head and shoulders and told her to leave her shoes behind, but when he was not looking, she tied the laces together and slung them around her bruised neck and hid them under the bulky shawl. He put on his cloth cap, pulled the peak down over his eyes and walked briskly out into the cool morning.

There were few people about—a milkman and two bakery workers returning home after a night's work. They walked through a maze of narrow streets until they reached the river. Marita knew they were not too far from the place where she and the Wagontrapers encountered the horsemen on their way to the ferry.

"We were so close to the river when the soldiers came!" she thought. "If we had left the hotel a couple of minutes earlier, we would have been well clear of it all; a few minutes later and we could have avoided it. It was bad luck that we went at the time we did."

They walked along the quayside. Though it was very early, there was plenty of activity on the docks. Coal was being unloaded from two ships, and there were great piles on the quayside as if the men had been working through the night. Across the river, cattle were being loaded onto another vessel, drovers shouting obscenities and lashing out at the terrified animals with sticks to force them up the narrow gangway.

In the cold dawn, they walked upriver, carefully avoiding a magnificent bridge with steel supports that were still shiny and new, until the docks and the city were left behind. Her bare feet were sore from the stony quays, and she was glad to feel the cool dampness on her soles when their journey took them along a grassy bank. They walked nearly a mile along the river until they came to a patch of tall reeds at the water's edge.

He told her to sit down, disappeared into the reeds and in a couple of minutes called her. She pulled up her long skirt and waded to a small boat he had dragged to open water. She got in and he pushed the boat clear of the reeds and jumped in.

The river was half a mile wide, but the surface was so calm that Marita was able to look over the side of the boat and see her reflection clearly in the water. The only disturbance came from the slow forward motion of the boat and the oars making dimples on the glassy surface as he rowed with strong even strokes. In midstream, it got a bit rougher because of the current and he had to pull harder on the oars to avoid being carried back downstream to the bridge that he had been so careful to avoid. Once they were clear of the fast-moving water, it was easier to maintain forward momentum and soon they reached the other side. He hauled the boat ashore and concealed it in another patch of reeds.

He rested a while on the riverside, and she watched as he bathed his arms in cold water to ease the ache in his muscles from pulling the oars. She sat on a stone and dipped her bruised feet in the river. The soreness eased and she felt better. He lay down on the grass and covered his face with his cap to keep the sunlight from his eyes.

If her mind had not been preoccupied with other things, she could have enjoyed the rest, for it was a pleasant place. She moved around, exploring the water's edge and discovered a small stream flowing into the river, which was full of minnows. She tried to catch them with cupped hands, but they slipped through her fingers, and eventually she gave up. She rolled down the front of her dress and splashed water on her bruised face, shoulders, and breasts. It smarted at first, but after a while the cool liquid soothed the ache from the welts he had inflicted on her.

Her heart skipped a beat when she spotted dark grey leaves growing on the bank of the stream. She picked a few and chewed until she was sure they were the same as the ones her grandmother had shown her. She was filling her pockets with them when he called her. It was time to go.

"Sulix," he said matter-of-factly, when he saw the leaves in her hand, "good for the hunger but trouble for the belly." She said nothing. If she got an opportunity to make some of her grandmother's brew, she could make sure that his rape would not leave her with a baby. The last thing she wanted was to bring a bastard child of this animal into the world. The leaves would not protect her from his lust, but they might prevent her from becoming pregnant.

Away from the river, the land began to rise gradually through a fertile landscape of lush grass and tilled fields bursting with summer growth. Hawthorn hedges surrounding the fields were in full bloom, and the scent of their white and crimson flowers filled the air. There was a strong smell of woodbine and honeysuckle. Wild rose bushes flourished in the overgrown ditches, flower-laden branches cascading to the ground like a waterfall. Along the divisions between the fields were rows of magnificent trees with dark green ivy clinging to the stout trunks.

Cows lay close to hedges, enjoying the cool morning air, waiting for the farmer to relieve them of the burden of milk that bloated their udders.

She was intrigued by the variety of trees and bushes—so different from the monotonous evergreens that clothed the hillsides of alpine valleys. High hedgerows had all sorts of foliage, including bushes with fruit at various stages of development. It was strange to see so many fruit trees growing wild in the open countryside—raspberries, gooseberries, blackberries, plums, and wild apples.

To avoid farmhouses, they walked across country through fields of flowering potatoes, their white, pink, and purple blossoms resembling a giant patchwork quilt stretched over the landscape. In the shelter of the ditches were yellow primroses, and in the fields, buttercups and daisies and cowslips and bluebells and sweet-smelling purple clover jostled for space in the lush, moist grass. Here and there, thistles towered above the growth around them, striving to flower and scatter their seed before the farmer got around to felling them with his scythe.

Apart from the swish of feet as they made their way through the high grass, there was hardly another sound to indicate the presence of human life. Only the birds could be heard, mostly crows cawing as they squabbled over snails caught out in the open after a night of meandering. The steady hum of insects, especially bees, was most noticeable. They flitted from flower to flower, gathering pollen for their secret honey store, fertilising a new generation of flowers that would provide them with next year's food store.

The smell of new mown hay hung over the countryside, and it was this scent more than anything else that reminded Marita of her valley home.

There were plenty of large farmhouses; as the morning wore on and the farmers were up and about their work he motioned to her a couple of times to stop and crouch in the tall grass to make sure they were not seen. They avoided roads, travelling instead through overgrown lanes and animal tracks. Her feet became swollen from walking on stones and from nettle stings; when he went ahead to check if the coast was clear, she sat on a rock and slipped on her shoes.

Marita lost track of time, but when the sun was directly overhead, she heard church bells ringing. They stopped to rest in a clump of laurel bushes. He hopped over a ditch and returned with a turnip and carrots. He washed the carrots in a stream and knocked the roots off the soft turnip with a sharp stone, then stripped the skin with his teeth. The turnip was juicy and sweet, and she crunched the raw carrot with relish. He lit a small fire, and when it was red, he hoked some potatoes in a field with his hands and placed them on the burning embers until they began to sizzle. He showed her how to peel off the scorched skin to get at the soft, hot flesh inside. She had never eaten potato before, but it tasted good and satisfied her hunger.

As they walked upwards, a range of high mountains came into view, shimmering like a mirage in the heat but still a long way off. The hills had rounded tops and took on a purple hue in the heat. Unlike the jagged peaks and snow-clad hillsides of her valley home, these mountains had greenery almost all the way to the top.

A light breeze played across fields of green oats and barley, sending ripples over the shiny grain like waves on water. Farmers with scythes were cutting hay, felling the green swards in neat rows to dry in the heat of the day. Others sprayed potato crops, the steady action of their arms pumping misty blue liquid from tanks strapped to their backs as they nudged their way between deep drills.

They climbed, and the land became poorer. Thick hedges gave way to stone walls surrounding fields of stunted grass; patches of rushes appeared where the water table burst out of the mountainside to create large areas of swampy ground. The only animals about were sheep, occasionally goats, and here and there, a dishevelled farm horse feasting on clumps of new grass growing in the shelter of ditches.

Late in the evening they reached a roadway running along the side of the mountain and, when there was nobody in sight, he quickly pulled her across and they entered a village. They approached a house beside the church, and he let himself in by a back door, beckoning her to follow.

They were in a large kitchen, and a woman standing at a black stove didn't even turn around when they entered.

"I suppose ye're hungry as usual," she said, continuing with what she was doing. She spoke matter-of-factly to him as if he had just come in from work in the fields. He sat down on a bench at the table and began to tell her how he had been to Derry and was on his way home. They could do it with a bite to eat and a place to stay for the night.

From a steaming black pot hanging over an open fire, she ladled soup thick with vegetables and potatoes and lentils and barley and slivers of white chicken mixed in. It tasted good, and the girl was hungry; when she scraped the bottom of the bowl with the spoon, the woman took it back to the pot and filled it again. She put slices of fresh scone bread down beside them and a plate of deep yellow butter. It was just like the bread her grandmother used to bake, but the butter was salty and felt funny on her tongue.

The woman said little: "Himself is on his rounds and will be back late and if he says so ye can stay the night."

"I hope ye had nothing to do woth that bother in Derry on Sunday," she said. "Did anybody see ye coming in here?"

"No," he said in reply, which left her none the wiser about Derry, but from the tone of her voice, it was clear she had her suspicions.

She sat down and they drank tea together. She was pudgy with bright red cheeks, stout arms, and swollen fingers. Marita's grandmother said the redness in country folk came from drinking milk and eating too much butter and cheese. She warned her grand-daughter to be careful, for boys preferred girls with pale skin. Marita's mother had a different explanation.

"Red cheeks come from too much blushing," she said. "Country girls have red faces because they are much shyer than town folk and more easily embarrassed." Marita wasn't sure who was telling the truth.

The woman neither looked at nor spoke to Mrita but directed all her talk to boney face. After eating her fill, Maria needed to relieve herself, and the woman pointed to a shed in the yard. His eyes tracked her as she got up from the table, and when she went into the outhouse, she quickly bolted the door in case he attempted to follow her. There was a wooden seat with a hole in the middle and a strong smell of lime from the pit, and she held her nose until she was out in the fresh air again. In the kitchen they had been talking about her. As she came through the door, he was telling the woman that the girl had got caught up in an ambush and he had to take her with him.

"If the soldiers got their hands on her she would be done for," he said.

They sat for a while enjoying the food, and when he had nothing else to say to her, the woman got up from the table:

"Well, ye can sit about all day but ah have work tae do. Ye better move intae the parlour out of mey way."

She led them into an adjoining room furnished with a mahogany table and chairs and a long leather couch. The place reeked of strong tobacco and alcohol. On a sideboard were decanters for whiskey and brandy, bottles of wine and sherry and a selection of drinking glasses.

When Marita sat down on the sofa, he shut the door quickly and came over to her. He pushed his hand roughly through the buttons of her dress and squeezed her breast. She was taken aback by his daring but made no movement. He opened more buttons until he exposed one breast, then took the nipple between his bony fingers and squeezed hard until she cried out. The woman called from the kitchen, and he quickly moved away. Marita buttoned her dress and drew the shawl tightly around her. She was shivering from the pain.

She wondered whether all his talk about the soldiers was just a bluff to frighten her, to deter her from trying to escape, but she was still confused and unsure what to do. If the soldier who grabbed her on the street had reached safety with her, he might have set her free, and she would now be well on her way to America instead of the prisoner of this animal. But the soldier had almost choked her to death as he dragged her along the street; he might have killed her anyway when he reached safety or handed her over to the police. Whatever about the soldier, she had no illusions about this animal; he would slit her throat and think nothing of it.

"Maybe the only reason I'm still alive is because he wants a woman to satisfy his lust," she thought. "Otherwise, he would have killed me in the house before we left Derry."

Marita sat alone in the musty room sobbing quietly. She was completely disorientated by the sadistic abuse she suffered at the hands of her captor; she had nobody to turn to for help, nobody even to talk to. Her family in Hoffenfeld was dead and her home gone; she had been separated from her adoptive family; she had no money, no clothing except what she wore; and her English was so poor she was unable to understand what was going on around her. How long could she go on like this?

Even in the depths of despair, however, there was still a spark of defiance. She could do nothing about the murder of her parents and sister, but she might still have a chance to get revenge on this man, and if the opportunity came, she would put a knife in his back or a gun to his head and gladly watch him die.

The woman came into the room at dusk to draw the curtains. She lit two oil lamps that brought a warm glow to the room.

"Are ye hungry, wee cutty?" she asked. "Dae ye want something tae ate?"

Marita shook her head.

Later, when it was dark, she heard somebody arrive on horseback and voices in the kitchen. The sitting-room door opened, and a tall priest came in. He took off his hat and heavy coat and gave them to the woman to hang up. He looked at Marita, then turned abruptly and strode through the open door back to the kitchen.

"What in God's name are ye doing wey that wee cutty, Eamonn?" he demanded. "Have ye no titter of wit about ye? If the police get their hands on her she'll blow the gaff on the whole lot of ye. And if they catch her here it's me that will have a power of explaining to do!"

"Ah git off yer pulpit, Father, and be quiet" replied Eamonn, annoyed at the onslaught. "If we're caught, we'll all hang together. Anyway, we'll be well gone by the time ye're up in the morning. We'll be no bother here the night."

Later she heard them laughing and the clink of glasses and several times the woman tried without success to get them to go to bed.

"Amen"— that's what the priest called him. She heard him telling the priest what happened at the Corpus Christi procession in Derry and how the bishop and his cronies were forced to flee with their tails between their legs when the Fenians started to sing "Faith of Our Fathers."

The priest laughed heartily. He would have given anything to be there just to see his pompous old bishop having to run for his life.

Eamonn mentioned only briefly about the soldiers firing on the crowd but described in detail how the Fenians ambushed three mounted patrols in the City in one day and killed the lot of them. The silver-haired cleric, with nearly half a bottle of whiskey in him, speculated that the killings at the procession were not a bad thing, as they would bring more support for the rebels.

He was intrigued to hear how Eamonn came by the girl when she got caught up in one of the ambushes.

"She says she came from a place called Bavaria in Germany and seems to have little or no understanding of English," he ventured. "She sez she's on her way to America. The fix she's in, she'll hardly make it now."

The two men talked for hours until the whisky bottle was empty before they broke up the party. She heard her captor come into the room and take off his clothes. The woman peeped through the partly open bedroom door, asking Marita if she was all right. She saw her nephew.

"Yer bed's upstairs," she said to him.

"I'll have tae stay down here and keep an eye on her," he lied.

The woman stared coldly at him and left. Every muscle in the girl's body contracted in fear as the door closed, leaving them alone in the darkened room. He whispered to her to take off her clothes. She did as she was told and lay naked and shivering on the couch, but when he came towards her, she stood up and faced him.

"I will shout!" she said. "I will shout!"

His fists clenched, and he raised his right arm as if to hit her, but he drew back, not sure if she was bluffing.

"Ich werde schreien wenn. Du mich beruhrst," she repeated her threat, more conviction in her voice. He did not understand the gibberish, but he knew what she was at, the bitch.

"Ye'll pay dearly for this night," he rasped at her. "Nobody gets the better of Eamonn McKee." He stood unsteadily in the middle of the room, glaring at her, his animal lust frustrated. She stood naked in front of him daring him to call her bluff; she stayed there until he flopped on the rug beside the sofa and fell into a drunken sleep.

When she was sure he could not hear her, she put her clothes on and sat in a corner of the room as far away from him as she could get. This time, she had outwitted him.

She awoke in daylight to find the red-faced woman standing over her.

"Ah was just about tae get ye up fer a bite tae eat," she said. "Come on in the kitchen."

The woman seemed surprised to find the girl huddled in the corner fully dressed and surmised that her drunken nephew had been pestering her.

Marita put on her shoes and followed the woman out of the room. There was a bowl of boiled oats on the table but when she tried to eat, it tasted like paste. The woman saw her grimace as she tried to swallow and laughed. She spooned sugar into the oats and some jam. Marita tried again and found it palatable. When she had finished, the woman put a plate of thick slices of salty bacon and fried eggs and potato bread down in front of her. She was hungry and ate everything; the food was delicious, not unlike the breakfast her grandmother used to give her before she and her sister set off for school on winter mornings.

When she finished, the woman said: "That'll do ye a power of good."

She was the priest's maid, and she was friendly. She asked Marita her name and where she came from and where she was going. The girl was in no mood for talking and grudgingly volunteered only that her name was Marita Muller and she came from Bavaria. The woman could see that the girl had great difficulty with the language.

By the time she finished eating, her captor came out of the room, shaking himself and rubbing his eyes to try and get rid of the effects of too much alcohol. He threw her the shawl, told her to put it on and left through the back door of the house without saying a word to the woman. It was cool outside in the morning air, and she put the shawl over her head and pulled it tightly around her shoulders to keep warm.

The woman waved to her as she walked across the yard. She was sorry for the girl for she knew that nephew of hers had a cruel streak in him and he had her terrified. But some things were better left alone. They were going to the farm in the mountains, and if he was forcing himself on the girl, it was up to his mother, her widowed sister, to sort out the problem.

The terrain got a lot rougher after they left the priest's house and they had to rest every fifteen minutes to ease the strain on their legs. It was all uphill and part of the way they had to trudge across wide stretches of marshy ground. The landscape was dotted with stacks of brown turf cut by farmers and left to dry in the summer sunshine.

He sat on a rock and ate food his aunt gave him when he was leaving, and he cupped his hands and drank water from a stream. He offered her nothing but when he moved off, he left what remained of the buttered bread and cheese on a stone. She ignored it and walked on. She would not eat scraps, like a dog. In any case she had a good breakfast and was not hungry.

The hot sun burned her face, and the muscles of her legs were sore from the steep climb. Her arms ached trying to keep the heavy shawl from slipping off her shoulders. At midday, they hid in a clump of bracken when they heard shots in the distance. It turned out to be gunmen hunting grouse in the heather, but he took no chances and stayed hidden until the shooting party was well out of sight.

She noticed for the first time how high they had climbed. Even with the heat mist she could see all the way down to the river where they had crossed in the boat the day before and the hazy outline of mountains beyond. Ahead of them was a fast-flowing stream and he stopped for a while to drink and she could see fish jumping over the rocks. Her father used to trap trout in a stream just like it as they struggled to the spawning grounds at the top of the valley.

They followed a narrow path along the gushing water until a farmhouse came into view. As they got closer, she could see it was a substantial two-storey place with several outbuildings attached. High steep roofs of dark grey slate reflected the sunlight; around them the air shimmered in the heat.

The stream bounded the farmhouse and buildings on one side and to the rear and on the other sides were huge, rounded boulders among which a few stunted trees had taken root. Only the front of the farmhouse was exposed, looking westwards from the mountainside over a landscape stretching for miles right down to the river and beyond. Where the buildings stood seemed to be the only piece of level ground in the rough mountain side. The place was more barren and rugged even than the mountain behind Helmut's farm. She wondered how anyone could survive in such isolation. The last house they had passed was more than a mile downhill.

As they approached, a woman emerged from one of the outbuildings carrying a bucket. When she saw them, she waved, and he called out to her. She was obviously his mother, and she gave him a long hug when they met.

"I see ye got yerself a woman," she said, eyeing the girl. "She looks a nice wee cutty."

"She's a furriner," he said, smiling. "She got into a bit of a tangle wey the army and ah had to bring her wey me fer safety. Her name's Marita but ah canny pronounce her other name. She's from some place in Germany."

Marita knew they were talking about her in their strange dialect. As they chatted, she recognised some of words like 'wife' and 'Marita' and 'army' and 'German' but little else.

The house was spacious and comfortable inside with bright white-washed walls catching light from the windows and splashing it around a big kitchen that occupied most of the ground floor. There was a stone chimney brace with a shiny new stove. The kitchen had solid wooden furniture, and the black beams in the ceiling stood out sharply against the whitewash between them. A proliferation of metal pots and pans and copper cans and pitchers hung from the beams, and they swayed and knocked against each other in the gentle summer breeze that wafted through the open door. Each window ledge had an oil lamp, and on opposite walls were cupboards displaying blue willow delph and polished brass ornaments. Copper swans hung in pairs where there was space for them to fly on the white walls.

The woman talked directly to Marita, and the girl answered her briefly, but neither understood much of what the other said.

A couple of times Marita said: "I do not understand." But the older woman still didn't know what the girl was saying.

"She doesn't know how tae spake the Queen's English," she said to her son. "Imagine bringing a wee girl like that here."

When they had eaten, he told her the story about the ambush and how the girl got mixed up in it. He told her about the soldiers shooting people dead during the parade and about the Fenians killing for revenge but never mentioned that he himself had taken part in the killings and had to flee Derry. The older woman cursed the English soldiers and vowed that if there was a God in heaven at all he should make sure every last one of them burned in hell for killing innocent Catholics going about their Sunday worship.

Eamonn told his mother the girl might have to stay with them for the winter for her own safety but added she should be well able to help with the daily work and earn her keep.

Marita understood when the woman asked if she could milk a cow or bake bread or wash the floor, but she shook her head because, at first, she was unwilling to have anything to do with these people. It wasn't the thought of working on the farm, no matter how hard it was, that troubled her. She was terrified of what lay ahead, of the torture he would inflict on her to satisfy his animal instincts if she had to stay there.

In the days that followed, she relented and helped the woman. She milked cows, fed the animals, and fetched baskets of hard black turf from the stack outside to fire the stove. She watched as the woman baked tasty scones, white and brown loaves, and spicy potato cakes. She talked to the girl as she went about her chores, for she was glad of the company of another female. Marita understood little and said less.

The older woman complimented her son. "That's the grand wee girl ye brought with ye. She's as good as any man about the farm. Ye could do worse than marry a girl like that."

He laughed at his mother: "No way I'm hanging a furriner like that round me neck. I have enough problems of me own."

Summer passed and autumn nights brought a chill, but the house was warm and the woman friendly and Marita ate well and quietly did her work. The days were pleasant enough, but the nights she dreaded. A couple of times every week he came into her room when he knew his mother was asleep.

His sexual appetite was insatiable. Even worse, he seemed to get as much pleasure from hurting her as he did from raping her. Sometimes he treated her gently as if trying to win some affection, but she always rebuked him. She spat at him once at the height of his passion when he whispered that he had taken a shine to her. The more she rejected him, the more sadistic he became.

There was an abundance of the dark leaves growing along the stream, and she picked supplies regularly, and every time she got a chance, she made the brew and stored its black pungent liquid in bottles among the rocks. She drank some every day. It was the only protection she had against him, against having his baby. She was determined this would not happen. After a while, the brew made her ill in the mornings, and she stopped taking it regularly. Instead, she took it only at the time each month when she was most vulnerable and again when her period was due to make sure she bled. It never failed.

The days passed quickly because there was a lot of work to do at that time of the year—digging and pitting potatoes to see them though the winter and harvesting corn, turnips, and kale for feeding the animals. Marita and his mother had to work in the fields alongside him. Occasionally he left them working while he went down the mountain to meet his Fenian cronies.

Autumn came to an end without a single visitor from the outside world except for the priest who arrived at Halloween to say Mass in the house and drink whiskey with Eamonn. He brought news about Fenian activities in the neighbouring counties of Donegal and Tyrone, but nothing had happened in Derry since the summer ambushes.

The farm survived almost entirely on what it produced—milk, bread, butter, cheese, salted bacon and pork from their own pigs, mutton from lambs he slaughtered by the stream. They had corn, potatoes, and fresh vegetables right through the winter, for the woman was wise in the ways of harvesting and storing food. Stock was kept indoors from November. The animals were housed in warm sheds and spent their days chewing sweet, dry hay, and every morning and evening, Marita brought them rations of corn, turnips, and kale to augment the fodder.

They needed only a few items from the outside world, such as tea, which they drank copiously, and luxuries like jars of honey and pots of sweet jam. Marita got used to drinking tea with sugar and milk and found it palatable. In fact, she also discovered that sugar in her black herbal brew took away the worst of the sickening taste. She tried milk with it too, but it turned sour. When the priest came, he brought chunks of spiced beef and marinated herring and whiskey, which Eamonn and he drank late into the night.

The stream, with its sparkling clear water, was her favourite place. She sat for hours in the evenings dangling her feet in it, enjoying the pressure of the current swaying her ankles from side to side. She drew a bucket of the chill clear water every evening and sponged her body from head to toe to refresh herself after her daily chores and cleanse herself of the stench of him. If it had not been for the torture that he put her through at night, life on the mountain farm could have been bearable.

She listened, watched and waited her chance. Sooner or later, he would rejoin the Fenian gang, and he would have to leave her behind. The first time he left her alone, she planned to make her own way down the mountain to the broad river and find her way back to Derry. She clung to the belief that there might still be money or a letter at the hotel for her; if not, she might get enough for her passage to America from the sale of the trunk of clothes. Otherwise, she would have to find work until she earned enough for the boat. There was also a chance that Helmut had already paid for her; maybe it was only a matter of making contact with the hotel manager or the captain of the *Clyde Clipper* and she could leave immediately to join them.

In November there was a fall of snow and she had to go with him into the mountains to bring sheep to lower ground. They made several trips to the bog to bring back cartloads of hard black turf to see them through the winter.

A couple of weeks later came another fall of snow, this time much heavier and huge flakes driven by strong winds caused drifts several feet deep on lane-ways and behind stone ditches.

When Marita woke the next morning and went to milk the cows, she discovered he was gone, and there were tracks made by the horse going downhill in the direction of the river. She decided this was the chance she had been waiting for to escape.

She dressed warmly, put on her shawl and left the house as usual with the milk pail for the cowshed. Once out of view, she dumped the pail and worked her way around the farm buildings until she found the path his horse had made. She began to walk downhill. She had to lift her legs high to clear the deep snow, and soon they became so heavy that they felt as if her shoes were filled with lead. She moved as fast as she could to get as far down the mountain as possible. So long as she had daylight, she was sure she could find her way back to the river and get across in the boat he had hidden in the reeds. The days were short, and if she was caught outdoors in the dark, she would shelter in a farm shed for the night and continue her journey to the river the next day. She knew that as she descended, the snow would not be so deep, and she would make better progress. She had no food and no money, but she was not deterred, remembering how she had found her way to Helmut's house on the mountain in far worse conditions.

Marita had been walking for more than an hour when a lone horseman came into view, coming towards her. She had been so preoccupied making plans for what she was going to do when she reached Derry that by the time she recognised the rider, it was too late to hide. She stood knee-deep in the snow until he reached her.

"Stupid woman—ye'll nivver git sense. The soldiers are looking for ye. They'll torture ye and then they'll hang ye and me with ye if they git the chance. Back ye go the way ye came," he shouted at her.

He made her walk in front of him and when she stopped to rest he used the horse's head against her shoulders to force her to keep moving.

His mother stood anxiously in the doorway when they arrived back at the farmhouse.

"I didn't know she was away until ah heard the cows going mad for milking," she said nervously.

He unloaded flour and other items from a saddle and stomped around the farmhouse, ignoring his mother, angry at her for letting the girl slip away.

He didn't speak to either of them for the rest of the day but when Marita went to bed that night, she heard him shouting at his mother in the kitchen.

"Ye're a terrible mean man, not like yer father, God rest his soul," she shouted back. "And I know ye're giving dogs' abuse to that wee girl."

"None of yer fucking business!" he shouted back to her.

Marita knew she was going to be punished for trying to escape and decided that whatever the consequences were, she would have to do something to stop him. She stripped naked that night and stood on top of the bed when she heard him coming to her room. He smiled when he saw her standing there.

"Ah knew ye'd git fond of me," he chuckled.

"If you touch me, I'll shout." She said it slowly, deliberately, so that he was in no doubt, she meant it.

He laughed nervously at her. "Ye'll take what's coming to ye and enjoy it. Ye don't think ye can threaten me in me own home."

"If you touch me, I'll scream," she said again, coldly.

He took off his shoes and socks and jacket. He slowly removed the leather braces from his trousers and wrapped one end around his right hand. He came towards her and lashed out. The leather end of the braces caught her across the face and shoulder, stinging her flesh. But she stood her ground. She took a deep breath and let out a long piercing scream that shattered the silence of the house. He flailed at her again, and she let out a second scream.

"Ye stupid bitch," he roared. "I'll kill ye." He lounged at her with the braces, knocking her backwards on the bed, and she fell out the other side onto the floor.

The bedroom door opened, and his mother burst into the room.

"What in God's name are ye doing Eamonn?" she shouted at him. "Have ye lost yer senses?"

She helped the girl up off the floor, and when she saw the red welts on her body, she couldn't contain herself. She flailed at him with her fists and kicked at his shins. "Ye're nothing but a savage. Even an animal wouldn't carry on like that," he shouted at him. "What kind of a son did I rear in God's name?"

She put a sheet around the girl and quickly ushered her out of the room. Both women were crying, and Marita was shaking from the cold; the welts on her body had started to bleed.

The woman brought her to the kitchen and gave her tea with whiskey while she rubbed melted butter on the sores. When the sobbing ceased, she took her upstairs, and they got into the same bed. For the first time, Marita felt safe between the warm sheets and fell asleep as the whiskey numbed her brain and her pain.

She awoke late next day to find her clothes neatly folded over a chair at the foot of the bed. The woman brought her porridge and tea and scones.

"Ye'll sleep here from now on," she said.

Marita had a headache from the whiskey, and the sores on her body were hurting, but it was worth it. She had got the better of him. Her attempt to escape had come to nothing, but she was out of his clutches for the moment. After that night, the woman stayed close to her.

The days got colder and darker and there was little to do outdoors so they sat in the warm kitchen and the woman taught her to knit and crochet and use a sewing machine. She showed her how to make different kinds of bread, how to save the thick cream from the milk for butter and cheese and bend rushes to make crosses and pound oats for the porridge. The flashing points of needles in the woman's hands reminded her of her grandmother, who used to sit for hours in front of the fire on winter evenings, knitting thick woollen pullovers and socks for family and friends.

The woman got used to talking very slowly to the girl to try and get her to understand and when she had difficulty with words or phrases gave her a practical demonstration until the meaning was clear. Marita felt she was beginning at last to get a grip of this difficult language. She knew this would be invaluable to her when she got to America.

The woman talked about the Fenians and tried to explain how the English had come to Ireland three hundred years before and made it part of their empire. Ireland was a very Christian country then with strong Catholic faith and loyalty to the Church of Rome and monasteries and seminaries flourished. Thousands of priests and religious brothers and nuns trained in Ireland had travelled all over the world spreading the Word of God.

But the Irish fought among themselves at home and the English found it easy to pit one against the other until they took control of the country and they had ruled with an iron fist ever since. They moved thousands of families—called Planters—from England and Scotland and Wales to farms in Ireland forcing the Irish off their land.

"Now the Irish want their country back, and that's what all the killing is about," she explained. "The English still refuse to give it up because it is part of their Empire."

She explained about the hungry 1840s when the potato crop failed and nearly a million people died of starvation and twice as many were forced to leave the country to survive.

"There have been many rebellions against the English, all failures. The Fenians are different from previous rebels. There are a lot more of them, they are well organised, and the Irish forced to flee to America because of hunger and deprivation during the Famine are sending them money and guns."

Marita listened but she had little interest. She told the woman in broken English what happened in Derry when they were on their way to the boat and how she was taken hostage and separated from the others. She did not know their fate, but she was sure they were in America somewhere and she wanted to go there to find them.

"I don't know much about America," said the woman, "except that it's supposed to be a wild, lawless place, not the sort of place for a defenceless wee cutty like you. Ye'd be better staying in Ireland. And ye nivver know—maybe ye'll meet a nice young fella and settle down here.

"They're not all like my fellow," she added. "He's been in the Fenians for five years and he cares about nothing else. He's the last of the McKee family and he'll nivver marry and have a child of his own the way he's carrying on."

Marita agreed. 'What woman in her right mind would want to bear a child for that animal?' she asked herself.

He left the farm on horseback a few more times, but she never tried another escape for he always came back the same day. The weather was bitterly cold and for weeks dark black clouds hung over the farmhouse and at times the mist was so heavy she could see no further than the cowshed.

Falls of snow came suddenly and were washed away by rain almost as quickly. When the wind came from the North, it was so cold that even the stream froze, and you could stand on the ice and see fish swimming under your feet. The woman took Marita outside one night, broke a hole in the ice with an axe, and placed an oil lamp beside it. When a fish appeared in the light, she casually put her bare arm into the cold water and lifted it out. She did it again and again until she had all she wanted. They were brown trout, which were plentiful in mountain streams and lakes, and they were easy to catch when the light attracted them. The fish were fried in butter until they sizzled in the iron pan and were eaten with wedges of fresh brown bread washed down with tea. After the normal diet of cured pork and mutton, the tasty pink flesh made a welcome change.

Just before Christmas he returned from one of his trips and told Marita to pack warm clothing and food. The soldiers were patrolling along the foot of the mountains and might come to search the house. He took his revolver and rifle and they set off on foot through the snow. They walked upwards and when it was nearly dark came to the cabin that she had seen before when they were rounding up sheep in the autumn.

"We can hide here until the danger passes," he said. "And ye can scream all ye like," he added, smiling at her. "There isn't even a bird up here tae hear ye."

Marita smelled whiskey from his breath and realised he had tricked his mother to get her away from the farmhouse. She sat down on some hay and pulled the shawl tightly around her. He lit a lamp and, as its warm glow filled the cabin, took off his coat and jacket and told her to lie down. When she made no move, he pushed her roughly backwards on the hay and knelt on top of her. He pulled the shawl off her shoulders, caught the collar of her dress, and tugged until the buttons flew off. He grabbed her cotton vest and pulled it up around her neck to bare her breasts.

He put her arms by her sides and pinned them to the ground with his knees. He took one nipple between each forefinger and thumb and pulled hard, stretching the tender purple flesh until she arched her back off the ground to try and ease the pain. He pushed her down again on the hay.

She clenched her fists and closed her eyes to try and blot out the pain. He got up off her, and when she opened her eyes, he was standing over her, removing his trousers. He pulled her knickers down until the material caught on one of her shoes, and in his rage, he yanked hard until the soft material gave way.

She kicked backwards and caught him with her shoe on the side of the head, and he had to roll her over on her back to stop her flying feet. He put his knee between her thighs and forced them apart, and she did not resist. She was in so much pain she hardly noticed when he forced his way into her.

Her buttocks were wet with blood and urine, her nose was bleeding, and she could feel it trickling down one side of her face to her ear. When she coughed, blood splashed on her chest and on his shirt, but he didn't stop until the last ounce of lust had drained from his heaving body.

"Ye bitch. Ye won't git the better of me," he smiled, "As far as ye're concerned, I am yer lord and master, de ye hear? Ah want no more nonsense from ye."

She lay on the straw bed for a long time, numb from shock and cold, unable to move. She used her torn vest to wipe away some of the blood on her body and pulled the remains of her clothing together under the black shawl. She used the remnants of her knickers to try and stem the flow of blood oozing from her thighs.

He sat calmly, eating bread and cheese and drinking milk from the can she had brought. He offered her some, but she refused. He turned over on the hay and went to sleep. She stayed well away from him, sitting upright throughout the night, holding her knees tightly together with her aching arms, her body shivering from pain and the intense cold.

When he awoke the morning was still dark; he smoked several cigarettes until there was enough light in the sky to travel. He offered her food again, but she shook her head.

She asked for a cigarette, and he gave it to her. She fumbled with the matches until she succeeded in lighting it and then coughed as the acrid smoke entered her lungs for the first time. He laughed at her. She took a few more pulls and put it down on the floor.

They set off down the mountain. She deliberately left the milk can behind and had to go back to the cabin for it. Inside she poured oil from the lamp onto the hay, found the still smouldering remains of the cigarette she had lit and set it alight. By the time she caught up with him, the cabin was ablaze. When he looked back and saw what she had done he hit her again on the face. Painful as it was, she smiled. He would not be able to use that place again to torture her.

"Ich werde Dich toten.... Ich werde Dich toten.... Ich werde Dich toten." She spat the words at him, but he did not understand her threat to kill him.

"Ye're as bitter as the soldiers, ye fuckin' witch," he laughed nervously. He was worried about the wily bitch setting fire to the cabin, as the smoke could be seen a long way off and might attract attention.

His mother knew there was something wrong the moment the girl returned. Marita showed her the blood and teeth marks on her body, and the woman vowed he would never get the chance to hurt her like that again. If they ever had to leave in future, she would go with them. The woman bathed her in warm water and smeared the cuts and bruises with oil to ease the swelling and the pain.

She ranted at her son, calling him a pig, but she knew she was wasting her breath. He didn't care.

Christmas came and went without celebration, for neither woman would even talk to him. A few times when Marita was working in the outhouses, he came up behind and grabbed her, but she screamed until his mother emerged from the house, and he was forced to let her go. At night, he drank whisky from the bottle and, when he got drunk, swore at the women and threatened Marita.

In March the weather turned milder, and primroses and flowers sheltered by ditches brought a touch of colour to the bleak landscape as it emerged from the cold wet winter. A few clusters of daisies appeared, delicate white petals still tinged with purple from the cold nights.

Since she arrived on the mountain, Marita had not seen a single bird, but in early spring, she noticed a huge one circling the farm. The woman told her it was an eagle, and it always made an appearance at the lambing season. The bird often swooped down to grab a lamb in its huge claws and soared off to its nest on the mountaintop to devour its helpless victim. Eagles ate the flesh and used skin and wool to pad their nest for the arrival of chicks in early summer. They also killed and carried off rabbits, hares, kid goats—anything they could catch out in the open on the exposed hillsides. Mothers with babies never left prams outdoors at that time of the year, for there were stories of youngsters disappearing without a trace. Nothing was safe from the eagle's claws.

He left one morning, telling his mother he would be back before dusk, but did not return for four days. When he eventually appeared, he had three other men with him. They were on horseback and led two smaller animals with boxes strapped to their sides. The heavy cases were dragged into the barn, and one of the men removed the lids to check the contents. Inside, packed in oily black paper, were rifles with shiny brown butts and sleek polished barrels. The men unpacked, examined the contents and carefully put them back and nailed the lids. They dragged the crates away from the farmhouse and hid them in a cave among the rocks.

The strangers talked among themselves about an attack on an army patrol two days earlier, on St. Patrick's Day. They boasted that they had killed fourteen soldiers and lost only three of their own men. The police knew that the Fenians retreated into the Sperrin hills after each attack, and sooner or later, Eamonn was sure the army, smarting after their heavy losses, would try to flush them out.

The rifles were American—the very latest—capable of holding six bullets in the breach; they would be very useful if an attack came. They were part of a shipment from Friends of the Fenians in Boston. So many weapons were coming across the Atlantic that the rebels had trouble finding safe places to store them.

Experience in other parts of the country showed that the British army was not prepared to make a full frontal assault on remote areas where the rebel bands were hiding. They preferred to send out patrols and use the same hit-and-run tactics as the Fenians. They shot sympathisers, burned houses, slaughtered animals in the fields and set corn and haystacks alight as a warning to the general population not to provide food and shelter for the rebels. They hoped this war of attrition would isolate the troublemakers.

Eamonn discussed plans with the others to attack any patrols that ventured into the mountains. One good ambush and he believed the army would pull back altogether leaving a kind of 'no man's land' in which the rebels could operate unhindered and from which they could launch attacks. The Fenians had the advantage in that they knew every lane and tree in the area, and of course, they had allies and spies everywhere to alert them to danger.

The four men settled down to a lazy routine on the farm. They spent the time cleaning their rifles or smoking and sometimes went behind the rocks and came back with jars of a clear liquid called poteen, a substitute for whiskey which they produced themselves from potatoes and grain. They drank the foul-smelling spirit until they were merry; after a long session, they ended up in a drunken stupor, unable to stand up.

As the days got longer, Eamonn and his cronies carried out regular patrols on the mountain. Marita watched them set off in the late mornings in single file, long overcoats touching the ground, rifles slung over their shoulders. He had a pair of binoculars and at regular intervals scouted ahead on his own to do a sweep of the countryside before signalling to the others to follow. They returned before dark and when they had eaten sat around the stove and discussed what they had seen and heard.

There was much more activity than usual along the main road that skirted the foothills. Army and police patrols were scouring the district searching for rebels and arms, offering good money for information leading to arrests. Eamonn had a map on which he marked the location of the soldiers, their numbers, and how they were armed. At the end of each day, they examined the map, making notes on what they had observed. They also picked up information about informers, for they had seen police make regular visits to particular houses. Some of the families concerned were already under suspicion and what Eamonn saw confirmed that they were selling information. Some of them would be shot in due course, but in the meantime, they could be useful to channel false information to the police.

In May the four left for Derry and a week later three returned. The oldest of his companions had been killed when an ambush near the bridge over the River Foyle went wrong. The Fenians shot two soldiers, but as they left the scene, they ran into a second patrol, and three members of the ambush party were shot dead. They also lost valuable rifles and some small hand-thrown bombs—part of a shipment from France. The Fenians who escaped, including Eamonn and his two companions, had to jump off the side of the bridge in midstream and let the current from the flood tide carry them upstream to safety.

Marita thought how unfortunate it was that he was not among the dead. When she went to the barn to get potatoes the next day, he pushed her against the potato sacks,s and while one of his companions put a rag in her mouth and the other kept a lookout for his mother, he raped her again. When he had done with her, he offered her to them but they shook their heads and walked away.

They had a lone visitor on horseback one day, a grey-haired man in his sixties who discussed the bridge ambush and what went wrong. He told them that it had been decided to stop all further action in Derry because a new system of back-up patrols by the army was in operation and the Fenians were finding it difficult to get accurate information about what was going on. Instead, they were to concentrate on attacking patrols in the countryside. The stranger warned them, however, that the police were paying good money to informers and getting a lot of information. Even though it could cost them their lives, there were people still willing to take the risk.

After he left, Eamonn studied the maps they had made to see if they could find a good ambush site. They marked the routes of army and police patrols and frequency. The patrols never ventured beyond the main road that ran through the village, where they had good cover from trees and hedges; an ambush there was out of the question. What the Fenians needed was some way to entice soldiers further up the mountainside to open ground. Since there were now only three of them, any attack would have to be set up so that little was left to chance. After days of discussion of various options, Eamonn came up with an idea himself.

"But ah canny let the women know what's in me mind," he warned the others, "fur me mother would throw us out o' the house if she heard it."

He then outlined a plan to use the girl as bait to lure one of the patrols up the mountain. He knew exactly how and where it could be done and though he knew his mother would object strongly the wee cutty herself might be more than willing to play her part if she was promised the one thing she wanted more than anything else—her freedom and enough money to pay for passage to America.

CHAPTER TWO

THE KILLING POOL

The mountainside was mainly sheep-grazing land, sloping ground dotted here and there with clumps of bracken and occasionally a hawthorn bush that survived the harsh climate by growing sideways rather than upward, pushing its stout thorny branches along the ground to lessen the impact of winter storms. There were no trees on the landscape. Division of farms was marked out by stone walls two or three feet high.

This lack of cover allowed army patrols an uninterrupted view for miles around. Through binoculars they sometimes spotted rebels moving along the mountainside, but they could do little about it. The moment they left the cover of hedges and trees close to the river, they were exposed, and the rebels could spot them from a long way off.

Eamonn explained his plan to the others. The stream that ran by the side of the farmhouse tumbled downhill until it reached a ribbon shaped pool from which gravel had once been excavated for road building. When the pit closed, villagers altered the watercourse to create the pool, which was used by children in summer. Water tumbled in at the upper end and gently overflowed at the other to continue its course downhill. A few small trees and bushes had taken root in the grassy banks around it, giving it the appearance of an oasis, a pool of deep blue water in verdant surroundings.

As a boy, his father often brought him there and because the pool was on their land, he regarded it as his own private place. He learned from an early age that you had to be careful to check how deep it was every time you went for a swim for it was as unpredictable as the weather. During heavy rain the volume of water plunging into the pool from the swollen stream gouged the bottom to a depth of six feet or more. In fine weather there was a gentler flow and sand and small stones carried down the hillside raised the bottom until the water was only knee deep.

Eamonn's idea was to create a diversion that would entice soldiers to leave the safety of the road and venture up the hill to the pool. Once they arrived there, the Fenians would have them at their mercy. The plan was to use Marita as bait to lure them, but she would have to be convincing. If they could get her to strip off and go swimming, it was only a matter of time before she would be spotted, and soldiers, being what they were, would come after her. Lonely young English conscripts were suckers for a pretty woman, especially if she was on her own with the promise of a sexual encounter. If they had to use a bit of force who was there to see it? In any case, they regarded all Irish women as Fenian bitches, fair game.

"An innocent wee cutty bathing naked in a lonely mountain pool would be too much for the soldiers tae resist," Eamonn told the others.

The problem was how to get Marita to co-operate with the plan. He knew from previous experience that the bitch hated him because he beat her into submission. He could not force her to strip off at the pool—his mother had put an end to that. He needed to get her to go along with his plan by offering her something she could not refuse—a promise of sending her to America.

Remembering the way he raped her in the barn, the others were sceptical. Since that day, there has been only contempt in her eyes for all of them.

Eamonn was confident, however, that she would do it. He told his mother he wanted to have a meeting with the girl because the time had come when he might be able to get her away on a ship to America.

At first Marita was wary of having anything to do with him but in the end agreed to meet if his mother was present. When she came into the kitchen the three men were already seated around the big wooden table and his mother moved over so that the girl could sit beside her.

Eamonn explained that he needed a favour from her, and if she agreed, the Fenians would give her money and get her aboard a ship for America. If she trusted them and did exactly what she was told, within a month or six weeks she would be on her way to join her friends.

It was like music to her ears to hear that at last there was a possibility of getting away from him, from this God-forsaken country. The favour had to be a big one for the mean bastard had never done anything to help her since the day he grabbed her on the street in Derry and made her his prisoner. "What do you want the wee girl to do?" asked his mother anxiously.

When he explained, she jumped to her feet at the table and flew into a rage.

"How could you even think that this wee cutty would belittle herself like that," she shouted at him. "Fenians or no Fenians she won't do it—I won't let her!"

"Let her make her own mind up," he shouted back. "You mind yer own fucking business. Either she goes to the pool and gets a free run to America, or she stays here and rots!"

"Ye'll get her killed! Then ye'll be happy," his mother said. "Ye and yer Fenian friends."

She turned to the girl: "Ye'd be mad to get involved wey that crowd," she said firmly. "They want tae kill soldiers, but they don't want tae risk their own necks!"

"I won't do it," Marita said. She got up from the table and the two women left the room.

"Ye're an interfering auld bitch," he called after his mother.

Eamonn had no intention of giving up. After a talk with his cronies, he rode off that same evening and returned next morning with the priest who asked to speak to the girl alone.

The old man explained to Marita that he would have nothing to do with the killings but gave his solemn oath that if she did this thing, once the ambush was over, he personally would see to it that she got her freedom and passage to America. He would take her to Derry himself when the time was right, see her safely aboard ship and give her the names and addresses of Fenian sympathisers in New York who would look after her until she found a job and a place to stay. He took out a Bible, put his hand on it and swore before God that he would honour his promise.

It was what she wanted most and, though puzzled how a priest could be involved with open rebellion and killings and still swear on the Bible, she realised it might be her only chance to get away from her mountain prison. She didn't trust the Fenians or the priest either for it was clear from the first time she met him that he was a Fenian too. She said she would think about it.

"Ye have to make up yer own mind," said the grey-haired cleric, "but to my mind, it's the best opportunity ye have of getting back with yer family. They must be worried sick about ye after all this time."

The following morning, Eamonn approached as she was milking the cows and asked her: "Do ye want to hear more now?"

She nodded her head. "But if you touch me again, I won't do it for you, priest or no priest And I want money before I do anything."

He explained what she had to do. She would go down to the pool when the weather was fine and spend a bit of time there until they were sure she was spotted by the soldiers who would be watching the hillside through binoculars from the village. She had to take off her clothes, swim around in the water for a bit, then lie on the grassy bank and sun herself.

"Ye might have to do that for a couple of days," he warned her, "before they are tempted to leave their hiding place".

If the soldiers did come to the pool all she had to do was keep their attention, chat to them for a couple of minutes, and he and his companions hiding nearby would capture and disarm them. He lied that the purpose of the ambush was to get their hands on army rifles. They wanted her to tease the soldiers so that they could be separated from horses and weapons. That's why she had to take all her clothes off and walk around. Once they got into the pool where she was swimming, he and his companions would commandeer the horses and rifles and take the soldiers prisoner. When it was over, she would return to the farmhouse the way she came and that was the end of it. As soon as they had their prisoners, the priest would get her to Derry and onto a ship.

"And what if the soldiers don't come to the pool? What if they are too cute for ye?" asked his mother. "What happens to the girl then?"

"A deal is a deal, woman," he said. "The priest will take her to the boat and we'll be well shut of her."

That night, when she thought about what he had said, she suspected it was not going to be as simple as they made it out to be. What if it went wrong and the soldiers started shooting? She had no doubt he and his cronies would abandon her to save their own necks. And if she got in the way, the Fenians would kill her if they had to, and it wouldn't cost them a thought. But the thing that worried her most of all was that even if she did manage to escape from the pool unharmed, there was no guarantee they would honour their promise. The priest was not to be trusted. His mother was the only one she could rely on.

Marita was desperate for some way out of her predicament; she had to get away from the bloody country in which he found herself. If she didn't co-operate with him, she might have to spend years in this awful place used and abused by this sadist. If she did not go along with his plan, America would never be anything more than a dream.

In the morning she told the woman to inform them that she would do it but wanted money for the trip to America before the ambush—enough for her fare, clothes and food and lodgings when she got there. If she did manage to get to America, the last thing she wanted was to be dependent on Fenians. He gave her the money that same day and she gave it to his mother for safekeeping.

The three men sat down with a large map of the area and explained the plan again until she understood every detail. He warned that if she did not carry out her part of the bargain if she baulked at the last minute or did something stupid that put them in danger, she was on her own. The soldiers would rape her and probably drown her when they finished with her, and nobody would lift a finger to save her.

He took her to the pool and showed her exactly what they wanted her to do, how to position herself when the soldiers came. She had to make sure she was on the opposite side of the pool from them so that they would have to put down their weapons to keep them dry or walk all the way around the pool to reach her. She understood and told him so.

"There's a clump of gorse on your side near the water," one of the others said, "and that's where we will be hiding. When we challenge the soldiers to surrender, you can make a run for it. Keep going up the hill the way ye came and ye'll be back at the farm in no time at all."

They made it all sound so simple, but Marita had no illusions. There would be no prisoners—only dead soldiers—if their plan worked.

Early in June, police raided the priest's house and took him and his housekeeper to Derry for questioning. They were held for two days until the bishop intervened, demanding their release so that the priest could resume ministering to his flock. But the police would not let him go until he swore on the Bible in the presence of his bishop and District Inspector Mehaffy that he knew no Fenians, that to the best of his knowledge, there were no Fenians in his parish, and if he ever got information that there were, he was duty bound to inform the police and have them apprehended.

The priest took the oath in a clear voice, his hand on the Bible as if he was in a court of law. It meant nothing to him—he regarded himself as an Irish patriot and the only oath that bound him before God was the one he took when he joined the Fenians to fight for the freedom of his country.

Nevertheless, the bishop was impressed by the clear and concise way in which the oath was taken and reprimanded the police for embarrassing one of his ministers who was a loyal subject of the Crown.

"It's clear that you acted in haste on the word of an informer," he chided Mehaffy, "the word of some malicious busybody who has a grudge against the priest or the Catholic Church."

The bishop made the police pay for a coach to take his priest and housekeeper back to their hillside parish. Eamonn went to the parochial house that night, and they drank a bottle of whiskey while the priest told him all that happened.

"Eamonn," said the old man solemnly, "you'll have to git yer hands on that informer before he gits us all in serious bother."

Eamonn knew who it was but said nothing to the priest or to his aunt. It was a woman who lived within a stone's throw of the church, and she would be dealt with when the ambush was over.

On a fine day towards the end of June, Marita made her first trip to the pool. She lay down in the sun, but it was so hot she tucked her dress inside her knickers and walked around in the cold water to help cool down. A couple of times she left the pool and stood on top of the bank so that anybody on the road would have a full view of her. She had another stroll around the pool before she sauntered back to the farmhouse. She wondered if Eamonn and his companions had been watching her if they were nearby; obviously, they were well concealed, for she neither saw nor heard anything.

On her third visit she undressed and went into the pool for a swim, wearing only her knickers. It was cold, and when she got out she took off the wet undergarment and quickly dried herself. She lay in the sun until her body warmed again.

When he returned to the farmhouse later, Eamonn told her that the soldiers had spotted her. He saw them watching her through field glasses.

Marita was more apprehensive when she went to the pool the next day. She was curious about where the soldiers were and kept a sharp lookout as she strolled around the pool naked to her waist. A few times she saw sunlight reflected from glass, but she was not sure whether it was the soldiers watching her or the reflection of the sun on a window in the village.

She felt uneasy at the thought of the soldiers' prying eyes on her naked body for the wet knickers clung to her skin as if they were part of her, showing every curve and crevice. She was given the usual whistle signal to get dressed and made her way back to the farm.

Marita was warned to be ready for action, for it was likely that the soldiers would come to the pool the next day if the weather was good enough for her to go swimming.

"Once you hear their horses coming," Eamonn told her, "get yourself into position on the right side of the pool. And remember, no matter what happens, you are not to shout for help, or the whole thing will go wrong," he warned. "When we think the time is right, we'll be nearby and ready and it will be all over quickly.

"What you have to do then is git yerself back to the farm as quick as yer legs will carry ye." The more he reassured her, the more suspicious she became. He was such a devious, lying bastard.

In the morning a heat mist hung over the mountain, and it took the sun a long time to burn it off; the church bell was ringing the Angelus at noon while she was walking to the pool, much later than usual. The three armed men had already left the house and set out on foot across the side of the mountain using the mist as cover.

She was tired, for she had slept little during the night, worried about the ordeal she had to face at the pool. The mist drifting slowly across the mountainside was cold and she was wearing a light dress. She had a towel for the pool, and she put it over her shoulders to keep warm.

When she heard the soldiers might come that day, she wrote a letter to the priest in Innsbruck telling him briefly how she had been separated and held prisoner by rebels in a country called Ireland. She realised she was in danger, and if she was killed, at least somebody in Hoffenfeld should know what happened to her. How ironic it would be, she thought, if a survivor of the valley massacre should die a violent death in a strange country in a cause she knew nothing about. She handed the letter to the woman and asked her to make sure it was posted if she did not return from the pool.

At least she was not worried about leaving anybody behind she explained to his mother, for she was the last surviving member of her family.

"Hush, girl, sure what would happen to you? Ye'll be back this evening and I'll have a nice hot dinner ready for ye."

The woman knew the danger. Before the day was out, she could lose both her only son and this girl of whom she had become so fond. She made the Sign of the Cross on the girl's forehead and splashed some Holy Water on her face as she went out the door. She prayed silently to God to bring the girl back safely. Marita couldn't understand being blessed by anybody when she was about to break the most important Commandment of all—"Thou shalt not kill."

Her walking dream was interrupted by the glint of sun on glass from the same place she had seen it the day before. If it was the soldiers they would wait until she reached the pool, then watch as she took off her clothes. She was very late, yet they had waited patiently for her. She felt this was the day they would come and if they did it might be their last day on this earth. It might also be hers.

Before she left the house, she decided to wear only her knickers and a dress because it would be easier to get rid of wet underwear and slip on the dress when she had to leave in a hurry. The only other thing she brought was a red flannel towel wrapped around her shoulders.

When she reached the pool, there was no sign of life, no movement in the bushes or around the rocks where she knew the Fenian gang was lying in wait, watching the soldiers watching her. She was terrified of the ordeal ahead but excited too at the prospect that, before the day was out, she might be free and ready to resume her life and put the wide Atlantic Ocean between her and these Fenian killers. She hoped her tormentor would die in the ambush, but if he did, the chances were that she would be killed too, for the soldiers would know it was she who had led them into the trap.

She spread the towel on the grassy bank and lay down on her back until she could feel the hot sun tingle the skin of her face and burn her bare shoulders. She sat up, took off her shoes and turned around to face the roadway where she had seen them watching her. She unbuttoned her dress from top to bottom as he had told her to and slipped it off her shoulders. Though tense and scared, her body felt good as her bare skin took the full heat of the sun's rays. She folded the dress carefully and placed it beside her shoes. She stood up and waded into the pool.

The water was ice-cold, and she shivered when it reached her knees and gradually crept up her thighs and buttocks as she moved into deeper water. She lost her footing a couple of times on sharp stones at the bottom. By the time the water reached her hips, she had goose pimples on her arms. But when she lowered her whole body below the surface, it felt warmer, and soon she was splashing around, enjoying the buoyancy. When she stood up her body felt good as it caught the full heat of the sun again.

She held her breath and listened for the sound of approaching horses but there was nothing. She swam back to the bank, dried herself and lay in the sun, waiting for the signal to dress. She began to think about what would happen if the soldiers did not take the bait and never came to the pool. She had the money and one way or another, she would get her freedom. She had kept her part of the bargain, and his mother would make sure the priest kept his.

She felt good lying in the hot sun and was so preoccupied by her thoughts that she dozed off and was awakened by the noise of horses' hooves clattering on stony ground; she opened her eyes to find the soldiers were already there, on top of the bank on the other side of the pool, calling to her and whistling, excited at the sight of her naked body. Her heart began to race, and her body froze as she stood up on the bank. She turned her back to them to hide her nakedness. When she went to get her knickers, they whistled and shouted all the louder. There were four of them leering at her, the buttons on their bright red tunics glinting in the sunlight. They each held the reins of a horse in one hand, rifle in the other. The one who was doing most of the shouting had a sword dangling by his side.

They dismounted and tried to coax her to their side of the pool, but she shook her head emphatically as she tried to cover her nakedness with the knickers. On impulse, she dropped the undergarment, waded into the pool, and crouched down until the water covered her shoulders. She shivered from the fright of their sudden appearance and the cold water.

"Come on, missy, be a sport. Stand up and let us see you."

"Come on, colleen, we only want a bit of fun."

"Be a sport, ma'am"

"You're a beauty."

"I'll make it worth your while....."

They kept up a continuous barrage of words, urging her to stand up so that they could see her.

"Please don't hurt me," she called out, and slowly moved backwards out of the water again, still facing them, not knowing what to do next. She felt trapped and there was no help coming from Eamonn and his cronies. They were supposed to protect her.

The soldiers had a quick chat amongst themselves; three of them got off their horses, hastily undressed on the bank, dumped uniforms unceremoniously on the grass and waded into the pool completely naked; the fourth dismounted and held the horses' reins. He cradled his rifle in his arms and shouted obscenities at his companions, annoyed that he had been left to stand guard.

Marita took a few more steps backwards and crouched lower so that the water covered her legs and thighs. She was shaking with fear and there was still no movement or noise from the Fenians; were they nearby at all? She could hear her heart thumping against her ribs and her breath came faster and faster.

For all the shouting and whistling, when they reached her in the pool, they kept their distance at first. They swam around a few times before one of them plucked up the courage to touch her. Another lifted her up in the water until her breasts were exposed. She felt one of them behind her, pressing his body hard against her, and he put his hands around her stomach. A red-haired soldier picked her up in his arms and slowly moved through the water to the bank. She said nothing and made no effort to protest or struggle when he set her down gently on dry land. After what happened to her at Hoffenfeld, she vowed she would not allow herself to be abused again, but it had happened with the animal Eamonn, and now it was about to happen again. The soldiers were aroused by her nakedness and made no attempt to hide the fact that she was theirs for the taking, and they all wanted to have a go.

Marita was terrified. Where were the others? She had separated three of the four soldiers from their weapons; this was the time the Fenians were supposed to come to her rescue.

The red head forced her down onto the towel she had been lying on before they came. Then he stood up and they discussed briefly who was to have first bite of the cherry.

They were going to take turns raping her. She knew it. One of them took her hands and forced them back until her knuckles were on the ground, her body spread-eagled. The redhead knelt astride her stomach.

The soldier on guard called to them but they made no answer.

"Give it to her," he taunted the others. "She wants it and there's enough there to satisfy all of us. Get a bloody move on!"

She made no effort to resist, for she knew it was useless. She lay still as the soldier rolled down the wet knickers covering her thighs and cast them aside.

The bastards had gone and left her! She was sure of it!

When he leaned over and kissed her stomach, she suddenly said: "No! Tell them to go away. Only you stay." She was trying to gain time in the hope that the others would come. The redhead said something, and his companions reluctantly backed off into the water to wait their turn. She could see the fourth on the other side, still in his uniform, standing at the water's edge, rifle cradled in his arms, watching them. He shouted that he wanted a go too.

Something was wrong. What if they didn't make it to the pool? Was there a change of plan when the soldiers brought horses with them instead of coming on foot? She should have known things never worked out the way they were supposed to. From the very start, she suspected things would not happen the way Eamonn had said they would. He was such a liar. She was in worse danger now than she was the night of the massacre. They would rape her and maybe kill her when they were finished with her. And if the Fenians' attack failed, the soldiers would kill her anyhow when she realised it was she who led them into an ambush.

The soldier was drying her wet thighs and stomach with her blue dress. He stroked her gently, and when she didn't resist, he touched her thighs. Still, she did not move. The bitch was beautiful, and she loved what he was doing to her. He kissed her lips lightly and prised her thighs apart with his cold hand.

She closed her eyes when she felt the full length of his warm body on top of her, waiting for him to rape her. There was no point in resisting further—the cowardly Fenian bastard and his cronies had fled and abandoned her, just as she knew they would.

She gasped for air and struggled against him when he forced his way into her. His lips were soft on her neck, and his hands caressed her buttocks, and he was whispering that she was beautiful and telling her how much he loved her. She lay still with her eyes closed and let him have his way. He was gentle with her; she felt none of the pain she had experienced with Eamonn.

A heavy sickness engulfed her body. It started in her legs and flushed through her veins all the way up to her brain until her head was swimming. Her arms instinctively tightened around his neck, and she pushed back her head and gasped for air.

When he began to move up and down on top of her, she started to move with him; she could not help herself. His hands tightened on her buttocks as his movement quickened, and she felt her own breathing come faster and faster; her head was in a whirl. She put her arms around him and pleaded with him in German to be nice to her. In her passion, she bit his shoulder hard until she tasted salty, hot blood on her lips.

He let out a loud moan and collapsed on top of her. She clasped him tightly to her, pushing against him; she did not want him to stop.

Suddenly, she heard shots ring out and opened her eyes, but her body was in the throes of passion, her vision blurred and her head still spinning. His face was on her shoulder. She screamed when she saw blood gushing from the side of his head. It spurted over her arms, face and shoulders until the whole top of her body was wet. She pushed him off and sat up. The naked bodies of two soldiers floated face downward in the pool; the third, still in his uniform and clutching his rifle, lay on his back beside the frightened horses at the edge of the water on the other side.

There was blood everywhere—on her body, the towel, on her dress, on the grass. It ran from the soldier's head down to the water's edge and spread outwards across the pool like a cloud of red dye until it joined the blood of his dead comrades. She was paralysed with fear.

Eamonn grabbed the dress, towel and shoes and threw them at her. "Get up and get out of here, woman!" he shouted. When she did not respond, he dragged her to her feet and roughly pushed her up the bank and threw the clothing after her.

"I said get out of here, ye stupid bitch."

Dazed, she bundled up the dress, lifted her shoes and started to run in the direction he pointed, completely naked. After the first few steps, she fell on her knees, and he shouted at her until she got up again and staggered forward along the grassy path. She tried to run, but her legs were so heavy that she could not lift them. Her bare feet caught on every stone and clump of grass in her path. The smell of blood on her body and clothing was sickening, and the more she tried to wipe it off with the dress and towel, the more the sticky mess clung to her. She knelt on the pathway and vomited.

Eamonn's mother heard the shooting, and she was standing at the door twenty minutes later when Marita stumbled into the farmyard naked and covered in blood. She thought the girl had been shot. She made her lie down on the kitchen floor and washed away the blood; there was no sign of a wound. She put her on a chair and forced her to drink a cup of tea and whiskey. She sponged her matted hair until the blood was gone, then helped her upstairs and into bed. In deep shock and drugged by the alcohol, Marita fell asleep.

She tossed and turned in the bed, bad dreams alternating between the ecstasy of the soldier's lovemaking and the terror of seeing his blood and brains flowing from the gaping wound to his head where he had been hit with the butt of Eamonn's rifle. She would never forget the fixed stare in his dead eyes when she pushed his body aside. Eamonn was standing over them and struck him a second blow in case the first did not do the job.

It was late the next day before she had the strength to get out of bed. The woman had laid out her blue dress, washed and neatly pressed, on a chair. But she shied away from it and pointed to the one she had brought with her from Germany. She would never wear the blue dress again.

Downstairs, the three men had already packed their belongings and rifles and were ready to leave. They planned to get down to the river and across that night and in the morning make their way to County Donegal and hide with friends in the mountains along the rugged Atlantic coast.

The army would take swift revenge, Eamonn warned his mother. The police would be active too, for after burying the soldiers in the bog, the trio had gone to the village and shot the woman informer.

"My advice," he said to his mother, "is to pack yer bags, the pair of ye, and git yerselves as far away from here as ye can. Am going and ah don't know when ah'll be back fer I'm a marked man, according to the informer. The soldiers know me and they're out tae git me.

"Ah'll tell the priest on me way down the mountain to come and git yis tomorrow. He has a safe house in Tyrone where yis can stay for a while tae things settle down. It might be a good idea fer both of yis to head for America."

Marita protested bitterly. They had promised she would be taken to Derry and put on the boat after the ambush.

"Ye can go to Derry if ye want," he said, "but the army is looking for ye, for they know ye were at the pool, and if they catch ye, they'll try ye and hang ye before the week is out."

Only now did she realise the enormity of what she had done; she knew that this time he was telling the truth. She was no longer his prisoner, but she was still trapped. It would not take the army long to find out that a naked woman had been used to lure the young soldiers to their deaths at the mountain pool. From her bedroom window, she saw the three of them leave the farmyard on foot carrying their belongings, rifles slung over their shoulders. They set off northwards to avoid the village and eventually disappeared towards the priest's house.

Eamonn's mother went to the outhouses and turned all the animals loose, driving them towards the higher reaches of the mountain so that the soldiers could not shoot them if they came.

They spent the night packing their belongings. The woman was sad to see Eamonn go, for God knows when she might ever set eyes on him again. She was sad too about leaving the farm to which she had been brought as a bride twenty-five years before. She was forty-two years of age, and between the death of her husband when Eamonn was still in his early teens and the boy getting mixed up with the Fenians when he was old enough to carry a rifle, she had nothing but worry for as long as she could remember.

The past decade had also been a lonely existence for her. She had married when she was seventeen and was only thirty when her husband died. She often felt hungry for the company of a man. A few had propositioned her, and she would have loved to strike up a relationship with them but baulked at the idea of bringing a stranger to the farm that rightfully belonged to her son.

When Eamonn first arrived with this young girl, she had hoped he might have found somebody to settle down with at last and leave her free to meet someone and marry again, but it soon became clear that this foreign girl meant nothing to him. He treated her like a slave, and she hated him.

It was four o'clock in the morning by the time they put together what they wanted to bring with them. They dragged two heavy bags full of clothing and keepsakes to the kitchen and put them behind the hall door. During the long night, the full impact of what had happened by the pool hit Marita, and several times, the older woman had to shake her awake to interrupt the nightmares.

Every time Marita closed her eyes, she imagined she could smell the hot, sticky blood of the young soldier on her body. The memory of his naked companions floating in the water reminded her of a time in the valley when farm waste in the river killed all the fish; she had stood on the bank with her grandmother and watched the pathetic upturned bodies float downstream.

Eamonn's mother was frightened, as she was firmly convinced that the soldiers would come that night to burn the house and kill them both. That was why her crafty son and his companions had fled so quickly—to get themselves and their weapons well away in case they were cornered on the mountain farm.

The girl had not told her much about the killing at the pool, but it must have been a terrible ordeal. She had stumbled up the mountain completely naked, clutching her dress, covered in blood from head to toe. While sponging the blood from her hair, the older woman had asked several times if Eamonn was okay, but Marita just stared at her; it was hours before he came home.

His mother was glad he was alive but sad that the boy who was once the pride and joy of herself and her husband had turned into such a monster. He used to be a timid boy, so much so that when animals were being slaughtered on the farm, he refused to help because he could not stand seeing them stunned with a hammer before the butcher slit their throats.

The Fenians changed him. They had convinced him he was a patriot and that it was his duty to avenge the great Irishmen of previous generations who had been murdered by the forces of the Crown. What frightened her most was that even among the rebels, her son had acquired the reputation of a cold, calculated killer who had no regard for human life—that's why he had been appointed a leader.

The two women drank cups of strong tea to keep them awake during the hours of darkness, and occasionally, Eamonn's mother went outside and peered down the mountainside through the moonlight for signs of approaching danger.

At first light, she saw two horses approaching, but there was a misty haze hanging over the hillside, and she was not sure who it was. She called Marita and they grabbed shawls to keep warm and together they fled the house to the safety of a cave in the rocks that Eamonn had used as a hiding place for the rifles. They waited in silence to see who the horsemen were.

A man's voice called out in the semi-darkness. "Is there anybody up yet? If ye are, git yer things together and be as quick as ye can, for the sooner we get out of this place, the better."

The older woman recognised the voice at once.

"We're all right," she said. "It's the priest come to take us away."

He was surprised to see them emerging from the rocks, but the older woman explained that they thought it better to hide in case it was soldiers coming to search the house.

"They'll be here soon enough," he said, "but not this quick. They'll turn the village upside down first and it's me that'll be the busy man before this day is out. The soldiers won't rest until they find the missing soldiers. and when they do, they'll kill rings round them".

They loaded their belongings onto one of the horses and the priest rode the other and the two women walked down the mountain behind the animals. They had only gone a short way when Eamonn's mother remembered that the oil lamps were still lit in the kitchen, and she wanted to go back to douse them but the priest wouldn't hear of it.

"It's bad luck to turn back anyway," she said to Marita. The girl glared at her. Ordinary bad luck would be welcome after what she had been through since she set foot in this damned country.

Although she was setting out on another journey into the unknown, another one not of her own choice, Marita was glad to see the back of that mountain farm where she had spent a year of torment, where she had been degraded and abused and then bribed into taking part in the murder of four people.

As they walked down the pathway, Marita winced several times when she thought she smelled blood. She saw some on the ground where she had used grass to try and wipe her body clean. When they reached the pool, the girl covered her head with a shawl and stumbled along blindly. Even with her eyes closed, she could see it, and she could still smell the blood that stained the blue mountain water.

It was early when they reached the village and there was nobody about. The priest led them into the parochial house through the back door. While his maid fussed over the two women, he unsaddled the animals and turned them out into a field. He dragged the heavy bags to the church, put them in the porch and locked the door.

Army patrols would not arrive in the village until later in the morning, he told them; he impressed on them the need for secrecy because the police had spies everywhere.

Few words were spoken between them, and there was no mention of the ambush, as if it had never happened. Both priest and housekeeper knew all about it, for Eamonn and his pals had stopped for a meal the evening before on their way to the river and boasted how they used the naked girl to lure the soldiers to the pool to kill them.

The priest's maid was a great supporter of the Fenians and proud of the fact that her nephew was one of them. She had no qualms about killing the soldiers. She knew that he couldn't have done it without the help of the girl. Several times she told Marita: "Well done girrel. The Fenians will look after you when you get to America."

The housekeeper took them from the parochial house to the church at dusk and told them they would have to make themselves comfortable; it was the safest place in the village. Later, she came back to see how they had settled in, and she had whiskey with her. She and her sister had a couple of glasses each, but Marita refused, for she hated the taste of it. The girl felt she had to keep her wits about her in case an opportunity came to slip away from these people and resume her own life.

After the whiskey, the two older sisters prattled on about the Fenians and how the British army could not keep going with all the men they were losing, and it would not be too long before Ireland was free of the English murderers and their lackeys.

But behind it all Eamonn's mother was far from proud of what her son had done, especially for the callous way he had used the girl. Killing for your country was one thing, but asking a young girl to strip naked and expose her body to strangers was another. It was against all her Catholic upbringing had taught her, for the sin of impurity flew in the face of God.

The next day brought news that the soldiers had recovered their comrades' bodies from the bog hole where they had been dumped, and several farmhouses were burned in revenge. Eamonn's place was still intact according to the young man who was looking after the animals. The soldiers were afraid to venture into the mountains in case there was another ambush.

Days passed without any news of their departure, and the two women remained cooped up in the small room high up in the church bell tower. It was hot during the day when the full force of the sun's rays fell on the large expanse of slate roof above their hideout. The church bells were rung twice a day at noon and six in the evening, and while the racket of the Angelus was going on, the women had to put their fingers into their ears to try to deaden the noise. At night, swallows nesting in the eaves also made such a racket that the women found it hard to sleep.

When the church doors were locked late in the evening Marita ventured from the loft and walked down the stairway and ambled up and down the aisles to get rid of the stiffness in her limbs. It was a strange place at night this House of God. There was complete darkness except for a solitary candle burning in a small red lamp over the altar.

Once her eyes got used to the dark, she was able to make her way about without difficulty. When the moon shone through the tall stained-glass windows, she could make out all sorts of things—a crucifix hanging from the high ceiling and the Stations of the Cross around the walls beautifully etched in wood, and rows of oak pews neatly arranged like drills in a potato field in spring.

She had always wanted to see what it was like from the other side of the communion rails, for in the valley, women were never permitted to pass beyond them. The marble rail was cold to touch as she climbed over to enter the consecrated ground, and when she stood on the altar steps and turned around, she was in awe at the size of the place. The aisles were so long she could not see all the way to the back, but she could make out the organ pipes in the gallery just below their hiding place.

She climbed into the pulpit to get a better view, resting her hands on the rail in front of her just like the priest did when he started his Sunday sermon. No wonder clergymen felt so superior; she understood for the first time how, from this vantage point, he could see everything that was happening, who was falling asleep and who was talking or laughing at the back of the church.

In the morning, the maid told them posters had been put up in the village naming Eamonn McKee, Peter Donnelly, Manus McStay and an unidentified woman as the Fenians who murdered the soldiers; a £100 reward was offered for any information leading to the capture of any of them. Detailed descriptions were given of the three men and woman who lured the soldiers to the pool where the Fenians were lying in wait to murder them. The girl seen with the rebels had a foreign accent.

The priest told them the false information about the girl being an American was deliberately fed to an informer to try and protect Marita if she should be found. However, any strange girl discovered in the area could not escape suspicion, so she had to remain in hiding in the church for another few days. Marita realised that trying to get to Derry on her own was out of the question, as she would be arrested before she got out of the village. Obviously, more than one patrol of soldiers had been watching her from the roadway in the days preceding the ambush, and no matter what the maid said about laying a false trail through an informer, she would be recognised. Some of the villagers might also have been watching her prancing around the pool naked. If an informer found out she was hiding in the church, she was finished.

She and Eamonn's mother were as quiet as mice, talking in whispers in case people visiting the church during the day overheard them. In the daylight hours, Marita passed the time rummaging through old pictures and books that had been stored for years in the dusty room and discovered a prayer book in German written by a Jesuit priest. Tedious as it was, she read it to pass the time. It brought back memories of her schooldays and the prayers she used to say with the nuns. It all seemed such a long time ago.

On Sunday they had to be particularly careful when the congregation arrived for Mass. All the movement down below and the thumping of the organ sent clouds of dust upwards in the warm air until they almost choked; they tied cloths over their mouths to filter the air and stop them from coughing.

The priest gave a long, rambling sermon, mostly about the brutal killing of the young soldiers, and laid down the law of the Church that nothing could excuse the taking of the life of another except in times of war. The laws of the country had to be obeyed; otherwise, there would be anarchy. Marita found it hard to believe he could be such a hypocrite, preaching about the Commandments and the Word of God when it was he who had recruited her to lure the soldiers to their deaths.

After Mass he paid a brief visit to tell them to get ready, as he had found a driver to take them to Tyrone. They would be safe there, and when things settled down he would get them to Derry for the ship.

When a cart pulled up in front of the church door a short time later, the two women hurried down the spiral stairs and quickly loaded their belongings. Within minutes, they were on their way. The housekeeper had filled a basket with buttered scones and cheese and a can of fresh milk and placed it under the driver's seat. In a cloth was a cooked chicken with a small bag of salt. She waved from the parochial house window as they passed, but the priest did not allow her to say goodbye in case she attracted attention.

They followed a rough road along the side of the mountain, keeping the peaks of the Sperrin Mountains on their left and the long winding river Foyle far below on their right. Here and there, mountain streams had washed parts of the roadway away, and they had to get out and walk while the driver coaxed the frightened horse across deep cuttings.

The driver was pleasant enough but did not have a lot to say. Clearly, he had undertaken the job as a favour for the priest and wanted to move as fast as he could and deposit his passengers at their destination to be rid of them. Marita wondered if he knew why they were fleeing. When the older woman asked him what Tyrone was like, he replied that it was a lovely place that they were going to live with nice people and they would have a comfortable home for the winter. It was a farm on a hillside overlooking a place called Mournebridge, a busy town and well worth a visit on market days.

He stopped occasionally along the way to look towards the river to see if there were any soldiers about. When he spotted them in the distance, he pulled the cart off the road into a field and waited until they had moved on. If they were stopped, he told them to give their names as Annie and Mary O'Donnell and say they were mother and daughter from County Donegal on their way to the hiring fair in Mournebridge. The soldiers would be none the wiser, since thousands of young girls and boys from poor families came to the hiring fairs in Tyrone at this time of year looking for work. In any case, they needn't have worried, for he cleverly dodged all the patrols during the day. When he thought a patrol was getting too close, he stopped and used the time to water and feed the horse.

CHAPTER THREE

SURRENDERED DREAMS

The Irish countryside changed as they moved southwards. Stone walls and boggy land along the foothills of the Sperrin Mountain range gave way to more fertile lowlands adjoining the River Foyle. High hedges sheltered fields flush with grass and heavy crops of grain and potatoes. The further they travelled, the more fertile the land and the more substantial the houses and buildings dotting the landscape became. Farm homes had shelterbelts of high trees, mostly oak and birch, but there was plenty of mountain ash, voluminous cedars and occasionally a stand of giant Scotch Fir planted a century before by settlers who came across the Irish Sea. The evergreen trees stood straight and tall; the deciduous native species leaned away from the prevailing westerly winds.

There was plenty of hay in the cart so that the women were able to make themselves comfortable as it bumped and swayed along the stony mountain roads. When Marita was tired of lying on the hay, she sat on the open back of the cart, dangling her legs above the road and humming Bavarian folk songs. People they passed waved to her, and she waved back. She felt good with the heat of the sun on her face, happy at last to be rid of the animal that had made her life hell for more than a year. Now, she had time to plan her journey to America, and she was determined not to let anything get in the way. She had the money for her ticket and a bit to spare, and that's all she needed. Even if the priest welched on his promise to take her to Derry and get her aboard ship, she would find her own way.

They travelled all day until late evening when the cart suddenly wheeled to the left, and by the time the women regained their balance the driver pulled up in a farmyard beside a large white-washed house.

"Gather yer things together," he said. "We're here."

The women got down from the cart and had a look around. The place was larger than the McKee house in Co. Derry, but instead of rocks and a stream, it was surrounded by high evergreens on three sides. The front had a splendid view west over the River Foyle and the mountains beyond. Between the road and the house was a fine, well-kept garden bordered by rhododendrons in full bloom and neat flowerbeds filled with roses and tall lupin and scented stock.

The driver helped them unload their belongings, shook hands and wished them well. They barely had time to thank him before he led the horse and cart out of the yard and disappeared the way they had come.

Everything was still after he left and there wasn't a sound except for the receding noise of cartwheels grating on the stony road. After a while, even that died away, and an eerie silence enveloped the farmyard.

The older woman went to the house and knocked at the front door but did not get an answer. She went to the rear and walked around the outhouses; there was no sign of life. The occupants were obviously still working in the fields; there was nobody at home.

They sat on their bags and waited for somebody to come. It was a beautiful summer evening and though they were tired and stiff after the long cart journey it made a pleasant change just sitting there watching the sun set slowly in the evening sky, leaving a trail of flimsy pink clouds behind as it retreated across the River Foyle over County Donegal and westwards to the broad Atlantic ocean.

Marita rambled around the house. At the rear, she came across an orchard with maturing apples, pears and plums, rows of red and black currant bushes, gooseberries, and raspberries all neatly staked and tied. Beyond the trees to the rear were outbuildings—a cluster of high barns and sheds in front of which was a wide yard. Carts and farm implements were parked along one side.

The house was surrounded by fields bursting with summer goodness. Hawthorn hedges, neatly trimmed, defined each field; the flowers had gone, and the bushes were laden with maturing haws. Huge tracts of wheat and barley and corn were beginning to turn golden and bend under the weight of the grain. Cows stood beside the gate of an adjoining field, waiting to be brought in for milking; the animals walked with difficulty, swollen udders swinging from side to side, teats hanging so low that they brushed the long grass. Nearby stood stacks of hay weighted down with heavy stones and thatched with rushes to withstand winter storms. The fresh country smells were overpowering.

The place was so quiet they could hear swarms of insects sounding off in the heat, doing what they had to do before dark. Flies and midgets darted around, and occasionally a bee or a dragonfly hovered briefly to peer at the strangers before continuing on about its business. Despite occasional swipes by the women, the midgets managed a few bites on bare faces and hands, stealing tiny drops of human blood before the last frantic bout of acrobatics that would bring their short lives to an end.

At dusk two men came into the yard leading horses. They glanced at the women briefly as they passed but continued to the barn without a word. They removed the harnesses from the tired animals and proceeded to brush their sweaty coats with water and feed them as if the women did not exist. They poked at the horses' hooves, dislodging small stones and soil with sharp knives. The horses were led into stalls in the barn and the door bolted for the night.

It was getting dark when one of the men called the women to bring their bags up to the house, and he showed them the stairs and the room where they would sleep together in a big brass bed. When they came downstairs again, the second man had a pot of stew and potatoes hanging from a crook over the fire. The goodness of what was in the iron pot permeated the whole kitchen; to the hungry women, it seemed ages before he lifted it off the fire and began to ladle it into large bowls. Everybody had a second helping, and the men used slices of brown bread to wipe their bowls clean.

"I'm Peter," said the friendly one, "and this is mey younger brother Joe, and we're glad to welcome ye. Ye'll be all right here fer yer time with us. We have no woman in the house so any help ye can give us will be welcome, like a bit of cooking and cleaning and maybe a hand wey the milking if ye have a mind to. This is a busy time of the year for us, but there'll be no work fer ye in the fields, fer that's a man's job."

Joe raked the fire with a long poker until the ashes disappeared and the logs glowed red. "Two fine-looking women they are, two fine specimens of womanhood," he said to his brother, loud enough for them to hear. Marita did not understand but the other woman clearly did and smiled.

"What is this talk about us staying here?" Marita asked the woman. "You have to tell him we will be leaving in a couple of days."

"Keep quiet for the present," she replied. "We'll sort it out later."

Lying in the big bed that night the women talked for ages about the fine house and the way it was furnished, the large Persian rugs in the bedrooms and heavy drapes on every window. The furniture was mostly oak, very old but well looked after. An oval mahogany table in the dining room had so much polish you could see your face in it. There were pictures, mostly portraits, in the sitting room, which looked as if they had been hanging there for a long time. As far as furnishing the house was concerned, it was clear no expense had been spared. It reminded Marita of the fine hotels in Milan and Liverpool. Before they fell asleep, they heard the brothers downstairs cleaning and tidying around the kitchen and the sound of pots and pans being hung up in their proper places.

"Getting ready for the morning," said Marita.

"And we didn't even introduce ourselves—My God, they'll think we're powerful ignorant," the older woman said.

They fell asleep, still not too sure about the brothers and wondering what sort of a life was ahead of them among total strangers.

In the morning, Marita reminded the brothers that she would be leaving soon to go to Derry with the priest for she was on her way to America.

"Ah know nothing about that," said Joe. "That's yer own business. The priest will come when he comes and that's his business and we don't want to have anything tae do wae that. But ye'll be safe wae us until the priest says its time tae go."

In the days that followed, the women settled down to a routine of house-work, and when Marita offered to help out with the milking in the evenings, the brothers were delighted, for it saved them doing it when they came home from the fields. The men ate and drank well but never sat down to a meal without first attending to the animals, especially the horses that did all the heavy work around the farm. They had six in all and treated them like humans, calling them by their names, praising them for their hard work and occasionally cursing them for doing something stupid.

The brothers worked from Monday to Friday, and only when the weather was very bad was there a break in the routine. They had a strict rule that no work would be done in the fields on Saturdays and Sundays. Saturdays were devoted to caring for the animals and Sunday was a day of rest. But the household was up early on these days just the same, for there was still the milking to be done and animals to be fed.

Peter and Joe spent Saturday morning washing and grooming the horses, and Marita marvelled at the respect they had for the dumb animals and the way they looked after them. They poured buckets of warm water over their coats and dried them with old blankets, starting at the ears and working all the way back to their tails and down to their hooves. Special attention was paid to the manes and tails that were combed patiently until every last bit of tangled hair had been straightened out. When the animals were nearly dry, their coats were brushed until they shone as if they had been polished. Hooves were inspected one by one, cleaned out and washed, and the iron shoes were checked to make sure they were not loose. Finally, the hooves were painted with black polish and brushed until they shone like army boots on a parade ground.

The brothers went through the same routine with each horse, talking to them all the while as if they were human. When the grooming was over, they were turned loose in a field for two days of grazing and rest.

They inspected the cattle, checking them for injury and disease. They examined the udders and teats of the milking cows to make sure there was no swelling or soreness, as bee and wasp stings were a problem at that time of the year. They checked young cows and suckling calves and discussed any problems and what to do about them. Only if it was serious did they call on the services of a vet.

Unusually for brothers, they were great friends, and the women could hear them talking and laughing together as they worked in the yard. They discussed weather prospects for the following week, what work should be tackled next, what animals they might sell and what they should buy. They picked up bits of news from the farmhands in the fields about what was happening in the neighbourhood and in the town—about political meetings, police raids, army patrols, who got married and who had emigrated to England or America.

When the women were not within hearing, the men talked about how good-looking they were and joked about their chances of getting one of them into the hay for a bit of fun.

On Saturday afternoons, the pony and trap were harnessed, and the men disappeared down the hill to the town. They always came back late, quite drunk and on a couple of occasions the two women had to steer them safely into the house and unhitch the pony from the trap. They brought meat from the town butcher in bloodstained brown paper parcels tied with twine and a crate with two dozen bottles of dark stout. Sometimes, they had a glass jar of hard-boiled sweets, a couple of local newspapers and a wooden chest of tea; they drank a lot of tea.

The women did the cooking, and at the weekends, they sat down together to eat and talk. Afterwards, the men drank a few bottles of stout, each with a couple of glasses of whiskey. Joe had a book of ballads, which he took out occasionally and sang for them, and Peter joined in when he remembered the words. These were the happiest days either of the women had experienced for a long time. But Marita got more and more worried as time passed, and the priest did not come for her.

After they had gone to bed and left the brothers poking the dying embers of the fire, the women lay awake mulling over the day's events. They had to choke back the laughter when they remembered the unfortunate pony arriving back from the town with the drunken brothers fast asleep in the trap, depending on the dumb animal to find its own way home. The older woman recalled how when she tried to get Peter out of the narrow door of the trap, he put his arms around her and mumbled:

"There's no finer woman in the county of Tyrone than the women we have on our farm. Ye're a beauty and I'd love tae have ye in my bed." He held her tightly and would not let her go until she gave him a kiss.

"I wonder what he would say if I told him in the morning what he was at?" she joked.

"Ah, don't embarrass him," said Marita. "He did not mean any harm."

A couple of nights later, Marita was awakened by the noise of the bedroom door opening. She sat up with a start, and though everything was black, she was conscious of somebody in the room, for she could hear breathing. She shook the woman beside her. "There's somebody in the room," she whispered. "I can hear him."

"Sadie McKee. Are ye awake? I want ye to come in wi' me. I'm terrible lonely. Do ye hear? Are ye awake?" It was Peter's voice, and he sounded the worse for drink.

"She's sleeping," whispered Marita. "Go back to bed and she'll talk to you in the morning." She heard him shuffle out of the room and close the door.

As Marita slipped back under the blankets, Sadie got out of bed and gathered her clothes from a chair in the darkness.

"You go back to sleep, I'll be all right," she said and quietly left the bedroom.

'Sadie McKee' he had called her. Marita realised that it was the first time she had ever heard the woman's Christian name, even though they had been living in the same house together for more than a year. Marita had not really seen her as a woman, a separate person, all that time. She existed in the girl's mind only to shield her from the savagery of her son. On the mountain farm in Derry, she had been just part of the furniture.

She was a good-looking woman who kept herself neat and tidy, and most of the time, she was good-humoured and an excellent manager in the house. Although still in her early forties and the mother of a grown-up son, she had the soft blue eyes and clear skin of a much younger woman, especially when she got rid of her sedate bun and let her long chestnut hair fall around her shoulders. She must have looked good when the normally shy Peter plucked up enough courage to come into their bedroom in the middle of the night and ask her to come to bed with him. The girl was amazed at the way the older woman had gone the moment he called her, as if she had been expecting him.

Sadie never returned to Marita's bed after that night, and as the days passed, she could see that the older woman was happy about the new arrangement, though she never spoke about it. Joe joked a couple of times that he couldn't get a decent night's sleep with all the racket going on in Peter's bedroom; they had a good laugh and Peter proclaimed that he was only sorry he hadn't met Sadie twenty years before.

"Ye would have been had up for child-snatching," quipped Joe, "sure she was no more than a slip of a girl then."

Peter wanted to take Sadie and Marita with them to Mass on Sunday morning, but Joe warned that it was too soon, as the police and army where still very active in the area and wagging tongues might draw attention to two strange women in the locality.

As the days passed, Marita became more and more anxious about her situation. She wanted to know when she would be able to leave for Derry to get the boat to America.

"Ye'll have tae wait tae the priest comes fer ye," insisted Peter. "It might take a bit of time for there's a lot of trouble going on in Derry. The priest is the best man tae decide that."

It was clear that Peter did not think she would be leaving for some time, and Marita was certain that when the time came, there would be no question of Sadie going with her; Peter and Sadie were lovers, and it was unlikely they could be parted.

Joe spent more time with Marita because Peter spent all of his free time with Sadie, and the girl began to get worried that he might get the wrong idea and appear in her bedroom some night, thinking he could carry her off like his brother did Sadie. If he tried, she knew she would have no alternative but to leave the farm and take her chances with the police and the soldiers; she was determined she would not be used by another man against her will, no matter what the consequences.

Her fears about Joe were groundless; he was just being nice to her. He took her around in the pony and trap on Sunday afternoons to show her neighbouring towns and villages. It was late summer, and the countryside was at its brilliant best in the sunshine. They drove along lanes where trees and bushes formed arches of green to shade them from the sun; clouds of pollen and scented petals enveloped them as they disturbed branches hanging from tall ditches that lined the narrow country lanes.

The villages they passed through were warm and friendly places with thatched roofs and whitewashed houses that reflected the sunshine so strongly that she had to shade her eyes with her hand. He took her to the church and graveyard and pointed to a Celtic cross.

"My mother and father and grandparents are buried there," he said. "May God have mercy on their souls."

They met people he knew on the road and he introduced Marita as a relation from England. She and her mother had come to stay at the farm for a while. They exchanged greetings in Gaelic and parted.

"Nosey bastards, them Duffys," he said when they were out of hearing after one chance meeting, "they're terrible talkers. I'll have to tell Peter we ran into them. He won't be wan bit pleased."

When they got back to the farm, neither Peter nor Sadie was to be seen. Later in the evening, they arrived in the kitchen from upstairs; they had spent the whole afternoon in bed.

"We had a couple of bottles of stout and felt drowsy," explained Peter. They looked relaxed and happy.

"Ah, sure, we understand," smiled Joe.

"There's no fool like an old fool," he whispered to Marita.

The weather stayed fine, and life on the farm was so good that Marita and Sadie felt it could not last. At harvest the brothers spent all their time in the fields and ferrying casual labourers between the town where they lived and the farm. The brothers handled the entire harvesting operation between them, supervising the cutting of wheat and corn crops, binding sheaves for the labourers to tie into stooks ready for the thresher. Potatoes were tossed out in long rows with a mechanical digger, and an army of girls and boys free from the shackles of school picked them off the fresh brown clay, sorted them by size and brought them to pits to be covered for the winter. The brothers sold potatoes in the spring when supplies got scarce and the price was good. Turnips were drawn by the cartload to barns for storage; they would be used to supplement hay as winter feed for the cattle.

While the harvest was in full swing, the two women had to do a lot of extra work. They had to prepare meals for up to forty workers and bring them in the pony and trap to the fields twice a day. They brought cans of tea, pails of fresh milk and buttermilk, iron pots of thick stew with meat, potatoes, carrots, turnips, parsnip and onions. As soon as the women appeared in the fields, all work stopped and did not start again until everybody had their fill to eat and drink and a smoke. The younger men teased Marita about her fine figure and good looks, and she got several invitations to local dances and a few offers of a roll in the hay, but they gave up when she showed no interest.

With all the extra work they had little time for idle chatter or relaxation and when bedtime came were glad to put their heads down and get some sleep.

The harvest was over, and still, the priest did not come.

Peter and Sadie spent their spare time together, either rambling through country roads or in bed; they had clearly formed a permanent relationship.

Sadie bought new clothes and they transformed her appearance. She was no longer the plain woman with the worried face who had arrived on the cart at Knockavoe Farm a short time before. Marita was genuinely happy for her. At first she was worried that Joe might resent this woman coming between him and his brother but it soon became clear the younger man was delighted for Peter and treated Sadie as if she was the lady of the house.

Joe told Marita that she was a beautiful young woman and he would have no trouble finding a good match for her, but she laughed it off, saying she was too young to settle down.

In September, Marita realised that there was something wrong with her. She was tired going to bed at night and still tired when she got up in the morning; when she mentioned it to Sadie, the older woman put it down to the fact that they had so much extra work with the harvest. When the crops were in, they would be able to rest during the long, dark nights of winter. But Marita was still worried. She had missed bleeding the month after she arrived at the farm but thought nothing of it at the time because of the trauma she suffered after the killings. It had happened to her once before after the ambush on the street in Derry, but everything was back to normal the next month. This time, she didn't bleed the second month. She had a sensation of fullness in her stomach and imagined her breasts were swollen.

She searched until she found Sulix plants on the bank of a farm stream, made a brew from the leaves and waited for the bleeding to come. Since she was eating very little food, the acid liquid made her feel ill, and she began to vomit. She continued to lose weight and became so weak that in the mornings she struggled to get out of bed. The brothers were worried and offered to take her to a doctor in Mournebridge, but she refused, saying it would pass. And eventually, it did.

She began to eat normally again and resumed her work about the house but realised she had more than a feeling of fullness in her stomach. She had a sizeable bump where her waist used to be. In desperation she made the brew stronger and stronger as she became more and more anxious, but in the end she had to accept that she had a baby growing inside which refused to be dislodged.

She never wanted a baby, and she didn't want one now. When she was being abused by Eamonn, it was what she feared most, not just because he was an animal and had tortured her so much, but a baby could put an end to her dream of America. There was no provision in her life for love or sentiment or marriage, and especially not for babies.

She had no doubt whose baby it was. The young red-headed soldier had made her pregnant literally with the last breath he ever drew. Like a salmon desperate to expel its seed on the riverbed before floating away on the current to die, the soldier had sown his seed inside her before a rifle butt split his skull and the lifeblood ebbed out of him. Was this his way of getting revenge on her? How could she ever hold a baby in her arms knowing she had helped murder its father?

She knew when she lay with the soldier at the poolside that it was different from Eamonn, who had tormented her while he raped her. The minute the soldier held her from behind in the water, her body had reacted to him. When he lifted her up in his arms to carry her from the pool, she had instinctively put her arms around his neck and held on to him. And when he placed her on the towel and stood over her, she did not have the same feeling of terror as with Eamonn.

If he was going to rape her, she wanted him to do it tenderly, and he did. By the time he lay down with her, Marita had become a pliant and a willing lover, and even though she knew that the killers might strike at any moment, she had allowed him to take her. It was the way she had always imagined a man would make love to a woman, slowly and tenderly until they moved as one being. With this strange soldier, she had lost control, and when he pressed his lips to hers, she was filled with such longing that she put her arms tightly around his neck to keep him close. She had never experienced pleasure like it before.

The baby inside her was the result of that brief, loving encounter by the lovely mountain pool that Eamonn McKee turned into a killing field.

She cursed the dead soldier, the Fenians, the priest, this awful country, and most of all, she cursed Eamonn McKee, who stole her future and destroyed her life.

Marita continued drinking great mugs of the black brew and worked harder than ever about the house and farm. She even persuaded Joe to let her ride the pony, as she remembered Helmut saying that it was dangerous for pregnant women to ride a horse. She also took baths so hot that her skin was red when she stepped out of the tub. She drove the trap over bumpy roads, even tried wild mushrooms to make her violently ill—anything to get rid of the parasite inside her. But the baby kept growing and pushed harder against her clothes so that even her apron could no longer hide the bump. She started to put on weight.

Confused and frightened by what was happening to her body, Marita had a panic attack and fainted in the kitchen one morning when the two women were preparing a meal for the men working in the fields. Sadie put a cold, wet towel on her face until she stirred back to life.

Marita knew she would not be able to keep her predicament secret for much longer. Sadie would be sympathetic since she would assume it was Eamonn's child, but Marita was not at all sure how the brothers would react to the prospect of a bastard child born on their farm.

Marita told her that day that she was going to have a baby. She had felt something happening to her for more than a month but was afraid to tell anybody, hoping that it was not true. She never mentioned any of the remedies she had tried to get rid of it. Marita cried, pleading that it was not her fault since the father had forced himself on her. She never mentioned the soldier, and Sadie assumed that she was talking about Eamonn, whose abuse his mother was well aware of.

Sadie stared at the girl when she blurted it out, and Marita could see her turn red. She covered her face with her hands. Marita waited for her to say something. After a while, Sadie took her hands away, and Marita saw she was laughing nervously at first, then louder until her whole body was shaking and tears were streaming from her eyes, and she could not stop herself. Marita stared at her, not understanding. Sadie put out her arms and hugged the girl tightly, whispering not to worry, for everything would be all right.

She looked straight into Marita's eyes. "I might as well tell you, and you are the first to know, and I don't want you laughing at me, but I'm pregnant too," she said. The girl looked at her in disbelief.

"I'm forty-two years of age, and I'm going to have a baby, and I'm worried sick what Peter is going to say. I don't even know how I am going to tell him. He's a man of sixty years of age and it never dawned on me that anything like this could happen."

"Are you sure?" asked Marita when she recovered from the shock.

Sadie nodded. "Remember, I've been through this before," she said.

They spent the rest of the morning sitting at the kitchen table trying to come to terms with this new twist in their lives, especially how, when and where they were going to tell Peter and Joe. Should they break the news gently when the pair returned from town on Saturday night, the worse for a drink, or should Sadie tell Peter in bed some night and see what the reaction was? The women were worried how the brothers would feel about two bastard babies arriving at Knockavoe Farm practically at the same time, for Sadie figured they would give birth within weeks of one another. The situation was further complicated because the brothers had told friends and neighbours that Sadie and Marita were mother and daughter from England. There was bound to be a lot of gossip in the parish about two pregnant women living in the same house with two bachelors.

Sadie broke the news abruptly at the dinner table the following Sunday. She stood up halfway through the meal, looked across at the brothers and took a deep breath.

"There's something I have to tell you and it has to be said and it's so important that it can't wait so I'm going to tell you now right this minute and ye can think what ye like."

Marita was taken aback by the sudden outburst and pushed back her chair to get up and leave. Sadie caught her by the shoulder and pushed her down on the chair again.

"There's no point in running away, for it's as much your concern as mine. Sit where ye are until I'm finished."

The brothers stopped chewing their food and stared at Sadie, wondering what was so important that it could not wait till they had finished their dinner. She was red with embarrassment.

"What's going on here?" said Peter. "What are ye playing at, woman?"

"I'm going to have a baby," she said in a clear voice and sat down before the legs gave way under her. "I'm pregnant," she said.

The brothers looked at each other and then at Sadie. Joe opened his mouth to say something, but words would not come. Peter got up from the table, walked quickly to the other end of the kitchen, and stood with his back to them. Sadie turned around, staring after him, the colour draining from her cheeks, waiting for him to say something.

When he turned around again, tears streamed down his weather-beaten, ruddy face and his outstretched hands were shaking. He walked back to where she sat, put his arms around her and hugged her tightly.

"I'm the proudest man in Ireland this day," he said, his voice unsteady with emotion. "There'll be a wedding in this parish before Christmas if God spares me, and with the help of God, there'll be a new generation of the McKennas in this parish next year to keep the family name going after I'm gone."

She put her arms around his neck and clung to him; she could feel his wet tears on her neck.

"I think ye better ask that woman to marry ye first," said Joe. He went to the dresser, took out a bottle of whiskey and four glasses and poured generously. "Let's all have a good drink to settle our nerves."

Before the others had time to sip, he put the glass to his head, drained it and poured another.

"This'll be the first baby born on this farm since I came into the world fifty-eight years ago," he said and tipped the glass to his mouth and let the whiskey slide down his throat. He poured himself another.

Marita was delighted with the brothers' reaction, especially for Sadie, who stood smiling and happy with Peter's arm around her shoulders. She wondered what they would say when they found out that she was going to have a baby as well. That would have to wait for another time—it was best to give the brothers a chance to enjoy the news that Peter was to be a father.

But Sadie decided that this was the time to tell them everything and came straight out with the fact that Marita was going to have a baby too and quickly explained that the girl had been badly wronged by her own son, Eamonn, at the farmhouse where they lived in Derry. The two men had trouble taking it all in, but Joe poured more whiskey, and the more they drank, the more they were taken with the idea of two babies arriving at Knockavoe House in the spring.

The four of them talked far into the night when all sorts of plans were made, and the brothers decided that the women would do no more farm work, not even the milking, so that no harm would come to them. Peter and Joe insisted that because of her age Sadie should take extra care and make regular visits to the doctor in town to make sure everything was going well.

"You may as well go too, Marita," said Joe, laughing, "for the doctor will charge as much for one as for two".

Marita hoped that the priest from Derry would not come at that time because she was in no fit condition to travel anywhere, least of all to a country on the other side of the world where she knew nobody. She would have to postpone her departure for another year at least until her baby was strong enough to make such a long journey. She felt cheated again, robbed of the opportunity to get away from this country to start the new life she so looked forward to. And unless she could persuade Sadie and the men to keep her baby or maybe even adopt it, starting over again in America with little money and no friends and lumbered with a baby was going to be difficult.

The most immediate problem was Peter's wedding. Sadie knew if they got married in their own parish, it would set tongues wagging, so they arranged it for the church in Mournebridge to avoid scandal.

Sadie and Marita made their own dresses, and the brothers went into town and bought new suits. They were married quietly one morning with only the four of them present in the huge church. The young priest who officiated complimented the women on their good taste. When they went to sign the register, Marita saw him cast a cold eye on the bump where her waist ought to be. He stared at her and at Joe beside her, and she knew he was thinking there ought to be two weddings in the church that morning.

Joe saw the priest eyeing Marita. "I might want ye to do a christening for me at the farm in the spring," he said, winking. The priest glared at him and turned away. The four of them laughed about it afterwards during a meal and drinks in the town hotel.

They went home that night on the pony and trap, the brothers well under the weather from drink. Peter refused to carry Sadie over the threshold because he was unsteady on his feet and terrified he might let her fall. Joe insisted that the bride had to be carried through the door by somebody and hoisted her into his arms. The others watched anxiously as he steered her through the hallway, bumping off door posts and furniture as he struggled to get her inside.

Joe went to the hiring fair in Mourne in October and, without a word to any of them, arrived back with two young sisters, Sheila and Aine O'Donnell from County Donegal, to do the housework. It took Sadie a month to train them, and thereafter, Marita and herself lived a life of leisure. They whiled away the time driving to and from the town and on trips through the countryside in the pony and trap while the young hired girls did all the housework. The days got shorter and cooler, and they had to spend a lot more time indoors, but between knitting for the babies and making maternity clothes, they kept themselves busy.

There was no scarcity of money at Knockavoe Farm, and the women could have anything they wanted. The brothers kept a locked money box in one of the cupboards. The key was hidden in another cupboard and Sadie was shown exactly where it was and told to take money as she required it, either for the house, herself or Marita. The only stipulation was that when they took money out, they had to put in a note showing the amount they had taken; every week, when the brothers went into town, they brought back whatever sum was needed to make up the shortfall in the cash box. This was money to pay casual workers, like engineers who came occasionally to repair machinery, the blacksmith who came regularly to shod the horses, tinkers who called from time to time to repair or replace pots and pans and milk pails and journeymen, tradesmen who did odd jobs about the farm that the brothers could not do themselves.

The girls from the hiring fair had to sleep in a barn, even though it was winter. Marita felt sorry for the youngsters, as they were both in their early teens and away from home for the first time. But they were used to a bit of hardship and content with their lot. The brothers had been hiring girls for years at the fair and never allowed them to sleep in the house. It was the custom in that part of the country, and it was as much to protect the girls from being taken unfair advantage of by unscrupulous farmers as anything else.

They were from a place called Gweedore and often talked about their home overlooking the wild Atlantic Ocean. They had very poor English, even less than Marita, for they spoke only their native Gaelic language at home. What English they had was picked up from friends and neighbours who migrated to England and Scotland in summer to find work. There were ten children in their family living on a small farm. Their brothers were fishermen, and some older sisters had already emigrated to America and found jobs.

The girls were scrawny and badly clothed when they arrived, but they ate the same food as the rest of the household and after a couple of months in the countryside developed into healthy youngsters, full of antics and chatter. Sadie and Marita altered old dresses for them, and the girls were delighted with the lovely new clothes.

At Christmas they were particularly lonely without family, and Marita took them to the town to post a letter to their father to tell him they were being well treated and how much they looked forward to getting home in the spring. They brought back a Christmas tree and decorations and presents for everybody.

The girls loved Marita telling them stories, especially about her adventures after leaving Bavaria and the great cities she had visited and the things she had seen—hotels and ships and snow-capped mountains. She repeated everything until she was sure they understood and sometimes even drew pictures, for they would not allow her to continue with a story until she cleared up questions they had for her. The girls had tears in their eyes when she told them about the night the horsemen came to the valley and killed her parents and sister and all her friends. They listened in awe as she described the awful days in Derry which ended in her being separated from the family she had been travelling with, probably forever, for she had never seen or heard of them since.

The girls knew all about America because so many people from their home parish had emigrated there. During the Civil War in that country a lot of young Irishmen had joined the Union Army and when it was over were rewarded with land. The tradition in the West of Ireland was that once one member of a family got to America and began to earn money, he paid the passage for another brother or sister and in this way whole families emigrated over a period of years, leaving only elderly parents at home.

Everybody they knew who emigrated had done well. The girls said there were thousands of lonely Irish lads farming and working on cattle ranches in America who were looking for wives and they preferred to marry somebody from their own country and their own religion.

The girls' infectious enthusiasm made Marita all the more determined to keep to her original plan to get to America; even with a baby, she could find work, and with the money she saved, she might even be able to get a place of her own to live, maybe start a dressmaking business. Selling herself for money might no longer be feasible, but she was an accomplished cook and had become quite skilled as a dressmaker. If she could persuade Sadie to look after the baby in Ireland for a couple of years, it would give her a chance to get herself established.

The women and girls had great fun making themselves understood as they passed the long winter nights. They laughed heartily as Marita tried to teach them some German words and phrases, and they in turn tried to get her to speak Gaelic. They sat around the open fire, enjoying the heat radiating from the red coals; now and again, the brothers would get out the ballad book and sing. The hired girls knew most of the airs and sang the words in their native tongue. Sheila asked if they had a fiddle in the house since she could play, but they had none, and though Joe made a special trip into the town and tried every shop, he couldn't find one for sale.

There was not a lot of activity on the farm at that time of year except for milking and daily feeding of the housed animals. There was some excitement when merchants arrived from time to time to buy wheat, barley, potatoes and oats that had been bagged and stacked in the barns at harvest time. Wagons hauled the grain away, teams of stout horses grunting and snorting as they struggled out of the farmyard, puffing clouds of white breath into the cold air like a railway engine letting off steam.

The brothers demanded cash payment for everything they sold because the dealers and merchants often came from towns far away, and some of them were not to be trusted. They were particularly careful when selling cattle; many of the buyers were rogues whose cheques were as unreliable as their words. Every penny they earned went into the bank for safekeeping.

"Hoarding money on the farm," Joe warned the women, "is just an invitation to thieves and robbers."

On March 17, St. Patrick's Day, while the brothers, Sadie and the two hired girls were at Mass, Marita felt the first pangs of labour. By the time the others got home, she was in such pain and distress that Joe went to the town to fetch the doctor and midwife. Because it was the national holiday, the doctor was already well under the weather from drink, and when he arrived at Knockavoe, he was more interested in where Peter kept his whiskey bottle than in Marita's condition.

"If there's one thing I learned in all my years as a medical man," he said as he poured himself a large glass, "it's not to interfere with nature except as a last resort." The midwife made the girl as comfortable as she could and stayed with her, reassuring her that it would all be over soon and not to worry.

Though she did everything the midwife asked of her, labour continued throughout the day, and Marita began to imagine there was something wrong. When darkness came, she was so exhausted she could no longer make the effort to keep up the pushing that was demanded of her; even her screams became muted and she drifted off several times, coming to her senses again when the pain increased.

Just before midnight, when she was so weak and no longer cared whether she lived or died, the pain ceased, and through hazy eyes, she saw the midwife holding a baby in front of her face. "Ye have a lovely daughter," Sadie whispered. "Go to sleep now. Ye deserve the rest."

It was daylight when the baby crying in the room awakened her.

"Yer wee girl is hungry. Come on and I'll show ye how to feed her," said the midwife. She propped Marita up in bed with pillows, opened her nightdress and placed the baby in her arms, its tiny face close to one of her breasts. The baby bawled until its lips found the swollen nipple and began to suck hungrily, choking when the milk came too quickly. Gradually the baby got used to the flow and, after drinking its fill, slept contentedly.

Marita was so exhausted that she slept for the best part of two days, interrupted only by the midwife waking her to feed the baby. It was the third day before she felt well enough to tend to her daughter.

She was as lovely as Sadie had said, a perfect little girl from the tip of her tiny nose all the way to her miniature toes. Once she was fed and changed regularly, there was no more crying. Everybody made a great fuss over the new arrival and Joe went to town and brought back stout and whiskey and stone beer to celebrate. When the midwife left, Sheila and Aine took turns to stay with Marita, seeing to her needs. The girls were confident looking after the new arrival, as they had washed and changed younger brothers and sisters at home since they were nine years old.

The parish priest came to the house for the baptism, and Sheila suggested they should call the baby Breige, but Marita wanted a German name and eventually it was decided to call her Brigitta, the German version of Bridget, which in Gaelic was Breige, and everybody was happy.

"That was my mother's name too," said Joe. "She was Bridget McKenna, God rest her soul."

After the fright with Marita, Peter decided that he would take no chances with Sadie, so he arranged with the midwife to come and stay with them two weeks before the baby was due. The nurse thought it a good idea, especially since Sadie was not a young mother. Sheila and Aine did not understand what all the fuss was about because their own mother was as old as Sadie and had babies every other year, and they never saw a midwife in the house.

And they were right. Sadie woke up on a Saturday morning in pain and two hours later she presented her husband with a fine baby boy. Peter was overjoyed and relieved that it was all over so quickly and his wife and baby were fine, and Joe brought out the whiskey bottle to celebrate the arrival of a son to carry on the family farm at Knockavoe.

When the Lenten season of fasting and abstinence was over, they threw a party at the house and invited friends and neighbours to celebrate the safe arrival of two babies. The boy was named Leo after his paternal grandfather and his mother was complimented on how well she looked and more than one of the guests remarked that the two women looked more like sisters than the 'mother and daughter' they were supposed to be. Sadie had never been so happy in her life, and she had never felt better.

A couple of weeks after the party, the old priest arrived from Derry to tell Sadie that Eamonn had been wounded in an ambush in Donegal on St. Patrick's Day and, though he escaped, he had to be smuggled aboard a merchant ship bound for America. She was not to worry, however, for he would be well taken care of in New York.

"Good riddance," Marita muttered to herself, but she said nothing because she did not want to offend Sadie. There was no justice in this life, she thought, when that animal who had made her life such a misery and prevented her from going to America was now on his way there while she was still stuck in Ireland. But at least he was gone out of their lives forever, and that was something to be thankful for.

The priest said he was now in a position to honour his promise to get Marita to America too, but not from Derry. She would have to travel to Queenstown on the south coast of Ireland to catch a steamship for New York.

Sadie explained that Marita had been ill and was not ready to go just yet, but as soon as she was able to travel, they would write to him to make the arrangements. Before he left the priest was given instructions to sell the mountain farm for the best price he could get and send the proceeds to Eamonn. Sadie pleaded with him not to tell Eamonn that she was now married and had a baby son, and especially not to mention that Marita had a baby daughter. The priest gave her his word and said he was delighted that both women had found such a good home.

He blessed the babies before he left, and the whole household went out into the yard to see him off as he rode through the farm gate and turned north towards Derry. The priest was gone, Eamonn was gone, and soon her farm would be gone.

"I'll be glad to see the back of that place," Sadie confided in her husband. "I have had nothing but trouble since the first day I went there."

After the party, the hired girls finished their contract and packed their belongings to return home. Joe counted out their wages, making sure they understood exactly what they were getting. He gave them a lift to Mournebridge in the trap and was surprised by how much luggage they were going home with compared to what they brought when he hired them. Sadie and Marita had filled sacks with discarded clothing and shoes for the girls and their sisters.

Joe paid the train fares so that they could keep their wages intact and told them if they wanted work next winter to come straight to the farm and he would look after them, no bother. In the meantime, he promised he would make it his business to get his hands on a fiddle somewhere, even if he had to travel to Dublin for it.

The girls were sad to leave, but by the time they were ready to board the train in Mournebridge they were bubbling with excitement at the prospect of being home with their mother and father and brothers and sisters before the day was out, and so much to tell them. Joe bought them a big paper bag of sweets to pass the time on the journey and two bottles of stout as a present for their father.

The girls had tears in their eyes when the kindly Joe shook hands with them for the last time.

The house was a sad place after the girls departed, especially for Marita, who had found them great company. However, a lot of her time was spent with the baby because the girls weren't there anymore to see to her daughter's needs. She took an interest in reading newspapers and what was going on in the world and also to help improve her English. She used a dictionary when she ran into difficulties, for neither Sadie nor the brothers were much help.

She also started to write a diary in German, and because there was so much to write about, she bought a ledger in town and began to set down as best she could things about her childhood in Hoffenfeld and what happened the night of the massacre. She described the long journey from Genoa until she was stranded in Derry and the difficult life on the mountain in County Derry before they moved to Knockavoe Farm. When it came to the incident at the pool, she wrote a full account of how she was coerced by Eamonn McKee into luring lonely soldiers to their death on that desolate mountainside—and all for the promise that she would be set free with money to get her to America. She kept the ledger wrapped in brown paper under the dressing table in her bedroom with a note explaining that if anything happened to her, it was to be given to Brigitta when she was twenty-one years of age.

The two women had every comfort on the farm and anything they asked for was provided without question. They shared house duties after the departure of the hired girls but there was not a lot to do because the brothers were busy on the farm ploughing the land and planting new crops. The men took turns getting up during the night to check on the sheep , as it was the lambing season.

The mothers spent all their time with the children, feeding and changing them, comparing size and progress; the brothers made plans to rent a house by the sea for the summer.

Marita spoke less and less about going to America, and Sadie was glad; she would sorely miss the girl if she ever left.

They cut patterns for dresses from the newspapers and reproduced the finished article with such perfection that when they appeared outdoors, they were much admired for their up-to-date style. Marita had become so adept at dressmaking that she could copy almost any garment she saw in a newspaper or magazine.

They paraded their fine clothing to Church on Sunday mornings and occupied the front pews to make sure everybody got a good look at them; they had a laugh afterwards about the reaction of various people in the congregation.

"Even the priest gave the pair of ye the glad eye," chuckled Joe. The brothers were as proud as punch of the two women who were turning the heads of every man in the parish.

Sadie's milk began to fail when her son was only six months old, and it was discovered she was expecting another baby. She was shocked that it could happen so quickly or indeed at all, but Peter thought it was great news that he was going to be a father again at his age. Marita took on the job of feeding both Brigitta and the boy and eventually most of her day was taken up nursing two babies and changing nappies.

Sadie had a second son, Patrick, born in June of the following year when she was forty-four years of age and her husband sixty-three. The midwife remarked that Knockavoe Farm was busier than the maternity ward in the local hospital. But the two women enjoyed all the attention they got with the babies, and the brothers were so grateful to God for the gift of a second son that they gave the parish priest five hundred guineas to put a new roof on the church.

Peter and Joe and Sadie and Marita made the most of each day and lived contentedly as the children grew up together on the farm. Friends remarked that the two women were getting younger looking, while Peter and Joe began to slow down noticeably as old age and hard work gradually caught up with them. Peter complained that his limbs were stiffening, and although he was still doing a full day's work in the fields, it took more and more effort to do things that, for years, he had taken in his stride. Joe had rheumatism, and when the days were cold and wet, he could not venture outdoors. The happy years had passed so quickly.

Peter began to suffer from bouts of depression, worried about his children and how Sadie would manage if he died while they were still infants; it got so bad that some days he could not summon up enough energy to get out of bed in the morning. The doctor said his condition was due to worry and also to ageing after a lifetime of hard work.

Events in the outside world quickened as the end of the 19th Century approached. There was political upheaval and turmoil throughout the British Empire, with uprisings and rebellions in the colonies. British forces were sorely stretched trying to maintain order in places like India, Egypt, and South Africa, even Australia. Their biggest problem was much closer to home. In Ireland, the Fenians, now calling themselves the Irish Republican Brotherhood, engaged the British Army and armed police daily in guerilla warfare. There were large areas of the country where neither soldiers nor police could enforce the ageing Queen Victoria's rule.

New political figures emerged in the British Isles, and attempts were made to work out home rule for Ireland. The rebel leaders were in no mood for compromise—they refused to settle for anything less than an independent Irish Republic, but the British Government would have none of it.

More than anything else in the world, Peter McKenna wanted to live to see his sons working the land, but when the boys were still at school, he collapsed in the cornfield one day as the Angelus was ringing and died in his brother's arms without opening his eyes or uttering a word. Joe whispered an Act of Contrition in his ear, asking God for forgiveness for his brother's sins and made a sad journey back to the house with the prostrate body of his brother on the cart. Peter was in his seventy-seventh year.

Sadie had lost another, much younger husband to tuberculosis many years before, and though it had left her lonely and isolated with a young son to bring up, she accepted it then as God's will. She consoled herself that at least Peter had led a full and useful life, and although she was again left with two young boys, she did not feel the need to grieve over him. Marita found it hard to believe that the shrunken remains in the huge open oak coffin was the same man she had seen striding into the farmyard sixteen years before when she and Sadie arrived from Derry.

After the funeral, Joe took his brother's will from the cupboard and read it to them. After providing for the payment of all his debts, his funeral expenses, one hundred guineas to Marita, and one hundred guineas to the parish, he left his half of the farm and his share of the money in the bank to Sadie for her life, the remainder to be divided equally between Leo and Patrick on her death.

Soon afterwards, Joe had the farm surveyed and divided into two equal parts. He built a small house on his own half and moved away from the main house. When the women protested that he should stay in his home, he joked that at his time of life what he needed most was peace and quiet. He hired men to do the farm work and keep the place going, and when the boys were old enough, he imparted to them the knowledge he had accumulated during a lifetime on the land.

Inevitably, Joe missed his brother. He particularly missed his company in the fields where they had worked together since they were boys. He also missed the company of the two women and the children but refused all pleas to move back to Knockavoe. He put on weight, and his hips began to give him trouble; eventually, he had great difficulty walking.

He told the women many times it was his dearest wish to live to see the dawn of the 20th Century, although when it finally arrived, he was far too ill to appreciate it. He suffered a stroke at Christmas 1899, and a week later, Sadie and Marita and the children were at his bedside on New Year's Day 1900 when he slipped quietly out of this world.

In his will he left his land and money to Sadie in trust for his two nephews, to be divided equally between them when Leo reached the age of twenty-five years. His house and all its contents, two acres of a garden and the pony and trap he bequeathed to Marita in the hope that she might remain in Ireland. In a sweet jar in his cupboard, Marita found two envelopes, one for her and one for her daughter. There were notes inside saying that accounts had been opened in the bank with two hundred guineas deposited in each in appreciation of the happiness Marita had brought to Knockavoe Farm and the two lonely bachelor brothers.

The McKenna boys grew up and began to take more interest in running things, so Marita decided to move to the house that Joe had left her, which was already well furnished, comfortable, and within reasonable walking distance of the town. Brigitta was disappointed, for she had grown up with the boys as if they were her brothers.

Marita had to take stock of her situation and decide what she was going to do in the future. She felt she had been robbed of the best years of her life by events outside her control. The opportunity to go to America never did come her way as the children grew up and the old men became ill. She was forty-one years of age, with a twenty-one-year-old daughter. She had a home of her own and enough money to ensure she could live fairly comfortably. Although she still lived among strangers in a country that was not her choice and which she did not like, she felt she was past the age when she could start a new life somewhere else. Apart from Sadie and the McKenna boys, she had no friends.

Marita finally had to accept that her dream of going to America was over. Fate had intervened over and over again to frustrate her plans, robbed her of the chance to make a new life. She had a daughter, and her home was in Ireland; she had to resign herself to the fact that this was where she would spend the rest of her life.

CHAPTER FOUR

YEARS OF TEARS AND ROSES

Brigitta grew up so fast that Marita felt she hardly had time to get to know the girl. She boarded with the nuns in the convent in Mournebridge while she was being educated, and when she arrived home at the end of term discarded the school uniform and spent all her time at the McKenna farm.

She had grown up into a lovely and accomplished young woman, taller than her mother and slimmer. She spoke perfect English, excelled at Spanish and German and was constantly praised for her piano playing and her artwork. She was a favourite with the nuns who were convinced she would make a name for herself as a pianist. The girl had fine features with high cheekbones and a graceful neck and shoulders. She had a mop of dark brown hair, a feature Marita knew she had inherited from her father.

When Brigitta first went to school in the convent, her mother fabricated a story for the nuns that her German husband had been killed in Derry during the Fenian troubles and because of the sad background the girl was given special treatment. What would they say, she wondered, if they knew the real story—that the girl was the bastard daughter of an English soldier whom her mother had lured to his death? The nuns might not have been as shocked as Marita thought. Long after the brothers died, she discovered that the McKennas had sheltered rebels for years. When the police and army became active in the area, the brothers moved their fugitives to the safety of the convent where the nuns looked after them and asked no questions.

Unknown to Marita and Sadie when they first arrived at Knockavoe, the nuns were made aware that the pair were hiding from the authorities, that they were Fenians or connected with active members of the rebel movement. And because of their background, when it was time for the children from Knockavoe Farm to go to school, they were welcomed with open arms as special children and given extra special treatment.

In all their years together, the McKennas never once discussed the Fenians with the two women nor did they ever ask why they had been sent to the farm in Tyrone. The brothers were aware that the pair had been spirited away from County Derry for some reason but knew nothing about the part that Marita had played in the notorious murder of the English soldiers at the mountain pool.

After Brigitta left school, Marita began to feel bored and made plans for herself and her daughter to do something different with their lives, particularly since she had abandoned the idea of emigrating to America. She discussed with her whether she would be interested in returning to Bavaria. They could buy a house in Innsbruck and perhaps start a dress-making business. Brigitta was taken with the idea but was reluctant to leave the McKenna boys. When she talked to Leo about leaving, he said it was a matter for herself and her mother to make up their minds but warned that trouble was brewing in Germany, and there was talk of them taking up arms against their neighbours. If war came, Germany would have to stand alone against its traditional enemies—the French and British.

The situation in Ireland was not good either; the country had become very unsettled, with shootings and bombings a daily occurrence. Marita decided to postpone her decision about leaving; the last thing she wanted was to go back to Germany and find herself in another war. She had enough of killing and violence.

She became an avid reader of newspapers and kept herself up to date on changes in the world outside the sleepy Irish countryside where she lived. She regretted more than ever that she never got to America, for she felt she could have made her mark during the boom years there. The New World was going through a period of unprecedented economic growth and the dollar had become the strongest currency in the world. This brought dramatic changes to the lifestyle of the people. Carriages called automobiles replaced the traditional horse, and carriages and tractors replaced the horses that had always been used for farm work. New winged craft called aeroplanes appeared in the sky, and their inventors predicted that one day, people would travel through the clouds and complete hours of journeys that by rail and sea took days. Great steel ships called liners had engines powered by oil with underwater propellers that drove them through the waves. The sea journey from England to New York had been reduced from weeks to days.

By Irish standards she was a wealthy woman in her own right and there were plenty of men in the town who would have given their right arm to get a ring on her finger. She was still a pretty woman and could turn a few heads when she walked the streets on a Saturday afternoon. But she never considered getting involved with any of them. She had too many bad experiences with men.

To occupy her time, she purchased a small shop in Mournebridge to sell ladies' clothing. To add to the stock bought in Belfast and Dublin, she produced dresses and skirts to her own design, blending traditional Bavarian and Irish styles, with neat waistline and bust and long slim skirts trimmed with leather. The nuns taught her how to make white blouses and edge them with intricate lace; the garments were no sooner in the shop window than they were sold.

The Sisters tried to persuade Brigitta to go to Dublin and train to be a teacher and guaranteed her a job the day she qualified. Despite her gift for languages and art, she did not fancy such a life and instead went into business with her mother. The girl had a good eye for style and her ideas brought orders from younger women in such volume that they had to engage and train seamstresses to keep up with the demand.

Brigitta worked alongside her mother and gradually they built up a fine trade and their reputation for taste and excellence spread far beyond the borders of the county. Wedding clothes were a speciality, and the two of them made occasional trips to Dublin and Belfast to find out about the latest styles.

People in Ireland were generally poor, but when it came to a wedding—or a funeral—no expense was spared. They ordered costly materials for dresses and booked receptions in the best hotels and many couples did not settle for a honeymoon nearer than Dublin or London. Marita wondered where the money came from to pay for such luxuries; generally working people were badly paid and many had no work at all. But there was always lots of money in the farming community, and they paid extra for something special for a daughter on her big day. Even among poorer people, money never seemed to be a problem for these special occasions; if they didn't have enough, they borrowed and spent years paying it back.

Like her mother, Brigitta had little interest in men or in socialising. She had lots of invitations to parties and dances and weddings but always declined. She was conscious of the fact that she did not have a father and worried that if she became serious about a boy, sooner or later there would be awkward questions about her background. Even her best friends at school were hurtful about such things.

She spent weekends at home with her mother or at the McKenna farm with Sadie and Leo and Patrick where she had such happy times. Brigitta settled into a humdrum routine content with her lot. She was only interested in her work, her mother, and happy days with McKennas. Her thirtieth birthday came and went, but there was still no romance in her life.

The dreaded war in Europe materialised as the McKennas had predicted, and Marita was glad they had stayed in Ireland. The horror of the carnage in France was brought home to Brigitta on a visit to London with her mother in 1914. She met some friends who had volunteered to look after wounded soldiers returning from the war. Although settled in her ways and a rock of sense, she became completely infatuated by the work of these dedicated women playing Florence Nightingale to the wounded. Despite the best efforts of her mother to dissuade her, she decided to stay in London with two of the girls she met there and joined the volunteer nursing organisation.

Brigitta did six weeks' training at the City Hospital before she was posted to Dover to care for men coming off Red Cross ships. She wrote regularly about the terrible injuries she saw and complained that she was having trouble sleeping.

"I only keep going because I feel I am doing something useful with my life," she wrote, "but when you see men arriving without arms or legs or burned or blind, it's almost too difficult to bear."

Months passed, and Marita was happy that Brigitta had coped with the drastic change in her life. She seemed to be settled in London, and as time passed, she wondered if her daughter would return to live in Ireland when the war was over.

Then came a letter with news she did not want to hear. Brigitta was in France. There were so many wounded coming from the Front that it was decided to set up hospitals across the Channel to treat the wounded; as far too many of them had died during the sea journey back to England.

On visits to the Front to collect the wounded, Brigitta saw the carnage at first hand: stinking water-filled trenches, rats feeding on the dead bodies, men walking around like zombies after days of bombardment from German artillery. The nurses referred to the soldiers as walking dead — men who could still follow orders and even fight but not able to fully comprehend what was happening around them.

Brigitta realised the danger she was in, but she also knew she had no prospect of getting out. She wrote that she had applied several times to be sent back to England with the wounded but had heard nothing from her superiors.

Marita was annoyed that the Army sent such an inexperienced volunteer to the Front and wrote to the head of the Volunteer Nursing Service, demanding that her daughter be brought back to England immediately and given work there.

Eventually, Brigitta got word to her mother through a friend that she was going back to Dover with a boatload of injured servicemen and intended to resign from the Volunteer Service as soon as she delivered the injured to the hospital.

The next news Marita had was a note that she was working as a nurse at a hospital in London. But instead of returning home to Ireland, Brigitta said she had befriended an injured officer whom she had tended in France, and she was going to look after him until he was well.

It soon became clear that she and the officer were more than just nurse and patient, and when Captain Peter Anthony Couchy was discharged from the Army on medical grounds a few months later, Brigitta wrote that they were in love and wanted to marry. After the wedding she would bring him home to Ireland to meet family and friends.

Marita was shocked by the news of the romance. It was too rushed for her liking, and she pleaded with the girl to take things easy, give herself time to get settled back in England, and if she was sure she wanted to marry, there would be plenty of time to make arrangements. There were other considerations, she pointed out.

"If you go ahead with this marriage," she wrote, "you cannot even consider returning to Ireland. There is a lot of rebel activity, and everybody's talking about an uprising in the South. Any British soldier, whether on active duty or not, is not safe in Ireland. He will become a target for rebel gunmen."

But Brigitta was so besotted by her first love that she went ahead with the wedding and wrote to inform her mother that she was now a married woman. Marita threw up her arms in disgust. She had a bad feeling about the affair from the start; she hoped her daughter would not regret a decision taken in such haste.

The McKennas had troubles of their own. Young Patrick disappeared from the farm one morning after a row with his older brother Leo and returned in the evening to tell his mother he had joined the British Army and was off to Belfast to train with the Inniskilling Fusiliers.

Patrick had never settled into life on the farm as his older brother had and was always threatening his mother that someday he would head for America or Australia or New Zealand. He was fed up with the daily grind of farm work and the boredom of living on the edge of a small town, especially when the world outside was changing so fast. He did not want to end up like his father and Uncle Joe and die of old age and hard work without knowing anything outside of their own farm.

He had six weeks of training before he was shipped out to France in the autumn of 1917. Instead of shouldering a rifle, he was handed a shovel and assigned to a burial party. His job was to prise dead bodies from where they had been buried by mud in the trenches. While he and other Irish men dragged the mangled remains to new graves behind the lines, Kitchener's army advanced and retreated, leaving more dead behind them every time the Front changed.

In September of that year the British fought the Battle of Ypres. There was heavy shelling by both sides, and casualties were so great that the recovery of bodies was suspended, and burial parties were disbanded and brought back into active service. The problems with the number of dead bodies in the trenches became so bad that men preferred to lie in open ground and risk being shot rather than spend time below ground with the stench of rotting flesh and the plague of rats. Torrential rainstorms that month were the worst in living memory in France and turned the network of trenches into water-logged ditches. Patrick's unit was re-assigned to ferry explosives to a special squad of demolition experts tunnelling under the battleground to reach the German trenches.

Aeroplanes were deployed in large numbers on bombing missions over the battlefield as the stalemate in the war on the ground continued. On September 16, 1917, Patrick and his companions were unloading explosives from wagons at a railway siding when their position took a direct hit from one of the bombs. The shell set off a chain reaction among explosives, killing or wounding everybody working within a radius of fifty yards.

A British officer arrived at the McKenna farm three days later while Leo was busy with the harvest. When he saw his mother being driven across the field in the pony and trap, he knew something was wrong. Even after she told him his brother had been killed in action, he found it hard to believe.

"Did they say he was killed in action or that he was missing in action," he asked. "He might be lying injured somewhere or he might even have been taken prisoner."

"There's no hope," sobbed his mother. "It didn't happen in the fighting. It happened at a railway station some miles away when a bomb was dropped from a German aeroplane."

For a long time afterwards, the mother and son had great difficulty coming to terms with the fact that Patrick would never be home again. It had happened so far away, so soon after he left, and there was not even a body to bury in the family plot. Sadie was glad that neither his father nor his doting Uncle Joe was alive to see that day.

Sadie was heartbroken over the loss of her son. She had tried every way she could to keep him at home—money, holidays, a motorcycle and freedom to come and go as he pleased at Knockavoe—but it wasn't enough. He wanted excitement, and in the end, it cost him his life.

Leo threw himself into his work on the farm to try and overcome the loss of his younger brother. He was well able to manage the land on his own, for he had inherited much of his father's canny intuition on how to get the best out of it. He also had a good education in the town's agricultural college and kept abreast of the latest developments in farming—particularly hardy new strains of grain and potatoes developed abroad were better suited to Irish soil and climate, and new methods of planting and fertilisation secured maximum yields at harvest time. Leo persuaded a small group of farmers in the neighbourhood to put up the money to buy a Ford Tractor between them to do the ploughing, and it proved such a great success that they formed a small co-operative and bought the latest attachments to use with it.

Brigitta wrote to her mother regularly with news of her husband and a lovely house they had rented, and when she discovered she was pregnant, life could not have been sweeter. She had a daughter whom she called Penelope, and the couple were hardly over the excitement of the new arrival when she became pregnant again. In the next three years she had another daughter, Lucy, and a son, Edward, and the letters became shorter and less frequent as she tried to cope with the daily grind of looking after three infants. When a letter arrived pleading with her mother to come and see her grandchildren, Marita detected a degree of desperation creeping into Brigitta's life.

She decided to rent out the shop and move to England to be with them, but while still finalising matters with the solicitor, she had another letter telling her to postpone the visit. Brigitta explained she was having financial problems and had to vacate the house they were renting and move to temporary accommodation in a council flat. Marita sent money to keep her going until things took a turn for the better.

In the months that followed, it became clear from Brigitta's letters that the situation in the marriage was much worse than she had imagined. Captain Couchy had women trouble as well as money problems and disappeared, leaving Brigitta alone with the children and mounting debts. It transpired that he had to flee after the owner of a mill discovered that his nineteen-year-old daughter was pregnant and Couchy was the father.

Marita went to England the moment she heard that Couchy had fled. Brigitta herself was very confused but still clung to the belief that her husband would never abandon his wife and children. She also refused to return to Mournebridge; she did not have the courage to face friends and admit that her marriage had broken down. When her mother failed to persuade her to change her mind, she gave Brigitta money to move to London to find a place and see if she could resume her career in nursing or get a job as a seamstress. Marita took the three children back to Ireland.

Brigitta moved to the capital and found a job, but in her letters to her mother, it was clear that she still clung to the belief that her husband loved her and would soon realise what a terrible mistake he had made and would come home, and they would all be happy again. She made excuses for his misbehaviour, stressing the physical and mental anguish he had suffered in France.

Marita read the letters and knew that her daughter needed medical help for her mental state; she was living in a world of make-believe. Couchy was gone and he would not be back. Marita felt that was not the worst thing that could happen for his conduct since the beginning of the marriage left a lot to be desired.

When Sadie McKenna heard about Brigitta's marriage breakdown she was sad for the girl whom she loved like a daughter. She visited Marita and offered help with the children. Leo arranged that the youngsters would come to Knockavoe every weekend to give their grandmother a break. Sadie thought the presence of the youngsters might help to recapture the happy days when Leo and Brigitta and Patrick were growing up there.

Since the death of the two old farmers, however, things had never been the same. The world had moved on, the children had grown up, and the death of Patrick had cast a shadow over everything. When the two women met, all they seemed to have for one another was bad news.

Marita hired a girl to look after the children and began to spend more time supervising the clothing business. She was glad she still had the shop both for the income and the interest it gave her. She had orders from all over the north-west of the country for clothes—enough to keep four seamstresses fully employed. When Leo McKenna decided to get married to a local girl, Marita made all the clothes for the bride and her maids. This was her present to the couple, and the designs were so chic that the wedding was the talk of the town.

Although the war in France ended in victory for Britain and its allies, and thousands of Irishmen who had fought with the British army returned home to celebrate, the political and military situation in Ireland became very volatile. Many of the returning soldiers found that while they were fighting with the British Army in France to uphold the rights of small nations, other British soldiers—among them criminals recruited from British prisons—had been waging war against the Irish civilian population, murdering innocent people and burning their homes.

Many of the returning soldiers were so disillusioned by what they found that they joined the rebels and fought against the very soldiers who had been their comrades in France. The war was over in Europe but was just beginning in Ireland. A bloody new conflict gradually took shape as the country sought its freedom after centuries of occupation by England.

The hated Black and Tans regiment, which got its name from the colour of their uniforms, appeared in Mournebridge briefly on the day of Leo McKenna's wedding and fired several volleys over the church roof while the couple exchanged vows inside. The priest locked the church doors and kept everybody inside until the soldiers left.

The campaign of terror and intimidation by these uniformed ex-criminals strengthened resistance by the people as a whole, and the British Government was forced to look for a political settlement to extricate itself from a costly war in Ireland, which they no longer had the resources or the will to fight.

In Dublin and Cork, Republican politicians like Eamon de Valera, Michael Collins and Cathal Brugha openly demanded an independent Irish Republic—even if it meant an all-out war against the British. A growing faction in the North, who wanted to keep Ireland in the Empire, opposed them. When the London Government showed signs of yielding to the Southern rebels, a Unionist leader, Carson, rallied the descendants of the Protestant planters in Ulster to arm themselves and fight to prevent the northern province from being ruled by a 'Fenian parliament' in Dublin.

The Republicans wanted the country to cut all ties with the hated Empire; the Protestants demanded that it be partitioned and the most northerly of the four Irish provinces remain in a United Kingdom of England, Scotland, Wales and Northern Ireland. Political rallies and meetings were held in cities and towns in support of one position or the other, and the country as a whole tottered on the brink of civil war.

In Mournebridge, the police tried to arrest some of the speakers at a meeting of Republicans, and there were riots and baton charges for two days. At these meetings, Volunteers were openly recruited for the rebel Irish Republican Army; young men eager to fight for the freedom of their country joined in their hundreds.

The Unionist leader Carson formed his own army to counteract the growing strength of the Republicans. He played on the fears of the largely non-Catholic population in the North by insisting that in an all-Ireland Republic, the huge majority of Catholics from the South would swamp them. Carson's slogan was "Protestant Ulster for Protestant People", and he procured large caches of arms abroad and made it clear he would use them to retain the link with Britain.

In the end, there was an unhappy compromise—twenty-six counties formed an independent Irish Republic, the remaining six a new State of Northern Ireland loyal to and an integral part of the British Empire. Tyrone and Derry, where Republicans had put up some of the fiercest resistance to British occupation, were excluded from the new Irish Republic and forced against their will to remain part of the United Kingdom.

There was such disagreement among the leaders of the Republican Army over the compromise that a bitter civil war ensued in the South between different factions, and hundreds died before an uneasy peace was restored. While this feud was going on among Republicans, Protestants in Ulster consolidated their position with the help of the British Government and a border was officially established between the northern state and the Irish Republic.

Brigitta wrote that she was in hospital in London and needed to come home, but her mother advised that because of the political situation and the fact that she had been married to a British officer, she should stay where she was until the country settled down.

The desperate woman arrived unannounced a couple of weeks later, saying that she wanted to be with her children. Marita was shocked to see the change in her daughter. She had grown frail, ashen faced; her hair had turned prematurely grey, and her legs were so thin they could not support her body; she was so weak that she could not stand for more than a few minutes. Marita knew there was something terribly wrong with her.

Brigitta had tuberculosis. She told nobody in London because she desperately needed her job, and when she collapsed at work and they discovered how advanced the disease was, she was beyond medical help.

TB was highly infectious, and to protect the children her doctor ordered that she be taken to a sanitarium in Derry.. Her mother and the McKennas took turns visiting every couple of days, but as the weeks and months passed it was clear that she was not going to recover. The children watched their grandmother come and go to the hospital. When was their mother coming home?

Seven months after she returned to Ireland, Brigitta Couchy's lung ruptured one night while she slept, and in the morning a nurse found her dead in bed. She had drowned in her own blood. The McKennas were given the bad news when they arrived for their usual visit and made immediate arrangements to bring her body back to Mournebridge. The first Marita knew about her daughter's death was when the hearse pulled up outside her shop and Sadie McKenna came through the door sobbing.

Health regulations did not permit the lid of the coffin to be removed in such cases, so the only way the children could say goodbye to their mother was by kissing the bright silver nameplate embedded in the stout oak coffin that lay for two days and two nights in the sitting room of their home. Marita did not allow the children to attend the funeral to see the lovely Brigitta, who had been the light of her life, lowered into the cold, wet grave.

After that, the fight went out of Marita. She was sixty-five years of age, her body and spirit drained by suffering and grief, and she had the responsibility of bringing up three grandchildren. What would become of them if anything happened to her while they were still so young?

She spent the next few years trying to cope with the lively youngsters; she could not have managed without the ageing Sadie, who came to visit several days a week. Sometimes, Leo and his wife took the children to Knockavoe for a few days so that their grandmother could attend to her business.

Marita sent them to the same school where their mother had spent the happiest days of her short life, and a new generation of nuns took a special interest in the orphans. In the evenings, Marita taught the elder girl, Penelope, how to make the beautiful Carrickmacross lace. As he got a little older, her brother Edward cycled to and from Leo's farm and became wise in the ways of farm life. The younger girl, Lucy, had trouble coming to terms with the death of her mother and stayed close to her grandmother. The old woman often woke in the middle of the night to find her curled up beside her. She kept up a constant barrage of questions about her father and asked over and over again if he would be coming to fetch them now that mummy had gone to heaven. Marita lied that he was a soldier and spent his life travelling around the world wherever men were fighting wars. Eventually she would have to tell them the truth, but not until they were older.

When the pressure of looking after the children became too much, she considered putting notices in the English newspapers informing Couchy that Brigitta was dead and asking him to contact his children in Mournebridge, but Sadie McKenna convinced her that he could never be trusted with the children after the way he had treated their dead mother.

"Don't worry your head about the children after you are gone," Sadie comforted her, "for the McKennas will always be here to look after them; they are just the same as our own family."

"But the McKennas have a family of their own to bring up," insisted Marita. "It's too much to expect Leo and his wife to rear another three as well."

"Marita," replied Sadie, "remember there wouldn't be a McKenna family if you had not come into our lives."

Penelope, Lucy and Edward loved Granny Sadie, the old lady of Knockavoe Farm with the wispy white hair and the eternal good humour, who gave them sweets and fruit every time they visited. She took the children for long walks through the fields in the autumn to gather blackberries for jam and filled baskets of white mushrooms that grew in abundance in the dewy grass to take home to their grandmother.

Sadie McKenna lived to see four grandchildren running around the farmhouse and died at the ripe old age of ninety, nearly half a century after the pair of them arrived at Knockavoe Farm. The priest in Derry was long since dead, and so was her only sister, and she had heard nothing further about the sale of her farm or about her son Eamonn after he fled to America. Although she often wondered what had become of him, she never made any enquiries about his whereabouts. She never forgave him for the hurt he had caused to Marita.

When she died, the McKennas held a wake for three days, during which hundreds of friends and neighbours called to pay their respects. The old woman, her face wrinkled and sunken and her Rosary beads entwined in her bony fingers, was laid out on her marriage bed dressed in a long black shroud trimmed with white Carrickmacross lace made by Penelope. Her head had been raised almost to a sitting position and she looked so fresh and lifelike that the children thought she was just sleeping and shook her arm to wake her.

Leo McKenna observed all the family traditions. Each evening at her wake, the Rosary was recited in Gaelic, and everybody who came was given tea and cigarettes and a drink if they wanted it. Because there was music in the house from the time his father and Uncle Joe were alive, fiddlers were invited to play, and people sang ballads, and now and again, there was an Irish reel or a jig to pass the long hours of darkness at the wake. Leo McKenna was sad about the death of his mother, but he remembered when his father had died, she would not allow any crying in the house, for she believed grief kept the soul from reaching its eternal reward in heaven.

When the old woman was finally laid to rest in the family plot, the children placed flowers on the bog oak coffin before it was lowered into a grave lined with green moss.

Marita felt as if she had lost an older sister. Sadie had protected her when she needed it, gave her support when she found she was pregnant and companionship during the happy years at Knockavoe. She had lost her parents and her sister and even the Wagontrapers, and if it had not been for Sadie's friendship and help it might all have been too much to bear. She was gone, as were the kindly brothers and the impetuous young Patrick and her own beloved Brigitta. Now, there was only herself left with three precious grandchildren and her friend Leo McKenna and his family.

She kept busy with the shop and dressmaking and gave a lot of time to the children and their homework. The three progressed through school and were doing well according to the nuns who urged their grandmother not to let them throw away their lives as their mother had.

She kept a tight rein on them, especially the girls, for she wanted them to complete their education and go out into the world as accomplished young people.

The Twenties was a decade when it became the fashion for girls to let their hair down and live life to the full. The problem was that a lot of them got into relationships with men who had no intention of marrying them and ended up with babies that had to be farmed out for adoption. Marita was terrified in case either of the girls would get caught in this way and watched them night and day to make sure there were no boys hanging around. The only time they were out of her sight was at Knockavoe Farm, where Leo McKenna and his wife looked after the trio as if they were their own children.

The elder girl, Penelope, grew up a strikingly beautiful young woman. She helped her grandmother in the shop and dressed with such good taste that she was known in the town as a 'living doll'. She was invited to lots of parties, but Marita was so overprotective of the girl that she discouraged her from getting involved in social activities. She was afraid her granddaughter would be ruined by some local fly-boy looking for a cheap thrill at the girl's expense.

While the family was on holiday in the seaside resort of Bundoran, Penelope met and fell madly in love with Thomas McVeigh, a land steward from County Donegal, and although she was advised by her grandmother, as was her mother before her, to take her time and not rush into things, Penelope married six months later when she was still only eighteen. Marita felt that her granddaughter had made the same stupid mistake as her mother and wondered how she could do such a thing after all the advice she had been given. She took some consolation from the fact that the new husband was a good bit older and more sensible than Penelope, a go-ahead type with ambitions to have land of his own someday.

But the bad luck that ran in the Muller family caught up with the young couple soon after they were married. Penelope arrived in the shop one afternoon to say that the estate had changed hands and her husband had lost his job and they had to be out of the steward's cottage inside a month. Then she broke the news that they had decided to emigrate to America and make a fresh start rather than become a burden on the family. They had been told that America was booming and there would be no problem getting work. Parcels of land had been allocated to a new wave of immigrants from Europe after the war, and Penelope's husband thought he might be able to set up a business advising these new farmers how to get the most out of their holdings. He had ideas about setting up a co-operative modelled on the co-operative movements that had done so well in Ireland to bulk purchase seed and machinery and market farm produce.

Marita was devastated by the departure of her eldest grandchild but hoped a new start in a new country might change her luck. And she felt good that at least one of the Mullers made it across the Atlantic in her lifetime. She gave Penelope some money to get them started and they sailed from Derry for the new world on the very route that she herself had planned to travel more than half a century before.

Lucy was the direct opposite of her outgoing sister. She was a plain girl who did nothing to enhance her appearance by the clothes she wore. Her grandmother had suits and dresses specially made for her, but even these could not rid the girl of her shabby, unkempt appearance. Marita eventually gave up trying to make her look attractive.

The old woman sensed the insecurity in the girl; she was always asking questions about what she would do if Granny died, with Penelope so far away in America. Marita decided it was time to tell her the truth about her father, how he had abandoned their mother and went off with another woman; the girl became even more introvert and lapsed into long periods of silence.

Lucy did everything that was asked of her at school and at home; she did it because she was asked and not because she wanted to. The old woman sometimes felt the girl was holding her life in suspense, waiting for somebody or something dramatic to change it.

The boy was different. Edward was full of enthusiasm for everything he did, whether it was writing an essay for school or dressing up to play with the local hurling or football team. He spent his summers with Leo on the farm, and his grandmother rarely saw him. But when he did return home, he made a great fuss of the old woman and hugged and clung to her and told her she was the greatest grandmother in the world. She enjoyed every minute of his company, for he was a breath of fresh air about the house. He was also very tender and understanding towards his sister.

Penelope and her husband settled in a small town near Dayton, Ohio, and went into the business of advising farmers. He borrowed from the banks to supply seed and farm implements on credit, and in the fall, he sold the crops and paid the farmers after deducting what was owed to him. She wrote regularly to her grandmother, describing their success in business and the fantastic lifestyle of the American people. Everything was on such a large scale, overwhelming. In some of the towns there were so many cars you could hardly walk across the street; trains ran the length and breadth of the country; and more and more people were taking to the air for long journeys. Thousands crossed the Atlantic every week in planes just to do business in London or Paris. Things were changing so fast it was hard to keep up with them.

Reading the letters as she rested in the evenings, Marita wondered where she herself might have been had fate not intervened as they walked to the ferry that evening in Derry. Would she really have gone ahead with her plans to set up a brothel? Or would she have stayed with Helmut and Rosa after all and married a farmer?

What had become of Helmut and Rosa and Johann? She had not completely forgotten about them, but she thought about them less and less as the years passed. It was difficult to imagine little Johann as a man well past the prime of life, as he would then be. Helmut and Rosa would be in their seventies. She did not know if they were dead or alive or if they had ever bothered to find out what had happened to her. After she moved away from Knockavoe Farm and had time on her hands, she wrote to the Jesuits in Innsbruck and asked if they would inquire through the church in Hoffenfeld if anybody had any contact with them. Unfortunately, so much time had elapsed that a new generation of valley families knew nothing about Helmut and Rosa Wagontraper.

Every time Penelope wrote, she suggested that Marita and Lucy should come to see her and the wonderful country that America was. Eventually, with another Irish winter approaching, Marita decided at the ripe old age of seventy-six and after constant pestering by her granddaughter and with the threat of war again looming in Europe, to visit the country about which she had dreamed all those years. She and Lucy travelled to Foynes in the West of Ireland in the summer of 1937 and boarded a Pan Am Flying Boat called "Caribou" to New York.

Grandmother and granddaughter were terrified from the moment the big seaplane lumbered through the choppy seas for take-off. And as they flew high above the vast Ocean buffeted by high winds, the old woman found herself praying for the first time since she was a child. She had no fear of death but dearly wanted to live long enough to hug Penelope again. When they landed at Gander in Canada to let some passengers off and take on fuel for the long flight south to New York, they were so air-weary that they had to be coaxed by the hostesses to come back on board for the final leg of their trip with the promise of a birds' eye view of the greatest city in the world—New York.

The flight overland was much more comfortable, and the air hostesses so friendly and helpful that the second leg of the journey seemed to pass more quickly than the first. The old woman was terrified when the "Caribou" finally came down through the clouds to the capital of America over buildings so high it seemed that the plane could not avoid crashing into them. When they landed on a broad river the buildings looked even more terrifying from the ground, as if they might fall over and bury the streets and the throngs of people beneath them. They stayed the night at a hotel not too far from where they landed, and in the morning, a taxi took them to Grand Central Station to board a train for Iowa. The station was crammed with people trying to get aboard trains lined up on different platforms. The noise and the bustle reminded the old woman of the first time she saw the majestic *Garibaldi* standing in the station at Milan; she could still remember the shriek from the burst of steam that sent them running for their lives. Somehow, it did not seem so long ago; she remembered it clearly.

The visitors had no conception of the journey that lay before them. They spent two full days on the train watching the great American plains and mountains drift by in daylight through the carriage windows. Lucy got a headache looking at telegraph poles flipping past. Day changed quickly to night, and they slept in bunks as the carriages rattled through the starry darkness. Fifteen hundred miles later they arrived tired and completely disorientated at their destination.

Penelope was waiting at the station to greet them, and when they complained about the journey on the train, she confided that she had deliberately misled them. If she had told them about the distance they had to travel from New York, they might never have come and she wanted so badly to see them.

They set out in her open-topped car and drove for hours until they reached Dayton and arrived at Penelope's home, a breathtaking mansion on the edge of town.

The visitors hardly had time to recover from the long journey when a round of parties began. First, there was a homecoming to which neighbours and friends were invited, and everybody fussed over the old lady from Ireland about whom they had heard so much. This was followed by invitations to other grand homes owned by business associates of Penelope's husband, and by the end of the first week of their stay, they had to take a couple of days to rest. Penelope stayed close to her grandmother everywhere they went, and nobody was in any doubt but that she loved the old woman dearly.

During the second week Penelope had more time to sit and chat with them and they brought her up to date on all the news from Ireland and especially about the McKennas. Marita also took the opportunity to ask the one question she had been afraid to ask in her letters. When was she going to start a family?

Penelope had no children and sadly explained to her grandmother and sister that she had been advised that it was unlikely she would ever have any. She and her husband were resigned to the idea at this stage, and although they had discussed the possibility of adopting a child, he was not keen on the idea. So she gave a lot of her spare time to organising charity events to aid the local orphanage and other needy institutions.

That was the last time the subject was mentioned by any of them, but Marita felt that the absence of children was a heavy burden for them to bear. It did not affect their marriage, however, for she and her husband were as madly in love with one another as the day they were wed.

Penelope liked driving, and the visitors spent happy hours motoring through cities and towns and the expansive countryside. The old woman enjoyed the grandeur of everything and was greatly excited by the hustle and bustle in the towns. Out in the country wide roads rolled right up to the horizon with hardly a bend. There were few trees and bushes, no hedges or stone ditches, just parallel strips of land like stamps on a letter that came from the other side of the world. The countryside had no flowers, no bees and few birds. The ground looked parched, and they did not see a drop of rain all the time they were there.

When they had a few days to spare towards the end of the holiday, Marita asked Penelope if there was any way they could check to see if the Wagontrapers might have settled in that State. The girl said it was like looking for a needle in a haystack, but they all went to her husband's offices one morning, commandeered the services of a secretary and started checking phone exchanges and directories for people named Wagontraper. They found dozens listed and rang every one of them, but none had any connection with Hoffenfeld, nor were they aware of the existence of Marita Muller. Still, Penelope did not give up, and for two more days, the girls tried calls to neighbouring states. When their efforts turned up nothing, they contacted the immigration authorities in New York and got them to check for any record of the family, giving the approximate date when they would have landed in America. But it all came to nothing, and although several agencies promised to make further checks and write back if they got any information about the family, nothing was ever heard of them again. Helmut and Rosa and Johann seemed to have vanished into thin air after the *Clyde Clipper* sailed from Lough Foyle.

The threat of another war in Europe forced them to cut short their visit; they were advised to return home in case travel was restricted. When the time came to go, there was a sad parting; Penelope realised for the first time that she would probably never see the old lady alive again. Nevertheless, she promised that when her husband got some free time from the business they would return to Ireland for a holiday. If her grandmother felt well enough, they would all go to Bavaria to visit the valley of their ancestors and say a prayer at the grave of their great-grandparents and their great-aunt Maria.

But Penelope never made it back to Ireland. The fertile countryside in Iowa experienced a severe drought that same year that turned the fertile black soil into a dusty desert on which no crops would grow. When credit ran out for impoverished farmers, they abandoned their holdings and migrated to the West Coast looking for work. Penelope and her husband were left holding useless pieces of paper, promises to pay for seeds that had never yielded a husk of corn or a stone of potatoes. The business collapsed and the bank seized their home, their cars, everything. They were forced to seek shelter in the very orphanage for which Penelope had worked so untiringly during the good years. The nuns gave them a place to sleep and their meals for a couple of months, a charity that they were glad to accept when many of their friends went hungry.

Frantic notes written by Marita to her granddaughter were returned marked *"Not known at this address"*. In the weeks that followed, Lucy tried every way possible to contact her sister. She wrote to the Mayor of Dayton and the Postmaster at the General Post Office, but they were no help. The orphanage where the couple had stayed had no information of their whereabouts. A nun wrote that even though Penelope and her husband had lost everything, the bank's lawyers still pursued them for outstanding debts, and rather than face the prospect of going to jail, the couple just up and left and never made contact again. There was no forwarding address, as they did not want the bank to trace them. The nun wrote that they were both very depressed when they left, but they were a loving couple and, with the help of God, would work their way through this crisis in their lives.

The old woman lapsed into long periods of silence after the letter from the nun and never really returned to her former self. She caught influenza, from which she developed pneumonia and became quite ill. She had a nurse with her all the time, but the doctor told Edward and Lucy that the fight had gone out of her; it would be a miracle if she survived. The two grandchildren and Leo McKenna took turns sitting by her bedside night and day.

The doctor managed to control the fever, but the illness had weakened her and for weeks she hovered between sleep and waking. When she spoke, it was in her native German; she imagined she was back in the woods in Hoffenfeld talking to her grandmother. She also conversed with Helmut and Rosa and Johann and argued with the Jesuit priest Fr. Damien about religion and God.

When she mentioned Brigitta and Penelope, she reverted to English. She asked over and over again if Penelope was coming to see her, but all Lucy could say was that they were still trying to make contact with her. The grandchildren and Leo McKenna watched Marita deteriorate, hardly able to believe that this was the same strong woman who was once the focal point of so many lives. Lucy and Edward each held a limp snow-white hand when she eventually slipped into a coma for the last time in the autumn of 1938 and died. Leo McKenna put his arms around the two of them and the trio held on to each other for support. They were all that was left of the two families, and Leo vowed they would stick together.

"It's what Sadie and Marita and Peter and Joe, God rest their souls, would have wanted us to do," he said sadly. "It's such a pity that she did not see Penelope before she died."

Their grandmother always said that if at all possible, she would like to be buried in Hoffenfeld, in the same grave where her parents and sister had been laid to rest so long ago. She had no affinity with Ireland, regarding it only as the place where she had been forced by cruel circumstances to remain against her will until it was too late to leave. And apart from her time at Knockavoe Farm, they were for the most part years of pain and hardship.

Going through her grandmother's personal belongings Lucy found the ledger wrapped in brown paper and tied with string addressed to Brigitta. The girl could hardly believe her eyes as she translated her grandmother's account of her life before the birth of her only child at Knockavoe Farm.

It was clear that she only started to record her thoughts long after she came to Ireland, when Brigitta was still a baby and she had time on her hands, but events were set down as if she had written them as they occurred a long, long time before.

The first was dated June 17, 1872: "*Wenn ich endlich diesem liebenswerten tal den rucken kehren werde ......"When I turned my back on the lovely valley which had been my whole world my stomach felt as if it had slipped down to my knees. But I never turned to look back and I never shed a tear. I just wanted to remember it as it was before the massacre and not think of all those new graves beside the church nor the burned-out shells of houses that had once been filled with simple, happy people.*"

She obviously had a vivid memory of the long journey to Ireland and there were many entries describing the countryside and what they ate and drank and the trains and the ships and the great ports they visited and the people they met.

The diary recounted snatches of the hurt and loneliness she felt after her kidnap in Derry and the sexual and physical abuse she suffered at the hands of Eamonn McKee. She wrote fondly about the McKenna brothers and Sadie and the happy days they spent together, especially the shock when it was discovered they were going to have babies at the same time.

It was in one of these notes that she gave a brief account of the events that brought them to Knockavoe, and Lucy could hardly believe her eyes when she read about the incident at the pool that ended in the killing of the British soldiers. She realised, to her horror, that the father of her only child, Brigitta, was the English soldier who raped her before the Fenians killed him.

She wrote lovingly about Brigitta, a bright, outgoing girl for whom she had such high hopes and whose life had been ruined by another English soldier.

The last entry was made after she returned from her holiday with Penelope in America, when she recorded her sadness that the girl had everything in the world except a child. *"Leben kann schon sein, aber Natur grausam ...... Life can be good, but nature can be cruel,"* was the last line she wrote.

To fulfil her grandmother's wish that she should be buried in her native Bavarian valley, Lucy arranged with the undertakers to embalm the body in preparation for the long journey back to Germany. Edward travelled with the remains by sea to Liverpool and on to London by train. The British authorities were very uncooperative, for as the year came to an end, there was a great deal of diplomatic bickering and distrust between them and the Germans.

Eventually the documentation was cleared and the remains were put aboard a cargo flight to Munich. At that end, there was more paperwork to be completed, and Edward himself was subjected to intense questioning by the German police before he was authorised to hire a hearse to take the cask to Hoffenfeld.

The heavy coffin lay in the valley church for two days and two nights while arrangements were made to have the Muller grave opened. All the victims of the massacre had been re-interred in a commemorative plot in the valley many years before. He had another long wait and had to swear affidavits to the effect that Marita was the only survivor of the massacre before her remains could be interred there.

Edward was surprised on the morning of the burial to find the cask covered in wreaths and fresh flowers. Though it was nearly seventy years since the massacre, it was still remembered as the worst tragedy that had befallen that part of Bavaria and had been commemorated every year with the celebration of an open-air Mass. The burial plot was well tended; before the old priest died, he had ordered the mountain farm to be sold and the proceeds used to tend the communal grave in perpetuity.

Penelope felt bad about getting up in the middle of the night and leaving the convent at Dayton without a word to the kindly nuns who had taken her and her husband in when they lost everything. They had no option but to go; they were being hounded by the banks over unpaid loans and had become an embarrassment to the Sisters.

Her husband thought it very wrong to go without at least telling them why, but Penelope was adamant.

"If we do that, we are just putting them in a more difficult position. They will have to lie to the banking agents about our whereabouts. If they don't know where we are going, they can truthfully say they don't know."

They carried only a small suitcase each when they made the short walk from the convent to the bus station in darkness. They took turns sleeping in the waiting room until the ticket office opened and paid for the first leg of their journey to what they hoped would be a new beginning in California.

Thomas had a contact there who promised them work on a fruit farm, and he was as good as his word. They were given a one-room cabin on the farm and one day to get settled in before they began work. And it was there in the San Fernando Valley that they remained for the next two years.

Penelope was grateful for the work but hated the primitive conditions in which they had to live and the pressure of stretching their meagre income to keep themselves fed and clothed. She was glad they did not have children; couples that did live in poverty, and if they had sickness, their situation became even more desperate.

She collapsed in the field one day from exhaustion, and Thomas helped her back to the shack they called home.

"I've had enough of this," she confessed. "We are getting nowhere with our lives. I think the time has come to swallow our pride and go back to Ireland. We may still be poor there, but at least we will be poor among friends."

Thomas agreed. "But we still need to work and try and save the money to get there," he pointed out.

"I could write to Granny Muller—she would help us out."

He was adamant. "No," he said "we are not beggars. We have to work harder and save harder. War is coming in Europe and America will soon be involved and the country will need more food and they will have to pay us more to provide it. Once we get the fares together, to Ireland we will go."

But wages did not improve. There was plenty of work, but it was still poorly paid. Unions saw their chance to organise the fruit pickers, but their intervention caused a strike and blackleg labour was brought into the valley to do the work.

It was all too much for Penelope. She had enough of the fruit fields and hard labour and watching their savings disappear when they were out of work. She was desperate and had nobody to turn to for help. She had lost touch with Granny Muller and the McKennas—the only people she might have asked for help—and was too ashamed to go begging to them. She felt isolated and desolate, but worst of all, she had lost confidence in Thomas—she finally had to admit to herself that he had neither the drive nor the enterprise to get them out of their disastrous situation. She made up her mind that she would have to do something about her predicament, take hold of her own life and carve out a future for herself.

While her husband was at a meeting of striking workers one night, she sat down and wrote him a letter:

"Thomas, I cannot take any more of this life. I have been thinking about it since all this union trouble started and finally made up my mind what to do. By the time you come home, I will be gone. My plan is to go south to the Mexican border and make my way to South America, to Argentina. I know you will feel that I have betrayed you, but time changes everything, as we know from bitter experience. The hurt will go, and you will only have yourself to think about in the future. There is no point in saying that I will write you when I reach my

destination, because I am not sure where that destination even is. South America is a very big place and I understand a very poor place, but I intend to get involved in charitable work rather than look for a job. When I did charitable work for the nuns in Iowa, it was very rewarding and I feel that's where my future lies.

"There is another reason, Thomas" she continued, *"I feel that the bad luck which has dogged the Muller family since Granny left Bavaria is still with me and you are suffering because of it. I firmly believe you will do much better on your own. Let Jonah follow me—It's my bad luck and I will have to cope with it."*

She packed her suitcase and took half of what dollars they had left and set out on foot once again in the darkness with nothing but a stout pair of walking shoes and a map on which she had marked out the road route across to the Mexican border—a distance of 1,800 miles.

"If my Granny could make it all the way from Bavaria to the Mediterranean when she was only thirteen," she said determinedly, "surely I can make it to the border."

She had no money for fares, so she hitched her way across the country and used her dollars to buy food. After two weeks of hitching and sleeping rough, she reached Texas and turned south towards the Mexican border. It was winter, and there was a chill wind blowing across the prairie, and she was caught outdoors in several rainstorms.

She began to run a fever. She collapsed in a roadside eating house where she stopped to have hot soup and woke up two days later in hospital in a small town called Madison. She was there for two weeks before she was well enough to get out of bed and back on her feet but still not strong enough to resume her journey to Mexico.

She explained to the nuns in the hospital that she was on her way to Argentina to do charity work and asked if they could find her a job in the hospital and a place to stay until she was well enough to continue her travel. She was assigned to the hospital laundry and given a place to stay in the convent.

Work in the laundry was hard, slowing her recovery, and after nearly two months it was clear she still was not well enough to travel. She was moved to other work in the hospital and months passed; the Superior at the convent suggested that she could make better use of her time there training as a nurse. If she still felt she wanted to do missionary work, what better way to prepare herself than a nursing career?

Penelope never did leave the Hospital of St. Joseph in Madison nor the convent of the Sisters of St. Francis. She could never aspire to be one of the Sisters because she was still a married woman, but she stayed with the community, lived with them, prayed with them and worked in the hospital with them. For the first time in her life, she felt happy with what she was doing and with the company of the community in which she lived. She still felt guilty about leaving Thomas but convinced herself that God would forgive her. She did not leave for selfish reasons but to help other people and that's what she was now doing with her life.

She was too ashamed to make contact with Granny Muller and tell her that she had left Thomas, or to make excuses for not making contact for so long. Neither did she ever try to contact Thomas—that part of her life was over and done with. Neither did she want anything to interfere with the useful life into which she had settled.

Locals were intrigued by Edward Couchy's account of how his grandmother had been caught up in a rebellion in Ireland while on her way to America and forced to spend the rest of her years on an island on the edge of the Atlantic Ocean. The story was published in the newspaper in Munich, and he became a celebrity with invitations to meet various groups and talk about the adventures of the old woman. Nothing had ever been heard of Helmut and Rosa and Johann Wagontraper. Over the years, the Munich paper advertised far and wide in America to try and make contact with them to get a first-hand account of what happened the night of the massacre, but without success.

Edward decided to stay a while with the friendly valley people and learn to ski, for Bavaria was a favourite place for winter sports. He became so adept on the slopes that a friend persuaded him to train as an instructor. He was offered a job and wrote to his sister that he felt very much at home among the valley people and intended to stay until the end of the winter sports season.

Lucy begged him to come home for there was talk about another war between Germany and England. Edward knew his father had fought the Germans in the First World War and his uncle Patrick had died fighting for the British in the same war, but since his arrival in Bavaria, he felt closer to the German people than he ever had to the English or Irish. He joined a local volunteer force and was one of a group honoured by the local mayor by being sent to Munich to act as a guard of honour when Herr Hitler came for a big political rally.

Edward heard from the leader's mouth how wealthy Jewish families had tried to bring the Fatherland to its knees and humble the German people. Germany was now stronger than ever and would never again be forced to bend the knee to England or France or the Jews. Hitler vowed to take back for the Fatherland all the territory that had been annexed by neighbouring countries after the First World War with the connivance of Britain and France. Like thousands of others who gave the grand salute at the rally, Edward was so impressed by the man's eloquence and his call to arms to defeat the efforts of their European neighbours to destroy the Fatherland that he made up his mind that if there was to be a war, so be it; it would be an honour to fight for the Fatherland, now his homeland.

He wrote Lucy that he had formally changed his name to Eamonn Muller, describing himself as born in Ireland to Brigitta Muller, daughter of Marita Muller of Hoffenfeld Bavaria and Eamonn McKee, Volunteer in the Irish Republican Army, of Derry, Ireland, and warned her that if any enquiries were made about him not to contradict his story.

He let it be known that as an Irishman and a German, he had a deep hatred of England and all things British and hoped the day would come soon when the Fatherland would be victorious in Europe and give occupied Ireland back to the Irish people. He made no mention of his real father, Captain Couchy.

He was recruited into a special unit that monitored English language radio programmes beamed at Britain and eventually was moved to Berlin and appointed to the section that translated German propaganda scripts into English. When war came in the autumn of 1939, he was vetted as a foreigner and questioned closely about his parentage; he felt the SS men were not completely convinced that the details he gave them were true.

Lucy hated the name Couchy, especially since she learned how badly her father had treated her mother. When her brother changed his name back to Muller, she hired a solicitor to do the same for her, and thenceforth used the name Lucy Muller for all personal and business transactions. She felt a weight lifted off her shoulders once she had made the change, glad that the name Couchy had been erased from the public record once and for all, and happy in the knowledge that she and her brother could carry on the family name of the Mullers of Hoffenfeld.

Early in 1940, Edward wrote that he had been transferred to active service and posted to the Russian border. That was the last news she had from him or about him. In the following four years, she wrote dozens of letters to the German authorities, the Red Cross and even the Russian authorities, desperately seeking information. The German authorities in Berlin simply replied that they had no record of Edward Muller and the International Red Cross informed her that very poor records existed in relation to soldiers who were missing in action in Russia. Edward had given her the names of friends he made in Hoffenfeld, and she wrote them to try and get news, but so terrorised were they by the SS that they were afraid to make any inquiries.

Lucy lived life virtually as a recluse during the early war years, hoping against hope that she would hear from her lost brother and dreading the prospect that he might be dead. She became so withdrawn that when the McKennas came to visit, sometimes she pretended she was not at home; when they came to the shop, she scurried out of sight to avoid them.

Some of her neighbours were aware that her family originally came from Germany and that she had recently assumed a German name; they were also aware that her brother had gone to Germany with the remains of their grandmother and had not returned, choosing instead to stay and fight with the Germans. She knew people were talking about her, pointing the finger at her, boycotting her dressmaking business. She retreated further into a world of her own.

When war finally ended, she renewed her efforts to find her missing brother, writing to the Red Cross, the Allied authorities in Berlin and several organisations dealing with the repatriation of prisoners, but in vain. The Red Cross replied that although they had procured some records of German soldiers who had died or were taken prisoner in Russia, they could find no trace of her brother after he left the English translation department in Berlin in February 1941. He was listed simply as "Missing in Action", but it did not say whether this was in Russia or on the Western Front, or indeed whether he might have died in Berlin.

It was assumed that he was one of thousands who perished in the winter of 1941. Whether he died in the snow in Russia or at the hands of the Gestapo before he ever left Berlin, she never knew. She had to resign herself to the fact that she might never see her only brother again. She was completely alone.

Edward Couchy had been enjoying life as a ski instructor in the autumn of 1939 when Germany went to war, preparing for a busy winter season when the authorities ordered the closure of all ski schools. Foreign skiers who had been the lifeblood of the region for years were no longer welcome.

He had several letters from Lucy begging him to come home before he was trapped in a war in Europe, but Edward felt he would be labelled a coward among his own people if he left, and in any case, he had a duty to serve the Fatherland in its hour of need.

He joined the Hitler Youth Movement and soon afterwards was one of a small group of English speakers selected to go to Berlin to help the propaganda war being waged on the airwaves with the British World News Service. He worked there for two years preparing English language news bulletins and teaching English to trainee announcers until he let slip to one of his colleagues that his father had fought with the British Army in the Great War. The following day he was interviewed by two members of the Gestapo.

"Yes," he admitted, "my father was English and called Couchy, but he abandoned us when I was still very young and we never saw or heard from him again. That's why we changed our name to Muller, which was our grandmother's family name. "

"So you gave false information in order to join the Youth Movement," said one of the officers. "That is a serious crime in these times."

"I joined the Youth Movement to serve the Fatherland, not to spy on it," he insisted.

The report from the Gestapo to the head of the English Language school stated that Herr Muller had arrived in Bavaria in suspicious circumstances in 1938 and had given false information in order to be admitted to the Youth Movement.

"In the circumstances, he is to be relieved of his duties immediately and report to the Bavarian Division HQ to join the Wehrmacht."

In the autumn of 1943 Edward trained for six weeks with hundreds of other recruits in the Alps just as the first snow of the season was falling. The tide of war was turning against the Germans and he was just one of thousands of young men sent East to try and stop the Russian advance westward.

Edward arrived at an Army Camp in Kyiv, the capital of Ukraine, in September and was assigned to guard an industrial estate where factories were churning out winter clothing for the German Army. He was there only one day when the estate was overrun by the Russians and he and several hundred others were taken prisoner without firing a shot. They were marched off eastward to join thousands of other German prisoners and were put to work rebuilding roads and railways destroyed by the fighting.

They were forced to continue this work for two years until the war ended. In July 1945, they were marched into Kyiv, and Edward thought the time for the repatriation of prisoners had come. Instead, they were humiliated in front of the city population and then informed that they would not be going home until they had made good all the damage they had inflicted on the Ukrainian people. Some prisoners were publicly executed for war crimes; the remainder were divided into groups of 100 and assigned to different projects. Edward's group was sent to a small town north of Kiev, which had put up fierce resistance when the Germans first invaded. Most of the town had been reduced to rubble, and the population was forced to live for three years in makeshift hovels. Edward spent the next five years there, rebuilding homes by day and returning to a prison camp at night.

In 1950, the prisoners demanded repatriation, which was refused. Instead, they were split up into smaller groups and sent into the countryside to work on farms. Edward was given into the custody of a war widow, Elana Markova, mother of three young children; his job was to help her rebuild the farm and produce food for the Collective. When she complained that she was lonely, he moved into the farmhouse and they lived together until his five years of detention ended. She proposed that instead of returning home, they should get married, and he agreed. He was thirty-five years old; his wife was three years older, and they used her married name as their family name.

BOOK III

CHAPTER ONE

A TIME TO LIVE

Lucy Muller's self-imposed isolation led to loneliness and depression, but instead of taking the advice of her closest friends and seeking medical help, she turned instead to alcohol. Leo McKenna and his wife and their grown-up children tried in vain to help her, but she kept them at a distance, determined to deal with her problems in her own way.

She wallowed in a sea of self-pity, convinced that she had inherited the bad luck that had dogged her family from the moment her grandmother arrived in Ireland. The curse had followed them all the way from Bavaria, and it seemed there was no way of avoiding it. In the evenings she found that brandy was the only way of blotting out the demons that had made the lives of the Muller family a living hell for the best part of a century. When the effects of an evening's drinking wore off the depression returned; the only antidote was more alcohol.

For all her shyness and lack of social graces, Lucy was quite attractive, even good-looking, to those who got close to her. She had grown tall, and although alcohol and lack of sleep had paled her skin, she had much of the graceful movement and stylish poise of her missing sister Penelope. She had soft, sad eyes and a sensuous mouth with lips so red she never had to wear lipstick. There was little of the Muller family in her makeup; rather, she had the fine features of her father, the same inviting looks that made her mother throw caution to the wind and spend her nights sleeping with him in his hospital bed.

However, fine features could not make up for her lack of self-confidence and the vulnerability that went with it. Financially, she was well off by any standards. A businesswoman in a small town was considered a "good catch" for some enterprising young man, but she never let anybody get close enough to become romantically involved. Lucy acquired the reputation of an orchid—lovely to look at but not to be handled.

A week after the Japanese surrender finally brought an end to the war in the Pacific, American soldiers billeted in Mournebridge organized a huge victory celebration with marching bands parading through the streets and bunting and American and British flags flying from every lamppost. Amid the euphoria, Lucy was persuaded by one of her shop girls to go to a dance in the town. When her friend called to collect her that night, Lucy insisted that they have some drinks before venturing to the celebrations, and the pair were a bit tipsy when they arrived at the dancehall.

The place was full of young people and the band music and the dancing and singing and the sight of hundreds of men in American and British uniforms was infectious and they joined in the merriment. Lucy found herself amid a boisterous crowd of revellers swizzing around the dance floor until she felt dizzy; she enjoyed the anonymity of being part of such a large gathering.

Then she literally bumped into a young Irish soldier on leave from England who danced with her for a while and let her drink from his hipflask; they sang and waltzed around the floor until the early hours of the morning and when the music ended her new-found friend insisted on walking her home.

The effects of alcohol and the air of gay abandonment that permeated the evening helped her shed some of her shyness, and as they walked, she told him how difficult it was for her family during the war with Germany because her grandmother was from Bavaria. Her brother Edward was in Germany when the war started, was forced to join up and lost his life in Russia in 1941. Her own father was a British officer who fought in the First World War and was badly wounded, and her cousin, Patrick McKenna, was killed fighting with the British Army in France.

"In spite of all the sacrifice our family made in two wars," she said sadly, "we were still regarded as Germans, and townspeople pressed the authorities to have me interned for the duration of the war. When they failed, many of them boycotted my dressmaking business.

"The sad fact is that none of our family ever visited Bavaria except Edward when he went there with the remains of my mother to bury her in the family plot—a task that cost him his life because he had to join the German Army."

The young soldier had coincidently been in Bavaria during the final months of the war, and as they walked, he told her all about it, about the chalets, beautiful Alpine valleys and picture postcard vistas.

On the way home, they drained a brandy flask, and when they reached her house, she invited him in for one last drink. She closed the door behind them, and he put his arms around her and held her tightly against him. Lucy felt apprehensive at first, for she had never been that close to a man, never had a man's arms around her. It was a nice feeling. Gradually her body warmed to him, and she put her arms around his neck and rested her head on his shoulder.

"Let's have that drink I promised you," she whispered.

"No," he said without moving. "I have had enough. It's you I want."

He put his mouth close to hers, and she could feel his breath against her face; her legs felt weak, and she leaned against him for support. Then he kissed her full on the lips—a long lingering kiss that ended when his hand opened the buttons of her blouse, and he gently held the cup of her bra in his palm. When she did not resist, he slid the strap of the bra off her shoulder and put his cold hand on her bare breast; she gasped, and he took it away again.

Lucy Muller had never experienced such feelings before in her life. She was wise enough in the ways of the world to know what he was doing to her, and her brain told her she should stop him, but her body did not want to be parted from him. He was gentle and she had not felt so good or so relaxed for a long time. Though she had several drinks during the evening, her mind was clear; she knew exactly what he was doing to her, and she did not want him to stop.

He pulled her so close that her feet were no longer touching the ground. She felt weak and shivered with excitement when he pressed her stomach hard against his thighs. She parted from him so that she could open the remaining buttons on her blouse to take it off. She slipped the strap of her bra off her other shoulder, unhooked it behind her back, and it fell to the ground. She took his hand and led him to the bedroom, where they stood together at the side of the bed while he undressed and told her to get into bed. She watched as he took off his clothes, revealing muscular arms and broad shoulders. She could not take her eyes off him; he looked so handsome, so strong. She pulled back the bed covers so that he could get in beside her.

She shivered, and he asked her if she was cold.

"Not cold," she said. "I'm a bit scared—I've never been with a man before."

"A beautiful girl like you and no boyfriend?" he asked.

"Since the disappearance of my brother, I have not been very well," she said.

"A beautiful girl like you should never be without a boyfriend," he said.

They lay quiet for a while, touching and kissing and squeezing each other, and when he felt her relax, he pulled her close and caressed her naked body with his hands and they made love until passion flared between their hot, sweating bodies.

They did not talk for a long time afterwards, content to lie in each other's arms and feel the closeness of one another. Lucy was so overwhelmed by their lovemaking that she just wanted to lie on the bed and let the wonderful feeling in her body linger on. She had never thought too much about being with a man, what it would be like. Now that she had experienced it there was nothing in this world so wonderful.

What happens now, she wondered as she stared at the ceiling. She had no idea what to do.

"Do you want me to leave?" he said. "I don't live too far away."

Lucy didn't want it to end like that. "You don't have to go unless you want to," she said.

When he made no reply, she turned around and pressed her body against him. She wanted him to make love to her again, and she told him so: "I had a lovely time tonight, the best time of my life," she said. "Let's make the most of it, for we may not see one another again." They made love again and she fell asleep in his arms.

Sometime during the night, Lucy awoke and found herself entwined in the stranger's arms. The light was on, and she had a good look at the man lying beside her. When she tried to extricate herself from him, he awoke and kissed her again on her lips, caressing her neck and shoulders. She put her arms around him and they made love again.

Exhausted, they fell asleep and did not wake again until daylight. She got up and dressed and made him a cup of tea and told him she had to get to her work in the shop.

She kissed him once more in the hallway on her way out of the house.

"Am I going to see you again?" she asked. "Does this mean I am your girlfriend now?"

He nodded his head.

Lucy felt as if she was walking on air. Could this be the turning point in her life, the event she had been waiting for? He did not sound too convincing when she asked about being his girlfriend, but even if she never saw him again, she would remember that night for the rest of her life. She hoped his reticence was not because he already had a girlfriend —or worse still, that he was already married.

She put it out of her mind. She wanted him to keep the affair going; she wanted his lovemaking and the ecstasy that went with it. For the first time in her life, she felt like a complete woman—no more self-pity, no more alcohol, no more feeling sorry for herself. In one evening of happiness, she had rid herself of the feelings of inadequacy and depression that had turned her into a virtual recluse.

In the event, it turned out that he was a single man and had no girlfriend. He came to her house in the evenings, and she could not get enough of him. The days seemed endless in the shop waiting for the time to go home, but from the moment he stepped through the door they were in another world. Sometimes they were so hungry for one another that as soon as the front door closed behind him, he took her on the cold floor of the hallway.

His name was Patrick McLaughlin, and though they both had a lot to drink the night they first made love, he was completely overwhelmed by the passion of the shy girl he met by chance at the dance. When he first showed an interest in her, his pals warned him that he was wasting his time for she was "a cold, stuck-up bitch". But he wanted a woman badly that night, and despite what they said, he felt that if he got as far as her hall door, he was in with a chance. How wrong his pals were. She turned out to be a warm, passionate girl, and he continued the affair in the belief that she might, after all, be the woman for him. She gave herself willingly to him every time he wanted her, and he could not get enough of her.

He was twenty-five years of age and Lucy was twenty-eight. He had fought in France and in Germany and had been with women before but never experienced such intense lovemaking as with this strange, quiet girl.

Three months after their first meeting the doctor told Lucy she was pregnant and had better get herself married as soon as possible. It had never occurred to her that it would happen, and she wondered how she could have been so stupid. If her grandmother was still alive, she might make some of the famous brew she wrote about in her ledger, the potion she gave Rosa Wagontraper to cause an abortion.

For a long time, she was afraid to tell him; she felt the shock would put an end to their lovemaking. Her grandmother had warned often enough that nothing cooled passion faster than having a baby, whether a girl was married or single. So she said nothing at first, preferring to enjoy him as much as possible, and if he didn't want her with a baby, at least she would have a little more time with him before he found out.

When Patrick remarked that she was putting on weight, she told him. He was taken aback at first but to her surprise, continued the affair with more passion than ever. He became very protective of her and the baby. There was no more rough and tumble on the floor. He insisted that she make regular visits to the doctor to make sure she did everything right for herself and the child.

Patrick knew what wagging tongues got up to in small-town Ireland and the hurt they could cause to a girl having a baby out of wedlock, especially a loner like Marita, who already had to suffer Nazi taunts during the war years. To avoid the inevitable gossip and the complications and problems the affair was going to cause him with his own family, he suggested they elope to England as soon as possible and get married when the baby was born. They would make a new life for themselves. Lucy was so happy with her new love and having his baby and the prospect of getting married that she asked Leo McKenna's daughter to take over the shop and quietly left for London with Patrick.

She had money and they found a flat and he had no trouble getting a job, and when a baby boy arrived, Lucy felt she was the happiest and luckiest woman in the world. They called him Patrick, and even though they still had not married, Patrick McLaughlin was registered as the father. They planned to find a nice house, and once they had settled in, he would find a decent job and they would get married. Neither of them had any regrets about leaving Ireland.

Their passionate love affair resumed immediately after the baby was born and continued unabated, as if they had to make up for lost time during the pregnancy. They made love whenever and wherever they felt like it, and Lucy's whole world revolved around their home, her baby son and a strong man with a sexual appetite that matched her own.

He wanted to make her pregnant again and got annoyed when Lucy insisted that they should first find a permanent home and get married. Though he earned only a modest wage as a labourer on building sites, they lived well on Lucy's money. Soldiers were returning from war in their hundreds of thousands to find that they could not get work, and the fact that Patrick was Irish didn't help his chances of getting a permanent job. All that was open to him were lowly paid building site jobs, often doled out by fellow Irishmen who demanded bribes in return for the work. Patrick realised he had little chance of improving his position and became unsettled in London. He urged Lucy to move with him to some other part of England where there was a prospect of finding better work. When she refused, he became argumentative.

"We have a nice place here," she insisted, "and we have the means to maintain a decent lifestyle. Why should we uproot ourselves to move to a strange place?"

"Because," he said dolefully, "I am your husband, and I have to provide for this family."

That was the start of their troubles. There were frequent arguments about who the real breadwinner in the house was. and as the months passed, his ardour cooled.

He wanted her to have another baby; she insisted they would have to wait until they were married. She wanted him to go and look about getting a mortgage for a house, but he knew he would not even be considered because he did not have permanent work. He felt she was putting him under pressure to take on a financial burden he could not afford.

They argued when he came home in the evenings, which soured their lovemaking. Lucy had a lover and a baby; she still did not have a husband. She felt that Patrick had reneged on his promise to marry her and was unwilling to provide her with a permanent home. He told her she made him feel like a kept man; she resorted to blackmail by rationing her lovemaking.

He developed the habit of dropping into the pub on his way from work, arriving home later and later in the evenings with the excuse that he was delayed on the job. When she discovered that he was drinking when he was supposed to be at work, she railed at him for lying to her. He tried to force her to make love, but she resisted, so he stormed out of the house and went missing for two days. When he came back, she demanded to know where he had been. He told her it was none of her business; he took some clothing and left again.

His absence went from days to weeks and then it was a month; she realised that the relationship was breaking up. He phoned her from various pubs to see that Patrick was okay, and when she asked when he was coming home, he answered that he needed time to think. She tried to reason with him and mend the growing rift between them, but he did not respond.

When she buried her pride and pleaded with him to come back, he told her it was too late. He had met an old girlfriend from Mournebridge and moved in with her.

Lucy was devastated. She knew by his attitude that he was gone for good and, just as her grandmother had warned, she was left with a baby and no husband. Apart from the loss of her lover and the stress it put on her life, her money was depleted, and there was no way she could work and look after a baby. But neither could she return to Mournebridge with her illegitimate son and have herself branded as an unmarried mother and her child shunned as a bastard. She remembered the hurt it had caused her and her sister and brother as they were growing up, having to put up with jibes about not having a father.

When Patrick next rang her, she told him he would have to accept his responsibilities and support her and his son. But he said that was not possible since he and his girlfriend had decided to set up a house together, and he could not afford to keep two establishments. He advised her to go back to Ireland, where the shop would easily support her and the baby. When she railed at him for leaving her and the child destitute, he put down the phone.

Weeks passed before he made contact again. His tone had softened, and he wanted to meet her to discuss the future of the boy. He had a proposition for her.

He brought his new girlfriend, Marie, with him. She was no more than twenty, a timid girl who nodded her head while Patrick did the talking. He repeated that since he was getting married, he could not support her and the boy, but if Lucy wanted to go back to Ireland Marie and he would adopt him and bring him up as their own. Lucy was so angry she struck him with her fist and the pair fled the flat.

Her financial position became more desperate, and she started to drink again even though the doctor warned that alcohol could affect the baby she was still nursing.

She wrote to Leo McKenna for money and promised to repay him out of the estate of her missing brother Edward when he was officially pronounced dead. Patrick McKenna sent money by return post, saying it was a gift and there was no obligation to repay. He urged her to come home, telling her she was welcome to stay at Knockavoe until she got back on her feet.

The next time Patrick McLoughlin rang to inquire about their son, she was so desperate that she told him to get the necessary papers to adopt the boy, and she would sign them. A meeting was arranged at which Patrick appeared with his solicitor; she had to sign an undertaking that she was agreeable to have the boy brought up by his natural father. She would make no effort to contact the boy before he reached the age of majority, which was twenty-one years. Patrick signed a similar agreement that he would not reveal to the boy the identity of his real mother until he was twenty-one and then only if he first secured her written consent.

A distraught Lucy handed over her baby and all his toys and clothing to Patrick's young wife and walked out of the solicitor's office in tears. She went home to the flat, packed a few things in a suitcase, left the front door open so that neighbours could help themselves to what she had left behind, and walked to the station to get a train to the Holyhead ferry. She bought a bottle of gin and finished it on the sea trip to Dublin. She arrived in Mournebridge that evening, disillusioned, drunk, lonely and bitter.

She continued to drink to relieve the boredom of life in a small town as she tried to cope with the loneliness and emptiness that again filled her days and nights. The loss of the baby she had so unwillingly given away caused her great pain and remorse. She tried to console herself that even if Patrick McLaughlin no longer loved her, he doted on his son and would look after him well.

It was during one of those periods of loneliness and heavy drinking that she had one more fling, this time with a commercial traveller, a married man from Dublin whom she met while sipping gin in a hotel in Derry. She slept with him the very first night they met and, in the morning, lied that he was the best man she ever had. After that, every time he was in the area on business, he contacted her, and they carried on their affair in seedy hotel bedrooms in Derry and Donegal for more than a year. Then she discovered she was pregnant. He almost had a seizure when she told him.

She was not really surprised that she never saw him again, as she suspected from the start that he gave her a false name to make sure that if the relationship turned sour or if she became pregnant or any other complication arose, she could never trace him. She didn't care; it had never been more than a fling. Once she knew she was pregnant, the drinking stopped, and this time, she made up her mind there would be no slipping off to London or Dublin. She would stay put and have her baby at home, and to hell with the consequences. She was not the first girl to get caught, and she wouldn't be the last.

Lucy ignored the indignant stares and the gossip as her pregnancy progressed; she worked in the shop every day with the McKenna girl until swollen legs forced her to rest. She had another son, a blonde, blue-eyed boy whom she called Hans Dieter Muller, for in one of her darker moods she imagined she would someday leave this hellhole of a country and return to live in the land of her ancestors, the Mullers of Hoffenfeld.

Thereafter, her life revolved around the shop and the boy. She resigned herself to the fact that, like her grandmother and her mother, she was unlucky in love and vowed she would never compromise her independence again. There would be no more men in her life. She regretted the circumstances that forced her to part with her eldest child, but it was too late to do anything about that now because he had been legally adopted. She consoled herself with the thought that perhaps when he got a little older, the boy might come looking for her, but anxious as she was to see him, she honoured her legal undertaking not to contact him.

When miniskirts flooded the rag trade and took the fashion world by storm in the Sixties, the demand for formal wear by young people dropped dramatically, and Lucy had to let most of her dressmaking staff go. Big stores were mass-producing garments at a fraction of what she charged. Seven years after the war ended, her brother Edward was legally presumed dead, and his estate settled. She sold the shop to the McKennas, and when the proceeds were added to her brother's sizeable estate, she had sufficient means to take care of her son and live comfortably for the rest of her life.

Hans was very much a loner like his mother. She knew that his pals teased him about not having a father, and the taunts hurt him more than he showed. He concentrated on his studies and, like his grandmother Brigitta, turned out to be an exceptional student, taking top marks consistently for languages. In addition to Irish and English, he studied German, for the nuns advised Lucy that Continental languages would become very important if plans afoot to unify Europe after the war came to fruition.

Lucy teased him about the handsome young man he was and how he would turn all the girls' heads when he went to university in Belfast. She really hoped he would come out of his shell on the campus and get into the swing of student life. But her hopes were not realised. At student parties he talked about nothing except politics and got the reputation of being a complete and utter bore. He did not drink or smoke and spent all his pocket-money acquiring books on political movements, on politics and democracy, on the merits of the democratic process rather than passive resistance or violent confrontation as a means of overcoming corruption and tyranny.

He prided himself in being a disciple of Gandhi and had tremendous admiration for the Israelis and their struggle against the British to establish a homeland in Palestine. He read every book and newspaper article he could find on the decline of the British Empire and was conscious that as an Irishman his oppressed and long-suffering kinsmen had the honour of putting the first nail in the Empire's coffin when they fought and won the War of Independence in the early part of the century.

Among his student friends he acquired the reputation of being "a textbook revolutionary, the shadow of a gunman."

CHAPTER TWO

A TIME TO FIGHT

The Sixties were a period of great change in Ireland. Culturally the romance of the post-war years exemplified by the great musicals of the fifties gave way to a more rebellious age of Rock and Roll; restless youngsters looking for a different way of life asserted their independence though mass protest demonstrations against war in Vietnam and the threat posed to mankind by the build-up of stocks of nuclear weapons. It was the age of the Cold War, and no people and no country was safe from the threat of the nuclear bomb.

Out of this mass protest grew the Flower People, young people who set up communes throughout America and Europe, fuelled by alcohol, hash and LSD and a devil-may-care attitude to life itself, especially to authority. They did not care what the police forces or society as a whole thought of them—it was their way of escaping the reality of a world that after two World Wars had turned ugly again.

Hans was different from other people his age. He had no interest in music or the angry youngsters whose slogan was "Make Love, not War" and who battled with the police every weekend at "Ban the Bomb" marches. He had other more important things on his mind.

Nearly half a century after the 1916 Rebellion in Ireland and the Civil War that followed the partitioning of the country, Nationalists in the north who believed in a United Ireland were ruled by the iron fist of a Protestant majority, who in turn were terrified of being overwhelmed by the Roman Catholic majority in the country as a whole. The Northern Protestant majority held firm in their loyalty to the British Crown and the United Kingdom and manipulated politics in the province to ensure that the union with Britain would be maintained at all costs. In many cases, voting rights were denied to Nationalists, and where they did have a vote, electoral boundaries were blatantly manipulated to minimize Catholic influence, even in areas where Nationalists were in the majority. To protect themselves, Catholics congregated in particular areas of cities and towns, and this, in turn, created impoverished ghettos. These areas had no industries allocated to them, and with no work, thousands of men and boys had to emigrate to earn a living. The more people who left the ghettos, the easier it was for the Loyalist Protestants to maintain control of the political situation.

Taking a lead from the black Civil Rights movement in the United States in the Sixties, oppressed Northern Irish Nationalists launched a campaign of civil disobedience as part of a struggle to right the wrongs they felt had been committed against them.

This was the kind of movement that Hans felt he could subscribe to because this was an area in which he had done a lot of research while at college. He became actively involved in the Irish Civil Rights movement from the start. He organised protests inside the Protestant-controlled Queens University until the college authorities warned that if he caused any further disruption on campus, he would be suspended. But the student campaign attracted so much attention in the national and international media that when he ignored the threat of expulsion, the governors were afraid to act against him and other student movement leaders, even when they were pictured in newspapers grappling with police at barricades and roadblocks.

When the Unionist-controlled government at Stormont ordered the police to use heavy-handed tactics to put down the peaceful civil rights campaign, hundreds of supporters were beaten, jailed and threatened with internment without trial. The situation then changed. Remnants of the Irish Republican Army, which had largely lain dormant since the end of the struggle for Independence in the 1920s, procured weapons and explosives and started a guerilla war similar to the one in the early part of the century that forced the British out of southern Ireland.

The beginning of the new war in the North of Ireland coincided with a period in world history when the only major conflict was the Vietnam War, which had been going on for so long that the media had tired of Southeast Asia and were looking for something new to report on. Their prayers were answered with the conflict in Ireland where the Irish Republican Army, whose members could be counted in hundreds, pitted itself against the military might of the British Army. Under the spotlight of the world's press, an urban war unfolded on a scale not seen in Europe since the end of the Second World War. For the first time, the car bomb appeared on the streets. Family cars with boots filled with hundreds of pounds of explosives were detonated with sophisticated devices in areas where they did the maximum damage. The effect of the car bomb in crowded thoroughfares was devastating in terms of loss of life and destruction of property. As the conflict continued, the bombs got bigger and bigger and casualties among the police, army and civilians mounted.

The bombings were as spectacular as they were devastating; the Republicans who planted them often waited until the world's media were in position with cameras and microphones before they were detonated. And because of the car bomb, back-water cities like Derry and Belfast, which were hitherto unknown to the world outside Britain and Ireland, became household names.

When gunmen displaced the Civil Rights Campaign, Hans pulled back from the brink, still believing that Gandhi's civil disobedience was the way forward. He settled back into college and his studies long enough to complete his degree but refused to attend the conferring ceremony because it included the playing of the British national anthem.

He took part in major confrontation between Civil Rights marchers and the police that ended in street battles and riots. He was present at a huge protest in Derry on January 30, 1972, when a British Paratroop Regiment sent into the city to prevent civil disorder opened fire indiscriminately on Civil Rights marchers and killed thirteen unarmed civilians. This came to be known as Bloody Sunday.

After the killings, Hans's enthusiasm for peaceful protest waned. He believed that what happened in Derry was nothing short of mass murder.

He read and re-read his great-grandmother's account of what happened in Derry on that fateful day of the Corpus Christi procession in 1877 and decided nothing had changed. Believing the Civil Rights campaign to have failed, he joined the IRA with hundreds of other young men and swore to defend the Irish people against the brutality of the hated army of occupation.

He was among the first new recruits to be spirited away to remote areas of the Sperrin and Mourne Mountains for indoctrination and military training. They formed the nucleus of a new breed of guerilla fighters trained to operate not in remote country areas like their predecessors, the Fenians and the Irish Republican Brotherhood, but to engage in urban warfare in heavily populated areas.

They were given extensive instruction in the use of firearms—pistols, Belgian FN rifles, Russian Kalashnikov assault rifles and M1 carbines and powerful heavy caliber M-16s from America. They learned how to handle explosives and detonators and how to put together the devastating car bomb. They were taught basic principles governing the successful operation of a guerilla force, how to gather intelligence and, in particular, how to maintain security to protect their units and weapons.

Hans and his comrades were kept in the mountains for weeks until their training was complete then sent back to their home towns to recruit and train more Volunteers and form active service units.

While training in the mountains, Hans was no more than twenty miles from his hometown. When his mother asked where he had been, he lied that he had been in Dublin looking for a job, but her suspicions were not allayed because he seemed to know little or nothing about Dublin or the people who lived there, nor could he explain why efforts to find any kind of work had failed. It was not until he began to disappear for periods of two or three days at a time that she first suspected something sinister was going on.

Once, after an absence of three days, he asked her where exactly his great grandmother had spent her years hiding. They looked up the diaries, which referred to a farmhouse two or three miles up the mountainside from the village church in Crannamoe, County Derry.

Hans smiled: "I think that house is still there," he said. "I passed one just like it a couple of days ago."

When she demanded to know where he had been and what had brought him to such a remote part of Derry, he told her he was helping the Republicans to protect Catholic areas from attack by Loyalists.

"But the less you know, mother, the better," he warned her. "People are being picked off the streets at random and questioned about their families and friends."

"This family has had enough trouble," she said sternly. "I don't want you mixed up with these Republicans, for sooner or later, they will all come to a bad end."

But when she tried to get him to promise he would have nothing more to do with them, he said that he was an Irishman and proud of it and he would do his duty to his country.

Every time he went missing from home after that, even for a night, there was shooting or bombing somewhere in the area, or some building was burned down. Soldiers were killed, policemen were constantly under siege both in barracks and in their homes; punishment squads of Republicans were on the streets at night dealing with informers. Most of them had their kneecaps blown off as a warning, crippling them for life. If they were caught giving information to the police a second time, they were shot in the head.

Lucy realised the deadly game her son was playing. A new band of highly trained soldiers called the Special Air Services had been introduced into areas where the IRA was most active. This covert force operated completely independently of British Army Command in the North of Ireland. They were answerable to a higher authority in London. They moved around the border area, searching for Republicans and liquidating suspects. Because they had no contact with the police or with other regiments on routine patrol, it was inevitable that the SAS would make mistakes. Innocent people were killed, and on at least two occasions, they opened fire accidentally on regular army and police patrols whose path they inadvertently crossed during operations at night.

Lucy spent a lot of time on her knees praying that Hans would get some sense and give up the life into which he had allowed himself to be drawn.

One night while returning in the dark from a nearby shop, Lucy was ordered by a voice out of the blackness to stop, turn to face the wall, and place her hands against it. She put down the bag she was carrying and obeyed, frightened but still curious to see if it was the IRA. She was aware of somebody standing behind her and felt a pair of gloved hands under her armpits and moving slowly down her sides to her legs. There was a rustle as he rummaged through the plastic carrier bag. She heard him step back.

"On your way, madam," said the voice. When she turned around and picked up the bag, there was no sign of them. But she knew instinctively it was the SAS. That was the way they operated. She had seen nothing because public lighting had been switched off at night in the town since the bombings and shootings started to protect army and police patrols from ambush by the IRA. The only light reaching dark streets came through the windows of houses where curtains were not drawn. She hurried along towards home using a shortcut through a neighbour's garden to get there more quickly. As she approached her house, she saw the dark outline of two men kneeling on either side of the roadway and stopped instinctively. Another patrol.

"Keep going, Missus," said one of them. "But remember ye nivver saw nothing."

She started to walk again and passed between two men. They had rifles on their shoulders, barrels pointing upwards. They wore Balaclava helmets with slits for their eyes and mouth; they were not alone, for she heard rustling in the long grass nearby. She knew from the accents they were locals. This was Hans's gang, she was sure. Was he somewhere in the darkness watching her?

She turned around and whispered into the blackness: "The army is in the next street; they're just after searching me."

"We know," said the voice, "we're watching them. Go on home and don't come out again tonight."

In bed, Lucy lay awake, listening for gunfire. But the adversaries never made contact with one another that night, and she heard nothing until the front door opened sometime in the early hours of the morning. She thanked God he was back safe and fell asleep.

Hans knew exactly the risks he took and the dangerous game of cat and mouse he played. For some time, he had been trying to get the drop on an SAS patrol. The British Government boasted that they were the best anti-terrorist force in the world, and he knew that a successful hit on them would bring immense benefits to the IRA in terms of propaganda. Hans had no fear of the SAS. He was confident that the training he and his Volunteers had in urban warfare was as good as any given to the British force. He was probably far better educated than they were, and he had the advantage that this was his patch, his town, his people, and he knew every street corner and every ditch and tree. He would choose the time and the place to hit them, and when that opportunity came, he would make damn sure none of them survived to tell the tale.

Hans registered as unemployed after university and went twice a week to the local labour exchange to collect his benefit. This was his pocket money; his mother kept him at home for nothing. Mostly he bought books, for which he still had an insatiable appetite, but it also paid for trips across the border into Donegal to meet IRA officers from time to time. Otherwise, he spent his days on a bicycle around the town, visiting shops, meeting acquaintances, or lying on the riverbank on fine days reading newspapers.

He watched armoured cars coming and going from the town's police station, helicopters ferrying troops and materials to remote army outposts along the border that were dangerous to service overland. He familiarised himself with regimental markings on army trucks and uniforms and passed information about troop movements to IRA headquarters in Dublin. He was especially on the lookout for the parachute regiments who had been responsible for killing the Civil Rights marchers in Derry on Bloody Sunday. Hans regarded retribution for those killings as a priority. It was a score that had to be settled before the struggle for independence ended and he wanted to be the one to do it.

His unit had been supplied with FN rifles when it was formed, and explosives were procured from a cache hidden across the border in County Donegal. At his last meeting in Dublin, he had been promised delivery of a new weapon—an American rocket-propelled gun powerful enough to penetrate steel-plated personnel carriers. He was told that with proper training, it might even be possible to attack low-flying helicopters. Hans hoped it would also be powerful enough to blow a hole in the metal gates of the police station when the time came for an all-out assault.

For a short time, he got a job helping out as a substitute teacher in the local school and experienced first-hand the depth of hatred among the boys for the British Army and the police. There was stone throwing at the soldiers daily as the pupils went to and from school, despite warnings and threats of expulsion by their teachers if they were caught. The army, well aware that many of the schoolchildren were either in the IRA or had older members of the family in the organisation, retaliated by lining the boys up by the roadside for searches.

In the classroom the boys often discussed the activities of the army and what they got up to, especially their social activities and what pubs they drank in and where they went to find women. In this way, Hans picked up a lot of useful information. The youngsters knew what routes the patrols regularly took, the buildings they used as hiding places, and where they stopped to smoke or drink from their canteens; some of the boys even knew the first names of soldiers who stopped and searched them regularly. He got a blow-by-blow account every morning of what happened in their areas the previous night, and though he had to make allowance for the fact that some of the boys let their imagination run away with them, a lot of what he heard was good, solid intelligence.

When it was decided to form a new Company of Volunteers in West Tyrone Hans was the choice for OC He crossed the border into Donegal to meet his superiors who briefed him on how the company was to be structured to make sure security was not compromised, the tactics he was to employ, where weapon dumps were located and how to procure more when he needed them.

Thereafter, once a month, he was expected to attend meetings arranged by his Brigade Staff at which targets were identified and intelligence pooled. The main intelligence group for the organisation was located in the South of Ireland, near the capital city of Dublin. Information was co-ordinated by this group, which also had access to information from spies in London, from paid informers and from Republican "sleepers" working at the highest level of government in Dublin and Belfast. In this way intelligence officers were able to keep abreast of both political developments and military initiatives and take measures to counteract them.

It was during one of these briefing sessions that he first learned about a new explosive, Semtex, which had been bought in sizeable quantities from Yugoslavia. Used as a catalyst with more conventional fertilizer explosive it was very effective. Initially it had been bought for use against targets in London, because even a quantity small enough to fit into a holdall or backpack was capable of causing major structural damage. He requisitioned the new explosive for two targets that up to then had proved impenetrable.

The biggest problem Hans had when it came to attacking military and police establishments was the detonation devices. Timing devices such as watches, crude alarm clocks and even Mercury tilt switches had proved notoriously unreliable. He had lost three men to bombs that had gone off prematurely; in a few cases devices failed completely. A lot of planning and preparation went into bombing missions, and failure meant months of intelligence work down the drain, for it was nearly impossible to mount a second attack on the same target.

In the autumn of 1972, when he took the first delivery of Semtex, he was told about a new electronic device for safe, sure-fire detonation. It was called Trigger Release 1, or TR1 for short. It was based on an ordinary hand-held remote control for a television and had been developed for IRA sympathisers in America. With the modified zapper, a bomb could be detonated at a distance by remote control so long as it was within range of the radio signal.

When he took delivery of four TR1s, Hans went into the mountains to test them and found they had a 100 per cent success rate. For the first time, he was confident that bombs could be properly controlled from the moment they were planted until detonation. A Volunteer could wait to make sure civilians were clear of the target area but also had the option to detonate at any time if the British Army bomb disposal units attempted to disarm it. The only disadvantage was that at least one Volunteer had to remain in the vicinity of the target to use the zapper, as the radio signal would not operate beyond 150 yards. Where there were obstructions like buildings or even cars or trucks, the firing range was shorter, and there was always the danger that a Volunteer operating too close to the bomb would be caught in the blast.

Hans used the new device to detonate a car bomb in Mournebridge with devastating results. The vehicle was parked, the usual warning given to clear the area, and when the Army tried to move two robots up close to fire charges into the car boot where the bomb was packed, he pressed the zapper. Car, robots and several buildings disintegrated in a cloud of debris, dust and smoke. A week later, a Volunteer walked past the heavily fortified police station, set down a sports bag he was carrying, sauntered off and without even turning around, pressed the zapper. The explosion lifted the high fence of corrugated steel and barbed wire up into the air and it came down in a tangled mess on the roof of the fortified building. Inside the compound, vehicles burned furiously, and the dazed occupants grabbed their weapons, expecting an all-out attack.

In Derry, a young woman wheeling a baby in a pram walked through a security checkpoint outside an army barracks and emerged at the other side carrying the baby in her arms. By the time the sentry watching the CCTV monitor realised she had left the pram behind, it was too late. The woman used the RP1 to detonate four pounds of Semtex. The blast demolished the high protective fence and toppled a watchtower, killing one soldier and injuring eleven others.

At their next meeting, Hans reported that the new detonator and the Semtex were working like a dream. But he was advised to be cautious.

British intelligence already knew about the device and had electronics experts working on something to counteract it. They were testing an electronic sweep that operated like the zapper and triggered any bomb once the device came within range. If a Volunteer was delivering a bomb and got caught in a sweep, it would detonate.

However, the Army ran into a problem. According to intelligence supplied to the IRA, the mobile electronic sweep also switched televisions and video recorders on and off in homes so that people watching their favourite programmes knew when the army was nearby.

Hans was advised to postpone further bomb attacks because a second, more sophisticated version of the TR1 was on the way from America. The chip used in the new zapper had just been developed and would not even be available to the electronics industry for six to nine months.

Hans was impatient as he had two prime targets already marked down for attack. One was the police station that had only suffered superficial damage in the most recent bombing, the other a 200-year-old stone fort built on one side of the river running through the town, used by the Army as their headquarters.

The fort was one of the most strategic positions the British had in the whole of the North of Ireland with a commanding view of the town and the countryside for miles in every direction. It was also the Army communications centre covering one third of the area occupied by British forces in the North. It was regarded as impregnable.

As a target, the police station was just as difficult. It could only be approached from the front, and sentries on duty had a clear view of everything within a couple of hundred yards. Huge concrete blocks were positioned to ensure that no car bomb could get close enough to do real damage. When police patrols came and went, armed officers took up positions behind concrete bollards to protect the gates as they quickly opened and shut. Tall houses on either side had been commandeered to make sure no attack came from that quarter and at the rear there was a concrete wall that the Dambusters would have found hard to breach.

Hans decided that his first major attack would be against the police station and devised a daring plan to penetrate the fortified building. If he could not attack it from the outside, then he had to get a bomb inside. If he succeeded he had the means to detonate it from outside with the RP2. He was confident his plan would work.

He had twenty pounds of Semtex and an electronic detonator packed into a metal beer keg. Two Volunteers crossed the border into the South, hijacked a helicopter and ordered the pilot to fly to a field a couple of miles from Mournebridge. Hans and a Volunteer put the beer keg aboard and ordered the terrified pilot at gunpoint to fly them over the town.

Radar in the fort picked up something flying towards them, and the Army ran a routine check with headquarters to try and identify it. The British soon established it was not one of their own but thought it might be an Army helicopter from the Irish Republic on border patrol.

They were still checking with Army Headquarters in Dublin when the hijacked helicopter veered away from the river that formed the border between North and South and, within seconds, reached the town square. Hans put a gun to the pilot's head and ordered him to hover over the police station, clearly identifiable by the high barricade surrounding it. When they were directly overhead, he shouted, "Now!" and his companion rolled the cylinder bomb out of the open door.

"Get the hell out of here," he roared at the pilot.

He pressed the zapper. Nothing happened. He pressed it again and again, frantically pointing it at the fast-disappearing target. Still, nothing happened. He took out his pistol and put it to the terrified pilot's head.

"Turn back and make another run," he shouted, and when the pilot pleaded with him that it would be suicide to try it again, he pushed the cold barrel of the gun into the man's ear and motioned with his arm to turn around. The helicopter banked and made a second run over the station. By this time, the police had identified the aircraft as a bandit, and when they passed over the barracks a second time, the terrified pilot could see soldiers taking up firing positions on the walls of the army fort nearby.

Hans saw the hole in the barrack roof where the bomb went through. They had hit the target right on the button. He pressed the zapper numbers

8-9 over and over again, disregarding the fact that they were right on top of the target and close enough to get caught in the blast themselves if the bomb went off. Nothing happened.

"You stupid bastard!" shouted the terrified pilot. "If that bomb goes off, it will blow us all to kingdom come!"

"Mind your own fucking business," Hans screamed back at him, frantically hitting the zapper against the side of his seat and pressing the buttons over and over again, cursing the stupid piece of plastic.

"Keep your fucking mouth shut and head for the border or you're a dead man!" he shouted and stood on the zapper with his shoe.

The pilot flew back along the river until he was safely over the border. Hans pointed to a field and told him to put them down.

"Don't attempt to use your radio to call for help," he warned him. "If we get caught by the police, ye'll open yer door some night to find a punishment squad outside. Do ye hear?" The shaking pilot nodded.

The two discarded their green Balaclava helmets and weapons in a ditch beside the helicopter and disappeared into the countryside. When he was sure they were far enough away, the pilot radioed his position and called for help.

The police station was evacuated while the army disarmed the unexploded cylinder bomb. The metal beer keg was undamaged, and explosive experts recovered the receiver for the IRA's latest electronic detonator, the TR2, intact. Hans was angry, for he knew there would be no second chance. His superiors were furious with him when they realised he had handed a unique piece of new equipment to the enemy.

As it turned out, the failure of the operation was more than compensated for by the worldwide publicity generated by this first aerial bomb attack. It also confirmed to the London Government that while the British Army was holding its own against the terrorists on the ground, it was losing the propaganda war.

CHAPTER THREE

A TIME TO KILL

Hans decided to hit the second target—the great stone walled army fort—immediately, for he was worried about the loss of the RP2 and felt sure it would not take the British Army long to come up with some device to jam the signal.

The Army emplacement had been attacked before. His predecessor had a car bomb placed against the front wall and the ensuing blast shook the place up a bit. Since then, however, a huge steel door operated by a hydraulic system had been installed and iron spikes were concreted into the ground for thirty yards around it. There was only one entrance—a narrow walled corridor through which patrols came and went quickly.

The door was designed like a drawbridge. It took twenty seconds to lift it high enough to let vehicles through and the same time to close it, but it also had a guillotine device and when there was any danger the ten-ton monstrosity dropped like a stone, crushing anything under it. He had seen it operating many times when vehicles were entering or leaving. When it was open there was just enough time to fire one burst from a machine gun or a rocket if you had one but it left the attacker completely exposed to riflemen on the turrets.

Hans felt local knowledge and the TR2 had opened up new possibilities. For some time he had been considering an attack from the river side of the fort where a high granite wall sloped steeply from the water's edge to old battlements eighty feet above. It was the last place the army would expect an attack to come from because the walls were unscaleable and anybody stupid enough to try to climb it could be picked off by one of the sentries before he could get anywhere near the top.

Growing up in the town he and his pals had used that stretch of river for swimming on summer days and were familiar with every foot of it.

As kids they had spent countless hours etching their names into the slabs of granite with nails.

Two large pipes protruding from the bottom of the wall disgorged raw sewage into the river. On hot summer days the boys cursed the soldiers for the stench of the effluent hung in the languid air forcing the bathers to move further upstream away from their favourite spot.

Steel doors fixed to the end of the pipes swung on hinges. The weight of the doors kept them in the closed position until sewage built up inside the pipe, and pressure forced them open to release the foul contents. The boys piled stones against the metal to keep the sewage in, hoping it might back up all the way into the barracks and the soldiers would get a taste of their own crap for a change.

Hans devised an ingenious plan to get a bomb into the heart of the fort using the sewage outlet, but the diameter of the pipes dictated that only a small bomb could be used. He had thought about it before, but the amount of conventional explosive capable of going into the pipe was so small that any blast would have been insignificant, and he could not get reliable detonators that would work in water. As with the aerial attack on the police station, he knew he would get one chance and one chance only. If it did not work the first time, the ploy would be discovered and could never be tried again.

The advent of the powerful explosive Semtex and the electronic zapper had opened up new possibilities. His idea was to put one bomb in each pipe, then block the outlet doors so that the bombs would float upward on the rising tide of sewage until they reached the living quarters of the soldiers. When they were in position, he would use his new zapper to detonate them. Semtex was the key—it was so compact that even a small quantity was powerful enough to cause major damage.

The concept was simple, but it needed a lot of planning and preparatory work. Hans briefed two Volunteers. Their job was to observe the rear of the fort over a period of several weeks and come up with a reliable estimate of the rate of flow of sewage from the pipes. Because cameras protected the fort, this was difficult. Any suspicious movement would result in the two men being hauled in for questioning and this could jeopardise the attack.

Two IRA scouts took every opportunity they could to stroll with girlfriends along the riverbank opposite the rear of the fort, stopping when the weather was fine. They also spent hours with binoculars sitting at the bathroom window of a house across the river watching sewage burst from the pipes at regular intervals.

Because of the diameter of the pipes and the variable speed of the flow it was difficult to estimate with any degree of accuracy from a distance how much sewage was released into the river. The rate fluctuated considerably, depending on the number of men in the barracks. The pipes were also used as a storm drain so that rainfall also added to the flow.

The two men reported back to Hans, explaining the difficulties and sought permission to make closer inspection of the pipes under cover of darkness. The first visit went without a hitch and then a second and finally they made one last sortie just before dawn—all in the same week.

The best estimate was a flow of between 120 and 150 gallons an hour from the main pipe and about seventy to eighty from the smaller one over a twenty-four-hour period, which did not include rainfall. He studied the figures to make sure they made sense. Even allowing for variation in flow, the time of day, rainfall and other factors, Hans felt that the degree of accuracy of their estimate was probably seventy-five per cent, good enough for his purposes. He figured that if the main outlet pipe could be blocked, it would take about fifteen hours to fill completely to the top. The second smaller outlet would take longer.

The timing of the attack was crucial. A Paratroop Regiment was due back in the area for another tour of duty. Hans had been waiting patiently for their return.

The Brigade Staff asked him to delay any attack to coincide with ceremonies in Dublin to commemorate the Rising in 1916. He was not happy about waiting but had no option but to agree.

At dusk on Easter Sunday, he and three Volunteers strolled along the river at dusk with rods and knapsacks as if returning from a day's fishing upstream. It was dark when they reached the wall of the fort, and they paused for a while to make sure they had not been spotted. They worked quickly and quietly.

The bombs consisted of two small gas cylinders into which Semtex had been packed. A screw top was fitted with a special valve through which air had been pumped under pressure to give the cylinders buoyancy.

They forced the hinged doors open, placed the bombs inside and while two men held the metal gates shut tight Hans jammed the hinges with crowbars so that no matter how much pressure built up behind them the doors would not open. They picked up their gear and before they moved off along the riverside in darkness heard the cylinders knocking off the inside of the steel pipes; the bombs were on their way.

For the first time in his life, Hans felt nervous as he closed the door of his mother's house behind him that Easter Monday morning and set out to walk to the church for Mass. He intended to detonate the bombs as he passed the barracks just before nine o'clock but decided at the last minute to give the second bomb a chance to get into a better position by delaying until he was on his way home again.

When he reached the church, a riot was in full swing. Police tried to arrest youths selling flags commemorating the Easter Rising, which were banned by law. Other churchgoers rescued the youths, and the police drew their batons and charged. They made six arrests in all. Hans watched them being taken away and followed the police vans into adjoining streets to make sure they were going to the police station and not the army fort.

After Mass he put his hands in his pockets and sauntered off towards the fort which was on his way home. As he passed the iron girders guarding the great steel gate, he found the off/on button on the RP2 in his pocket with his forefinger and flicked it. His body tensed as he searched with his fingertips for the 1 and 6 buttons.

"Remember 1916!" he said to himself and pressed the two buttons simultaneously.

W—H—O—O—O—O—O—M—B—A—H !

The deafening explosion came with a flash of red light and flame; Hans felt his eyebrows and the hair on the front of his head singe. The ground shook under him with such force that he was lifted off his feet and thrown onto his back on the roadway. He opened his eyes to see debris falling from the sky. Windows and doors from houses opposite the fort were sucked out and floated like leaves overhead. Chimneys of nearby houses toppled over and crashed through roofs, splintering wooden rafters and demolishing ceilings and floors.

People on their way home from Mass screamed and covered their faces to try and protect themselves from the searing heat of the blast; flaming debris and ash fell from the sky around them. Hans rolled over on his stomach and tucked his head under his arms and shoulders for protection. People ran from their homes into the streets as walls and masonry crumbled about them. There was panic all around him; people buried under rubble and the flaming ash screamed for help.

Still on the ground Hans fumbled in his pocket until his hand closed over the zapper. He was shaking so much he could not find the 7 and 2 buttons to detonate the second bomb. He let his fingers move around pressing everything he touched.

W—H—O—O—O—O—M—B—A—H !

There was another deafening explosion and debris still falling after the first blast went up into the air again; buildings that had withstood the initial blast collapsed in a heap of rubble. There followed a great rumbling noise that grew louder and louder as if an earthquake was beginning, then slowly died away like thunder in the distance. Hans got up, and as he and others ran for cover, he could hear shouting from inside the fort. A great cloud of smoke and dust hung in the morning sky blotting out the sun.

The bombs had not just destroyed the fort—they had rocked the town to its very foundations. People enjoying a late morning in bed on the traditional Easter holiday got a rude awakening as chimneys and roofs tumbled through bedroom ceilings and landed on top of them. The shock waves burst water and gas pipes and blew away the town's electricity supply; walls cracked and collapsed, exposing the interiors of bedrooms and their panic-stricken occupants to full view. People who had been up and about on the streets stumbled around in a daze, covered in cuts and bruises from flying glass and burned by fire flashes and flaming debris.

Hans brushed the dust from his clothes, wiped the blood from a cut to the back of his hand and struggled to his feet. The granite slabs at the entrance to the fort that had stood for a hundred years had collapsed, leaving only the great iron gate and its metal frame still standing.

Hans was stunned by the force of the blast. He never dreamed such small bombs could have been so devastating; the town looked as if an earthquake had hit it. He had left himself so close to the blast that he could easily have been killed.

He edged away from the scene. His face and neck smarted from the burns. Across the river astonished townspeople who had escaped the explosions gathered to see the devastation. The great granite wall that had protected the army base since it was built a century before had disintegrated and tumbled into the river and, with it, more than half of the parade ground. The communications mast and its forest of antennae were buried under rubble. The debris formed a dam across the river, holding back the water. In what remained of the fort, vehicles were blazing furiously. Soldiers walked around in a daze; officers screamed at them to take cover and secure the fort against attack.

Hans forgot about his singed hair and the burns on his face and neck as he viewed the demolished fort from a distance. The bombs could not have done all that damage on their own. The Army must have had some kind of explosives or maybe tanks of petrol stored somewhere behind the wall. Even Semtex could not have caused such devastation. The only other explanation was a build-up of methane gas from the trapped sewage that ignited with the bombs. Whatever the reason, the results had been spectacular, and he knew it would turn out to be a major propaganda coup.

He had demolished the Paratroop Regiment's base with twenty pounds of Semtex and a bit of canny planning. He felt good.

When the sound of fire brigades and ambulances filled the air, and the first medical teams arrived to tend to the casualties, he crossed the town bridge and walked towards his house. As he crossed, he calmly took the RP2 detonator from his pocket and dropped it into the water.

He was prepared for a barrage of questions from his mother for she knew of his involvement with the IRA. But she wasn't in the house, and he wondered where she was when the bombs went off. He went to his room, switched on both the radio and television and lay down on the bed. Only when cameras started flashing live film onto television screens that evening did the full impact of what happened begin to emerge. Before the day was out, the town was crawling with television crews and newspaper reporters from all over the world.

The blast and the killing of the soldiers, and the destruction of the town brought condemnation from politicians of all shades and church leaders of every denomination.

"They can condemn till the cows come home," Hans told his mother, "but there will be no tears shed for the Paratroopers. They did their worst on Bloody Sunday, and they have paid the price."

Journalists speculated that the death toll among members of the Parachute Regiment was in double figures. Five civilians, including three local girls who had been in the fort with the soldiers, also died; hundreds of townspeople were injured by the blast, caused, according to reliable sources, by the biggest bomb ever planted by the IRA —"probably in the region of 3,000 lbs".

Reliable sources be damned, thought Hans. What would they say if they knew that twenty pounds of Semtex did all that damage, that most of the soldiers were killed by their own shit? The more he thought about it, the more he was convinced that it was the methane gas in the sewage pipes that caused the fireball.

It appeared that soldiers servicing and refuelling vehicles in the parade ground had been killed immediately. But most of the troops were in the living quarters and restrooms when the explosion came and were saved by the stout stone interior walls that shielded them from the full force of the blasts. The British Government Cabinet Security Committee issued a statement: "A preliminary examination of the scene indicates that there was no breach of security at the fort. The explosion may have been caused by an underground gas leak."

While emergency services and Volunteers dealt with the aftermath, Special Branch police started a systematic series of raids on the homes of Republican families and arrested upwards of a hundred men, women and young people for questioning about the bombings. Some Volunteers were caught in the net in the general swoop, for a lot of them were active in Sinn Féin, the political wing of the Irish Republican Army and were known to the police. His second-in-command, the teacher Brendan Mullan, was arrested in the swoop, but he had witnesses to prove that he was miles away from the fort at the time playing golf.

The police raided a few houses in his street but never came near Hans's home. He heard the front door opening and closing, and when he came downstairs to have something to eat that night, he could see fear in his mother's eyes.

"There are a lot of sad families in this town, and I know you're the cause of it," she said coldly.

He made no answer, and they ate in silence. Lucy suspected his gang was responsible for what happened at the fort but found it hard to believe that her son could be a party to so much devastation, so much carnage. Where did all that hatred, all that cunning, come from? She remembered his father as a harmless, gutless man who did not even have the courage to face his responsibilities. What sort of young man could sit there calmly eating his dinner, knowing what he had done? If he had planned the explosions, he was a mass murderer, and a hypocrite. He had gone to Mass that morning and, on his way home, killed God knows how many people and wrecked hundreds of lives. She remembered her grandmother's diary and what she wrote about the Fenian Eamonn McKee, "a born killer, who justified his bloody work by claiming he did it in the name of God and the Irish people".

She wondered what granny Marita would have thought if she was alive this day knowing that her own great-grandson was as much a murderer as Eamonn McKee, as cruel and ruthless as the men who came to her peaceful valley home a hundred years before and raped and murdered her family.

❁

At midnight, the IRA issued a statement in Dublin:

At 11.55 a.m. today Volunteers from the North Tyrone Battalion of the Irish Republican Army carried out a bomb attack on the British Army Signals Headquarters in Mournebridge, Co. Tyrone. The fort was almost completely destroyed in the operation and casualties were heavy. The attack force sustained no casualties. P. O Neill, Rúnaí.

Damage to the army base was so bad that it had to be abandoned. Two officers and seven soldiers had been killed, five civilians died, and more than 200 townspeople were injured. The Army were satisfied that it was the work of the IRA, and investigations continued into how two powerful bombs were planted inside the fort. The high-profile attack filled television screens all over the world, and it was followed by a spate of mortar attacks by the IRA on police stations and army outposts along the border. In London, two women parked a van near the Parliament buildings at Westminster, and members of the Government War Cabinet had to dive for cover as a barrage of mortar bombs fired through the open roof of the vehicle exploded outside the window while a meeting was in progress in the Cabinet Room.

Senior officers in both the British Army and the Police Special Branch in England and Ireland were summoned to a top-level meeting in Scotland to formulate a new plan to combat the terrorists, but the helicopter carrying the officers from Ireland to the meeting crashed on a Scottish hillside, killing everybody on board. Nobody knew for sure what caused the loss of the helicopter, but the IRA claimed they had destroyed it in the air. Years afterwards, an inquiry into the crash reported that it was due to pilot error.

CHAPTER FOUR

A TIME TO DIE

The IRA felt for the first time that they were winning the war. Hans stood down his unit on the instructions of his superiors for they did not want any setbacks to mar the propaganda bonanza that came after the destruction of the fort and the loss of the helicopter. The British Army now had no base in the town, which was a great moral victory for the IRA but the police were leaning heavily on informers using threats and bribes to get information.

While Volunteers were moving weapons to a safe place the following week three of them were caught in an open field in the middle of the night and shot dead by an undercover SAS team. This was exactly what Hans had been trying to avoid and it was the turn of the British Army propaganda machine to get their own back. The papers were full of informal briefings from unofficial Army sources stating that the three shot dead by the SAS were the bombers of the army fort.

The IRA issued a statement to the effect that the Volunteers had been summarily executed by the SAS. The rifles they had been moving were still packed in the same wooden boxes in which they had arrived in Ireland months before. There was no ammunition with the rifles so that the three Volunteers had not returned fire when attacked. They had tried to surrender but had been executed as part of the British Army's "shoot to kill" policy. Hans knew the police had bought good information from an informer about the arms and brought in an SAS squad to do the killing.

Thousands of people lined the streets for the funerals of the young Volunteers. The local Catholic priest refused to say Requiem Mass for the dead until an undertaking was given that flags would be removed from the coffins at the church gate and there would be no shots fired in the graveyard at the burial, but after dark that same night, a four-man firing party slipped into the graveyard and fired a volley over the graves as a mark of respect to their fallen comrades.

Hans was angry at the loss of the three men and wanted to retaliate immediately, but the "stand down" order remained in force. Police stepped up raids and surveillance and anybody associated with the men who had been shot was hauled to the police barracks for questioning. In the widespread search of homes that followed, more weapons were found, and some members of his unit were arrested and charged with being members of the IRA. The Volunteers in custody took their punishment but kept their silence so that the remainder of the unit remained intact.

Hans was not idle during the period of enforced lull in activity that followed the shootings and arrests. He was already making plans for his next attack, this time on the police barracks. The element of surprise had gone since the fiasco with the helicopter bomb. The next attempt would have to come from a full-frontal attack, which could be costly in terms of the loss of Volunteers. He regarded the heavily fortified police station as the last bastion of English rule in the town, and if it could be destroyed, the IRA would have virtually a free hand to control the area.

By the time the green light was given to resume operations, he accepted that it was virtually impossible to attack the police outpost from the inside. Since the destruction of the army fort, more elaborate security arrangements had been put in place, including the construction of high lookout towers at the front and rear.

There was no way of getting a bomb close to the building. He had looked at all the possibilities and the only thing left to try was a car bomb parked as close as possible in the open square where the police station was situated. To have any real impact, it would take a huge bomb and, even then, one specially designed so that the blast was directed laterally rather than upwards. Otherwise, it would demolish most of the old houses around the square while causing only minimal damage to the police station. More importantly, there would have to be a substantial warning period so that the houses could be cleared of civilians to avoid a lot of casualties. The longer the warning period, however, the more time the

Army had to destroy a bomb before detonation.

Once the decision to attack was taken, Hans and members of the unit began to assemble the materials—fertiliser, Semtex and the detonator. Hans and Brendan Mullan brought the explosives across the border from the Republic in small quantities concealed under the leather saddles of their bicycles.

He persuaded a sympathetic farmer to let them use his milking parlour to assemble the bomb and install it in a van. It was an ideal location, just off a busy road and two miles from the town. The IRA sent two explosive experts from Belfast to assemble the bomb and test the RP2 to make sure there was no foul-up. They built the bomb inside the van bit-by-bit, carefully wired it and reinforced the roof of the vehicle with steel plating to deflect the natural upward force of the blast laterally. The RP2 was set to trigger on the 'James Bond' command—007.

When they had finished the job, the two men took off for Belfast on their motorcycle, and Hans was glad to see the back of them; he found it hard to trust people he knew nothing about.

The next day he had the van driven from the farm to a garage in the town and it was parked outside with other vehicles on the pretence that it was waiting for repair.

He collected it early next morning and drove towards the square, eager to get there before the place filled with parked cars. He needed to position the van as close as possible to the police station, with the rear pointing at the target. When he arrived, it was obvious some vehicles had been parked there all night, but there was still plenty of space for the van.

He parked it beside a container truck that he thought might help shield some of the old houses on one side of the square. A quick look around showed no police movement; the daily round of patrols had not yet begun.

Leaving the engine running Hans got out of the van and knelt beside one of the wheels as if to check for a flat tyre. All the tyres looked as if they needed air, so laden down was the vehicle with the huge bomb. He switched off the engine, took a tool kit from the cab and began to remove one of the wheels. He needed time to have a good look around and make sure other vehicles already parked would not shield the barracks from the blast.

The jack wouldn't lift because the van was overloaded. He stood looking at it for a while and then left as if he was going for help. There was nobody about; it was a perfect time to find a phone, put over the warning and get into position to blow the bomb.

He had only gone a few yards when he heard a shout: "Stay where you are or we'll shoot!"

Hans halted the forward motion of his body and stood still, arms by his sides. His heart stopped beating for a moment and he held his breath.

Though he had no idea where the voice was coming from it was clearly directed at him. Inside his head pulses of electricity surged through his brain as he tried to get a mental picture of what was going on. When the buzzing in his head ceased, he muttered to himself: "Probably just a routine check."

The voice was behind him, coming from a line of parked cars. Maybe the police had spotted him parking the van and radioed a patrol to check him out.

His head was telling him one thing, but he had a feeling in the pit of his stomach that it was more than just a routine check. Were they lying in wait for him? His brain began to race again, like a computer out of control. Did they have information from an informer about the bomb van? If so he was caught red-handed.

"Slow down!" he ordered his brain. "Slow down and think it through!" Only two Volunteers apart from himself knew about the bomb and the target. Well, not quite, as there were the two "experts" sent to help him assemble it. They didn't know the target, but they did know the van. If there was a leak of information, that was the most likely source; perhaps they had stopped in some pub. where a drink too many had loosened their tongues.

"Turn around slowly and put your hands on the roof of the van," said the voice.

An English accent, but was it an officer or a squaddie? Was it the Army?

Parachute Regiment? He could not be sure. Whoever they were, either they had been lying in wait and knew all about the attack, or they were about to do a routine check on the van and would discover the explosives in any case. The ball was in their court for the moment.

What bothered him most was that he could not get a proper fix on where the voice was coming from. When he put his hands on top of the van, the voice should have been in front of him, but there was nobody in view. About fifty yards away was a broken line of cars parked along one side of the square and beyond were high terraced houses with facades covered in various shades of red and green ivy.

The soldiers might be lying on the footpath behind the cars, but he felt sure he could not have missed them as he drove into the square. More likely they had been hiding inside the houses. If that was so they did have information; they had been in position for some time, and he was trapped. He heard movement behind him and recognised the whine of the engines of armoured personnel carriers. Their arrival confirmed his worst fears. He had driven the van into an ambush.

Strangely enough, once he realised he was cornered, Hans calmed down. He breathed more easily, leaning against the van, and he could no longer hear his heart pounding in his ears. He tried to recall what he had been taught in training about a situation like this. He should be able to remember.

"If you are trapped," he recalled, *"Get out in one piece, take the prison rap and live to fight another day."*

But there were situations where this was not possible. Volunteers had been executed by punishment squads for abandoning bombs on crowded streets to save their own skins and leaving them to go off without warning. Similarly, an OC who escaped from a tight spot and left his Volunteers to take the rap faced an IRA court martial. This was different; if it was the SAS, he was going to be shot one way or another—retribution for the destruction of the army fort.

He could see clearly over the van roof. There was an exit street in the corner of the square where there was no sign of activity at all. Surely they wouldn't be stupid enough to leave it unguarded?

There was still a slim chance that it was only a routine check; maybe they were just suspicious of the van. If he made a run for the unguarded exit, he needed to cover about 100 yards to reach safety. Part of the way had parked cars between him and the soldiers. If he could get to that exit, he would detonate the bomb and in the chaos he might even have a chance of escape. But a no-warning bomb like this would cause scores of civilian casualties.

He recalled his training: *Don't abandon a ticking bomb in a busy street just to save your own skin.*

It could be they had left him an avenue of escape in the hope he would take it and he would be shot before he got twenty yards from the van. That way, there would be no bomb blast. He had learned from experience to trust his own intuition, and in this case, he had a gut feeling that, one way or another, he was not going to get out of the square alive.

He pictured a huddle of Intelligence Officers somewhere nearby controlling the situation. They had their plan carefully worked out. They had the bomber in their sights and would dispose of him at the appropriate time.

They also had a major problem on their hands—how to make certain the bomb was defused. If it did go off and it was discovered that the Army knew about the operation in advance, a lot of questions would be asked about why the van had been allowed into the heart of the town in the first place when it could have been apprehended before it got there.

"So they need to get me to defuse the bomb," Hans said to himself. Bad and all as his situation was, he still managed a smile when he thought about it. They had set up the game but made the mistake of leaving him one throw of the dice. Let them make the move and who knows what mistakes they might make.

"Do you have a weapon on you?" shouted the voice. This was no squaddie, but a youngish officer, upper-middle-class accent, a touch of Scottish, maybe even Irish in it. Lots of Paddies from the South of Ireland joined the British Army. Hans did not answer.

He had no weapon, but they did not know that. They would assume he had but if they wanted to find out for sure, they would have to come and search him. Why make it easy for them? If they shot him in the back and no weapon was found, there would be more embarrassing questions about a shoot-to-kill policy. And if they came and dragged him away, there was always the chance that once he got clear of the van, he might get his fingers to the zapper in his shirt pocket and blow it. He would settle for that and prison camp for a couple of years.

"We know you have a bomb in the van, Paddy," said the voice.

Hans knew for certain now that he had walked into a trap. They had good information, but where did they get it? It would be up to his second-in-command, Brendan Mullan, to deal with that. He hoped Brendan would check out the two "Belfast experts" before he started pointing the finger at any of his own men.

He was angry at the prospect that the unit's security had been so badly compromised by the outsiders. It was the Brigade staff that had insisted on the pair from Belfast; otherwise, Hans's Volunteers would have put the bomb together themselves. After all the attention he had paid to security, those two clowns had handed the British Army their best propaganda stunt for a long, long time. An IRA Commander—he would be labelled the man who had planned the attack on the army fort—was caught red-handed planting another bomb. And as a bonus, the army could claim credit for saving the town from destruction by defusing the most powerful bomb the terrorists had ever assembled.

Hans put his hands in the air and slowly turned around to face the voice.

"Keep your hands on the van, Paddy!"

"Turn around again or we'll shoot!"

The voice had lost its cool. The young officer was jittery.

Hans stayed put, leaning his back against the van, fingers interlocked on top of his head. He could see soldiers kneeling on the footpath behind the parked cars, guns trained on him. There was movement on the upper floors of one of the houses. That's where the voice was coming from: an open window on the third floor, a good vantage point overlooking the scene.

More armoured cars arrived and blocked off side streets, clearing them of passers-by who had stopped to see what was going on. Word had got out that something big was happening in the square. Brendan Mullan would hear soon enough and if there was time maybe he could get a diversionary action going.

He knew he was being unrealistic, grasping at straws, for the area around the square was saturated with soldiers. His only hope of getting out alive rested with the chance of some kind of intervention.

"Stay where you are," screamed the voice. "You will follow my instructions to the letter, or you will be shot. For the last time I am ordering you to turn around and face the vehicle."

He made no move. He could hear the squawking of their radios. The bastard was in a fix and desperately seeking further instructions. There was no way they were going to shoot him in full view of onlookers. Somebody out there would be running a video camera, and a "live execution" would end up on every television screen in the world. No way were they going to shoot him—at least not yet. The flurry of squawking stopped.

Hans cleared his throat. "You have nineteen minutes to clear the area," he shouted. He was surprised at how cool his voice sounded. "Clear all premises in the square."

There was a brief silence.

"Nobody is going anywhere, Paddy," said the officer, his voice clipped and authoritative again. "If the bomb goes off, you are the only one who will have bought it."

"Clear the area, or there will be a lot of civilian casualties," Hans shouted, making sure onlookers appearing in the side streets could hear him. Some of them were already shouting at the soldiers to get people out of the houses. Police pushed the crowd further back into the side streets, away from the scene.

"There isn't going to be any blast, Paddy. You are going to be a good chap and disarm the bomb for us and spend the rest of your fucking life in a cosy cell at a prison holiday camp." New man, new voice this time. Probably somebody from the bomb disposal squad.

"Now I'm going to tell you exactly what to do," said the voice. He spoke as if giving instructions to a child.

"First, you can take your hands off your head and relax. Then move slowly to the rear of the vehicle and open the doors."

When Hans made no move at all, the voice said: "Be a good chap now and do as you are told."

"You have fourteen minutes to clear the area," he shouted back. "You hear me? Fourteen minutes." More squawking on the radio. Captain Cool was not sure what to do next.

Hans heard a whirring noise from one of the side streets. A robot came into view, moving slowly along the roadway until it drew level with the rear of the van. It made a right turn and came straight for the bomb vehicle. They were going to put a charge into the van to destroy the detonation device.

He put his hands on his head and walked slowly towards the bogey, bumping along on the uneven surface towards him. The officer screamed at him to stay where he was or he would be shot.

Hans kept going, and when he met the robot, he pushed it with his foot until it toppled over on its side. He walked back to the van. The only noise in the square was the whirring of the robot, wheels spinning at full speed, going nowhere.

A cheer went up in one of the side streets and Hans smiled. He was centre stage at the best show in town a real live Mexican stand-off. The adrenaline was pumping. Jesus, he was beginning to enjoy himself.

"You have eleven minutes to clear the area," he called out loudly so that both soldiers and spectators could hear above the whine of the robot. "You hear me? Eleven minutes."

Standing among the crowd on a side street, Brendan Mullan admired Hans's nerves. The OC was a born soldier, more than that, a born leader, but his days as top man in the unit were numbered, one way or another.

"He is one cool customer," he said to the people standing beside him. He knew Hans faced a life sentence in jail unless the soldiers decided to execute him before the morning was over.

"He is one fucking idiot," said a man behind. "He'll be brown bread by the time this is over."

Mullen could not understand Hans's strategy. There was no timing device on the bomb. It had been rigged to operate with a zapper, so what was he playing at? He had something up his sleeve but what the hell was it?

As second-in-command, he would have to pick up the pieces in the aftermath. Somebody had sold them down the river and Hans had driven the bomb into a trap. There were serious questions to be answered about the breach of security. Only Hans, himself and two Volunteers knew about the van. If one of the two did not own up he would have no alternative but to shoot both of them. That was another day's work.

The Army negotiator was silent. They were trying to figure out what to do next.

Hans felt like something to calm his nerves. If he smoked, he would have lit up at a time like this.

He knew it would take a miracle to get him out of his predicament. He didn't believe in miracles. Even though the soldiers had their rifles trained on him and one of them could squeeze the trigger at any moment and kill him, so long as he was in control of the bomb, he had the whip hand. His mind was as clear as a bell, and he had a curious sense of elation like at college when he experimented with LSD. He could feel the adrenaline pumping through his veins like a drug.

"You have eight minutes to clear the area," he shouted, breaking the silence. "Eight minutes!" he repeated. He had to keep the pressure on.

No response from the voice this time. It suddenly dawned on him that he could be living out the last minutes of his life. Who would tell his mother? He wondered if she was somewhere in the town, shopping. Maybe she already knew and was standing among the crowd in one of the side streets. Unlikely, though, for she had a saying that trouble came to your door without you going out to look for it. Even if she knew what was going on, she would stay put in the house, waiting and praying that he would come home safe. She didn't want her son to be a revolutionary. She gave him everything, and all she ever wanted in return was for him to find a nice girl and settle down and bring some grandchildren into the world to carry on the family name.

Hans had never seen eye-to-eye with her on that. He had no interest in girls, in women, even for one-night stands. Since he joined the IRA, his mind had been focused on one thing and one thing only—the deadly battle of wits he waged daily with British intelligence. He gave the impression to his superiors that he was a committed Republican doing no more than was expected of any true Irishman who loved his country, but that was just a front. Since he got a taste for confrontation during the civil rights marches, he craved danger and pitting his wits against an adversary. He liked to feel the adrenaline pumping through his veins and the excitement of the danger that went with it.

Hans had no regrets for anything he had done—the killings, maiming and destruction of property. When he lost members of his unit in action, it had no effect on him except that they had to be replaced. Never was there any feeling for the lads who gave their lives while carrying out his orders. Some of them were youngsters whom he had recruited himself, boys whom he had turned into hardened gunmen and bombers. They were his soldiers, and when they died, they were casualties of war.

When young Scottish, Welsh and English soldiers were killed, his mother reminded him that they too had mothers and fathers or wives and children whose lives were shattered by the loss, but he could not see it her way. They were all paid mercenaries of the British Government as far as he was concerned, and it didn't matter to them whether they were killing thick Paddies in Ireland or Arab wogs in Egypt. They took their pay and had no moral hang-ups about killing. And neither had he.

He was convinced his time had now come—they would kill him before the day was done, one way or another; if they did, he had a duty to take as many of them with him as he could.

His train of thought was broken by the appearance of a young officer who emerged from the doorway of one of the tall houses, flanked by two soldiers with rifles at the ready. The three advanced briskly until they were about fifty yards away, then stopped. The officer appeared well in control of the situation until a radio one of the soldiers carried suddenly started squawking.

"Turn that fucking thing off," he shouted at the soldier, "you fucking clot. Turn it off!" He was as nervous as a cat.

He told the escort to stay put and moved forward on his own until he was only twenty yards from Hans, pistol in hand.

"You're a contrary fucker, Paddy," he said. "I hope you're not a stupid fucker as well. If you disarm the bomb, you get safe passage to the police station. No fireworks. Just do the job and make it safe. If you refuse, the men on the roof will take you out, and the bomb squad will put a charge into the van and disarm it in the normal way. Understood?"

Hans stared at him; "The device is set, and I can't stop it. There's about two minutes left, give or take a minute, and you have left it too late to clear the civilians." He spoke clearly and deliberately.

The young officer's nerve broke.

"For Christ's sake, disarm the bomb, and let's get to hell out of here," he pleaded.

Hans did not reply. The two soldiers backing him up were nervous, shifting their weight from one foot to the other, edging slowly backwards all the time. If the bomb was going to blow, they wanted to be well clear.

"Permission to withdraw, Sir!" one of them sang out.

"Permission granted. Back off but keep him covered. Time to go. You stay put, Paddy. You have a date in Hell."

Beads of sweat began to trickle down the young officer's face as he slowly backed away, step by step, making sure he kept the bomber in view.

Hans smiled at him: "You forgot something, baby face."

The officer stopped and the retreating escort paused; maybe Paddy had changed his mind.

Hans raised his right arm and opened his hand to reveal the zapper in the palm. "This," he said with a smile on his face.

The three soldiers stood transfixed. The officer recognised the electronic device.

"Don't do it, Paddy! Don't fucking do it!"

The soldier was pleading, desperate. "Mother of Jesus, don't do it!"

Hans pointed the zapper at the van. One of the soldiers started to run; the other went down on his knee and took aim to fire but before he could get his shaking finger to press the trigger, Hans pressed the 0 button twice in quick succession, and then 7.

V—R—O—O—M !

The explosion lifted the van and the earth beneath and all the vehicles around it in a ball of fire and spewed the wrecked vehicles into the air like molten lava. Soldiers and their vehicles and cars parked on the perimeter of the square were sucked inward to fill the vacuum created by a mass of rising air that suddenly ignited to form a great fireball over the square; it rolled outwards, enveloping the surrounding houses. The tall, elegant buildings shifted on their foundations, cracked and collapsed disgorging their innards like a pig with its belly slit. The corrugated iron protection around the police barracks was wrenched from its stanchions and metal sheets began to swirl around in the air, like loose papers flying in the wind. The front of the police station was laid bare, doors and windows burning furiously. Slates disappeared from the roof like confetti at a wedding, exposing flaming rafters.

People who had been watching the battle of wits between the Army and the IRA man fled in panic when the ground shook under their feet, but they could not escape the clouds of burning debris and hot ash that descended from the sky, setting clothing alight, burning skin on faces and hands, threatening to envelop them.

Terrified people stumbled out of crumbling shops and houses in adjoining streets, and broken glass crashed onto pavements and roadways. A couple of streets away, the church bell began to swing out of control as the force of the blast rocked it. A great gaping hole appeared in the roof of the boys' school, and Brendan Mullan's noisy class was showered with slates and plaster.

The dull thud of the blast reached the river, and the water carried the sound so that it was heard more than twenty miles away. Fires broke out spontaneously as burning debris settled on roofs and ledges and trees.

Where Hans had stood there was a crater nearly forty yards in diameter and twenty feet deep, surrounded by a ring of blazing car wrecks. Nothing remained of the blue van, of Hans or the young officer and his escort.

Brendan Mullan picked himself up off the pavement, where he had been crouching under a lorry to avoid the worst of the falling debris. He was shocked at the extent of the devastation.

Hans was gone, and so were the three soldiers, their bodies incinerated. Snipers on the rooftops had caught the full force of the blast. Some of them were sucked from their vantage points and hurtled to their death on the pavement four storeys below. Others who had been crouching behind one of the armoured vehicles were crushed when it rolled over on them. But the worst devastation had been caused to the houses around the lovely old town square. They had been blitzed, in ruins, their occupants buried under the rubble.

Brendan Mullan was terrified. He turned away and walked back towards the school and the pupils he had left unattended. He had seen his comrade play out the final minutes of his life in a most dramatic and devastating way. He was a hero, but he was dead. Some day he himself might have to face the same situation, but he knew he would never have the courage or the foolhardiness to do what Hans had done.

While emergency services were trying to sort out the dead and injured and rescuers tore at the rubble with bare hands to reach frantic people trapped in their collapsed homes, Brendan steered his pupils around the bombed-out area. He ordered them to go straight home and not attempt to come back to the town centre while all the commotion was going on.

He made his way through narrow back streets to Hans's house and knocked at the door. Lucy opened it, crying.

"You have already heard the bad news," he said.

"No, but I know you are going to give it to me," she sobbed.

He told her Hans had been killed in an explosion and how sorry he was to be bringing her the news. Nothing more.

Later in the evening, as she sat alone in darkness, soldiers and police arrived in force and took her away at gunpoint while they ransacked the house for evidence of terrorist activity. She was taken to Derry for questioning and kept in a police cell while they ran a check on her background. But they could turn up absolutely nothing on either her or her dead son to connect them with the IRA. The family had German connections but no record of political or military involvement in Ireland.

She lied to them that Hans was an impressionable boy who was not mixed up with any organisation, either terrorist or political and must have been threatened by somebody in the IRA to drive the van into the town.

But by that time the police knew that the suicide bomber was a top IRA man, most probably the terrorist who had planned and executed the destruction of the Army fort and the helicopter attack on the police station.

A thorough search of her house revealed nothing and four days later she was freed and taken home. Neighbours stood around cheering as she was helped out of the armoured police van and made her way to the front door of the house; she ought to be proud of her son, they shouted at her. But she went inside and shut the door tightly behind her without acknowledging their presence. She wanted nothing to do with any of them.

Hans's known associates were pulled in for questioning. Brendan Mullan was among them, but he had proof that he was in school and only left briefly out of curiosity when he heard about the bomb in the square. He acknowledged that he had known the dead man from college, and a couple of times a year, they went fishing together, but that was all. He had never heard of him being mixed up with any terrorist organisation.

There was no body to bury, so there was no funeral, and the local priest refused to say a Requiem Mass for Hans because of the carnage he had caused.

Lucy closed her door and would not admit anybody except the police, who made several visits and asked her to try to identify items belonging to her son. Even when they were clearly his, she shook her head. She had no further interest in the police or the IRA or anybody else.

In the tense days after the bombing, notices in Republican papers described Hans as OC of the Mournebridge Unit of the IRA and paid tribute to him, saying that he had died on active duty. The police returned to the house again and again to question her, but she pleaded total ignorance of her son's Republican activities, insisting that he was an innocent youth duped into driving the van with the bomb. They kept a close watch on the house after that but didn't bother her again.

Brendan Mullan visited the distraught Lucy and brought a bundle of Irish and English newspapers in which Hans was described alternatively as another patriot who willingly gave his life for his country, or the 'Monster of Mournebridge', 'Mass Murderer' of Mournebridge, 'Callous IRA Killer', 'Monster from Bavaria'—depending on the political leaning of the paper. Lucy was polite to Brendan but made it clear she did not want to be associated with him in any way. She took the papers from him, thanked him, and he left.

When she finally got around to reading the details several days later the graphic pictures of what the bomb had done to the town shocked her.

"Death of a Town" and "IRA Carnage" and "Devastation" and "IRA Suicide Bomber" screamed the headlines. There were vivid accounts of the last minutes before the bomb was detonated; there was no shortage of eyewitnesses. Aerial photographs of the wrecked town centre showed in graphic detail the full extent of the devastation.

There was a list of soldiers and civilians who had been killed and injured in the blast, and it was only when she read the names of dead townspeople she realised many of them had been customers in her shop.

There was a young picture of Hans from his days at university and, on the same page, pictures of the officer and two soldiers who were beside him when he triggered the bomb with the zapper. The two young soldiers had been married, but the officer was single. Ironically, he was described as born in England of Irish parents, an only child.

Lucy glanced quickly again at the name of the dead officer. Captain Patrick McLaughlin (26) of Slough, Buckinghamshire. Her heart sank as she gazed into the face of the handsome young man smiling back at her from the page. She gripped the paper more tightly until the pages began to crumple in her hands. Her head began to shake, and blood drained from her face as the full impact of what had happened hit her.

Hans had not only ended his own life; he had also killed his brother, the baby boy she had given away to her former lover, Patrick McLaughlin.

Lucy's body stiffened, her eyes began to roll out of control, and numbness in her head gradually moved into her arms and legs as the onset of a stroke starved her brain of its blood supply. She tried to focus her eyes to rid them of the grey cloud in front of her, but it got gradually darker and darker.

She sensed the end was coming and it brought tears to her eyes. She tried to lift her hand to wipe them away, but it would not respond.

Relaxed, ready for the blackness that she knew was about to descend on her, she thought about her life, her sons, her mother and grandmother. She tried to focus on the good times they had together, but instead, her mind flooded with memories and pictures of the tragic events that had marred their lives for a hundred years.

It was all over now; granny Marita was at rest, Brigitta was at rest, Penelope and Edward had disappeared without a trace, and now she had lost her sons in one moment of time.

Whatever about the next life, one thing was now certain—there would be no more suffering for any of them in this world.

For Lucy was the last of the Mullers of Hoffenfeld, and she was sure she was going to die.

EPILOGUE

After the explosion that wrecked the town and killed her cousin Hans Muller, Leo McKenna's eldest grandchild Joan and her husband had enough of Ireland and the dirty war being fought between the IRA and the British Army and decided to emigrate to America.

She was a nurse and found work in a Catholic Hospital in Texas while her husband, a teacher, got a job as assistant principal in a Catholic Boys' school in the same town.

Soon after she started work in her new job Joan became aware of another Irish nurse working there who also came from County Tyrone. Her name was Sister Penelope and when Joan met her, she said she had been in America for thirty-five years, first in Iowa, then California, before coming to Texas.

When Joan said she came from a place called Knockavoe near Mournebridge, the Sister was visibly shaken and excused herself. Thereafter, even though the two women worked in close proximity in the hospital, they had no further conversations about Ireland until Sister Penelope plucked up the courage two months later to confront her past.

"We never got to finish our conversation about Ireland," she said. "I want to hear more about your family. I think I might know them."

Joan sensed the nun was uneasy.

"Before we talk," she said, "I have to tell you something. I am not a nun. I could not take my final vows because I was once married, and my husband is probably still alive and living in California. They call me Sister here, but I am a lay Sister, not a nun."

"That's not a big deal anymore," said Joan. "Your work is the important thing. Lots of nuns are leaving convents in Ireland and finding jobs as teachers, nurses and doctors. Many of them are disillusioned over the way women are being treated in the Catholic Church."

"Now you know about me," said the nun. "I have a couple of questions for you. "Do you know the McKennas of Knockavoe Farm?"

Joan smiled. "Do I know them? I am one of them. I am Leo McKenna's granddaughter! How do you know them?"

The nun put her face in her hands and started to cry: "I spent my childhood there—the happiest days of my life."

She lifted her face and looked at Joan: "My name is Penelope Couchy," she said, "I am Marita Muller's granddaughter."

"My God," said Joan, "we all thought you were dead!"

The two women embraced for a long time.

When it ended, they wiped the tears from their eyes.

"We must find time for a long chat," said Sister Penelope. "I want to hear all about our two families and how they are doing."

"I'm afraid it is not a happy story," said Joan sadly. "Unfortunately, the bad luck that followed your family from Bavaria did not end with the death of Granny Muller."

The nun shook her head: "I always knew it had to happen, but you are the first person to tell me that Granny Muller is dead."

In September 1974 Edward Martinov was among 121 people killed in a train crash in the suburbs of Zagreb in Yugoslavia. He was on his way to an international farming convention. He was fifty-six years of age. In his will he left a letter addressed to *The Occupier, Knockavoe Farm, Mournebridge, County Tyrone, Northern Ireland,* to be posted on his death.

Leo McKenna's son Peter still farmed the land and had to read the letter several times before he realised that this man with the Russian name was the long lost, long thought dead grandson of Marita Muller.

"If you are of the McKenna family or the Muller family, this letter will come as a shock to you because by this time, no doubt my family and friends will have thought me long since dead. How I survived the war and its aftermath is a very long story, and I have enclosed several pages that will help you understand why I did not get in touch before.

"I have been dead to my family for a long time, and when you receive this letter, I am dead for all time. That's why the letter comes not from me but from a lawyer in Kyiv. I hope I am not too late to say goodbye to you all, especially to my sisters Penelope and Lucy.

"Tell them they were always in my thoughts, even during the darkest days when I was in a Russian Prison Camp in the Ukraine."

Peter shook his head as he read the story Edward told of what happened after he was sent to War by the Gestapo and his treatment at the hands of the Ukrainians since he was taken prisoner and how they had to work for ten years as slave labour to atone for the sins of the German Army. When he was eventually given a chance to rehabilitate himself by marrying a war widow and helping to raise her children, he took it.

Peter put the letter down, took off his glasses and rested his head on his hands in front of him on the kitchen table. He was shocked by what he had read and worried about what he should do with the information. It was complicated. Edward had been pronounced dead, and his estate was devised for his sister Lucy. What would happen now? Could it be claimed by his widow in Ukraine? Lucy was ill and in a nursing home, and what money she had was going to pay for her stay there.

Should he tell Lucy about the letter from her brother? She had survived the stroke after the death of Hans but was in such a state that nobody could say for sure whether she understood anything that was said to her or recognised any of the people who went to visit her. He had told her about his daughter Joan meeting Penelope in Texas, but she gave no sign that she understood.

His own father, Leo, was in his nineties and bedridden. He cried when he was told about Penelope.

"A lovely girl wasted, a lovely girl wasted," was all he could say.

Peter discussed the letter with his wife, and together, they decided it had come too late to make any difference to the lives of the old people. He had taken custody of all the family papers after Lucy got the stroke, the papers that she had guarded so jealously. In the quiet of his bedroom, he opened the bundle of faded documents and placed the letter from Edward on top in its original envelope.

He put a cover note with the pile before he tied it together again and placed it in its original brown paper bag.

The note simply recorded: *This last letter completes the jigsaw. All the members of the Muller family are now accounted for.*

Lucy Muller died in 1975, exactly 100 years after the massacre in Bavaria that shattered the life of Marita Muller and forced her to embark on a journey halfway around the world to a strange and violent country and start a family which had to endure more than its fair share of suffering and hardship.

The last surviving member of the family, Penelope, died in the Texas Hospital where she worked for so long and was buried in the community cemetery. Joan McVeigh, née McKenna, was with her in her final hours.

THE END